BETRAYED

The Net Tightens

Enjoy the read

ALAN ROBERT LANCASTER

Alan RL

12/10/14

New Generation **Publishing**

I have to thank my family, Kath my wife, my daughters Joanne and Suzy and my son Robert for their forbearance and help with producing this book, and 'cleaning up' my laptop system. The assistance given by my offspring has been of a technical nature, whilst my wife's has been of a historical nature, furnishing useful information about the old Roman roads that were still in use at the time of the Conquest, and about London in the years 1066 and after.

Thanks also go to Barrie Nichols, my former Geography and Maths teacher and wife Shirley who have encouraged me to proceed with the saga, and shown interest in the project.

To some of my former colleagues at Mount Pleasant Sorting Office for their input and suggestions on the storyline and content whether used or not, thanks again.

Alan R Lancaster, London 2014

The king this year imposed a heavy geld on the wretched folk; but not withstanding, let his men always plunder the kingdom that they went over; and then he marched to Defna shire, and beset the burh of Exanceaster eighteen days

Saxon Chronicle € 1067

RAVENFEAST HISTORICAL BACKGROUND & NOTES

Historical Background

The historical characters of this saga are known from numerous sources, including Snorri Sturlusson's Icelandic Sagas and the Saxon Chronicles.

King Harold is known to have had many Danes and Anglo-Danes amongst his household troops, or *huscarls*. His mother, Gytha, was aunt through marriage to King Svein and Jarl Osbeorn of Denmark through her brother Ulf. There had been many Danes living in England, some first generation, others whose families had lived in Danelaw Mercia since the 9th Century division by Aelfred. Their ancestry was celebrated in the bringing of the BEOWULF and HROLF KRAKI sagas to England in the ninth century.

After the Conquest many English nobles, churchmen and warriors left for Denmark and Flanders, raiding with the Danes on England's shores. Others roamed further afield, joining the Byzantine emperor Michael's Varangian Guard at Constantinople - known to the Norsemen as Miklagard (the Great Fortress City) = changing the composition of this elite body. Having originally been composed of Swedes (Rus), the make-up of the Varangian Guard changed over the years via West Norse to Anglo-Danish.

Harold Haroldson was born to King Harold's queen, Aeldgytha in early 1067 at Chester. Mother and son were spirited away to Dublin to keep them from possible harm from the Normans.

Nothing is recorded of them beyond that.

Eadgytha 'Svanneshals' (Swan neck) fled from Winchester with her youngest son Ulf and daughters Gunnhild and Gytha to Exeter together with Harold's mother Gytha. They were joined there by Harold's older sons by Eadgytha, Godwin, Eadmund and Magnus. Even as the Normans gained entry to the city the family went their separate ways, the womenfolk and children initially to Steepholm in the Bristol Channel, and then to Flanders once the hue and cry had died down.

Godwin, Eadmund and Magnus left for Dublin, where they were given men and ships by King Diarmuid. They raided in the West Country, on the Bristol Channel coast of Somerset where Godwin's lands were, and were beaten off by the local *fyrd* and Normans under the Breton Count Brian. Godwin and Eadmund are known to have survived, but Magnus is thought to have died of his wounds. There is also a story that Magnus did not die of his wounds but lived out his days in his native Sussex as a monk. His older brothers are said to have left for Denmark.

Ulf, Harold's youngest son by Eadgytha is thought to have been captured and imprisoned by William, later freed under an amnesty in 1087. He was befriended, along with Eadgar the *Aetheling* by Robert 'Curthose', William's eldest son, and is thought to have gone with them on Crusade in the early 12th Century. King Eadweard's widow, Eadgytha retired to the nunnery at Wilton Abbey along with Harold's daughter Gunnhild after surrendering Winchester to William. Wulfnoth, Harold's youngest brother, was brought back to England long after the Conquest and taken to Winchester, where he died an old and lonely, broken man.

Harold's elder daughter by Eadgytha, Gunnhild, is believed to have been abducted from the nunnery at Wilton by Alan 'Fergeant', Lord of Richmond, who had received lands of her mother's. In fact she fled the nunnery to be with him. She later 'took up' with his kinsman Alan 'the Black', despite Archbishop Anselm's attempts to get her back to Wilton.

Harold's daughter Gytha began a dynasty when she married Prince Vladimir 'Monomakh' of Smolensk and later Kiev. Her eldest, a son called Mstislav – or Mistislav - Harold was born in Novgorod. From him stems King Valdemar of Denmark and later Queen Elizabeth II of England by way of Queen Margrethe of Denmark.

2 Historical Notes

To familiarise you with Anglo-Saxon terminology and place names used in the saga of Ivar:

Before reading on, you might like to know how to pronounce these words. A general rule of thumb should help:

Silent 'g', as in Leagatun, can be said as a throaty 'h' or as a 'y' = 'Leayatun'; throaty 'h', as in 'Burhbot', pron. 'boorhbot'; long 'u', also as in 'Burhbot'; 'y' is like the German 'u' with *umlaut*; 'cg' is as 'dg = bridge; Eoferwic pron. as '*Yorferwic*'; 'ae' pron. 'ey'; 'sc' pron. 'sh'; 'skj' as in 'skjaldborg' pron. 'shyaldborh'; 'cea' and 'ci' pron. 'cha' and 'chi' as in '*Ceaster*', Chester, or '*Cild*' (Eadric Cild) ; 'thegn' pron. 'thane';

Burhbot   work on burh (town/city) defences, alternative to *fyrdfaereld* when defensive work needed to be upgraded or replaced under threat of siege/invasion

Brycgegeweorc upkeep of bridges as part of defensive strategy under threat of siege/invasion

Butsecarl seagoing *huscarl*/warrior

Ceorl commoner, free peasant/freed man

Discthegn/Hraegle thegn household steward/general steward

Ealdorman Anglo-Saxon predecessor of Earl

Earl/Eorl Anglo-Saxon equivalent of Norse *Jarl*

Earldoms status given to former kingdoms of England from and including the time of Knut/Canute

Fyrd regional militia or territorial forces were raised by the king to defend the realm for limited periods only, to repel invaders – not for aggressive purposes

Fyrdfaereld territorial military duty, a form of national obligation for limited period from several weeks to a couple of months before being stood down

Hersir West Norse landowners, latterly household warrior retainers, similar to *huscarls*

Hundred a southern or south-western shire district, charged with upkeep of law and local defence (see also *Wapentake*)

Huscarl household warrior, often landed, Danish origin, introduced by Knut into England

King's thegn obligated to answer king's call to duty

Norns three old crones, seers, *Skuld*: Being, *Urd*: Fate/ *Wyrd,* and *Verdandi*: Necessity

Shire reeve later sheriff

Scramaseaxe scramasaxe, the weapon associated with the Saxons, a curved blade on the top side with a concave split-edged blade on the other

Skalds Norse hall poets, retained by kings and/or jarls to recite the heroic deeds of their paymasters

Skjaldborg Norse, shieldwall, literally shield fortress, defensive/offensive formation of overlapping shields, used both in England and Scandinavia

Thegns or thanes, commoners ennobled by the king, usually held *'book land'* from king or ecclesiastical establishment

Thrijungar or 'Thirdings' (Ridings), the divisions of Yorkshire and Lincolnshire, each with its own *thing* or parliament

Wapentake/Vapnatak district within 'Thirding' in regions of northern and eastern (Danelaw) England, similar to Wessex

Hundreds, literally *weapon take*, or weapon store

    Wyrd   fate, woven by *Urd*, one of the three *Norns* who sat at the roots of *Yggdrasil*, the World Ash Tree – decided the personal outlook of everyone born to man in *Midgard*, (Middle Earth)

I have attempted to maintain the early mediaeval geography in the saga with the use of the 11th Century communal and regional references or names. The spellings use modern-day characters, as some of the original ones were never translated into the Gutenberg alphabet when printing was introduced to England in the 15th Century by Caxton. The main place/regional references and names used are:

    Aengla, Aengle, Aenglish   Anglia, English – people, English language and collective noun for people inhabiting Aengla Land: England

    Andredesleag   Andreds Weald, the thickly wooded hills across southern Sussex and south western Kent

    Beornica   Bernicia, northern half of *Northanhymbra* (Northumbria), ruled from *Baebbanburh* (Bamburgh)

Bretland	Brittany
Cantuareburh, -byrig	Canterbury, capital of Kent
Ceaster	Chester, capital of Mercia
Centland, Centish	Kent, Kentish

    Danelaw   formerly Eastern Mercia, the lands east of Watling Street offered by King Aelfred to Guthrum and the other Danish lords as part of the Treaty of Wedmore

    Deira   the southern half of the kingdom and later earldom of Northumbria, ruled from *Jorvik/Eoferwic* (York), in 10th Century ruled as separate Kingdom of York by Eirik 'Blood-axe'

    Deoraby   Derby, one of 'Five Boroughs' of Danelaw, with Lincoln, Leicester, Nottingham and Stamford

Dyflin	Dublin, southern Ireland
East Seaxan, East Seaxe	East Saxon(s), Essex

    Eoferwic and *Jorvik*   York, the first is the Anglian, and the latter is the Norse name from which the modern York stems

    Five Boroughs   are the main towns of the *Danelaw*, Derby, Leicester, Lincoln Nottingham and Stamford (Lincs.)

Frankia	France
Laegerceaster	Leicester
Lindcylne	Lincoln

Lunden London, there were other versions in the Saxon Chronicle, this version was used in the pre-Norman era

Lunden Brycg London Bridge

Middil Seaxan, Middil Seaxe Middle Saxon, Middlesex

Mierca Mercia

Miklagard Constantinople, 'great city/fortress'

Norse the West Norse are the modern Norwegians and their colonists in the Atlantic islands, including the British Isles; the East Norse are the Danes, Goths and Swedes, historically also settlers in the *Danelaw* in England and Ireland; also Rus, an ethnic group largely absorbed by their Slavic neighbours, originally in northern and central western Russia/ Ukraine.

Northanhymbra Northumbria, see *Beornica, Deira*

Northfolc North folk/ Norfolk – a sub-group of *East Aengle*/East Angles - see also *Suthfolc*

Northmandige, Northman/Northmen Normandy, Norman(s)

Norwic Norwich

Seaxan, Seaxe Saxon(s)

Snotingaham Nottingham, one of the 'five boroughs, Snota's settlement

Staenford Stamford, Lincolnshire, another of 'five boroughs of the Danelaw

Staenfordes Brycg Stamford Bridge, East Yorkshire

Suthfolc South folk/Suffolk, East Angles

Suth Seaxan, Suth Seaxe South Saxon, Sussex

Wealas, Wealsh Wales, Welsh – term was applied by the Saxons, meaning 'foreigner'

West Seaxan, West Seaxe West Saxon, Wessex – abolished by the Normans as retribution for Harold's 'perfidy', he was regarded as a usurper, and traditionally he still held his lands in Wessex until his death

West Wealas name given by the Saxons to Cornwall

Wintunceaster Winchester, capital of Wessex

Alan Lancaster, 2013

KIRKJUVAGR

LJODHUS

SOME OF THE CHIEF SETTLEMENTS IN LATE 11th CENTURY

BRITAIN

SCONE

DINAS EIDIN DUNEDIN
BERUWIC
BAEBBANBURH

DUNHOLM

CARDEOL

HVITEBY
SKARTHIBURH
EOFERWIC JORVIK

LUNECEASTER

DYFLIN

CEASTER
MENAI

LINDCYLNE
SNOTINGAHAM
DEORABY
LEAGACEASTER
NORWIC

HLIMREKR

VEIGSFJORDR

STAEFFORD
SCROBBESBYRIG

CORK
VEDRAFJORDR

RHOSGOCH
NORTHANHAMTUN
LUNDEN

CANTUAREBURH

WINTUNCEASTER
EXANCEASTER
WIHT

HERETOFORE

Wulfwin feared the new king knew of the whereabouts of Godwin, his brothers and Ivar, and warned them to leave Leagatun. Being further from Lunden Naesinga was safer, he told Harold's sons.

'This is your doing, Ivar', Godwin chided. 'Abbot Ealdred has been summoned to Bearrucing by Willelm, and taken to task for allowing outsiders into the abbey church of West Mynster at his crowning. Dean Wulfwin at Wealtham has learnt of the king's distrust in him, too'.

Godwin took his household out into East Seaxe, out of the way of prying Northman eyes. Although the move would lead to new hardships, Ivar was still needed to help Godwin's men learn their fighting skills.

Then new ills beset them at Naesinga. Healfdan thought his bride-to-be unfaithful. She had been seen entering Ivar's bed-closet and he killed her with one blow of his war axe. Fettering Healfdan was foolish, everyone said, he ought to have been put to death. The women at Naesinga were now wary of him, would come nowhere near him, not even when he was fettered to a post.

'Did you bed Ingigerd?' Godwin asked Ivar, thinking he knew the answer.

The woman who entered Ivar's bed-closet had to be the hwicce-woman, the shape-shifter Braenda.

Theodolf next thought his woman Gerda had been bedded by Godwin's brother Eadmund. Yet he let himself be sworn to her in the church at Saewardstan with all the show of a thegn's wedding. Nevertheless mistrust soon undermined his belief in her love for him.

Father Cutha, Godwin's priest at Naesinga talked his lord into sending Ivar away from the camp. As a would-be king, he could not harbour anyone, even a kinsman, who had dealings with demons. To him Ivar was Godwin's, and therefore God's foe, to be cast from the fold. Unwillingly, Godwin sent his kinsman away with a couple of friends to go his own way.

Ivar knew where he was to head for. He would seek out Thegn Eadric 'Cild' in the west, where he sheltered with the Wealsh princes Bleddyn and Rhiwallon. Godwin and his brothers would ally themselves with the Hereford thegn anyway, so they would meet in Wealas in the weeks to come.

Close friends Oslac and Cyneweard rode with Ivar on his way west shadowed by Saeward and Theodolf, who they thought would sooner stay near Wealtham. When Ivar, Oslac and Cyneweard came to an inn in the west they were taken by Ivar's old foe Gilbert de Warenne.

Taking Ivar would be a feather in de Warenne's cap. The Northman thought he had him. There would be no way he could flee now! How wrong could a man be? Theodolf and Saeward were there to save their friends.

Aethelhelm the thegn from Oxnaford and Bruning the innkeeper would have to be dealt with for helping their sworn foe.

Ivar thought Thegn Osgod and Harding with their following to be Northmen until other riders were seen coming over the hills from the west. Osgod showed Ivar by waving his shield that he and his men were friends. On seeing a greater number of riders the Northmen turned back before they could close on Ivar.

In the wilds of Hereford shire Ivar and his friends were befriended by another innkeeper, Osferth, who told them the way to find Eadric. Saeward felt there was something of the uncanny about Osferth's hamlet. He was uneasy – more-so when he learnt the name of the innkeeper's wife, Rowena, steeped in hwicce lore. They learned later that instead of talking with the living, they had met the ghosts of Osferth, his sons and neighbours, slain by the Northman earl fitzOsbern's men for withholding their tithes.

They came to Rhosgoch, to be welcomed by Eadric. Ivar learnt from him of Copsig being made Earl of Beornica. Despite a warning from Harding that as kinsman of Tostig he would be as loathed as Copsig, he felt Gospatric should be forewarned.

Being a Dane and kin to Tostig, Harding warned, Ivar was as likely as Copsig to be slain by Gospatric or his kinsman Osulf. Not to be put out by the threat, Ivar rode north with Harding, Oslac, Theodolf and Saeward. Cyneweard would stay at Rhosgoch.

Their guide, the priest Aldo led them into a trap and they could only flee after a hard struggle in which Aldo was cut down by a Northman arrow. Another fight broke out with the Northmen further north in which Oslac, shielding Ivar, was slain by a crossbow bolt. Theodolf was wounded and taken by back for treatment to Rhosgoch by Saeward, Sigrid the wife of a dead king's thegn and her maid Aelfflaed whilst Ivar and Harding pressed on with Earl Willelm fitzOsbern and his friend Ricard fitzScrob as hostages, to be used to bargain for their own safety.

By the banks of the River Seoferna Harding let himself be drawn into a wrestling match with the Northman earl, and the two Northman nobles fled on their mounts after overcoming him. Ivar and Harding had to flee east across the river. Here they were helped by Eirik the ferryman. Thegn Eirik, as he once was, ousted by the earl from his lands, led Ivar and Harding through the uplands, over the spine of the *kingdom.*

Deep snow in the mountains hindered them as much as it did Copsig and his hirelings. In one of the upland inns Ivar and his friends find the earl as much taken unaware by them showing as they were to come across him so soon.

Saeward catches up with Ivar and Harding, having followed them by way of Scrobbesbyrig. Their number now greater by the strength of one sword-hand, Saeward was welcomed warmly.

Nevertheless further setbacks awaited them, and still Copsig had the upper hand. Even after being waylaid by outlaws he and his men overcame them and pushed northward through Deira to look for more men in Eoferwic. They rode on beyond the Tese to Nyburna on the River Tina where a welcoming feast awaited him.

Ivar's own welcome was frosty, as Harding had forecast. Although Gospatric and his kinsman Osulf threatened his life, they took Ivar and his friends with them to greet the new earl.

Copsig's blood froze when Gospatric and Osulf and their armed men stormed the earl's garth together with Ivar and his friends. Copsig fled to the church, only to be smoked out of hiding and into the hands of his foes. Copsig's end was quick, his head sheared by Osulf's axe. His men were offered – and took – quarter. Told to ride southward, away from Beornica, they fled with their lives.

Harding now took Ivar, Saeward and Eirik home with him, southward over a time-worn bridge across the Tese to Rudby where his wife Aethelhun welcomed them. All was not as it should be.

Aethelhun soon showed her true colours.

They rode on to Aethel's steading near Tadceaster, leaving Rudby earlier than Harding had told Aethelhun, yet she was there on the threshold, the tool of a powerful warlock, threatening Ivar in the doorway in her bid to foul Aethel's dwelling. Harding, as much afraid as Ivar, found within himself the strength to spear her, rendering Aethelhun to smouldering ash.

On the death of Aethelhun Braenda showed herself to Ivar, thankful for his and Harding's help. She would not stay with her lover, and Ivar was left to ride back to Rhosgoch with his friends.

Godwin and his brothers meanwhile rode west with their men to help Eadric and the Wealshmen Bleddyn and Rhiwallon, almost giving themselves away to the earl's men but for Ivar warning them. With the Northman earl away at Scrobbesbyrig Eadric, Bleddyn, Rhiwallon and Godwin's men took Hereford's stronghold easily.

Saeward found a chest in the earl's ransacked stronghold and hoped to use the key they found on the Frankish priest Earnald. Stiff to begin with, the key turned and a sheet of vellum was found in the box. Bleddyn, angered that Ivar might cheat him of gains he knew nothing of, threatened to harm Ivar if he next caught sight of him again anywhere in Wealas.

With Bleddyn's curses ringing in his ears, Ivar rode south with his friends, leaving Osgod and Harding at Hereford. Godwin, Eadmund, Magnus and their men rode with Ivar to Exanceaster, to be with their close kindred.

A new threat would soon raise its ugly head. Hearing that Exanceaster had been closed to him, King Willelm rode west to take the burh from the rebels.

With Exanceaster beset by Willelm, Ivar and Saeward took the priest Eadwig over the burh wall to learn what the king had in store for them. Eadwig knew the Northmen's tongue and would tell Godwin what he heard.

1

The night air is still again. Saeward crooks a finger at me and the three of us stride slowly past the outer tents of the king's camp. Wary of being caught, I shuffle behind the priest Eadwig and my friend, looking out from beneath the rim of my hood for anything that shows King Willelm's whereabouts. I feel that even though my beard and the crown of my head have been shaven, he will still know me. He is no bumbling fool. That is how he has kept his head through these years, and I believe means to keep this kingdom, whatever the cost.

A screech-owl takes to the air as we pass by a tree near the road below the *burh* walls. Father Eadwig falters, taken aback and is pushed forward by Saeward behind him.

'I am sorry, father', Saeward murmurs, 'you almost stepped back onto my toes!'

'*Forgive me, my son!*' the priest blurts. All is quiet again.

Saeward puts a hand over Eadwig's mouth, looks from left to right, back again and nods us forward, taking his hand away from the priest's mouth. We pass a great bell tent, wherein men talk, laugh heartily and begin talking again.

'*What was that about?*' Saeward hisses.

'It is nothing worthy, my son - men boasting of the women they took in Suth Seaxe. *That is all*', Eadwig answers under his breath. A twig snaps amid the trees to our right and we crouch, frozen. Nothing happens, no-one comes forth and I stand, ready to go again.

'*Stop -*' Saeward hisses at us both, and creeps into the undergrowth and small trees whence the sound came.

He shows again, grinning broadly, waving us on and telling us under his breath,

'It was a hind, more afraid of me than I of it, whatever it might have been. Still, it is better we see what stirs amongst the trees than be caught unaware, eh Ivar? – I forgot, you must say nothing'.

He chuckles and we walk on to the next tent. There is no-one outside to keep anyone away, but Father Eadwig crooks a finger at us both to stop and stands listening. Looking upward as if for counsel from above, he cocks an ear for what seems to me a lifetime.

'What was that?' Saeward rasps at Eadwig when we are waved on again.

'That was one of their warlords', Eadwig tells us after we have walked on further. 'He was talking of what they are to do in the morning'.

'What *was* he saying?' Saeward asks.

'He said something about bringing a *trebuchet* forward', Eadwig answers, and puts a finger to his mouth. One of the Northman knights passes and is blessed in his own tongue. He bows his head for the priest to touch his forehead, crosses himself and strides on. Eadwig smiles after him.

'What is a *trebu-* ?'Saeward asks, unable to finish the word. A bemused Father Eadwig answers simply,

'A *trebuchet* is a great catapult that throws stones at, or over high walls'.

'I might seem dim in your eyes, father', Saeward looks about before finishing, 'but I do not know what a catapult is'.

'I will draw one for you when we are safe within the walls once more. First we must know more. There may be another tent nearby where someone has more for us', Father Eadwig beckons us on. He seems to relish what we are doing now.

He stops us again close by the last tent, and stands staring into the heavens above. I look down at the scraped earth at our feet, unaware of what either Saeward or Eadwig are at until one of them pulls at my right sleeve.

On looking up, wide-eyed, my gaze is met by one of the Northmen. He asks something and is plainly irked when I do not answer.

Father Eadwig steps forward from the gloom into the light of the campfire the knight must have seen me by. He says something to the Northman and beckons to Saeward, stabbing a finger at the gold-encrusted book he carries at his waist. My friend raises the relic to eye level and Eadwig begins to read in what I think must be the tongue of the Church.

The Northman stands, head bowed as the last one had done, crosses himself and walks away.

'He was taken aback that Ivar did not answer when he asked for a blessing, until I told him he cannot speak', Eadwig tells us under his breath. He watches after the Northman until he vanishes into the blackness and shivers, looks over his left shoulder at us and turns back to the way ahead, 'Onward'.

We stride on behind him into the darkness.

I think I know who the knight was, who asked for Eadwig's blessing. When we are back over the other side of the wall I shall tell them. For now I must be the dumb Brother.

'Father –'someone calls from behind, '*Father*'.

Eadwig turns to look at the man standing beside me. It is the same Northman he blessed not long ago.

'My son, what is it you wish from me?' Eadwig is taken aback, but holds himself well.

'Would you hear my words of guilt?' the Northman looks long and hard at the priest, searching his eyes. I can see him shaking. 'You have a chill?'

'Aye, my son, I have a slight chill. What *can* you have done, that I should hear you out even before fighting has begun? Surely you should seek me out afterward?'

'This has nothing to do with the fighting, father. What are you doing, an Aenglishman amongst the Northmen?'

The fellow speaks in the manner of a man from eastern Aengla. I bite my tongue, to hold back from killing him. Guthfrith, whom I thought to be a friend, has been sent by Ansgar to fight for the king *against* us!

'I am a priest, my friend', Eadwig tells him sternly. 'God does not set men apart. His word is for all to hear'.

'*Forgive me father*', Guthfrith looks shamed, but I still feel I should kill him. Who else is with him? Does the king know he taught some of Godwin's men their fighting skills?

If asked, he would be able to tell Willelm their weaknesses. Does Saeward also know him? I know my friend has been staring at him in the darkness, I wonder also unable to believe his eyes. As Guthfrith turns to leave Saeward asks,

'What happened to Healfdan, Guthfrith?'

'*What-?*' Guthfrith wheels around to stare at Saeward. There is the glint of a blade in what little light the half-hidden moon affords and Saeward holds Guthfrith in his arms, as if greeting a brother.

'Take him, Ivar', Saeward struggles to pull the blade from Guthfrith.

'*Fool!*' I curse Saeward as we lower Guthfrith between us, and drag him into thick undergrowth yards away. With all these Northmen around us and God knows, whoever might be watching from the shadows, Saeward has to kill the fellow. Eadwig is as scared of Saeward as I am angered. Now we cannot stay any longer before Guthfrith's corpse is found!

'We have to get away from here, back within the walls! Come, we must get back to where we were lowered and hope we are not seen or even found out by any of Willelm's armed men. *Fool!*'

Saeward cannot even see why we must leave. He stares blankly at me until Eadwig mutters,

'I feel the chill worse than before, Ivar. Have we not enough for Godwin?' To my reckoning it is his way of steering Saeward away from clashing with me.

'Then, we must head back', Saeward answers. He blinks at me

before looking back at the priest.

We have not gone far before something or someone stirs to our left in the undergrowth. There are no tents here and even night creatures are unlikely to stir as we pass. Saeward puts a finger to his lips and points into the darkness. When I nod he enters the bushes one way, I pass behind Eadwig and between trees the other way. Not knowing what Saeward's thoughts are, I push stealthily between saplings and come eye to eye with another of Ansgar's men.

'Hemming, what are *you* doing here?' I murmur, hopefully loud enough for him to hear. Unluckily Saeward has not heard me and comes out of the bushes behind him with his right hand raised, holding a knife. I hiss, '*Hold, Saeward, this is Hemming!*'

'Who – *Hemming,* what are *you* doing-?'

He cannot finish, with my hand over his mouth.

'Quick, *get back to the wall!*' I hiss at both men and although we must have made enough noise to wake the Northmen from their slumbers no-one follows us back to where we began our spying.

Saeward makes his owl call. Nothing happens. He calls again, and still nothing. He looks over one shoulder at me and I shrug. Making owl calls was never one of my strengths. He looks at Hemming.

'What is it you are trying to do?' Hemming asks Saeward.

'I am meant to make an owl call', Saeward answers under his breath, angered either at his own shortcomings or at Hemming.

Hemming offers to help, much to Saeward's unease,

'Let me try'. He cups his hands, looks upward at the top of the wooden wall, and hoots so much more like an owl that Eadwig stares up into the blackness of the trees.

'Who is there?' Heads show over the wall above us, and when the moon shows again between the clouds one of Godwin's men sees us.

The rope chair drops and we ready Eadwig to be lifted. When the priest is safely over the wall Hemming and I help Saeward.

Once into his harness he is hoisted quickly up and out of sight over the wall.

'You are next', I tell Hemming.

'If you are caught it will be death for you', Hemming tries to talk me into going first. He is right, but he may mean to go back to his fellows and pull the harness onto him. There is rustling amongst the trees and he looks startled at me, '*You heard that?*'

'I heard. If you keep quiet nothing will come of it', I murmur into his right ear, then hiss, '*Be quiet and be lucky!*'

'Put your feet over my shoulders and we can both be lifted!' he croaks. When I look over one shoulder into the trees I see someone coming!

'Ready down there?' someone snaps. The rope tightens.

We rise and then stop in mid-air. Someone groans before we rise again, slower this time. I can hear men talking above our heads before another fellow asks, 'How many of you *are there* on the chair?'

'Keep hoisting!' Hemming barks.

'Who *is* that? Have you put a horse on the rope or something?'

The rope stops again. Shouting begins above us and below I can see men rushing about, pointing upward at us. One of the Northmen has a crossbow at the ready, *aimed at us!*

'Get us up there before we are killed!' I yell. There is no longer any need to keep quiet.

I hear Eadwig pleading with whoever is up there to get someone else to help pull us up. Saeward next looks over the top of the wall and shouts for help from another of the men with Godwin,

'Help get these two up before they are drilled by *crossbow bolts!'*

Another looks down at us and sees the Northmen below. Before the men above can haul the rope chair faster, the air hisses with both arrows *and* bolts. Someone hurls a spear that only misses my backside because he aimed at where it was a breath or two earlier. The spear clatters against the wall and falls quickly. I hear a stifled croak and look down.

One of the Northmen has been pinned against a tree by his comrade's spear. Men's heads show atop the wall and cheering breaks out. Arrows fly both ways and someone above – Saeward I think – calls for the men above to take care lest they slay us with their arrows,

'For God's sake watch where you aim your bows!'   Almost at the top of the wall, an arrowhead hits my right thigh.

'Aargh – I have been *caught!'* I call out. 'Can you haul faster, *before* I am drilled into the next world?'

'Get them up here, *Christ almighty!'* I hear Saeward roar like a bear.

'Come on, *faster!'* Godwin takes up the cry and looks over the wall just as another arrow narrowly misses me and hisses upward, missing his head by a whisker.

At last Hemming and I are safely over the wall. He helps Saeward manhandle me down from the wall.

The narrow wooden steps make it awkward for them to help me down together, so Hemming grasps me below my arms and Saeward takes me by the feet. The pain of the arrowhead in my thigh brings a yelp from me and Saeward looks upward over one shoulder at me just as a Northman's arrow from below clatters down on the steps beside me and threatens to bounce onto his left shoulder.

He pulls me away and loses his footing, pulling Hemming down behind me.

The three of us slide down the rest of the steps and we fall in a heap to the bottom, Hemming still holding onto me and Saeward lying back against me.

'*Saeward...*' I hear myself groan before passing out.

I know nothing else after that until I am awakened, I do not know how long afterward. I am on my back in a room I have never seen before.

'What happened?' I hear myself ask, as if I were someone else. When no-one answers I try to turn onto my side. Pain engulfs me and I cry out aloud.

'Lie back', an elderly woman tells me soothingly. '*I* am here with you'.

'Who is that?' I ask, trying to look around the room. Firm hands push me down. Not a woman's hands. There is a man with her. I cannot see, but try to think back on who helped me away from the wall. 'Is that Saeward – *Hemming?*'

'Neither – I am no-one you know', a man tells me. 'You are safe here, your wound is being treated and you will live'.

Who are these two? I try to crane my neck to look around but the man's hands push me back down onto this bed by my shoulders.

'*I* am with you, Ivar', the woman tells me, '*Gytha*'.

That is all I hear before the blackness comes over me again.

'Are you awake, Ivar?' a woman asks. It is not Gytha this time. My eyelids seem to be glued together and I try to blink. I screw my eyes tightly together and try again to open them. Someone bathes my eyes gently and I open my eyes at last.

'Ivar, it is Eadgytha. Can you hear me?'

I nod and try to look where I think she is. Pain shoots up my right thigh and I try to stifle the pain.

'Try not to stir, Ivar. You are safe, but you are still a long way from being in good health', Eadgytha tells me and comes to the foot of the bed where I can see her. 'See, I am here'.

She sounds soothing, as Gytha did when as a child I would wake from the nightmare I had lived through. The nightmare was seeing my dead father, sword wounds to his back, chest and stomach. I try to think back on those days, when Gytha helped me through my worst dreams. There had been nights I did not dare close my eyes to sleep until, tired out by crying, falling asleep in Gytha's arms.

Earl Godwin understood, although he could never have known how it felt to see my own father in a bloody mess, laid out on the bed he once shared with my mother. My young kinsmen, Svein and his younger brothers Harold and Tostig helped me through those early years after I first came to live with them at Bosanham.

That was long before Svein was given his earldom of East Aengla. Hereford had followed, and the days of his banishment for taking the abbess at Leofmynster. Meanwhile we had played at fighting until the time came for me to learn the crafts of war. Seafaring with my half-brothers Beorn and Osbeorn followed.

My uncle, Knut died whilst Osbeorn and I were in the Eastern Sea. I did not miss him, believing it was he who had called for the slaying of my father in the great church of Roskilde after they had fallen out over a game of chess in Knut's great hall nearby. That was how I saw it then. As no-one ever tried to tell me otherwise, my belief stayed with me, even after the great king died. Harthaknut, Knut's son by Ymme became king soon after – but only of the Danish isles. Harold 'Harefoot' ruled for him in Aengla Land, and when he died suddenly Harthaknut came and almost had Earl Godwin slain. He believed Godwin answerable for the death of Aelfred, Eadweard's younger brother by Ymme and Aethelred, but Godwin had given him a finely crafted warship. That was the end of that, then - until Harthaknut died 'in his cups' at the feast given by Osgod Clapa for his daughter's wedding. Eadweard was made king in his own right and Earl Godwin was again under threat for the same 'misdeed'.

Now here I am, my thoughts wandering again, not knowing where I am.

'What are you thinking of?' I had not see Saeward enter the small room where my sickbed stands beneath a long, wooden cross. He looks up at the timberwork that hangs there, threatening me with its weight. 'I would never have taken you for a Christian, Ivar'.

'Oh, *that*. I have little say in what hangs on the walls in here. Someone thinks my soul needs saving', I answer, craning my neck to look up.

'It is the Lord's will that Ivar is on the mend', Father Eadwig tells him, having entered behind Saeward. He must have been standing there, behind the door out of my sight, listening to us. He chides, 'Shame on you Ivar, taking the Lord's name in vain'.

'You know *me*, Father', I wink at Saeward.

'I know you to be a brave man, Ivar. Coming over the wall last almost cost you your life. The Lord will find it within him to you'.

'Can *you*, Father?' I test him sorely, but he smiles and shakes his head.

21

'No, Ivar, I cannot forgive you for taking the Lord's name in vain but aye, I can forgive a hero his sins for saving my skin first'.

'Father, the Viking in me hopes to be taken into Valhall'.

I laugh when Eadwig frowns darkly and looks away from me, at Saeward, shaking his head slowly like a forlorn lamb.

'Speak to him for me, Saeward', Eadwig pleads, rolling his eyes in torment.

'Little good will come of it, Father. For all I am a believing Christian I have been thinking of late that I took the wrong road many years ago, working for Wealtham's canons. It is only through meeting Ivar again a year ago that I know I have found my true path', Saeward lets a smile come to his lips.

Eadwig shudders and straightens. He wags a finger at us both as he leaves,

'The way of the sword is the way of Satan', he mumbles, shudders and blesses us both, sprinkles water on my sheeted legs and leaves, grumbling beyond the door. And then he is gone, through an outer door to the street.

'I am still in Exanceaster?' I ask Saeward and am given a nod by way of an answer. '*Where* am I in Exanceaster?'

'This is a small *hospitium* within the garth, beside the hall of Eadgytha, Eadweard's widow', Saeward murmurs as a nun enters, fixes him with a stare and scolds me.

'You should not yet have visitors, Ivar. Your wound must heal!' She turns her head towards Saeward, 'You heard me, I think?'

'I feel no more pain', I lie.

Her eyes turn back to me. Smiling oddly, she tests me,

'Then you will not be against riding away from here soon, if the Northmen win through'.

'That could be weeks yet'. I flinch as I shift on the bed.

'I thought you said you felt no more pain!' she snaps. She smiles oddly again before adding, 'That ride *would* be painful'.

Saeward raises an arm in farewell and leaves. I am left alone with the nun. I cannot think what Svein Godwinson saw in Eadgifu, the abbess at Leominster, if she was anything like this nun. I should think it seemed worthwhile to him to take her in a wilful show of foolishness that earned him his banishment by the old king.

'What is your name, Sister?' I ask, hoping to sound friendly.

'I am Sister Leofgytha', she answers, bustling around the room, tucking in the sheet around my feet, adding nothing more. She is not a woman, just a name.

Sister Leofgytha takes out a bowl and closes the door behind her. I am alone with my thoughts again, wishing I could read.

There is a book on the table I take to be a book of prayer. Would I want to read that?

I think right now I would read *anything* anyone gave me, as bored as I am. Can I think of something to keep myself awake? My head tells me 'no' and I fall asleep again.

When I wake again I hear someone talking outside the room, then the door opens and Sister Leofgytha shows her head, no more. It looks odd with her black hood, as if floating on air.

'You are awake', is all she says and vanishes behind the door again, pulling it to behind her.

I look up at the top of the wall and twiddle my fingers on my chest for want of something to do. I have heard no news for I do not know how long. Since being hauled up over the wall, being drilled by that arrow or crossbow bolt I have seen none of my kinsmen, neither Godwin nor Eadmund. Even Magnus has stayed away. Are they busy, or has Sister Leofgytha warned them off, as she did Saeward. Father Eadwig came to see how I fared, which I think was good of him. Whether he had anything to tell me I do not know. Saeward was unwilling to say out aloud that I am still in Exanceaster, *why?* How did *he* reach me if no-one but the priest was to look in on me?

Sister Leofgytha enters the room again, followed by a Brother. She has a bowl on a tray, with bread beside the bowl, nothing more. I feel starved of food. The arrow – or whatever – entered my backside. I could eat a horse, but I think I shall only see broth again for the time I am here.

The Brother waits for the nun to feed me the broth, break the bread and dip it, then wipe my mouth tenderly. She looks into my eyes and I feel something stir within me. Has Sister Leofgytha found feelings for me now? This is something new to me, when I think back on... when was it I last saw her, aside from when she looked around the door? The Brother closes the door slowly and quietly behind her and walks across the stone floor to my bed,

'How are you, Ivar?'

I cannot see his eyes with the hood down over his forehead, but I think I know he is no man of the Church.

'I have come with news', he goes on.

'Go on?' I ask.

'The Northmen tried their best to break into the burh', I hear him say, whoever he is. My thoughts go to where I heard this man.

'We have seen the king's ballistas being rolled down the dale', the fellow adds.

'*Ballistas* – what are they?' I have never heard the word.

'The Northmen call them trebuchets', the fellow enlightens me, half-smiling. 'I cannot keep up these games'.

The hood falls back to show Hemming.

'I shall have to pull up the hood again if she comes back', he tells me, adding, 'here is something I have brought you'.

From the long sleeve he brings forth a small packet and thrusts it under my sheet before Sister Leofgytha enters again, pulling forward his hood as he steps back. On seeing the Brother is still with me she leaves, closing the door behind her again.

'That was close', Hemming breathes out, grinning.

As there are no chairs in the room there is nothing for him but to stand as he goes on to say Ansgar is with Willelm.

'*Ansgar* is with the Northmen?'

'He could not rebuff the king', Hemming adds quickly. 'There is word Willelm has another Northman in line to be shire reeve of Middil Seaxe. Ansgar is at risk of being sidestepped if he tries to help anyone who wishes to oust his new Lord'.

'I understand. Do you know the whereabouts of Guthfrith?'

'Do you know something I do not?' Hemming's eyes narrow and he stares, disbelief showing in the way he straightens again. 'You would tell me *if you knew?*'

I nod, but I do not think he believes me. My answer is not full enough for him, I know, but he says nothing more about the matter. He seems aloof suddenly. An awkward stillness falls between us. What would he say – *or do* – if I told him Saeward killed his friend?

'I must go', Hemming pulls the hood forward as Sister Leofgytha enters again. He tells her, 'I must be leaving now'.

The nun nods gravely and stands aside for Hemming. As the door closes behind him she comes toward me, lifts the sheet and draws out the packet,

'I cannot allow you to take gifts', is all she tells me and leaves the unopened packet on the table in the far corner, leaving me wondering how I am to reach it without letting her know I am out of the bed. The nun looks sourly at me before leaving the room, 'Sleep, Ivar, and dream of your woman'.

My head jerks towards her as she passes behind the door. Did she see me look up at her? What did she mean? Sleep overcomes me as I lie on my back, staring upward at a spider weaving his highway trap.

In my wild dreams I see shapes leap across a fire. They come closer, and I see women with dark shadows around their foreheads. They beckon to me to enter their frolics and I rise, painlessly from the bed.

Hand in hand we leap across the fire towards someone seated on a small throne. Torchlight shows me only the lower half of her body, rotten, sagging flesh. A torch is held up for me to see who the woman is, and my jaw drops. The woman on the throne is Braenda! *Braenda and the goddess Hel are one and the same!* I twist away from the sight of my woman and her mocking follows me into wakening,

'Do you suddenly not like the sight of me, Ivar?' Braenda is *beside* me!

When I turn to her she smiles and shows what I have missed sorely these past months, her skin soft and firm. I feel pain on turning towards her to my left but that does not matter now.

My woman is with me, yielding once more.

2

'Your sheets are a mess and you are bathed in sweat, what *have* you been doing?' Sister Leofgytha is beside herself when she next enters the room. '*They are wet through!*'

'I had a restless night', I answer, trying to hide a smirk, but she can see through *me* as clearly as if I were made of Frankish glass. She bustles about the room, pulls off the sheet – leaving me covered in little more than a scrap of cloth – and laughs out loudly.

'What *have* you been up to?' She says again, shakes her head and bursts into loud, raucous laughter. 'Have you had a *woman* here without anyone knowing? Do not fear, I shall tell no-one, Ivar. You have plainly wrapped some foolish maid around your little finger, telling her she shall be wed'.

'Not that it is anything to do with you', I tap my nose.

'You might think of something you have missed', Sister Leofgytha turns to find another bedsheet from a chest in the corner.

'*Which is -?*' Has she thought of something I overlooked? I try to show I am not worried, but the look she throws me tells me I *have* missed something – not that she would tell me. She is not like that. Were I in need of something she might withhold it. She spreads out the sheet over my manhood and clicks her tongue,

'I think you know', is all she will tell me for now. 'For the time being you have your morning meal to come'.

'You are still going to feed me?' I try my wit on her, but she turns her back on me and strides from the room. Not long later I hear Sister Leofgytha's footfalls outside the room again and she enters the room with a wooden bowl.

'You can feed yourself now, Ivar', she dumps the hot bowl in my lap, dropping the spoon into the grey-brown mess she has put into the bowl, splashing me with hot porridge. Having shown me how helpless I really am, she strides back to the door and leaves again. Meanwhile I have to struggle with the hot bowl.

When I see her next she looks away from me as she takes the empty bowl. She tells me on her way out of the room,

'Lord Godwin is here to see you'.

'I thank you', I answer, half-smiling at her put-on coolness.

'I have done nothing', Sister Leofgytha says as if in fright, looks over my head, crosses herself with her free hand and stands back to allow Godwin to my bed.

'How much longer will you lie in bed, whilst we out there keep out Willelm's Northmen?' Godwin slaps my shoulder with the open palm of one hand and looks up at the nun. 'You can leave us now, Sister Leofgytha'.

She scowls and pulls the door loudly to behind her.

'For a nun, that one is hardly unruffled. What is she like the rest of the time?' Godwin grins broadly at me.

'I feel well, but for a pain in my backside', I begin.

'*We* have many of them, too', Godwin laughs. 'I was about to ask how you are when you brought it up yourself. Can you walk?'

'I have not tried', I have to allow.

'*God*, I thought you were here to gain your health! What are they doing for you? I think I should leave Saeward here to help you back onto your feet', Godwin stares up at the cross and groans, pointing it out as if I were not already aware of it. 'Fools – what do they think *that* piece of wood is going to do for anyone?'

'I have stared at it for hours on end, trying to think', I sigh, trying to prop myself up without bringing back the pain.

'What if it fell down on you?' Godwin raises the unlikely.

'How is that going to happen?' I am mystified, but I would like to know. I have heard of the ground trembling here and there in the kingdom, but not here, in Defna shire. He does not keep me waiting long for the answer.

'The Northmen have brought two of their *ballistas*. You know of them? They – the *ballistas* - throw stones, *heavy* stones, at the walls. Some over-fly the walls and hit dwellings, churches. Whatever is within a few yards of the walls is broken, flattened, or shattered. Walls shudder – I have seen it – and things fall'.

'Then take it down', I look up and shudder at the thought of being sent to my maker by a heavy wooden cross when I am on the mend.

He calls out someone's name and a tall, burly fellow enters the room.

'*My Lord*, you wish -?' he asks Godwin, sees me on the bed and looks quickly back at my kinsman.

'Take down that wooden thing from the wall, Arnhelm, be a good man', Godwin waves toward the wall and stands well back as the fellow lifts it off its hook and stands it in one corner of my small room.

Sister Leofgytha comes into the room just then and glowers.

'Is that at *your* bidding, Ivar?' she sneers, looking into the corner.

Arnhelm stares at me, shrugs and touches his forehead to her,

'My Lady Leofgytha-'

'Who *told* you to take down our Lord's emblem?' she howls. 'I shall tell Father Eadwig you are *fouling* this hospitium with your deeds!'

'I told him to take it down', Godwin strides back to the middle of

27

the room to catch her eye.

'But why, *why* – what harm has the Lord done you that you anger *him?*' Sister Leofgytha sobs fitfully.

I had not thought she would be so fretful at seeing the cross taken off the wall. Godwin tries to calm her, to tell her why the cross might be harmful but she flees the room, leaving Arnhelm standing with the cross. Godwin tells him to set it down,

'*Leave* it in the corner, man, with Christ looking into the room! In God's name, who does she think she is?'

'She is Queen Eadgytha's abbess, my Lord', Arnhelm tells him.

'I cannot see that my aunt would wish the thing to fall off the wall onto Ivar's head', Godwin groans, then laughs, 'Come, let us away before she brings the hue and cry down onto our heads! Ivar, I leave you in the caring hands of the abbess'.

Leofgytha is the abbess!

With no need to see a lowly priest like Eadwig, she could have the ear of the king, should she wish so. I slide onto my back and await Abbess Leofgytha. Who will she bring back with her, who can tell Arnhelm to put back the cross and threaten me with the likelihood of a rock knocking it onto my head? The wait is not long. Gytha comes into the room with the abbess.

'Why has my cross been taken down from the wall behind you, Ivar? You cannot do this sort of thing, do you know? I will have it put up again when I find someone. Meanwhile, you should stay in bed until Abbess Leofgytha tells you that you are well enough. What have you to *say* for yourself? This is shameful!'

'It was taken down, before it fell down on me, Gytha. Godwin told me the Northmen have *ballistas* –'

'The cross is God's word, Ivar!'

I sit upright in the bed with arms folded and jerk my head backward, towards the wall where the cross hung earlier. Trying to get around her with a little wit, I ask,

'*Would* God want his word to fall so heavily on me?'

She softens, smiles and then shakes her head,

'The word of God, Ivar, harms no-one who might believe in his love'.

I stifle a hollow laugh and try to make her see sense,

'Not unless it is nailed to a chunk of wood the size of a child. Gytha, listen. Godwin said the stones they hurl shake the walls. When he saw that', I point at the cross stood near the end of the bed, 'he had Arnhelm lower it before it was shaken down on me'.

'This is the house of God, Ivar. No harm can come to you here',

Gytha almost whines. The loss of almost all her sons in warfare has shaken her to the core and she needs to believe in something. Now is not the time to test her belief in God's skill in stopping his word from falling on me, who would suffer under its weight. Before leaving the room she stops at the door, stares back at me, shakes her head and vanishes behind the open door.

For the time being I am safe from the weight of the word of God, and I have Godwin to thank for that – the kinsman who sent me away for having a *hwicce* woman, just to calm his priest.

Is it not odd, how our *wyrd* brings us together and draws us apart? Godwin still wishes me to show my war-craft to his men, who are as yet hardly tried. Being here at Exanceaster they will undergo a test of their learning that will either stand them in good stead, or show them how *little* they have learned before they fall to Willelm's swords.

'Now you are well again, Ivar– 'Godwin begins when he sees me atop the wall, looking out over the Northmen's camp.

'I am not at my best, *yet*, kinsman', I have to put him right. 'I still have a limp, where that Northman tested his marksmanship on me'.

'You will not be hard-tested here', Godwin grins, 'not in the way you were tested in the hospitium. Grandmother must have tried you hard'.

'You heard? She has lost much, Godwin. Do not mock her'.

I look out over the wall again at the array of tents and weapons below us, a sea of grey mailcoats waiting to attack when the walls yield to their *ballistas*. *If,* might be a better word. There might be no churches or dwellings left standing within the walls, but the walls themselves would stand against an unending storm of rocks. Many of the rocks they bring to bear on the walls are sandstone and boulder clay, and shatter on the high walls in a red mess, showering the men below in a hail of red dust and stones.

Each time this happens it is met with mocking howls from the men on the walls and earns the Northmen a shower of arrows.

'Where do they get these useless rocks?' Magnus laughs, asking anyone who will listen amidst the roar of laughter around him.

'There are cliffs nearby, downriver, towards the sea I think', Eadmund has heard him over the noise but knows little of southern Defna shire.

Not that I am much wiser, but I keep my thoughts to myself and hope they do not take stone from the upland tors. That granite would shatter the walls and we could find ourselves having to fight hand-to-hand. Do they have the means to cut it and bring it down here? We will soon know, and then Godwin would see better how well his men had been taught to handle their weapons!

'Look out!' one of the men shouts from our left. We drop to our knees as a lump of rock as big as a horse flies over us and lands with a crash in the yard behind us. Shouting follows.

'The outlanders are loosing off their dead horses at us now, are they?' one fellow below us laughs hoarsely.

'*What* was that?' Magnus leans over, stopping himself from falling inward off the walkway by holding on to me. It is as much as I can do to stop myself screaming out in pain. I clamp my jaws together and grin at Eadmund, who looks back at his younger brother.

'They are sending the rotting carcasses of their dead horses over the wall at us!' the fellow yells up at him. 'Wash your ears out!'

Hemming roars back down at him, '*You* – wash your mouth out before you insult your betters! *Who are you, anyway* – what is your name? *Get his name, someone!*'

There is no answer. The fellow below us walks on quickly – abashed - lest we learn his name and he finds himself punished.

'So they are ridding themselves of their dead mounts', Godwin snorts, 'winter has made its grip felt. They must be low on fodder. Heave back the cadaver, and a bale of fodder with it. *We must show Aenglish hospitality to our guests!*'

The dead horse is hoisted with rope-and-tackle to the wall top, and a bale of hay brought from Eadgytha's stables.

'Do we set fire to the hay?' one of the men asks, torch at hand.

'How would *that* help them? No, as Queen Eadgytha is so friendly toward Duke Willelm, the fodder is a gift from my aunt to the Northmen. The Northmen are our foes, *not their horses!*'

Loud laughter along the wall-top drowns out the shouting from below when the dead horse is heaved back over the wall and the hay follows quickly after it. One of the men foolishly looks over the wall and is skewered by an arrow loosed off by a bowman with strong arms.

'I would have thought they would send their thanks by way of a flask of their apple ale!' Saeward scowls darkly.

'They *have* no manners!' I tell him as I watch another arrow arch into the sky from below, fall and hit the back of the walkway with a thud. 'Yet nor are they short of arrows, that they can waste them on us'.

'They are loosing them off blindly', Godwin notes drily, 'out of hopelessness'.

'More like fishing with bows and arrows', Hemming grins and risks looking over the wall, pulling his head back as an arrow soars heavenward and embeds itself in the top of the wall.

'They have a strong bowman down there, with the eye of a hawk', Eadmund adds, sucks in his cheeks, thinking, and clicks his fingers. 'What shall *we* do?'

'What ails, brother?' Godwin looks over one shoulder at him, and steps back as another arrow flies over the top of the wall, to thud into the walkway between us. 'He is getting better. Have you thought of something, Eadmund - that might befall our friend down there?'

'Who have we, who can pick off the bowman with a throwing spear?' Eadmund asks, not of Godwin but of Hemming.

'How would I know? I do not know any of – ', he stops, deep in thought. 'Is Ordeh still with you?'

'*Ordeh* – do I know someone by that name? Which one is Ordeh?' Godwin asks Eadmund.

'Best ask Hemming – or Ivar', Magnus enters the fray.

'Do *you* know him by sight?' Eadmund asks me.

I have to think back to Naesinga, a hard task after spending days in the sickbed and riding across the kingdom.

However something comes back,

'Ordeh – *I* know him, well enough to have been taken aback by the strength of his throw. As you say, Hemming, he was good with the throwing spear', I stretch my neck and scratch at the new growth of bristle.

'So – *where* is he, can you tell me?' Godwin looks hopelessly aside, and around at his men. 'Come, this is not the time for play. Where *is* he?'

'He is right there, *behind* you, Lord Godwin', Hemming smiles, as if talking to a child.

Godwin wheels and asks,

'Which of these three is he?'

'*I* am Ordeh, Lord', a tall, scruffy, dark-haired fellow answers.

'*Ordeh* – I might have known it was you', Godwin pulls back. Not only is Ordeh scruffy, he smells – of swine-feed and fish.

In winter he cared for Godwin's swine, in summer he caught and sold fish in the river near Maldun. 'How are you with the throwing spear – *still good?*'

'I can show you, Lord', Ordeh thrusts his spear forward.

He almost spears Godwin's right nostril before my kinsman pushes away the point and beckons the fellow to show us on those below,

'If you are as good with the spear as Saeward is with the axe, we have little to worry about. As long as we keep these bowmen's heads down, we need fret no longer about their arrows cutting down my men. How do we test you?'

31

'See that basket in the lee of the walkway?' Eadmund points

'Aye, Lord?' Ordeh seems to stare at my kinsman, something he would have to unlearn, if he wishes to forward a life as a warrior with Godwin. I wonder if he is deaf and needs to read my kinsman's lips as he speaks. 'You wish me to spear it for you, from here?

'That *is* what I wish', Godwin raises a brow when the fellow turns to take aim. We stand back to give him throwing room and watch, open-mouthed when the spear slices through the basket, scattering the clothing in it.

'What sort of fool hurled a spear into my washing basket?!'

A woman rushes out from one of the dwellings and stops short as an arrow thuds into the earth an arm's length way from her. She screams and runs back indoors. At least we no longer have to beg her forgiveness. Godwin eyes Eadmund, who shrugs and turns away,

'Brother mine, that arrow saved you from a strong tongue-wagging!' Magnus digs Eadmund with one elbow and laughs.

'It will be paid back', Godwin draws Ordeh back, then pulls his hand away again, quickly, taking care to smile winsomely when Ordeh looks his way. 'Take as many throwing spears as you wish. Be a good fellow and show what you can do with them'.

'I will help him, Lord', Hemming eagerly goes about looking for throwing spears.

'Then take him to the *weapontake*, instead of looting other men's weaponry here', I take three of the spears from him and set them back down against the outer wall. Some would doubtless ask where their throwing spears were.

Hemming nods jerkily and beckons Ordeh to follow him down the steps. They both vanish into the darkness of the nearing winter's evening and Eadmund assures his brother that they mean well. His belief in their well-meaning is not shared by Godwin. He would need more than just words if men took him to task for the loss of belongings left on the *burh* walls.

I ask Godwin when the din dies down,

'How long have Willelm's men been here now?'

Godwin looks upward as if in search of help. He squints at the setting sun and turns to Eadmund,

'Eadmund – *do you know?*' Godwin tests whether his brother is aware of what I have asked.

'Know *what?*' Eadmund has been watching one of the maids below in the street and looks blankly at both Godwin and me. He looks back to Godwin, '*Well?*'

'Do you know how long ago the Northmen first came?' Godwin

asks.

'Let me think back now – aye, I would say at least *twelve* days'.

'*Surely not* - it has to be *ten!*' Magnus frowns.

'Two days of your life will not be missed at your age, little brother', Eadmund sniffs.

'A *fortnight*, Lord', someone puts us right.

'A fortnight, who said that was so?' Eadmund looks over one shoulder and sees one of his men has raised a hand.

'Aye, Lord', another adds, 'and we have been here only two days longer'.

Saeward seeks to put them both right,

'Right, I might say - *and yet so wrong!*'

'How so', one asks, 'if you are so wise, I wonder you should tell us?'

'We have been here fifteen days, having come on the Sabbath, and yesterday was the third we have spent here, the second since the Northmen came'.

In the gathering darkness it is hard to read what the men around us are thinking. Godwin looks down at his feet and mumbles,

'Saeward is right. *Father Eadwig* will bear that out – not that it says anything either way. I mean, how is it we have so little do besides listen to rocks crashing against the walls. *Is Ordeh back yet?*'

'Lord?' Hemming comes up the steps first, laden down with armfuls of throwing spears. Ordeh – well we can smell him coming up the steps – is close behind with throwing axes tucked into his belt.

'Ah, *here you both are!*' Godwin looks Ordeh up and down and asks, *'Throwing axes too?'*

In the light of a torch I can see Hemming smiling brightly at Saeward,

'I thought we would let Saeward show off, Lord'.

'Well, Saeward, *will* we witness your skill with the axe?' Eadmund pinches his nose and takes an axe from Ordeh's belt.

'Now, *in this light* – there is no way I could see to throw!' Saeward folds his arms. He will not be swayed.

'Could *you* throw a spear in this light as well as you could *earlier?*' Godwin asks Ordeh.

'I would have to look over the wall, but that torch would need to be doused first', Ordeh nods toward one of Godwin's men.

'What if he holds it low?' Godwin presses a hand down in the air to show the fellow how he wants the torch held. We shall need more than one, anyway, to go down the steps when we are done here.

Ordeh looks down and shakes his head,

'Saeward is right. Early light would be best', he agrees.

'What if I threw a torch down?' Hemming asks, reaching for the one Godwin's man still holds at waist height.

'What would *that* do?' Magnus laughs.

Hemming looks sidelong at Magnus, almost as if pleading, 'Ordeh could throw his spear at the bowman whilst his comrades try to put out the flaming torch'.

'The torch would surely break apart when it fell to the ground!' Eadmund sputters.

'Unless we put pitch on it', I offer. We can but try.

'Do we *have* pitch?' Godwin asks.

'The smithy has pitch, Lord', one of the Exanceaster men speaks up.

'Go, fetch some pitch and we will have this out, one way or the other', Godwin tells Hemming.

Magnus raises his doubts about the wisdom of doing so,

'Has anyone not thought that we will be making a gift of burning pitch to the Northmen?'

'They *have* fire', Godwin rebukes his young brother.

'Aye, but if they had *pitch* they would have used it against us by now, *surely?*' Magnus will not be done down.

Godwin purses his lips,

'Pitch is easily made'.

'Only if you have the *means*', I shake my head wearily. 'If they had been able to make it down there, Willelm would have made ample use of it against us. There is enough timber around to make a kiln, I will give you that. However they can not have found the other parts. Stay your hand, wait for the daylight'.

'Very well', Godwin shrugs, unwillingly agreeing. He wanted to show the Northmen they are too easily hurt down there, as much as we are in here. There will be another day to shine. 'Set the watch, Eadmund, and we shall withdraw'.

We all leave the wall to the night men.

Little can happen on a dark winter's night. The Northmen will be only too happy to tuck themselves into their sleeping bags, out of the way of this bone-chilling cold. They will be downcast, unhappy with their lot. Instead of cheering themselves over the Yuletide they are here, deep in Defna shire, far from their homes in a warmer Northmandige.

In the morning we climb, laden with weaponry to the wall-top. Frost rime is everywhere and we must be careful on the steps. The cold gnaws at your very soul, as it does on the banks of Roskilde Fjord at this time of the year. The Yuletide, the Seaxan's Christ mass, has passed and the camp lights and fires below burn sullenly in the mist that creeps up along the river from the sea.

The Northmen seem barely alive, having to live under canvas these last two weeks, as Saeward rightly pointed out. There are a few gathered below, as one of them – the bowmen – readies to show off again.

'Ordeh, Saeward – *are you ready?*' Godwin hisses, rubbing his gloved hands. He dare not clap them for warmth lest he lets those below know we are here. We need to take them off guard, for our 'games' to be of any use.

Saeward raises an axe skyward, as if aiming,

'There is a dark cloud, Lord'.

'We know – his name is Willelm and he thinks he is king. Why do you bring that up now, of all times?' Godwin is at first irked. He smiles on our missing his show of wit and shakes his head ruefully, 'Aye, the day will be long, friends. We are all short of sleep and another long night threatens. I also see the weather closing, what of it?'

'If we wait for it to come over, they will not see us so easily from below. They will truly be thrilled if suddenly they are beset by spears and axes that they cannot see before they hit!' I read Saeward's thoughts. 'Be sure to wear no helms that might glow even dully in the light and give you away'.

'Ready?' Ordeh grins at Saeward.

'You can start,' Saeward answers, as if offering drink at a feast.

'Get on with it, you two! Keep your manners for your own kind', Godwin snaps at their foolishness and looks warily over the top of the wall. 'There are men gathering below'.

'What if I drop a log over the wall behind them?' Hemming asks, brandishing a hefty chunk of timber.

'*Do* that, but you will only bring it off once. For the next time, we will need to think of something else', Saeward thinks beyond what Hemming has put forward.

Whatever serves to take the Northmen's eyes from him and Ordeh must help. Hemming strides away taking long steps, and stops, looks over the wall without putting his head too far out, turns and waves back.

'When he drops the wood, be ready with your spear, Ordeh, and I shall throw one of these axes the other way. We will see how long it takes before these men of Willelm's understand what is happening. After that we must take care', Saeward licks a thumb and runs it along the short blade, drawing a thin line of red.

Godwin watches out for Hemming, who raises a thumb on dropping his log. Ordeh leans over the wall, takes aim and throws a spear. Before he can draw his arm back an arrow slices through it, near the wrist,

'*Aah -!*' Ordeh sucks deeply on the winter air. Saeward does not even bother to aim, happy just to let fly the throwing axe.

A loud scream of anguish rents the air from below and Saeward smiles gleefully, punching the air,

'I have got *even* for you, Ordeh! Fear not, I shall see to your wound. These Church folk here seem unable to bring men back to health quickly, eh Ivar? I shall have you walking – *running even*, like a child!'

Magnus makes to lean over the wall, but I pull him back.

'Godwin, do you not think the Northmen may be playing with us?' He asks.

'*That* was not playing!' Godwin assures him. Our grins do, too. 'That was too good for someone making out he was cut down to get one or more of us to look over. One way or another, we shall soon know'.

For some time rocks pound the walls, knocking the frozen snow from the wall-top. One or two pass over the top, at which we curse and crouch beneath to ensure we are not beheaded. Some clay clumps break on the walkway behind us, but most fall short and we hear them thudding against the bottom of the wall.

'Have they taken their *ballistas* further away, I wonder?' Eadmund asks. The thin winter air is quiet again, but I sense something is amiss.

'Why would they do that unless something was afoot – *under*foot, even?' I ask, and suck on my teeth, pondering why things have changed. 'I have yet to see Thegn Earnwin this morning. Does he have tasks in the *burh* that keep him?'

'No doubt he has', Godwin answers, and begins to chew on his upper lip. I have set him thinking. He adds, 'Thegn Ligulf should be here by now, however. His lands are beyond Exanceaster and he only stayed because he left it too late to leave for his hall'.

'What are you saying, Godwin?' Magnus is uneasy now.

He drills the cold air with a stare that tells me he has thought beyond his brother's answer. Have the two thegns feared the worst and are talking with Willelm about what they should do, hoping to hold onto their lands after they yield the *burh* to him?

'You are thinking the same as I, Ivar?' Godwin's right brow lifts as he asks.

My worst fears must be mirrored on my brow. He sighs deeply.

'I should not wonder Willelm will have asked for hostages', Godwin begins again. 'Whether the fools took him for one of them, I cannot say. I only know they will learn their lesson hard. With our friends

Ordeh and Saeward killing his men after the thegns asked him for a truce, he will not let them get away with thinking they can drag him in like a floundering eel'.

'You fear we have been *betrayed?*' Eadmund has seen the signs. 'Godwin - we need to help the others, the women, away with our younger kin, and *soon!* Can we get boats away to help them flee, and if so *where to?*'

'There is an isle to the north of Defna shire, Steepholm. We take them north and have fishermen take them across in their boats', Godwin had already thought it through.

He is every inch his father's son.

Whereas his younger brothers shake with fear he is ready to act. I like him more, even though he let his priest have me cast to the wind last winter. I should let bygones be bygones. For now we must be ready to leave before Willelm enters the *burh.*

'Saeward, Hemming - go with Ivar. See the womenfolk are ready. Mother may know of another way out', Godwin waves us off.

'There *is* a way out', Gytha tells me when I see her in the stone-built church. 'Father Eadwig knows of it, ask him'.

'Meanwhile can you be ready, and help Eadgytha with the younger ones?

'I *will* see to them. Do not fret about us, Ivar. Everything will be fine, trust me', Gytha smiles. She has forgotten about the cross in the hospitium now she has something to do. It will be as when Godwin had to sail for Flanders thirteen years since.

'Meanwhile I must find our horses –', I begin.

'Our horses will be where we come to, through the tunnel from within the church', Gytha tells me.

'I thought you said –'

She puts a finger on my lips and ushers me away,

'I only know it is there, I do not know where within the church', Gytha prods my back. 'Go quickly, find the priest and tell him we need to find the tunnel'.

I look down at her and she flaps her hands about,

'Go – *go!*' she ushers us away.

Saeward and Hemming seek out Eadwig and find him at the door, on his way in to see Gytha. He stares at me bleakly and asks,

'It has come to *this?*'

'It has come to this, aye', I nod, and ask him about a tunnel in the church.

'Who told *you* about that?' Father Eadwig seems suddenly to have misgivings.

'Gytha told me. She will help Eadgytha 'Svanneshals' with her youngest, Ulf. Her daughters will be able to pack what little they need for the few days – hopefully – that they will hide on Flatholm. Is it true there is a tunnel in the church?'

Eadwig stares up at me, still not trusting, and snaps,

'Leave that with me!' He will not tell me. 'Come with everyone else to the church at the allotted hour –'

'What is the allotted hour?' Hemming asks. He looks puzzled as to why Father Eadwig is being so guarded.

'Lord Godwin will tell you. Ask him', Father Eadwig brushes past us, into Queen Eadgytha's hall to find Gytha. Hemming throws his hands up and shrugs.

'We should find Godwin and tell him everything is in hand', I beckon Hemming and Saeward to follow.

'It is all we can do. Why does Father Eadwig not trust us?' Saeward wonders aloud, close behind me when we climb to the wall walkway. Godwin watches us near him and looks closely at me when I tell him about Eadwig's tunnel.

'We *must* trust him', Godwin sniffs, 'with so few ways out open to us. We have still seen nothing of the thegns, Earnwin and Ligulf. I fear the worst'.

'Father Eadwig said something about an 'allotted hour'. What is that about?' Hemming presses Godwin for an answer.

'An allotted hour – what is that? I cannot think what he means. We go when we can, when the womenfolk are ready', Godwin looks around. The men there know we are leaving. They will be true to their oaths and fight to the last drop of blood in their veins has ebbed. They are Defna men, and as Godwin's huscarls have done – for want of a better word - have given their word to uphold Seaxan rule within the kingdom. Their oaths may cost them their lives, but they say nothing.

'Are the men ready?' Godwin asks Eadmund.

'They are ready', Eadmund answers levelly, and we make our way back down, Hemming and Saeward following after me. Godwin, being first to the ground strides toward the church. On reaching the great oak door Eadwig opens up and we follow him.

'What is this Hemming tells me of an allotted hour, Eadwig?' Godwin tests the priest.

'Allotted hour? What do you mean, what is the allotted hour?' Eadwig stalls.

'Do not ask me', Godwin out-stares Eadwig and the priest steps back to the doorway wall. 'You told Hemming about an allotted hour at which we leave here. Tell me, what is meant by that?'

Eadwig swallows hard, his Adam's apple bouncing,

'Well, can you tell *me* the allotted hour when we can leave Exanceaster?' Eadwig flusters.

'Was there ever any talk about you leaving the burh with us?' Eadmund asks.

'As a priest you are safe with the Northmen', I add. 'Willelm will always need a priest to bless his men before they kill more Aenglishmen'.

'His men will know me from the other night, surely?' Eadwig is still set on leaving with us. Why?

'I hardly think so', Hemming folds his arms and looks Eadwig up and down. The priest seems to be at a loss and flaps his arms as if trying to fly like a bird.

'That night I would not have known my mother', Saeward tests Eadwig.

He peers in the early evening darkness at the priest '

'One priest looks much like another on a dark, moonless night'.

'*They would know if I spoke!*' Eadwig grumbles. He only spoke to one Northman, the other was Guthfrith, and he is no longer with us.

'Aside from Guthfrith', Saeward now smells the blood of his prey, and pushes Eadwig back onto a prayer stool, 'you only blessed one Northman. What do you say to that, priest?'

Eadwig is silent, afraid. Godwin stares down at him, trying to think of what to say next.

'What *do* you say, Eadwig? Have you brokered a pact with Willelm?' My kinsman, along with many Aenglishmen, cannot bring himself to say 'King Willelm'. That would mean allowing that the Northman duke has a claim. It is a better claim than he has, even though his father *was* king for most of the year. But Eadweard's real heir was bypassed then as he has been again. Where is Eadgar *now?*

'I have not', Eadwig stands his ground, but everything about him says he is lying.

'*Where* is the tunnel?' Eadmund asks Eadwig.

'I am *leading* you to it', Eadwig brightens. He may not be lying this time, but he is still unwilling to tell us everything.

'Lead us to the tunnel, Eadwig', Gytha takes his elbow and steers him, but the priest goes the other way. 'But *Eadwig*, you told me the tunnel was behind the altar'.

'You must have been thinking of someone else, dear Gytha. I have never told you about it being behind the altar, it would make no sense'.

'This church is side on to the burh wall, is it not?' Magnus sets about Eadwig now when he turns toward a corner.

'That corner would be toward the old gate', Godwin squints, trying to put himself outside the church, where he would be looking now. 'How well is the old gate guarded?'

'No-one would have thought it useful to anyone', Eadmund shrugs. 'It is blocked from within'.

'*Is* it indeed?' Magnus shakes his mane.

'It would not be too hard to see for myself', Godwin presses Eadwig back onto the prayer stool when he tries to rise.

'I will keep him here whilst you look', I stare down at the worried priest. Something is amiss, he knows, and he would like to leave before it is too late.

'Why are you so afraid?' Eadmund asks. 'If you led us to the tunnel at the outset this would not happen'.

'But I was going to *lead* you!' Eadwig blubs like a child.

'You *were,* but are no longer?' I smile.

'I still *would*', Eadwig tries to stand but the point of my dagger blade nicks his cheek.

His hand goes to a small gash the length of my thumbnail and when he feels blood there he looks fearfully up at me.

'I need to tend to my wound!' Eadwig whines.

'What you need is a good seeing to. A woman could cure your ills', Hemming laughs, unaware I wonder that Eadwig has talked himself into an early grave. Saeward would give him that seeing to, but not in the way Hemming means.

'Where is the *tunnel?*' Godwin has no time for this, saying each word as if speaking to a child.

'You said it is behind the *altar*, I *heard* you', Eadgytha starts on him now. 'When we first came here, you told Gytha it is behind the altar, in the end wall'.

'Look for it, Eadmund. Use a knife tip to find loose stones', Godwin pushes a now shaking Eadwig back onto the stool.

Saeward's keen eye searches the wall for breaks in the stonework,

'It may be easier to see than we think', he taps each stone near the floor with the butt of his axe blade and smiles. 'Did *you* hear that, Ivar?'

He taps a couple of stones for me to hear before hitting the next a little harder. It sounds loose, ready to come out, as does the next in line.

There is a faint line, filled with grey stone dust, in the floor partly hidden by a rug. Saeward lifts the rug and his smile widens. There is an iron ring here that he lifts with both hands. A stone slab is raised with my help to show a deep, long, dark tunnel. Eadmund looks irked at Eadwig. Frightened, the priest stands and pulls back, but is halted by the stool and Hemming takes hold of him to stop him falling backward over it – or leaving in a hurry.

'Bring one of the torches', Godwin points to a pair that flicker with a draught of fresh air from the tunnel. Hemming reaches and takes one down from its wall bracket. 'Hold it down'.

The torch flickers wildly in the tunnel mouth and Hemming straightens.

'Bring him', Godwin beckons me to lead Eadwig.

I know Saeward would dearly love to see him part from life's slender thread, but I think Godwin has further use for him.

'You know where this leads. Come', Godwin is not asking, he is telling the priest to take us through the tunnel, Eadwig to head us to its end. Who knows what awaits us there.

'There are loose stones in the corner, too', Magnus calls, 'higher up in the wall. Shall I look where it would lead?'

Godwin shakes his head and tells him to leave be. Whoever awaited us will come to look and wonder where we have gone. Someone will put the rug back again- but who will do that?

'One of Queen Eadgytha's Exanceaster household men will set the slab back again and put everything back again the way it was before, to look untouched', Godwin tells us. 'Ivar, can you ask Aelfmaer to come? He should be in the hall kitchen, helping the maids clean away before their new Lord shows. We will be in the tunnel, follow us'.

I nod and turn for the door when Aelfmaer shows, about to enter the church. I stare warily at him – *was he listening?* I wonder he may be in the pay of either of the thegns, Ligulf or Earnwin, but my misgivings are overlooked. Godwin is happy about him being here so soon and beckons me to enter the tunnel after the womenfolk and little Ulf.

'You know what to do?' Godwin nods after Aelfmaer, and drops two - then a third gold coin - into the elderly fellow's open palm, stuffs his coin bag back into a leather satchel and comes down into the tunnel. He tells me to go ahead of him, ahead of Magnus.

Eadwig is down there, waiting, shivering with fear, to be told to make his way forward, Hemming close behind, keeping Saeward from knifing the priest. Godwin wants him alive, but will be happy to leave him to Saeward when the time comes. Magnus has a second torch from the wall.

When Aelfmaer lowers the slab we are in a dank, narrow tunnel, thirteen of us shuffling slowly along past and below thick cobwebs.

There is little headroom for a full-grown man, and Hemming has to carry his torch low. He has a rope tied to Eadwig's midriff to stop the fellow getting too far ahead, too soon. I would say Hemming is right not to trust the priest.

On the whole the Church sees Willelm as the rightful king; some beg to differ, but they are few in number and would be unheeded if it came to a show of hands amongst the clerics, from Archbishop Ealdwin downward.

Ulf whimpers and is comforted by Eadgytha. In this narrow tunnel he would not be the only one to feel forlorn, but as grown men and women we keep any fears hidden. I think back, a little over a year ago to Akeham, when Hrothulf, Aethel and I followed another tunnel, only to come eye-to-eye with Brand.

The strong breeze we felt in the church seems to have died down now. I wonder if the wind has died down outside. There are so many other likelihoods that I would sooner not think about, but I still have misgivings.

My worst fear would be of falling into the waiting arms of Willelm. He makes Brand seem happy-go-lucky. Knowing him he would not harm me, not to begin with. There are too many others he could hurt, the weakest first, and have me watch as he did so. I try to think of other things, but am plagued by that one. The thought keeps coming back to curse me.

The breeze blows down through the tunnel again, a little stronger this time. Ahead of me, Eadmund's hair is blown back over his shoulders. I feel better for this freshening air and all seems well with the world. We come nearer to the end of the by now weed and root-ridden tunnel in the dark. Our torches are held down near the mouth so as not to betray us. Still no-one speaks, although the others must feel as uplifted as I am at being close to the open.

Godwin whispers hoarsely,

'Saeward go forward and see what is there at the end of the tunnel. Try not to show too much of yourself in the open, and leave Eadwig alone when you pass him!'

'Aye, Lord', Saeward murmurs and pushes past Hemming.

3

Eadwig pulls back against the tunnel wall and Saeward lets out muffled laughter as he passes him, pushing him against tree roots.

'Saeward, *what did I say?*' Godwin hisses, but Saeward is already beyond hearing. He comes back not long after and asks about the horses.

'What *about* the horses?' Godwin asks, nonplussed.

'I heard the Lady Gytha tell Ivar in the church that we would have our horses -', Saeward does not finish before Gytha breaks in.

'I was told by Saewulf that we would have horses waiting for us here, to take us womenfolk and the young ones to the coast.

'I know of no such thing, nor do I know a Saewulf here at Exanceaster. What does he look like?' Godwin is nonplussed, scratches his beard and shepherds us to the tunnel mouth.

'He is short, with close-cropped hair', Gytha tells him and on leaving the tunnel mouth looks about. The trees above us creak in the wind and she looks up, 'Who are *they?*'

'Who are *who?*' Eadmund asks her, ushering Harold's daughters out of the tunnel mouth.

'*They*, up there', Gytha stabs the air with a long, bony finger, 'the men - hanging there, above you'.

Her grandson wheels and catches sight of them.

'Godwin, there are townsfolk up there that I saw yesterday on the wall'.

'The thegns must have given Willelm hostages', he answers dully. 'Ordeh's spear-throwing and Saeward's axe-throwing must have angered the king. They could not have trusted us, to tell us what they hoped to bring off with the Northman bastard. I wonder whether now they will learn, know the creature they are dealing with.

'What sort of lesson is it, when we must learn from others of the slaying of friends?' Magnus rails.

'There *is* always that' Eadmund shrugs.

Magnus' eyes are filled with hot tears of anger. He tries to hide his tearful fury at the hateful betrayal by these Exanceaster thegns.

'Then they would surely have learned their lesson at first hand!' Magnus snaps.

'You might want to hand yourself over against *our* deeds', Eadmund laughingly tells his young brother under his breath, loud enough for me to hear.

'Eadmund we must make our way away from here', Godwin chides, 'instead of standing around talking. 'Mother we must hurry. We will have some way to go before we can buy horses. We will carry Ulf for a while between us, beginning with me. When we are far enough away, he can walk'.

'There are bound to be steadings, where we can find horses to carry us to the coast', Eadgytha agrees.

She catches little Ulf deftly and swings playfully him into Godwin's waiting arms,

'Your big brother will carry you', she tells him.

'I *am* big now, big enough to walk!' Ulf squawks huffily and Godwin cups a hand over his mouth.

'*Shhh* – we must be away from here quicker than *you* can walk!' Godwin hisses, tickling his ear.

'Who will carry my sisters?' Ulf writhes, and is gripped tighter. 'Ow, Godwin, *that hurt!*'

'Stop struggling, little brother', Eadmund growls at him, 'or when it is *my* turn to carry you, I shall tickle you and *tickle* you harder!'

'Quiet, both of you - 'Godwin hisses, 'there *is* someone nearby! Saeward go forward and see who is there. Kill them if you must'.

That is not the wisest to tell my East Seaxan friend, since he killed Guthfrith without asking me. I still feel the pain of the arrow in my rear. Had he waited, we would have been stronger by one man, and we could have withdrawn over the *burh* walls without Eadwig learning anything from the Northmen. Guthfrith could have told us.

Saeward creeps forward, vanishes into the undergrowth and shows again a little further uphill toward the high moor, waving us forward.

'What is it?' Godwin asks when we come closer.

'A man with horses is up there', he grins. 'It might be us he awaits'.

'It could be a trap', Eadmund counsels.

'Go forward again, find out who it is waiting and if he seems unwilling to part with the horses kill him',

Saeward smiles thinly and draws the blade of his dagger over the palm of his hand, drawing blood. He licks the blood and slips quietly into the undergrowth. I liked him better when he was at Wealtham. Now he is tainted, like the rest of us killers by our own choosing. He is a useful tool, however, skilled in his art.

When the undergrowth rustles madly we freeze, swords at the ready until Saeward shows with another fellow in the light of the moon. I do not know rightly how far we are from the *burh*, and I do not know how tightly Willelm may have drawn his ring of steel around Exanceaster and I would not want to test the Northmen's hearing as well as my kinsman and friends are doing now.

With Saeward is a stocky fellow, hair cropped almost to the line of

44

his skull, who leads our saddled horses, three more for the womenfolk and Ulf follow, led by a scruffily clothed stable-hand.

'This fellow says his name is Saewulf', Saeward tells us as he draws the horses forward to let Godwin and Eadmund take their bridles. The fellow with him has four horses.

'Saewulf', Gytha asks, 'where is Almaer?'

'I do not know, Lady Gytha', Saewulf does not meet her gaze. 'I have Ecgwin with me'.

Godwin still plainly thinks something is afoot and looks around warily, down the path we followed and into the undergrowth. He would like to ask – *as I would* – how Saewulf and his friend left Exanceaster and gathered our mounts – saddled *and* bridled, no less!

'Where did you get such wonderful horses, Saewulf?' Gytha asks, wide-eyed.

'And with such handsome Northman saddles', I stride toward the first horse Ecgwin holds in check for Eadgytha to mount.

Ecgwin squints as I close my hand on his crop.

'Why are you doing that, Ivar?' Gytha tries to pull my hand from Saewulf's throat. 'Let *go* of him, *poor man!*'

'You might ask, Gytha, why the saddles on these three horses are of the Northman art', I show her the front and rear pommels. 'Have you *ever* seen this kind?'

'King Eadweard and Lord Eustace had saddles like them, if you think back on it', Gytha tells me, still holding on to my elbow and Ecgwin's eyes are streaming, his body shakes with fear. I tell her both men spent many a year in Northmandige, in company with Willelm.

She lets go my elbow and Ecgwin looks up, as if hoping to be freed from my grip by someone above.

'Let him free, Ivar', Godwin asks. 'I shall speak with him. If his answers do not satisfy me I shall hand him back to you to be dealt with. We shall soon learn whether he is in Willelm's pay'.

Magnus and Eadmund stand to left and right of him, Godwin to his fore, and ask this and that. Saeward thinks little of their questioning, even less of Saewulf's answers. Godwin is less than happy with the answers he is given, although Eadmund and Magnus see nothing wrong in them.

'You have still not given a good answer as to why the saddles and bridles are not Aenglish'.

'Where do the three other horses come from?' I ask again, patting Braenda on her nose.

'Thegn Ligulf knows where they came from', Ecgwin tells Godwin when he can breathe again.

'How did *you* come by them?' Godwin presses.

'I brought them down from a steading below the moor-top', Saewulf answers Godwin and steps back when he sees the priest, Eadwig.

'Saewulf – how did *you* leave the burh?' Eadwig is taken aback by the sight of Queen Eadgytha's elderly discthegn.

The older man is as baffled at the sight of the priest,

'What are *you* doing here, Eadwig? I thought you were with the abbess Leofgytha'.

'They think I serve the Northmen. Tell them I do *not!*' Eadwig whimpers.

'Not knowing any better, I cannot say either way, Father Eadwig', Saewulf answers with a loud sniff. He has as good as sunk a knife into the priest's ribs, but he has still not said how he and Ecgwin came to be out here. Saeward eyes both men closely. His gaze rests longer on Eadwig wondering, I might say, when he will be let loose on the priest. I can read him well by now.

Having mistakenly seen off Guthfrith, he will not err a second time and awaits Godwin's say-so on either of these two.

Godwin is unsure. Eadwig as a trusted man of God, and Saewulf being of his aunt Eadgytha's household, is almost like kindred. But now there is a threat, and either discthegn or priest could bring it down on our heads, the womenfolk and child Ulf notwithstanding.

'Do not kill Eadwig', Godwin tells Saeward, knowing how near the priest is to being laid low. 'Bind him and gag him. The Northmen will find him in the morning'.

'*Godwin*, my son -' Eadwig pleads. When Godwin nods to Saeward he draws back.

'You are *not* my father, Eadwig! I cannot trust you not to bring down the wrath of this Northman king down on our heads. Wulfnoth, my uncle, would doubtless be happy to have some of us with him over the sea to share his gloom, but we must deny him for now and hope to bring him home soon. Be glad I have not told this fellow here', Godwin aims a thumb at my East Seaxan friend, 'to use his knife on you. *Saewulf* heed my words, that if you are found to have schemed with the Northmen I shall not afford you the same kindness!'

Saewulf nods. If he knows something about the priest, he hides it well. Saeward pulls Eadwig's hands together behind his back and binds them tightly. A clean rag is found to pull over his mouth and he is pushed backward to the ground, stumbling over tree roots as he tries to keep his feet. Saeward trips him and he lands in nettles.

'Feet together, Eadwig!' Saeward tells him, binds his legs at the knees and takes a length down to the priest's ankles. Task done,

Saeward stands and awaits further word, leaving Eadwig struggling in the nettle bed.

'Hide him behind the bushes there', Eadmund offers as little Ulf stares wide-eyed down at Eadwig. There will be others like Eadwig, no doubt, willing to do Willelm's bidding because the Church has thrown its weight behind him as Eadweard's heir and anointed king.

Ulf's eyes grow even wider as Saeward drags Eadwig by his feet to where Eadmund shows him. His mother, Eadgytha '*Svanneshals*' pulls him away to where Saewulf has brought the horses and hoists him onto the saddle,

'Stay there, son', she pats his back and goes to help Saewulf lift Gytha into her saddle. Harold's daughters are helped into their saddles by Hemming and Magnus, with some muted giggling from Gunnhild.

We are ready to leave and Godwin looks to where Eadwig has been left.

'He is safe, my Lord', Hemming tells my kinsman. 'He will be found when the Northmen come looking for stones for their *ballista*'.

Godwin is still unsure, but on a nod from Eadmund we make our way along the narrow dale to the uplands.

We men have a long walk ahead of us, leading our mounts, before we can allow a halt on the moor overlooking the sea to the north. How far Willelm sends out his horsemen to scour the land is unknown to us, and we have only until the dawn to reach the tops, and safety.

There is no snow in this part of the kingdom as yet, and we will leave no tracks, but the cold gnaws hungrily at our bones. Gytha, Eadgytha and her offspring are wrapped well against the weather, but they could begin to feel it unless we find shelter soon. There may well be snow higher up, I do not know. The wind has been coming from the west of late, and may have kept the moor snow-free.

As for Eadwig, he may have luck on his side and be saved from a cold death - or not. I shall lose no sleep over him - nor are Saeward or Hemming likely to – but Godwin is much his father's son. He cannot readily bring himself to believe a priest would turn him over to Willelm, however well meant his aims.

Our climb is made without talking. We must keep our strength for the way ahead, as food may not be found before we reach the northward-looking slopes. The outlanders may well have scoured the land to the furthermost steadings this side of the uplands, to keep their men and horses fed as they did on making landfall near Haestingas. Every ceorl and freeman within sight of the south coast had cattle, sheep and crops taken from them to feed the outlanders.

Godwin whispers hoarsely as dawn lightens the land.

'*What was that?*'

'What was *what*? What have you seen?' I murmur, taking in the hillside above us, where he points.

'I saw a glint of metal in the light of the rising sun', Godwin halts, one arm outstretched. The horses are reined in and we keep to the few trees that grow up here. 'There, *look!*'

I see the flash on sunlight on steel and halt sharply.

'Is it one of *them?*' Magnus cranes his neck to see, Eadmund behind him holding him by the shoulders.

'Who can tell? It seems there is one on his own, but there might be others lower down, ahead', Godwin shivers and tries to stop his teeth from chattering in the cold. Our breath hangs in clouds around our heads as we strain, open-mouthed to see whether the rider is one of Willelm's or -

'He has a *pennon*', Saeward growls. 'A Northman, I would say!'

'What is a *pennon?*' Magnus asks Eadmund, who shrugs and looks at me.

My breath wreathed in a thick, icy cloud I tell him,

'Their horsemen have long spears they call *lances*. *Pennons* are the flyers you see just below the spear or lance heads'.

'If you had them, why might it not be other Aenglishmen who have taken them from the foe?' Magnus starts forward, hands cupped over his mouth.

Saeward pulls him back sharply, hands over my young kinsman's mouth. Magnus struggles but is held tight until Godwin tells him to let go. We watch longer, as the horseman stops in his tracks, looks down into the dale-head, then presses his horse onward and out of sight.

'God, *I wish I had a sword in my hand!*' Magnus swears under his breath.

'Then I would have had to let Saeward hold you back!' Godwin swears, echoing loudly around the horseshoe of rocks below the moortop. We all stand, stock still in our tracks and Magnus pouts angrily like the child he still is.

'Hopefully *he* is out of hearing', Hemming wonders under his breath, and cranes his neck to look over hawthorn bushes for the Northman.

'He must be some way off, I would have th-', Magnus begins and finds Saeward's hand over his mouth.

There is the sound of heather brushing against a horse's hooves as the Northman passes close by in the half-light.

I can just about see him, standing in his stirrups, looking around. He reins in his horse and drops down from the saddle,   thumping down onto hard earth amid the short, sheep-cropped moorland grass. He stands stock still, listening.

Little Ulf whimpers, stiff with the cold. Whether the rider has heard him I cannot tell because now he is out of sight behind his horse. One of the other horses stamps the hard earth and I can hear footfalls. I dig Saeward with one elbow and show him with my arm outstretched that I want him to make for where there is a gap between the bushes. Hemming sees Saeward go and looks back to me, eyebrows arched, wordlessly asking if I wish him to go with Saeward. I stab a finger the other way and he follows there. I edge to the gap and wait, dagger in hand.

The Northman may be no fool, but he is now out of sight of the others. I hear his breath come in short bursts from walking fast - he must have come quickly to his side of the hawthorn. When he sees me he hisses,

'*En garde-*' he draws his sword on seeing me side-step with my dagger. He takes my grin to be sportsmanlike and stands sword in hand, grinning foolishly, lopsidedly, waiting for me to meet his sharp blade – as if I were so dim!

He does not hear Hemming behind him, but from the way he swings his sword arm he seems to know someone is behind him to his right. Hemming steps back deftly, beyond arm's length and brings his spear forward when the Northman falters.

Wearing his Northman war gear and helm, at first sight – were I one of theirs - I would have taken Hemming to be friend, not foe.

The spear is run hard into the outlander's throat, *through* the chain mail neckguard, too fast for him to cry out for help. The others behind the hill still do not know of his death.

I stride quickly forward just as Saeward shows from Hemming's left, and holds onto the Northman's sword before it clatters onto the rocks as Hemming twists the spear shaft. The grin has gone from his lips now, his eyes wide open in death.

'Close the man's eyes, *for God's sake!*' Godwin tells Saeward, who does as he is told, although I can well recall a time when he would have answered back that he was not the man's slayer. Between us, Hemming and I lower the dead man to the earth and Saeward strides to the end of the hawthorns to see if anyone else is coming.

'Where is his horse?' Eadmund asks, the only one to think clearly. 'He did not walk here, I would warrant'.

'Go, *fetch* the man's horse!' Godwin hisses to Saeward, who turns on his heels and vanishes into a thin, creeping moorland mist – to show again, pulling hard at the Northman's bridle. Not knowing the man who grips its reins tightly, the horse pulls back.

Hemming slaps its hindquarters and the horse veers round. Saeward has to press a hand hard down onto its muzzle to stop it from grunting, bringing down his comrades on us.

'*Fool!*' Saeward snaps at Hemming under his breath.

Hemming, taken aback, shrugs.

'He was helping', Eadmund brushes his whiskers, trying not to laugh and looks away, upward at Gytha on her horse. 'Grandmother, tell Saeward Hemming was helping'.

'Do not bring *me* into this', Gytha pleads, tired and cold. Eadmund presses his lips together and stares back at me, shaking his head.

'The sooner we get off this moor the better'. Godwin hisses, teeth set grimly against the bitter cold and asks Hemming, 'Can you see any others?'

Hemming has been watching the moor top, but from where we are we can see little. We would need to be higher.

'Shall I take Saeward up there and look around?' I offer.

'If you would', Godwin brightens, 'then we might pass over this damned moor to the north rise above the coast'.

'Saeward', I catch hold of his chain mail sleeve.

He follows me by way of a dyke let in to the moorside to the heights. We have to climb on foot so as not to be seen, but nor can we see as well as if we were mounted. It is some time before we reach the top of the moor, a mile or more away. From there we cannot see Godwin, Eadmund and the others, but at least we can be happy in knowing the Northman's comrades must have left without him. Nevertheless it is odd, this far from Exanceaster. They may be lower down, so we must take care not to be seen from below when we get back to the others.

'You saw no-one?' I ask when he is back with me, having crossed the open land. With a shake of his head he bears out my own thoughts. We have only just set off back downhill, clambering down into the dyke to stay unseen, when we hear talking. Whoever it is speaks throatily, but not in the Frankish tongue. They may be Flemings.

We have to clamber out of the dyke a short way, toward prickly gorse, to be able to see who is talking. Pressing ourselves against the low bank of the dyke we part the nearest bush a little. Six men, clad in mailcoats but with helms doffed, are hunched around a small, crackling fire. They break off from talking and one cranes his neck upwards, listening. He shakes his head and they go back to talking. I wonder if they are waiting for the one we slew. I push myself backward, away from the sharp gorse spikes and whisper to Saeward,

'Can you bring Hemming and Eadmund and we can deal with these'.

'There are *five* of them!' Saeward answers in a hoarse whisper. 'I should bring Saewulf and Ecgwin'.

'To what end? They are stablemen, *not* fighting men', I wonder sometimes what he thinks with!

'Numbers', Saeward offers.

'Then bring Godwin instead', I answer. 'At least he knows how to handle a sword'.

'What if their fifth man flees whilst we tackle the other four?' Saeward is still not thinking.

'They do not know we are here yet', I hiss, '*go, Saeward!*'

He nods unwillingly, yet understands. Is this the man who rode to fight the Northmen in Centland and Suth Seaxe? Whilst I keep watch on the outlanders he draws back and passes behind me, back to Godwin and the others.

'Saeward tells me you have lost your wits', Hemming thumps down on the earth bank beside me and parts the bushes without shaking them. 'He says you want to attack these Northmen here'.

'What would you say – *has he* told Godwin?'

'He told *me*', Hemming answers. He looks over one shoulder at me and shakes his head.

'I told him he should pass word to Godwin', I grind my teeth gloomily, wondering whether he has suddenly lost his spirit for fighting.

'Godwin was talking with Eadmund and Gytha', Hemming lets me know and slaps my back. 'He still does not feel able to talk to Godwin, as the king's son – albeit a *dead* king's son'.

'Will *you* tell him, before these five come for *us?*' I do not relish having to fight mounted men with lances.

'I will tell him, whether or not he is talking with my betters. I can see you are champing at the bit-'

Before he heads back I grip his sword arm and ask,

'Before you go back, tell me if you think I am misleading myself in thinking we can see them back to their maker with the men we have'.

'I cannot see why not', Hemming grins at me, 'if we catch them off guard, not knowing we are here'.

'Tell Saeward from me that I think he has lost his nerve', is my parting shot. With luck that will sting Saeward into fighting, bring him to the boil.

Crouching, Hemming swears under his breath,

'Fear not, Ivar. I shall not waver from that task'.

Awaiting Godwin, I keep watch over the five Flemings, hoping they do not mount before *we* are ready to take *them*. I need not fear being kept waiting, however. Godwin drops to his knees beside me, with Eadmund and Magnus close behind.

'Hemming tells me you have something aforethought for our outlander friends there', he jabs the now frosty air with an un-gloved finger and straightaway sucks in air, hissing. 'It has become *cold* so suddenly! The wind seems to come from the north-eastern quarter'.

'You will be glad of a short fight to warm you up, then', Eadmund smiles brightly.

'You will know then, brother, how good you are with that axe you carry – whether you carry it only to chop firewood', Godwin sneers almost.

'That will cost you one day!' Eadmund snaps, to be thumped by me. '*What?*'

'*Quiet!*' I hiss at him and point toward the Northmen, still out of sight, still hopefully unaware of our being here.

'What would *you* say we do?' Godwin digs me in the ribs. He does not like me having spats with his brother, I have learned. He would sooner pull him up himself.

Magnus looks worried behind Godwin.

'What *ails*, Magnus?' I ask, hoping to draw an answer from him before he loses his nerve in the close fight I think we will have.

'Nothing', he shakes his head, but does not lose his look of worry.

'Tell me before we take them', I plead, 'before it is too late'.

'What do you want us to do?' Godwin asks again, annoyed at the unsettled Magnus. He chides, 'He will forget his worries soon enough when he hears his sword sing'.

'Very well', I draw lines in the dirt, crosses where I want each of them before we attack. The Outlanders are in a dip in the land, with a rise all around them. Just as they thought they would be unseen there, we can stay unseen until we fall on them. When I am done even Saeward nods his head, glad at the thought of blooding his axe on these Northmen. 'Hemming, as you were so good with your screech-owl, can you do a Moorcock?'

He smiles, as if my asking him might be something akin to foolish.

'Very well, then. When the Moorcock begins his call we attack together?' I nod with the others and wave them away.

I stay where I am with Saeward beside me, Hemming and Saewulf make their way, still crouching, around to our right. Godwin and his brothers veer around to our left.

The call comes and we launch ourselves on the foe. Cries of woe and screams of pain greet us as our blades cut deep into them. Three of them put up a fight against my kinsmen, and Hemming goes to their aid, cutting down the nearest from behind. The last man standing stares me in the eye and stands with his sword, ready to fight to the end.

As with Brand I step sideways, around the dip in the land, to have him looking into the low sun. He shields his eyes with one hand as he slashes wide, hoping to keep me away. I sidestep as he scythes through the morning air and bring my axe at his neck – but my wound makes me groan in pain and I stumble sideways, away from his sword-blade as it comes at me, now downward.

Clearing the ground in sudden pain again, my right foot almost catches the stones around the Northmen's campfire. I think I see Theorvard, Ubbi and Karl watching me fight my corner. *This is the fight with Brand all over again!* Out of the corner of one eye I see the sword blade arcing through the air, downward at me. I stumble backward over the stones, onto my back and the Northman comes on at me. The blade of my axe lifts upward, almost of its own, and catches the man upward between his legs.

His scream of pain brings the womenfolk running. Eadgytha stands looking toward me at the rim of the shallow dip, making me think of Braenda in the way she stands there, hands at her side. Gytha's hands shield Gunnhild's eyes, but she pushes her grandmother's hand away and stands gaping at the flailing Northman.

He stares up at me, eyes pleading, mouth is like a hole torn from his jaw in suffering. Again, still seeing Brand on the ground, I bring my axe down onto his head. The blade buries itself in the crown of his skull and I have to put my boot on his chest to pull the blade out again.

'Ivar', Saeward is first to speak, 'I must see to your wound again'.

I close my eyes, trying to blot out the sight of Brand below me, and nod slowly. Godwin strides toward me, Eadmund close behind. My kinsman asks,

'Are you well, Ivar?' He rests a hand on my back, pats me twice and stoops to look at the Fleming, his jaws still wide open in his death agony, lying back against the slope. He would have been inwardly begging for freedom from the pain. This is Brand all over again – how long do I have to see him whenever I kill, man-to-man?

'I will live', I answer and let my axe drop to the dew-laden grass by my feet. Saeward takes me by one arm and steers me away from the others. I hear him speak, but his words are lost to me.

'I asked if you were in pain still', Saeward says again. '*Are* you?'

'As I said to Godwin, I will live. Once I am mounted I will be fine, honestly', I smile.

'I should look at your wound, you know?' Saeward presses.

'Later', I steer him back to the others.

Saewulf and Ecgwin bring the horses forward. Gytha and Eadgytha having mounted again, along with Eadgytha's daughters – Ulf having stayed in the saddle – press their horses forward. Saewulf hands me Braenda's reins and stands by whilst I summon my might to hoist myself slowly, wincing, into my saddle.

'Is there not something you can do for Ivar?' Eadgytha pleads with Saeward, knowing him to be gifted with herbs.

'He does not want my help - yet', Saeward answers, casting a look sideways at me.

'You foolish man', Eadgytha mouths the words at me, and turns to Gytha. 'Ivar wishes to be a dead hero'.

My ageing aunt looks scathingly at me but says nothing, and merely shakes her head.

Magnus grins and foolishly tells me,

'Women, they worry too much over nothing!'

His mother makes him mindful of his own failings,

'When you are in need, young man, you squawk loudly enough to make anyone think you were breathing your last!'

Magnus reddens when Eadmund and Godwin chuckle, yet Godwin looks back over one shoulder at their mother lest she has words of warning for him. She sets her jaw, saying nothing more, and he leaps spryly into his saddle.

We crest the hilltop in line, Godwin leading and Hemming taking the rear. The womenfolk and Ulf ride in the middle behind Eadmund, Saewulf and Ecgwin. Magnus, Saeward and I follow closely behind.

My thoughts are with Godwin's men back there in the *burh*. If the thegns who betrayed us point them out to Willelm, they could well fare badly, I wonder, being taken back through Lunden to be punished as I and my friends were after Willelm's crowning. There would be no-one to save them from being put to death, if the king had it forethought as their *wyrd*. Is Godwin thinking about them, I wonder?

'They will be well', Godwin nods. 'The thegns, Ligulf and Earnwin will not yield them to the Northmen. We, Eadmund, Magnus and I were wanted, not our men. They will make their way eastward, back to East Seaxe and Suthfolc, and melt away until needed'.

He may want to believe that, to ease his sense of right and wrong, and for his sake I hope he *can* believe it. I am not so sure he is right. They may be made to suffer, badly. Willelm is not known to be forgiving towards his foes – I hope I am wrong. I say nothing more on the matter and ride on through hazy sunlight, over the moor tops to

Defna's northern shore. Steepholm is still far away, northward off the coast of Sumorsaetan. There is a long ride ahead along the coast north-westward toward the mouth of the River Pedride, where there are marshes and fishing hamlets. We shall be able to see the womenfolk safely out to Steepholm from there.

The sea ahead of us is bathed in dappled sunlight as scattered clouds pass below the dull glow of the white winter sun.

Ships in the channel ply their way to or from Brycgstoth, their sails catching the late morning sun. Whose ships they are I could not say, but if they belong to the Northmen they will be well out of the way when Gytha and Eadgytha make their crossing to the isle. Word will be sent to Aenglish shipmasters not yet under Willelm's yoke, to take them to safety in Flanders. Gytha will learn there that she has at least one other son aside from Wulfnoth.

I cannot tell Harold's sons, lest word reaches the wrong ears.

Should Gospatric learn I helped Tostig leave these shores he would take steps to 'rid' the kingdom of me in the same way as Copsig was dealt with.

'I am hoping to take ship to Dyflin', Godwin tells me as we follow the track down to the coast. 'King Diarmuid of Leinster will help me in the same way he helped father and Leofwin'.

'Where will you find a ship to take you across the sea?' I ask, wondering how much Harold told his son about those days.

'Hopefully there will be – there *should* be - a ship from Brycgstoth', he falters on seeing me frown.

'We were near Brycgstoth on the way here, if you recall. Magnus went into the burh and you were fearful the Northmen would find us through him', I tell him wearily.

'There *are* folk there who are friendly toward *us*', Magnus cuts in, sounding hopeful, 'I met some of them in one of the inns, who told me there were ships whose masters the Northmen had not taken hostage. We may yet find a shipmaster willing to take us to Dyflin'.

'I hope you are right', I set my teeth, trying to keep myself from flinching from the sharp pain in my left buttock.

'You can have your wound seen to when we reach the rivermouth near Barnestapla', Godwin cheers me.

I stifle another sharp intake of breath and tell him,

'A rest would help. I am saddle-sore and the pain is numbing my leg. If I do not alight from my perch soon, I shall fall from it!'

'You should have told me!' Godwin pulls back on the reins, bringing a bad-tempered snort from his mount.

'We would have got nowhere if we stopped each time I felt a stab of pain in my backside', I groan in answer and ease my left leg over the saddle to slide down onto the track. Gytha looks back at me as I rub myself roughly to get the blood flowing along my leg.

'Let me look – *now!*' Saeward snaps at me and drops down from the saddle. His mouth twists in a wry smile when I look ahead at the womenfolk. '*No-one will be watching!* If you do not let me see the wound now, think how you would look without your leg'.

'Very well', I groan, giving in to him. With my breeks lowered after first looking ahead I clamp my jaws and Saeward peels away the old dressing. He mumbles something I can make neither head nor tail of and turns me away from the sun to see the wound in   the light.

'You should have told me earlier of your pain', Saeward hisses into my left ear when he stands again. He pulls up my breeks, letting me take the tops and fasten the fine leather belt Earl Godwin once gave me.

'*Well?*' I ask, irked by his clucking.

'You will not lose the leg, but you might keep the limp', he smirks. 'When did you begin to feel the pain again?'

'I have not stopped feeling the pain', I answer truthfully to his head-shaking. This is more than I can bear and demand, '*Now* what?!'

'I shall do my best...' Saeward shrugs and digs around in the pouch he carries to the fore of his saddle.

'*Do that!*' I snap.

'Ah-ah – best not lose your temper, Ivar!' Saeward wags a finger as he turns to me. 'You are beholden to me now. Lower your breeks'.

'You will not let me forget', I growl. 'Why did you pull them back up and let me belt up again?'

'I pulled them up to keep your *manhood* warm. I said nothing about fastening your belt!' Saeward is full of himself again - the only man I know who tends to the wounds of others and lets them *know* he is doing it for their welfare.

On my unfastening my belt again, he pulls the left side down and tells me to stand still,

'Take in the wonderful sea whilst I tend to your wound, Ivar. Think on what you wish to do at the Yuletide'.

As my thoughts stray to my woman, I feel a sharp stab in my left leg and cry out,

'What are you *doing* to me, in God's name?'

'Just that', Saeward answers. 'I did it in God's name, you heathen! Now stand still whilst I put on a new dressing'.

'Next time you slit a Northman's throat I shall ask if you are doing it in *God's* name!' I growl again as he fusses in his bundle, looking for muslin to make a dressing

'To which I shall answer that I am! Now pull in your cheeks whilst I do this', Saeward tells me.

'The cheeks on my backside or-'I begin to ask.

'Aye, *them* – what would sucking in the cheeks either side of your mouth do, may I ask?'

'What would *I* know? Get on with it before more Northmen come'. I am being humbled enough, with my friend dabbing around behind, me without him smirking over my lack of knowledge in health matters.

'There will be no outlanders here – *not yet'*, Saewulf tells me, nodding wisely.

'They are only in the south of Defna', Ecgwin nods with him. They look like a pair of wizened old monks, with their dun cloaks wrapped around them.

'You are done', Saeward packs away his things and stows them in his saddle bag.

I hoist my breeks again and buckle up. My next task is climbing back into the saddle. Ecgwin drops down from his saddle, Saeward smiling over one shoulder calls out,

'Even if we fall out, Ivar, you will still have one friend'.

Godwin's horse trots back behind Saewulf, its master grinning smugly. He watches as I struggle into the saddle, still smiling, and then wheels his horse about behind Braenda.

'Given time, Ivar, your wound will heal', he rides beside me and leans toward me to put an arm on my right shoulder.

'Had your man been quicker, hauling me up onto the wall top, I would not have felt that Northman's crossbow skills', I think back to the night we went around Willelm's camp.

'I am *sorry*, kinsman. My men did not know they had to raise *two* on the chair together', Godwin pats my shoulder and presses his horse into a trot. I follow with Saeward, Ecgwin and Saewulf and we catch up with the others. Eadgytha looks back, smiles and waves. I wave back at her, putting on a smile for her sake, although I cannot help thinking about keeping the limp, as Saeward said I may well.

4

Following the coast towards Sumorsaetan, we keep out of sight lest any of Willelm's ships were to pass close to shore and send word to their lord of our whereabouts.

We have eaten as guests of a freeman, our horses rested and we have been told of a boat that might be had for the crossing to Steepholm. The freeman who made us welcome turned away Godwin's silver, telling him,

'I am helping you because one day I would like to see one of your blood take the throne again', the fellow said.

Godwin was plainly heartened by these words, Eadmund and Magnus cheered that a rising would happen here, should they wish to stir Defna's men against their outlander lords. We rode on hopefully and even I forgot my pain for the time being.

We are to see a ship owner by the name of Wulfberht at the riverside at Barnestapla.

'How will we know his workshop?' Eadmund had asked his namesake.

'There is a sheltered millwheel against the river wall', the answer came. Easy enough to think of, I thought.

So now we are closing on Barnestapla, its roofline broken by the river. As we hunt for a bridge to cross, folk busy themselves in the fields on the west side of the river. No-one offers to tell us where we can find a crossing, so I call out to the nearest ceorl,

'Where do we cross the river, friend?'

'What is it you seek on the far bank, Lord?'

'We seek Wulfberht, to ask for a boat to Flatholm', I add. He stares at the women in their finery, at Godwin and his brothers, and back at me.

'There is no need to cross the river, Lord', he points his hoe northward and our eyes follow the line. A longhouse stands close to the river three ship-lengths away, a tall millwheel we did not see earlier turns slowly at the riverside, where a mill-race feeds the swirling water.

'I am grateful to you, friend', I salute him. Godwin turns his horse and the others follow him.

'*Are* you, Lord?' the ceorl smiles, and then sets himself back to his work.

'What did he mean by *that?*' Hemming scowls at the ceorl's back

'I asked *him*, not you', the answer comes from the ceorl before I can open my mouth.

Hemming draws his sword, but Saeward leans toward him and

pushes it back into the scabbard for him. Not wishing to be overheard by the ceorl, Saeward tells him under his breath,

'You would not do something you might be sorry about, Hemming? I thought not. He could really hurt you with a hoe that sharp!'

Hemming is about to say something, but thinks better of it and shakes the reins for his horse to trot on after Godwin and the others. I follow him and Saeward, looking back at the ceorl. The fellow is hard at work with his hoe again, and does not look up.

Godwin has already dropped down from his saddle when we catch up with him, and raps on the door of Wulfberht's workshop as we ride up. Saewulf has already been around the dwelling and its outhouses by the riverside, and comes back looking lost.

'There is no-one here, Lord', he tells Godwin.

A boat the length and breadth of a *karve* draws up beyond the mill, and a stout fellow steps onto the short landing stage beside it. Our womenfolk being nearest, he strides toward them, calling out,

'Do you seek me?' He stands by Gytha's mount, looking up at her as Godwin closes on him from behind. Startled by a snort from Godwin's horse as it is led toward him, the fellow wheels to look up at my kinsman behind him, 'Whoa, who are you, fellow? I was only asking this kind lady whether she sought me for something'.

'I mean you no harm', Godwin answers, 'are you Wulfberht?'

'Who wishes to know?' the fellow's brow knits, thinking I wonder, that Godwin is one of those Aenglishmen used by the Northmen to do their bidding.

'I am Godwin Haroldson', my kinsman begins.

'Godwin...' the stout fellow scratches his thick beard. 'Godwin, *our Lord?*'

'The same', Godwin grins, and hands the reins of his horse to Saewulf. 'As I said, are you Wulfberht?'

'I am, Lord Godwin – I *am* he! *Welcome*, Lord, to my humble home! What is it you wish from *me?*' Wulfberht seems to laugh and cry at the same time, overjoyed at seeing his lord for the first time in many a year I would warrant.

He rushes to his door, wrenches it open and hastens into the darkness within, shouting as he runs back and forth out of sight within. He shows again, breathless in the doorway, followed by serving men and women who cheerily throng Godwin.

'Would you tend to my mother and grandmother?' Godwin asks Wulfberht. 'My youngest brother and his sisters need warm food and drink, too'.

'The Lady Gytha is with you, the lady on the horse I spoke to?'

Wulfberht's eyes open wide and he looks from one woman to the other, not knowing what he is doing. I would have thought it plain which one is my aunt Gytha, but the women wear headscarves to keep them warm and neither looks very old if you cannot see their hair.

'Aye, Wulfberht, my grandmother is behind you, still mounted', Godwin grins broadly at the elderly fellow.

Wulfberht is trying to get on the right side of Gytha and himself. Eadgytha plays with him briefly,

'You thought *I* might be the young man's grandmother? Gytha should be glad you think *her* so young! I am the young fellow's mother, Wulfberht. What we *have* in common is that we need to sit by your hearth, as do my daughters and youngest son, Ulf. We need a boat to take us to Steepholm and from there a ship for Flanders'.

'Ah, Lady Gytha, let me help you from your horse!' Wulfberht turns to see my aunt bending to come down from her saddle, cold and hungry as we all are.

'*Do* you have a boat to spare, good fellow?' Eadmund asks Wulfberht.

'I have something *bigger!*' Wulfberht cranes his neck to look up at Eadmund beside him whilst fussing over Gytha.

'You have a ship?' Godwin looks happier.

'I do *indeed*, and she is due in a day or so – back from Brycgstoth', Wulfberht absently waves north-easterly with one outstretched arm.

'The Northmen do not watch you closely?' Magnus asks next as he, Godwin, Eadmund and Wulfberht enter the house behind Gytha and Eadgytha. Saeward, Hemming. I enter the warm dwelling behind them and in the middle of the great room Wulfberht's house-maids heap kindling onto an already roaring fire.

Saewulf and Ecgwin stay with the horses until Wulfberht calls them in,

'Come, friends. You must be chilled to the bone! My stablemen will take these horses from you and tend to their needs. *Come!*'

Saewulf and Ecgwin need no second bidding. They stand with us, slapping hands, kneading frozen fingers as the maids bring mulled ale for the men, mulled wine for Gytha and Eadgytha. Her daughters and young son are given warm milk and cakes. Godwin and Wulfberht talk about hiring a ship as the rest of us eat. Thick, hot lamb's meat and turnip broth have been brought, fresh bread is cut and soon the hall is filled with laughter and the buzz of chatter.

'Ralf is my shipmaster', Wulfberht tells Godwin.

'You have a *Northman* shipmaster?' Godwin is taken aback.

'Not Northman, *Norseman*. He is a Dane, from Fyn I believe',

Wulfberht laughs. 'He will be here in a couple of days. You can speak to him'.

'A *Dane*, you say? Our kinsman here, Ivar, is a Dane. Come here, Ivar', Godwin laughs.

'I am right here, kinsman', I tell him, tapping his shoulder, 'you need not shout'

'Ivar, Wulfberht says his shipmaster is a Dane', Godwin tells me what I have heard already, but I must go along with him.

'You say? Where does your Danish shipmaster hail from, Wulfberht?' I ask, knowing the answer already since it was shouted loud enough for me to hear from outside.

Nevertheless the stout West Seaxan is only too eager to tell me again, bawling as if he were outside by the river,

'He is from an island he calls *Fyn*, friend Ivar'.

I beam broadly back at him and take another gulp of the mulled ale. We shall be well regaled for the next few days at least, and I would say he can afford it when I hear him tell us he owns much of the land on this side of the river. Godwin's ears prick when he says he trades across the sea to Dyflin and Vedrafjordur.

'You would know King Diarmuid?' Godwin asks, echoing my own thoughts.

Wulfberht gulps down meat he already had in his mouth, burps and answers,

'I know *of* him'.

'Would you be able to take us, my brothers, my kinsman –'Godwin begins.

'Your kinsman-' Wulfberht looks up and around.

'Ivar', Godwin pats me on the shoulder.

'Oh aye, Ivar', Wulfberht nods and picks up a chicken wing to gnaw whilst Godwin goes on,

'You may be able to take me, my brothers, kinsman and friends', Godwin finishes, pointing to Saeward, Hemming, Saewulf and Ecgwin.

'I can', Wulfberht nods, and goes on gnawing. He puts down the bones, licks his fingers, swigs his ale and looks closely at Godwin, 'It will cost you – *I have men to pay*'.

'I understand', Godwin answers, patting Wulfberht's back.

'As long as that is clear', Wulfberht smiles warily. Not knowing my kinsman too well, he does not know whether he has crossed Godwin by demanding silver for taking him across the sea. This is the first time he has met any of Harold's sons, and is on tenterhooks here.

Godwin reaches for his ale cup and raises it to our host,

'*Wulfberht*, Wulfberht- *why* is it you are suddenly so unsure of me?

I raise my cup to you, and look forward to a long and worthy friendship. You are my eyes and ears here in the north of Defna shire, and you will be of more help to me than you can think without putting yourself or your kin at risk. Drink with me now, brothers, friends, and kinsman', he bends forward toward me, cup in hand, 'and look toward the new kingdom!'

'Aye', one of Wulfberht's men takes up what he thinks to be Godwin's lead, 'we should drink a toast to the *aetheling* Eadgar!'

There is a deathly hush in the hall. Wulfberht looks from the fellow to Godwin and quickly back again. He seems to turn white, but sweat runs on his forehead. It could be he has already had much to drink today, and he seems suddenly frail.

Hemming looks to Godwin, ready to draw his dagger on Wulfberht's man. Saeward merely stares at him dully.

'To the *aetheling* Eadgar', Godwin smiles and echoes the fellow's toast, 'and to Wulfberht's household!'

Cheers echo in the hall from the score or so of Wulfberht's men and household women. Hemming would have been unlucky, had he drawn his dagger, with us being so badly outnumbered. Now he sits, smiling, his dagger used instead to cut the core from an apple.

'What is your name, friend?' Eadmund asks of the fellow who told us to drink to Eadgar.

'I am Wulfberht's brother Eadwulf', the answer comes.

'You have met the *aetheling*?' Magnus asks.

'Aye, Lord, I have met him – more than once, too', Eadwulf nods.

'More than once, you say - how?' Magnus straightens up on the bench.

'I fought with the Middil Seaxe *fyrd* at Lunden Brycg', Eadwulf answers. Magnus has no answer to this and I listen closely to Wulfberht's brother, 'I was near Lord Ansgar in the shieldwall, not far from Lord Ivar there. His young friend brought down one of the Outlander horsemen who threatened the shire reeve'.

'You *saw* that?' I forget my ale and food for that short while, wondering why I do not recall seeing him.

'Aye, Lord Ivar', he tells me. It seems odd, being spoken to as 'Lord' Ivar. It could be he thinks that my being kin to Godwin – and to Harold through him – makes me a Lord. 'When I think back on it, I saw you roasting in your own sweat under your mailcoat and wondered how a man so high-born could fight as hard as one of us'.

Saeward slaps me on my back and laughs,

'There you are, Ivar, your good name goes before you!'

'You do not call him *Lord*?' Eadwulf sounds out Saeward.

'Ivar is no *lord*', Saeward answers back. 'He is not even a thegn. He is our friend, albeit a *lucky* friend!'

Godwin, Eadmund and Magnus sit staring sideways at Saeward. They cannot believe their ears, that their kinsman – me – is so close to his men that they forget his kinship with Harold, and therefore with them. I would say now they dearly wish to set themselves apart from me, but to do so would strain their friendship with Wulfberht. It might be better for them to 'lower' themselves a little in the eyes of these folk. With a hero in their midst these good Defna folk feel safer, with two – Eadwulf *and* me – they may feel they cannot lose to the Outlanders.

Having fought once against Willelm fitzOsbern they may think they have some standing as warriors, but it was Eadric, Bleddyn and Rhiwallon who shone at Hereford. Godwin and his young brothers had almost brought ruin on us when they rode almost into the Northman earl's lap. Nevertheless I stand, cup in hand, and wave my drink toward my kinsman,

'I raise my cup to my young kinsmen, Godwin, Eadmund and Magnus, who have shown themselves worthy in fighting the outlanders at Hereford when we fought side by side with Thegn Eadric', I nod to them to stand with me for all to see. 'They will be leaders of men against the outlander king. For now, with me, they will raise men across the sea, as their father did all those years ago. When we come back, those of you who wish to stand with us shall strengthen our shieldwall. That is not the only way to beat them, but their horsemen cannot cut through a shieldwall that stands and will not break. We learned that lesson at great cost'.

'Our king, their father', I draw my hand through the air toward them, 'Harold paid for our mistakes. We shall see to it that no more of our leaders need pay'.

Fists thump the wooden boards, platters jump, cups spill. Calls for Godwin to speak echo around Wulfberht's hall,

'*Godwin! Godwin! Godwin!*' they yell, still thumping the boards. When Godwin clears his throat they cheer again.

'I thank my kinsman Ivar', he begins to more cheering. 'Ivar went with father and Leofwin to seek help from King Diarmuid for Earl Godwin all those years ago. He now comes with us, bringing friends Saeward and Hemming, to raise men and ships and help clear the kingdom of the hated Outlanders. When this Northman king has been thrown back into the sea he came from, then our rightful king will rule over us!'

Harold's eldest son is thinking of himself, but hides his bitterness well when the men thump the boards again, calling out,

'*Hail King Eadgar!*' With cups raised once more, they drink to the *aetheling*, not to Godwin. He will struggle hard, if he cannot buckle down to the wishes of these good folk. Were he to try to bend them to his will, that road would lead to grief. How can I tell him that, despite his father reigning well and being better-known men see Eadgar as their true king?

Days later, with Gytha, Eadgytha and her younger offspring safely hidden from prying eyes on Steepholm, Wulfberht's trading ship, '*Defnas Heort*' sets out westward along the coast from Barnestapla. Aboard are Harold's sons, Saeward, Hemming and I.

Saewulf and Ecgwin have stayed behind on Steepholm to care for the womenfolk and Ulf, and will sail on with them to Flanders. With us is Wulfberht. He wishes to sail on from Dyflin after landing us, to head south along the coast to Vedrafjordur and Veigsfjordur. He will have goods to bring back to Barnestapla, should he be stopped and boarded by the Northmen.

Saeward's nose runs like the flood-tide, as yet unused to being on board ship and we have not left the coast of Defna behind us! West Wealas soon beckons to the south-west.

Sails can be seen way astern of us, and we must hope we can outstrip the ships they push after us.

Wulfberht watches, screwing up his eyes against the sun as his Danish steersman Ralf brings '*Defnas Heort*' about for the north-west. The sun glares at us over the hills behind the coast. We are aboard a *knarr*, a broad-beamed trading ship, but these are warships that seem to chase us into the open sea.

Their sails are broader and deeper than ours, and should their masters wish, they may overhaul us before we are halfway to Dyflin.

'We should take off our mailcoats', I tell Godwin, 'to look like crewmen'.

'Surely they would see this ship as over-manned?' Godwin shields his eyes, watching the sails with Wulfberht.

'The sea crossing to Dyflin is rough, kinsman. More hands may be needed on the oars, more men needed to stand by with pails to bail the water, should the wind prove too strong for the sail', I tell him.

'Will *they* know that?' Godwin points a thumb astern.

'We can tell them', Wulfberht nods.

'We must hide our weapons and chain mail before they come close enough to see us', Eadmund agrees with me.

Godwin turns again and watches the sails billowing, the ships nearing – closer, *closer*.

We pull off one another's mailcoats, stow our swords, axes and daggers in weatherproof cloths offered by one of Wulfberht's crew. Rough-sewn all-weather clothing is given to us as Hemming, Godwin and Magnus undo their leggings.

Saeward and I take off our boots. My fur lined and trimmed boots are too good to be those of a seaman, so I must hide mine. He still has the boots he took from a Northman, they will not be happy to see *he* has them.

We are ready to be boarded. Their ships will soon catch up with us and I can see men with crossbows lining the deck as their seamen slacken sail.

'*Sails ahead*', Ralf calls out to Wulfberht.

Are we to be beset by more Northmen?

'*Three sails!*' Hemming nudges me.

'Where are they?' Magnus peers around and is shown them by Eadmund.

'Danes', I tell them, 'not from across the sea to the east, but to the west!'

'Dyflin Danes, aye', Wulfberht nods and Ralf grins broadly.

Saeward thumps my arm to gain my ear,

'Ivar, *Ivar, the Northmen have come about!*' He pulls me around and shows me the ships turning in their own wake, wallowing in the waves, the wind threatening to heave them over.

Wulfberht's crew stands and jeers, fists are shaken and Hemming leaps to the sternpost to howl like a wolf. The Northmen's ships look helpless with waves washing over the deck walls, crews running out the oars to stop their ships overturning and to flee the new threat that closes on them. The Dyflin Danes fold in their sails as the steersmen pull the steerboard oars hard to the right and come around toward us. One of the shipmasters cups his hands over his mouth and bellows, but I cannot make out what it is he wants from us. Wulfberht cups a hand to his ear to show he could not make out what was being bellowed.

The ship comes alongside and the fellow calls out again, bobbing about on the heightening waves.

'Who are you?'

'I am Wulfberht of Barnestapla and have with me men who wish to speak with King Diarmuid!' Wulfberht shouts back over the strengthening easterly wind.

Another of the Danes' ship's company calls out,

'*Who* is it who wishes to see Diarmuid?'

'I am Godwin Haroldson, with my brothers Eadmund and Magnus. My kinsman Ivar Ulfsson is with us and we wish to know if King

Diarmuid will do the same for me that he did for my father and grandfather', my kinsman tells a tall, swarthy, big-chested shipmate of the Dane.

'That is a little before my time. I was a child in those days, not wise to the worldly ways of men. However, I am sure my father will hear you out. I am Murchad', the Erse aetheling tells us his name as he takes first Godwin's, and then Eadmund's and Magnus' hand. He looks my way and asks, '*You* are this Ivar Ulfsson?'

'I am', I answer curtly, weighing him up, and give him my hand in friendship. After all he and his Danes frightened off our Northman hunters. I did not know Diarmuid had a son, but then again as he says he was a child when I saw Diarmuid.

Having come about, the Dyflin Danes open out their sails once more. Murchad boards his own ship and Wulfberht calls for his sail to be opened out. We follow westward in the wake of Murchad's ships. It is late afternoon before we sight the ness to the east of Dyflin. No doubt, had we not slowed them down, Murchad's ships would have been berthed by the time we entered the bay.

We are taken to the king's garth. That is, the Danish king's garth where Sigtrygg '*Silkeskegg*'- he of the silken beard - held court in days gone by. This is where we met Diarmuid almost fifteen years ago when he called on his Danish underlings with his queen and offspring to gather his tithes.

'My father is on his rounds, but he will be here soon', Murchad tells us, showing us to rooms we would like for our own.

I cannot recall our quarters when I came with Harold and Leofwin, but I am sure they were as good as this. Saeward and Hemming, sharing a neighbouring room, can be heard laughing about the size of their beds. We had been so long underway before reaching Exanceaster that we had almost forgotten what beds were. Sleeping in Wulfberht's hall was like the old days again, after two long days on the moors - but this is *kingly!*

We are left to ourselves until early evening, when one of Murchad's underlings brings clothing for us to don,

'My Lord Murchad says it would be rude of you to wear your chain mail to the feast', he tells me. I can hear Saeward whooping next door at the sight of the clothing the Erse *aetheling* has sent him.

'Ivar, have you seen the *like* of this?' Saeward asks when he shows at my doorway in an outfit worthy of a noble. Hemming, standing beside him looks like a thegn at a feast. Saeward brims over with the thrill of being here, unused to living with this sort of finery. He looks me up and down before telling me, '*You* look much the Lord you *should* be!'

'I thank you, Saeward! I feel much better, but we have talks ahead of us, and I have to warn you against speaking out of turn with this king'.

The last time I met him I had shoulder-length hair and a full beard. Will he know me with short hair and stubble on my chin?

'They might look at your wound here before we go back to our own shores', Hemming sees me limp on our way.

'I would be glad of that', I answer, although I keener for ale and food. Since being at Wulfberht's hall I have become used to eating more than scraps once a day.

I do not know how things will be when we reach Sumorsaetan again with Godwin, nor how long it will be before I sit down to a square meal again after leaving here! We need to make as much of our time here as we can – who knows, we could find ourselves in dire straits!

Meanwhile, as we are led into the great hall I see my kinsmen seated close to Murchad, talking earnestly. The *aetheling* cuts short his talks and greets me,

'Ah, *Ivar*, come here and sit by me'. When he sees me look back at Saeward and Hemming he adds, 'Bring your friends'.

When we are seated, Murchad tells me he has been talking with Godwin about our fighting the Northmen. He tells me also that he has heard of my time as huscarl with Harold, and that I fought on Caldbec Beorg,

'You have done much these past months!' Murchad's eyes open wide in awe of a warrior who has lived through trying times.

'He also almost brought the wrath of the new king on us', Magnus shoves me playfully.

'*How* is that so?' Murchad looks from me to Magnus and Godwin answers for his brother.

'Ivar took some friends with him so that he could watch Willelm being crowned at the West Mynster!'

Murchad stares at me, and at Saeward.

'Tell me *more*', he asks me to go on.

Saeward tells of our way around the north of Middil Seaxe to Ceolsey and the West Mynster. He tells of how, clothed in habits of the Benedictine Brothers, we took the seats of two of the abbot's Brothers and were kept back whilst fighting broke out in the street beyond the doors. When I speak of meeting Braenda in the inn at Ceolsey his mouth falls open.

'This spay wife, she *seeks you out?*' he asks, breathlessly, taking a gulp of ale before pressing me for more about my woman.

'He has given his horse the same name', Eadmund laughs, speaking out of turn when I warned Saeward against it. Godwin scowls at him, but Murchad laughs out loud.

'*Just like a Dane!*' Murchad laughs long and deeply. Saeward and Hemming join in the laughter. I hear one man laughing louder than any other here and Murchad almost chokes before calling out,

'*Ketilbeorn*, come and tell Ivar the name you gave *your* horse!' Tall, flame-haired, built like an elk, Ketilbeorn strides from the back of the hall in answer to Murchad's summoning him. He plants a foot on the bench by Hemming.

'Tell him the name of your mount, Ketilbeorn!'

Murchad is already in tears laughing before the fellow tells us,

'*Apple Maiden*', Ketilbeorn tells me, grinning broadly. He laughs loudly again when he sees the look I give him, 'She is a filly. The apples are what she leaves as gifts to land workers – *horseshit*, in other words!'

Murchad wails, weak with laughter when my look of wonder turns to disbelief – before I burst out laughing, everyone around us bent double with mirth. Godwin is bemused, as is Magnus, but Eadmund sits head in hands, shaking. He will tell his brothers later. No doubt when he has drunk his fill, Godwin will understand the wit.

'*I like this!* It is a shame Guthfrith is no longer with us', Hemming tells me, wiping the tears from his cheeks. 'He would have loved that one!'

Saeward's laughter dies away, it seems to me he is thinking back to that night below the walls of Exanceaster when he knifed Hemming's friend. Hemming looks bemused at first, then, shakes his head and begins laughing again at Ketilbeorn's wit. It is unlikely he will ever know of his friend's untimely end.

Morning dawns crisply and the sun shines brightly onto the river as we leave the hall, where laughter still echoes. Hemming giggles like a maiden as we walk slowly back to our rooms.

He still recalls the name of Ketilbeorn's horse, '*Apple Maiden*' as he drags his feet across the earth yard, and then his legs buckle. We lift him for the last few strides, through the door held open by Saeward, up to his room and let him fall onto his bed.

'Do we pull his boots off?' Saeward asks when he enters the room he and Hemming share.

'Leave him sleep it off', I tell him, smiling, and leave for my own room, bed and welcome sleep. Am I out of Braenda's reach here? Unable to pull off my boots, I take off the tunic I have been given and let myself fall, backwards onto the bed. Sleep? I could lie here until kingdom come! Forgetting my aching back, my wounded backside, I drift off helped by the ale and mead downed over the past hours.

'Are you not going to kiss me and fill me with your seed, Ivar?' I grunt, turn over and almost fall onto the stone floor, but a hand catches my arm and pulls me back into the middle of the bed. Now I am wide awake! Someone asks, 'Will you plough my field, Ivar?'

I turn onto my right side to see who saved me from a more painful awakening to see my woman there.

'Braenda, how on earth did you get *here?!'*

'The way I always come to you – you *will* me to be with you', she answers. I ask myself, is it *that* easily done? 'I take it I have to pull off your clothes again, lazy man!'

She sets to pulling off the Erse *aetheling's* clothing as she listens to me telling her what has happened to me lately, although I think she knows. When I have trouble thinking back she tells me. Asking me to tell her is a way of bringing the everyday into her life. I think she yearns to be as other women, but then she knows that riding on my dreams, wishing her by my side would be a thing of the past.

'You have not always come', I chide as I drift back into sleep with her wrapped in my arms.

'I told you about the Centish warlock, did I not?' she answers back, but I am away from here in another world.

'Ivar, *wake up!* It is well into the afternoon, and King Diarmuid wishes to see you in the hall!' Hemming shakes me back into the world I share with my fellow man.

'What *day* is it?' I ask. Did I fall onto my bed early this morning or in another year? I feel as if I had slept through a lifetime since taking my woman in my arms. On sitting up I see I am the only one here, but there is a woman's shift on the floor. Was she *really* with me? My thoughts race back, to when she gave herself to me in the early morning. Was it *this* morning? Hemming sees it and smiles.

'What is the matter with you, Ivar? We have each of us slept the morning through but no more. Godwin wishes to speak to you before we go through to King Diarmuid, so you need to dress quickly - in your chain mail, this time', Hemming chides and throws me my undershirt.

'Where is Godwin's room?' I ask Hemming.

'Pull on your clothes and I will take you there', he searches for my breeks and throws me them before raising my mailcoat from the pile of shredded clothing on the floor, where I undressed yester-eve before the feast.

I am not long in readying myself to see first Godwin and then Diarmuid. For all I know Murchad will be there with him, ready to tell him of my lingering with a spay wife.

'Ivar, I am glad to see you!' Godwin lies. It is written as if in runes across his forehead that he wishes me on the other side of the world. He did not even seem keen to see me at Leagatun after many months as a guest of King Maelcolm, whatever else his brothers might have said.

'I was told you wish to see me before we meet the king', I reach out a hand.

He takes it limply and then straps on his belt before turning back to me,

'When we meet King Diarmuid, can you let me do the talking? I know you have been here before, but I have things to ask that were not raised by my father and uncle'.

'Oh, what do you think your father or Leofwin left out when they came here?' I ask, my eyes searching him.

'We did not have a Northman king then', Godwin tells me bluntly, 'and many of the folk in the lands grandfather and father raided were already on our side'.

'Why would you think they might not be with you when you go raiding in the western shires?'

'I merely wish to see things as they may be. It would be little use to me if, when I go raiding on the coast of Sumorsaetan, every man there wishes me in a cage!' Godwin is no fool, or else he has seen the writing on the wall.

'Then you should go with Eadmund and Magnus to ask Diarmuid for what you wish', I counsel.

'You come with us, Ivar. Diarmuid may ask things I cannot answer', Godwin presses me into going with them. I nod.

'I am nodding unwillingly, you must understand', I tell him, and follow him out of his room. Eadmund and Magnus await us in the yard. Drizzle has set in and the earth has softened so much that it is hard to walk. The early morning frost has turned into a fine rain and Magnus' hair hangs limp. Eadmund wears a cloak and hood, keeping him from the damp of an Erse mid-winter's day.

'Your unwillingness is not what matters, Ivar, as long as you nod at the right time!' Godwin smiles - it is not the smile of friendship, but that of a fox watching tame fowl.

Magnus shrugs and follows his older brother to King Diarmuid's throne room. Eadmund walks with me. He is not always at one with Godwin, but he knows to keep his thoughts to himself. He may one day gain from it.

'Good day, my young friend Godwin!' Diarmuid greets him warmly, hugging him, and then Magnus and Eadmund in turn. When I walk up to him his brow beetles and he stares. All is still for a short while as he walks around me. Godwin watches, fearful his mission will fail because of me.

Diarmuid has greyed over the years, grizzled would be a better word but then he is a king, and *looks* what he is. When he stops walking around me, looking me up and down as if I were a thrall at market he stares into my eyes – then breaks into a smile, broad and warm. His smile is that of an old, almost forgotten friend. He pulls me to him, hugs me bear-like, as Tostig did at Staenfordes Brycg, and pinches my chin,

'Ivar, what have you been doing to yourself all these years?! You do not remember, do you, when you first came here I pulled your beard to see if it was real! Leofwin was much younger than you and still had his baby fluff. Why is it your beard is not soft and silky, as it should be on a man of your years?'

'I needed to look like a Brother when we walked amongst the Northmen's tents below the walls of Exanceaster. There was no telling, that if Willelm saw me he would not see if I was shaven at the back of my head as well as on my forehead. He is no fool-'

'That I *well* know! He can surely be no fool, to beat your kinsmen in a long, drawn-out fight. With Harold and Leofwin both gone, Gyrth with them – I fear that is sad indeed! Your kinsman Godwin thinks he can alter the way things are now in the kingdom. Do you *share* his hopes?' Diarmuid clasps my right hand in his.

'I do, my Lord Diarmuid', I tell him. Can he read my misgivings?

'I hope you *believe* that, Ivar'.

Diarmuid reads me well. He cannot allow the Northmen to think they can rule a neighbouring kingdom without fighting tooth and nail for every mile!

If Willelm were to win the whole isle, Wealas and Aengla Land as well as Maelcolm's kingdom, would Leinster be next? Diarmuid may have thought along these lines when I came with Harold all those years ago, that greed would lead the Northmen across the sea. Had Eadward had his way in banishing Earl Godwin Wulfnothson, they might have looked his way before now.

'You are heavy with thought', Diarmuid wonders aloud to me. He must wonder why I am so downhearted. Could be I am worn from all this criss-crossing of land and sea. Yet having Braenda with me in the early morning gave me some hope. I turn to look at him,

'Forgive me, my Lord King. I forget at times where I am, or indeed who I am *with*'.

'I understand you drank well last night', he beams, elbowing me and cackling. Godwin shuts his eyes tight and looks upward, but Diarmuid pays no heed to him. He has *him* where he wants him. 'I also understand a woman looked into you in the morning before men were afoot. Fear not, Ivar, the maid Katriona told only me'.

And now my kinsmen also know. Still, why should it worry me what they think. This king of Leinster they have sought out to beg for help does not care that my woman is a spay wife, nor does Murchad. I hope Katriona does not suffer from too loose a tongue.

'It may be all over Dyflin by now, though'.

So she *was* seen. Braenda is losing her touch, letting mere maids see her come and –

'Katriona also told me the woman left after her candle burned to a stump. You *ought* to be happier now than you show yourself to be. I would be if the likes of her came to *my* bed!' Diarmuid sits up and beckons Godwin to him. 'You wish to ask me for men and ships?'

Godwin's brows rise and fall. He seems taken aback that Diarmuid should know, but then Murchad would have had words with his father.

'My son told me. He also told me of the Northman king's ships that Wulfberht was trying to outrun. They did not seem to care to tangle with our Danish friends. Guthrum and his friends are a fearsome sight to behold, I will allow... Where was I? Ah, *men* – how many do you think you will need?'

'Four or five ships should be enough', Godwin fiddles with his sword pommel. I, he and his brothers have been allowed their mailcoats again, now that we are no longer in the feasting hall.

Swords and drink do not mix well!

'Your father had ten', Diarmuid tells him, 'by my reckoning that must have been three hundred men or more'.

Godwin's mouth opens and closes, like a fish on land.

'Would you let us have *that* many?' he is taken aback, awe-struck that the king should think in such numbers.

5

Diarmuid's smile tells him he *was* thinking of more. I daresay he had been thinking of more, and Godwin's lack of years and skill as a leader took him aback. His father had plainly never passed on his own knowledge, but then he had been taken up with ruling the kingdom over the last year of his life. Even *before* Eadweard died, Harold was almost seen as king. Granted, there were the years when Harold could have taken time with him and his brothers, but even *before* Gruffyd raided Hereford alongside Aelfgar the kingdom was in a state of unrest.

'Ask Ivar', Diarmuid tells Godwin, 'to give you an insight into his warring years'.

Godwin looks pained. He does not want to hear this, he would sooner do things his own way, or how he *thought* his father had done. I am sad Tostig is no longer with us. Not only could he have set his brother right, but he could have given leadership to young Godwin, as he had shown his own sons, Skuli and Ketil. He had made men of them, notwithstanding their tender years!

Murchad is with us again now, having stolen into the room whilst his father spoke with Godwin. He had nodded when his father counselled the young Seaxan lord to seek *my* counsel. In this part of the world men look dimly on their fellows who will not seek the counsel of their elders when it comes to warfaring.

He offers his own outlook,

'You *should* listen to Ivar'. Godwin looks from him to his father, fearing the failure of his undertaking even before it is underway.

'Do not fear, Godwin. I *will* give you the ships and men. You tell *me* how many ships you wish, but I must warn you, that when you take on my men you seek the counsel of *my* Danes as well as of *your* Dane', Diarmuid points to me. 'I must warn you also, that Ketilbeorn will not risk the lives of his men if he thinks the prize or the risk unworthy!'

'I hear you, my Lord King', Godwin nods sagely.

'Will you *heed* my words, my young friends?' Diarmuid looks from Godwin to Eadmund and Magnus.

'We *will* heed your words', Eadmund assures him on behalf of himself and his brothers. His broad smile strikes a chord with Diarmuid and Murchad. They smile and nod back, and Murchad steps forward to shake Godwin's hand.

'We will bring in Ketilbeorn and Thored now, so that you can talk together over what you may have aforethought. They will give you some of their insight, and you *should* all talk with Ivar – *really!*' Diarmuid's handshake must be strong, as Godwin flinches but says nothing and smiles.

I think he will learn well!

Ketilbeorn and Thored are stirred by Godwin's thoughts on landing in Sumorsaetan.

'I have land in the shire, and followers', he even makes *me* think his landings will go ahead unbeaten, 'who will flock to my standard against their Northman masters. My friend Wulfberht –'

'Wulfberht is the old shipmaster?' Ketilbeorn asks.

'He is, aye', Godwin nods, wondering why the Dyflin Dane broke in. He pauses to listen, and when Ketilbeorn says nothing more Godwin goes on. 'My friend Wulfberht says the tithes his fellow landowners must give the Northmen have brought the Defna men to the brink of an outright uprising. I cannot think the men of Sumorsaetan will think otherwise when they see us'.

Thored asks searchingly, arms folded,

'How *many* men could you summon?' This younger man is dark-maned, as tall as Ketilbeorn, although not as barrel-chested, one of the Dyflin Danes with a Gaelic mother. He and Ketilbeorn talk briefly in the odd Danish-Gaelic their kind share in this part of Leinster amongst those many of mixed background.

'*Er* – there should be as many as the fyrd turns out at such a time', Godwin answers, not altogether as surely as Thored would like to hear. The Dyflin Dane flinches and stares.

I can see his thoughts written across his forehead as surely as if they were carved there,

'This is hopeless. The Aenglishman does not seem to understand his own undertaking'.

'The folk of Sumorsaetan will flock to my banner. Will no-one understand?' Godwin pouts like a maid and Thored stops himself from laughing out aloud.

I wonder myself if Godwin has thought it through. Has he left it to the Almighty to lend weight to his claim? Willelm will be more annoyed than angered, having let my kinsman slip through his fingers once already. Who *does* he have in Sumorsaetan to try to throw us back into the sea?

Doubtless we will learn sooner rather than later, but Thored wants to know what his gain will be. Whether Ketilbeorn has thought along these lines is not as plain. He may have heard wrongly, or he may have thought he and Thored could take Godwin in hand and steer him like a ship. Neither knows my kinsman well enough. He has the blood of Thegn Wulfnoth, Earl Godwin and King Harold coursing through him. Leaders cannot be steered that easily, as we found to our cost when

Harold pushed too soon to the south coast. I have said before that only one man could guide Godwin now, but he is in Flanders – or elsewhere.

Diarmuid sits with his chin on his right knuckle, his left hand under his cloak, deep in thought over Godwin. There is not as much of the seasoned warrior in this young man as there was in Harold. Back then Diarmuid was still a war leader himself. There must have been something in the young earl that drew him.

Were I brutally honest, I would say Godwin does not *speak* as a warrior. With his brothers he must look into what he wishes to do, thrash out something that sounds worthy to Diarmuid or he may be sent away with his tail between his legs.

'My Lord King', I speak out, much to Godwin's thinly hidden scorn, 'we will withdraw to talk over what my kinsman hopes to achieve'.

'I would say that is a sound offer', Diarmuid nods.

'Worthy', Thored adds. Ketilbeorn says nothing. He sucks in his cheeks, blows out again, shrugs and strides off with Thored.

They leave the king's room talking earnestly. It does not look good for Godwin, if he only knew. They were hoping for something better, such as knowledge of abbeys or churches where silver and gold could be had at little cost to them. The likes of Ketilbeorn and Thored do not mind losing men, if there is gain to be made. Nor are they afraid of dying, only of looking fools to their followers.

'What is the meaning of this?' Godwin fumes. He would dearly love to take me to task but Eadmund is between us, keeping the peace.

Diarmuid stands ready to leave the room and speaks up for me before he does so,

'Young man', he too stands between us.

Godwin listens, unwillingly.

'Your kinsman has many years of fighting behind him. He has known good leaders and can guide you, if you will let him. Listen to what he has to say, and come back to me when you have something you and I can talk over, together with Ketilbeorn and Thored". Diarmuid smiles wanly before walking slowly to the door.

'He is right Godwin', Eadmund puts a hand on his brother's right shoulder, staying him from doing something rash. Magnus nods and beckons me to his side. We stride from the room in pairs, and Murchad follows, to draw the door to behind him.

Diarmuid is seated in the throne room again, one elbow resting. His other hand strokes a heavily bearded, greying chin. To his right stand Murchad, Ketilbeorn and Thored. Godwin Eadmund and I stand in line abreast to his left. Godwin, his brothers and I have at last thrashed out something Diarmuid and his Danes should like. Hemming has come with us and stands behind me, ready to add another titbit, something that might bait the line for Ketilbeorn and Thored.

Murchad leans on the throne back to his father's left, looking down and speaking under his breath to Diarmuid. He nods and steps aside, folding his arms.

'You may speak now, Lord Godwin', Diarmuid beckons my kinsman closer. He looks to Ketilbeorn and nods when the Dane takes a step forward. To Godwin he says out aloud, 'I hear you have something to tell us'.

'Aye, my Lord King', Godwin is still edgy, but he can raise a warm smile. 'We – my brothers, my kinsman and I – think we have something to offer to Ketilbeorn and Thored. We will land on the coast close to Brycgstoth and gather men from the burh. The Northmen are weak around there, as their lord must watch the Wealsh. They are still worried about attacks by Bleddyn and Rhiwallon in aid of Eadric. From there we sail south-west close to the shore whilst the Brycgstoth men push along the coast into Sumorsaetan, where I have land of my own. I am told there are riches to be had where the Northmen have been gathering tithes to be handed over to their earl, Willelm fitzOsbern. They have amassed wealth from their own lords at Brygge near the coast, near the mouth of the Pedride'.

'That is *much* better, Godwin. You see how a gathering of boughs bears fruit?'

Godwin bunches his brow, not understanding.

'A tree has many boughs, Godwin. Your own tree - your kin - has borne fruit in coming together', Diarmuid smiles as if talking to a child. 'We must bring Ketilbeorn and Thored into the talks now. How do you say, friends? Do you think Godwin has been wise in talking over his thoughts with his brothers and Ivar?'

'I would say it sounds good', Ketilbeorn nods eagerly. 'I think taking the tithes their lords have brought together is worthy of a raid such as we can launch on their shore!'

'Much better thought out', Thored agrees, nodding. He then beckons Hemming toward us and asks, 'Hemming, what have you to say for yourself?'

'Lord Godwin asked me what my lord, the shire reeve Ansgar would do were he to be with us', Hemming starts.

'*Ansgar* – is he not one of this Northman king's pups?' Thored asks. 'Surely we cannot think of using the fellow to draw on for a line of attack, when he is in their pockets?'

'Ansgar *was* King Harold's stallari, as well as his shire reeve in

Middilseaxe', I put in, showing some friendship toward a man who outlived his king, only to have to bow like a whipped whelp to the man who beat his king.

'Who was answerable for King Harold losing to the Northman?' Diarmuid screws up his eyes at me, thinking I might know the answer to an oft-asked question.

'Surely a king's stallari must know something of beating back a foe with his back to the sea?'

'The Northmen had weapons never seen outside Frankia', I tell him.

'Weapons are still *only* weapons in the wrong hands', Thored tries to browbeat me. 'What made *theirs* so wonderful?'

'Crossbows and lances did much of their work for them', Godwin cuts in unwisely.

'Crossbows - and lances-' Diarmuid looks puzzled.

'Why should we fear them?' Ketilbeorn thrusts out his barrel chest like a cock-bird. 'These lances can only be carried by men on horseback, true?'

'Aye, true', I am heartened by this fellow Ketilbeorn, but Thored is not as brash. 'I was only warning you'.

'I have heard their horsemen can throw their weight about. Their lances, as you call them, can cut men down in swathes'.

'They are useless against a shieldwall', I answer, 'and our bowmen brought many of these Northmen down. I saw many horses riderless on Caldbec Beorg'.

'Then *how* did this Northman duke win?' Thored asks me, standing with his hands out wide. 'He had a shieldwall atop a high hill, the Northmen and their allies had a hard *climb* to attack you!'

'My kinsman did not wait long enough for men to flock to his banners, and the men of Suth Seaxe were mostly untried, their thegns unwise. They broke ranks to chase the first attackers downhill – straight into the arms, so to speak, of the duke's horsemen. Throughout the day he drew more of them. The lure was too much to withstand!'

'Are the men of the western shires any better, then?' Ketilbeorn asks Godwin. 'It is on them will have to fall back, after all, if these Northmen are stronger on the ground than you say

'You fear the Northmen - why?' Eadmund foolishly asks Ketilbeorn and is made to feel the man's wrath.

'Any fool who left his ships and crossed Frankia on foot would know never to do so again, *if* he came out alive!' Ketilbeorn looks sideways at Thored, who merely shrugs and looks down into the nearest dark corner.

'We will be no further than a couple of miles from the Seoferna near

Brycgstoth', I tell him.

Thored raises a hand and shakes his head. He tells Godwin, Eadmund and me a chilling tale from days gone by,

'That could still be too far from the ships. The Franks Ketilbeorn speaks of tore his uncle and his men to shreds. Only one man was allowed to live to take word to Ketilbeorn on the Seine, to warn him of what could befall him should he and his men set foot on their lands again', Thored stops to swallow. 'My father was with them, the ones into whom the Franks tore with their lances and maces'.

'Never again-'Ketilbeorn swears, '*never!*'

'Not even for the silver you will find in Brycgstoth?' Godwin taunts.

'It had *better* be there!' Thored warns, 'Should we not find it, we will leave your bones for the ravens to pick!'

'Why were your elders marching across Frankia?' Eadmund asks.

'They were heading toward a monastery they were told had gold and silver worth a king's ransom', Ketilbeorn tells Eadmund. 'The man who told them about it also told the Frankish abbot they would be on their way. We learned about that from the fellow himself before we made a feast of him for the crows'.

'You are Christian, are you not?' Magnus raises a brow. Thored's icy stare lets him know he should tread lightly. Ketilbeorn scowls at him.

'We gain from their raids on Frankia', Murchad smiles at me before Diarmuid adds something for Eadmund and Magnus to think on. With it he is telling them that all is fair as far as he thinks,

'*Our* Church and theirs are at odds with one another. When the Northanhymbran Oswald and his brother Oswy were given shelter by our kinsmen the Scots they took Christ and gave our worthy Columba the island of Lindisfarena so that their underlings could learn the word of Christ from his Gaelic follower. The Holy Father in Roma sent Augustine to take your kings away from Columba's teachings, and for that he was made a saint'.

'Surely that is no grounds for attacking fellow Christians?' Godwin pleads to closed ears. Diarmuid smiles, sets his teeth and adds,

'Columba was banished from Northanhymbra by a later king, swayed by his southern neighbours to bow to Roma. I gave these Danes a home, shelter from the storm – so to speak – and I turn a blind eye to them raiding Frankish abbeys. I want no more talk of 'fellow Christians' from you, Godwin. I can as easily counsel *my* Danes against helping you and leave you to the Holy Father's pup, King Willelm. He wags his tail to Roma now but will turn his back on the Holy Father when he thinks himself strong enough, and your fellow Aenglishmen will feel his wrath if he thinks you threaten his welfare with uprisings. Take my help by all means, and I will do all I can for you in the same way as I helped your father an uncle'.

The room seems suddenly smaller, threatening, even to me. I think Godwin must choose wisely. Diarmuid means him no harm, nor do Ketilbeorn and Thored. They *want* to go with us to fight the Northmen, but he has to understand their aims are not the same as his. Diarmuid does not need Godwin to understand why he wants to help, he only wishes him to acknowledge the Erse outlook.

'*Well?*' Ketilbeorn booms. Godwin steps forward to shake their hands. Diarmuid pulls Godwin toward him and hugs him tightly, as a father would a long-lost son.

Ketilbeorn hugs Godwin too, almost crushing the young fellow like a bear. Thored is a little stiff. He takes Godwin's hand and slaps him once on the back and steps back, as he does with my other kinsmen and me. Hemming earns a mere handshake from all here.

Hugs and back-slapping follow all around. Diarmuid has tears in his eyes when he hugs me after all these years.

'How many ships can you give me?' Godwin asks, to grins from Ketilbeorn and Thored. He *has* taken in their words.

'I can give you ten ships', Diarmuid answers, the others nod. 'My friends here will let you know how many men will go with them'.

Godwin knows now that Ketilbeorn and Thored will take us, whatever their thoughts may have been heretofore. He may have thought he would only be counselled by them. From meeting them, I knew these two would not want to miss out on raiding on Aengla Land with the son of an Aenglish king.

It matters little to them that many Aenglish lords thought of his father as a throne grabber. They smell gain, and that is what matters to them. Back in the days of Haesten, Ubbi and my namesake, Ivar 'the Boneless', Danes and Norsemen helped one Aenglishman against another - or against a West Seaxan even, with reward in the offing. We have slain one another for gain from time to time, when hired by different lords.

The evening is spent drinking, in hall sport, drinking and board games. Gael, Seaxan and Dane share one thought, and that is to drink until we fall down or pass out. Taste be hanged, not that we would drink anything that tasted as if a horse had pissed into it!

Hemming foolishly takes on one of Murchad's men in a drinking bout, and is beaten hollow. He has to pour what is left in his beaker over his own head. Saeward takes on the Gael, wins and lets no-one forget until he too slides under the bench some hours later.

'Your East Seaxan friend takes too much on himself!' Laughing, Thored strides past the dozing Saeward on his way to bed. Ketilbeorn behind him scowls down and steps over Saeward's outstretched hand. In the days to come there will be a lot less drinking and a lot more testing for the shieldwall. The time may come again for drinking, those who live through what we set out for.

My thoughts turn to Braenda. Not my woman, my horse, being rested and fed in Wulfberht's stable. She will be ready for me to go back and call on her strength in the months ahead.

I have to own, that only after thinking of my horse does Braenda the woman enter my thoughts. She might laugh if I told her, but I should keep it to myself lest she be insulted. After all, when she looks in on me she comes only for one thing. Of late she keeps asking me to fill her with my seed. She *has* a child of mine, but will not tell me where.

Is the child a daughter fostered on someone? Her longing may drive her to seek me out to give her a son, another Ivar to raise to manhood as she sees fit?

Diarmuid slaps my left shoulder,

'Well, Ivar, I see you are still with us. Shame your friend here does not have your staying power with his drinking'.

'We are each our own man', I answer.

Much of Diarmuid's time at the feast has been taken with talking, leaving the drinking to younger men now. He has sent out men to take word to the Danes and those Gaels around Leinster who wish to pit their skills against the Northmen across the sea. Within the next days we will see how many have answered the call to fill Godwin's ships.

Saeward groans, flops over onto his back and starts snoring. One of Ketilbeorn's men empties a pail of dirty water over him and bends down to see how Saeward takes it. In a flash Saeward reaches out his right fist and floors the fellow. He struggles to his feet and looks down at the unlucky Dane, muttering,

'Let sleeping hounds lie!'

'You see yourself as Diarmuid's hall hound now?' I ask, and duck as a clenched fist comes my way. '*Hey*, friend, watch where your fists fly! I wonder you would like to go back to sleep as quickly as you rose?'

'*Who* – oh, it is *you!* Help me to my cot, will you?'

My lips curl into a wry smile and I offer only so much help,

'I *will* help you to your door, Saeward, but if you want to be mothered ask one of the women here. One or two I believe might not fear to sleep under your fat belly!'

'Where is Hemming?' he asks, overlooking my slur on the size of

80

his belly, and looks down behind him to where my down-turned finger tells him his room-mate slumbers. 'Dead to the world, eh – could not make it back to his cot? How long has he been like that?'

'Since he drank himself under the bench with that Gael you took on and beat', I answer, sniff and pull his right arm over my shoulder.

He pushes me away, snapping back,

'*Not* like *that!* I can walk myself there, I just want you to steer me - like a ship in a heavy swell'.

'How heavy would this swell have to be before you lost your way?' I ask, tongue-in-cheek.

'As heavy as my belly', he snorts, almost falling over another of King Diarmuid's guests as he looks back at me.

I push him and he falls forward over another poor drunken soul. He raises himself on one elbow and reaches up his other arm for me to lift him. The task is made harder by a pair of Ketilbeorn's men trying to lift him between them. Beyond help themselves, they fall over him and knock themselves out doing so.

Both men lie on top of him now, and I have to heave them aside before I can hoist Saeward to his feet. If this was happening to someone else I would call it laughable. As it is I am the one who has to save him from anyone else trying to help. Ketilbeorn sits on a bench nearby, cackling like an old toothless spay-wife and I feel duty-bound to grin as I lead Saeward away from the darkening hall. The Dyflin Dane slaps a big hand down hard onto the bench in his mirth, and almost launches himself onto the floor. Were I not busy with Saeward I would be slapping my thigh with drunken glee, but he is several strides ahead of me and likely to bring down the wrath of the household men on him by mewing at their womenfolk.

'The fellow is well-sated', I tell them, 'harmless – almost legless!'

'*Just as well then!*' one surly young fellow spits, only drawing back from hurting my friend because I am there with him.

'I could take *you* on, sober *or* drunk', Saeward snarls, fists clenched ready to maul the fellow.

'*Another time*, Saeward', I head him off and grin cheerily at Diarmuid's man, who goes back to dousing torches in their wall brackets outside the hall door.

Saeward turns, only to be blocked by Thored.

'I'll beat the scum into *Hell*, so I will!' Saeward mumbles.

'Who is it your friend means?' Thored asks me, knowing that Saeward to be foolishly drunk.

'One of the king's men dousing the torches', I let him know whilst Saeward rests against one of the posts, breathless from the effort of staggering out of the hall.

'Do you mean the dark, heavy-set one?' Thored turns to see.

'He *is* the one', I answer wearily. By the time I reach my bed I shall be in need of rest!

'Oh, *I* should like to see *that!*' Thored tells me his name is Cormac, a fighter of renown who willingly takes on and beats any man foolish enough to call him out. 'I would put silver on Cormac laying your friend out in the first round!'

'Aye, well there will be no rounds', I nod at Saeward. 'I need his skill with an axe. He can hurl an axe fifty strides from the saddle'.

'An axe man, *him?*' Thored stands open-mouthed.

'You should see him!' I ruffle Saeward's tousled brown hair. 'He is also good at healing men's wounds. He has saved *my* life more than once in the past year or so'.

'Odd, what do *you* think, him being a healer *and a* slayer? You said he can throw an axe over two score strides?' Thored scratches his well-groomed beard.

'Fifty!' I tell him, wondering where this will lead.

'Cormac can do *three-score!*' Thored boasts on the Gael's behalf.

'Would you put silver on *that?*' I ask, getting Saeward into deeper water.

'Easily, I *would!*' Thored licks his lips, and looks at me as a bull might before it tramples me into the dirt!

'In the afternoon he might take you up on that offer, I wonder?' I can already taste the silver coins between my teeth.

'Done – and your friend *will* be!' Thored beams broadly and spits into his right palm. We shake hands. I can tell Saeward when he awakens, of the task I have let him in for. That will teach him to get drunk and put himself in my care!

'You did *what?!*' Saeward sweats. Deep red, his eyes glistening beneath beetling brows, he looks ready to kill me.

'I have put a bet on with Thored that you can beat his man at throwing axes – fifty strides, I believe', I tell him and put on a smile to cheer him. It does not work and he glowers still. 'Are you telling me you are *afraid* of this Gael – you, a man of the East Seaxan fyrd, who stunned Eadgar the *aetheling* with his axe-skills at Thorney?'

'He was young, easily stunned!' Saeward will have none of it.

'He was not the *only* one. Others – men at Naesinga who spent their lives fighting – said you were the best they had seen!'

He is silent, deep in thought, so I add,

'What about the young Northman you threw your axe at? He was easily *three-score* strides away and riding off!'

'*Hardly* – more like *two* score!' Saeward chides, still scowling, but I see a grin just below the scowl he is trying to hide.

'*You* can do three score – I know it, here', I spread my right hand across my chest, '*here!* You would never let me down, *I know you!*'

'What if I do not?' Saeward licks his lips. Is it fear? Or can he also taste the silver coins he knows will be forthcoming if he wins.

'You and I will share a *bagful* of silver', I tell him.

'Wait – *what* is this? You and I will *share* this bagful of silver, when *I* am the one throwing axes?' Saeward throws me a look of scorn.

'Who would have made this likely for you, if you were so *unsure* of your throwing skill?'

I stand square onto him, arms folded and at my full height – at *least* a head taller. I would not bully him, not a friend as he has come to be, but in browbeating him into this and taking some of the spoils I will have furthered his name as a true warrior. True, he will be the one who throws the axes, as he says, but I am the one who will suffer derision if he proves to be less than I made him up to be. He will just be forgotten by them – *however*, should he win they will talk about him here in Dyflin and around Diarmuid's kingdom for a long time to come!

Saeward's eyes narrow to slits. He sizes me up and tests me,

'Very well, then – three-score parts of the reward to me and two to you if I can throw that far in stride-lengths. Who will test the length?'

'Murchad or Ketilbeorn will rate your throw', I offer. He shakes his head enough to test its anchor. I ask, '*What* then?'

'A priest should do it', Saeward tells me.

His teeth are set firmly, he is unwavering.

'Very well, I shall ask a *priest* to referee for you', I nod and lead him out to the garth yard.

'Can it be *any* priest?' Thored asks Saeward. 'I can ask Father Donal. He is not from these parts, being a man of the northern isles'.

'Aye, ask him', Saeward beams.

'Osketil, fetch Father Donal', Thored asks one of the Danes. With a thumbs-up Osketil leaves.

'Whilst Osketil is away, Saeward, would you like to warm up for the match?' I ask, pointing to Cormac.

The Gael is already out on the rough earth, limbering up. He lifts an axe from where it has been embedded in a tree trunk and shows off with it for a short time, spinning it in his hand, tossing it from hand to hand across the width of his outstretched arms. Then he grasps the axe and looses it, away into the air. The weapon spins in its flight and lands some way off. A youth chases eagerly after it, and smirks as Saeward weighs his in both hands.

'The lad asks if the axe is your own', Ketilbeorn asks Saeward, who merely nods and gazes across the open ground at where Cormac's axe landed, the earth broken, turf turned upward by an oak sapling.

'How far would you say that is?' Saeward asks me, to be answered by Thored, who tells him,

'That is two score and ten strides from the line – there'. Thored shows him the line cut into the sandy earth a little way to his left. 'That is where you stand to throw for the bags of silver both Ivar and I have given King Diarmuid to hold. He in turn will put another bag of silver to ours'.

Saeward's eyebrows rise and he blows out his cheeks. He looks at me and asks,

'There is *that much* riding on this?'

I am taken aback. *Diarmuid* has been brought into this by either Thored or Ketilbeorn – or *both*!

'The king learned of the match from me', Thored smiles winsomely.

'As soon as Thored told me I had to be in!' Diarmuid crows, walking toward us, 'Few are the times a Gael can take on an Aenglishman in sport. When silver is brought into the game, it strengthens the bond between men, would you not agree, Ivar - or would you say otherwise?'

'It *can*, my Lord King – or it can make them bitter foes. When the gain is raised, the more a man might try to cheat', I answer.

'*How* would any man cheat here, with so many witnesses around him?' Diarmuid tests me, looking around us.

'For myself I would not know, Lord', I shrug, looking at him to show I have no such aim. I wish a fair match for Saeward's sake. It is his renown as a warrior that is at stake here, and the silver will help us both find a life when our struggle is at an end. My share would buy land. That is my dream. Saeward, for his part, would like land and I wonder he would buy a mill in East Seaxe. Our warring days would be over, and Braenda might come to live with me, bring our offspring with her.

'Well spoken', Thored rests a hand on my right shoulder. 'Is Donal here yet?'

'I *am* here', answers a young fellow. He pushes back his hood to show noble roots in his narrow jaw and brow. I would warrant he carries the blood of kings. He has the same fine reddish hair as Braenda.

6

'Ivar Ulfsson, this is my third son, Donal', Diarmuid beckons the young man to his side.

'This is the catch in the match', I tell myself under my breath. No wonder Thored put forward Donal as referee. He is one of *them!* Aloud I tell them with a smile, *'So be it!'*

Diarmuid, Thored and Ketilbeorn are wreathed in smiles, Cormac smirks, along with his young helper. This has to be the first time I have leant towards prayer in years and my thoughts to Saeward. I have said before that he has the makings of a fine warrior, even though at times he has shown himself to be a ruthless killer – a ruthless, *bloodthirsty* killer. Can he rein in his skill, knowing how much rides on it, without losing any of the raw strength and pluck that goes with it?

He would have made a great Viking.

I have never told him so, thinking he might be offended. Yet he stands there, stock still, axe in hand, girding his loins.

Cormac stands close by him, smirking at Saeward's first warm-up throws, counting the silver as each throw falls short of the oak sapling. His helper laughs into his hands, gleefully, un-checked.

Still Saeward pays no heed to them, weighs his axe and throws one last time before the match begins, to see it land – again – just short of the sapling. Is he toying with everyone?

Diarmuid plainly thinks highly of Saeward for his steadfastness, as much as he wonders at my gall for calling Thored's bluff. He watches each of Saeward's throws and claps loudly, keeping his own counsel on Cormac out-throwing him.

Donal calls for the match to begin when he stands well to the right of the sapling. Both men stride up to a line marked out earlier by one of Thored's men, taking care to keep behind it, allowing for the full stride they will need to letting loose their axes. Cormac and Saeward shake hands before readying themselves to throw, and Cormac rubs flour onto his dish-sized hands.

'In your own time -' Donal calls out, right arm held high. The arm drops and Cormac steps up to the line. He spins three times and lets go the axe, not so much a warrior but as a hammer thrower, a sportsman, much like the Scots in their games.

With three throws each, Saeward's next, he looks sure of himself. Unflustered, he weighs his axe to throw after Cormac's. Not having thrown an axe since we fought Willelm fitzOsbern's Northmen at Hereford, he nevertheless breathes evenly. He believes in his own skill, as shown well in his careful over-arm throw.

Where Cormac's easily struck the line before the sapling, Saeward's falls short – again. Shouting breaks out to cheer on Cormac, but is cut short by Diarmuid raising his staff. He nods for Cormac to throw his second, and the Gael throws again in the same way as his first. This time the axe flies out of his hand and almost cuts down Donal.

Shouting breaks out again. Diarmuid takes his hands down from his eyes, fearful of what might have happened. Had Cormac killed his youngest? He raises his staff again to still the cat-calls and rasping from the onlookers, and Donal – having shaken off his fright – calls for Saeward to throw.

Cormac's bad luck brings neither smirk nor laughter from Saeward. He steps forward, tongue between teeth, takes his axe from the young lad who holds it out to him, and weighs his axe in his left hand. His right grips the long handle and he spreads his arms, axe head resting in his left hand still, a warning for those standing nearby to withdraw. He brings the axe forward in front of him, bends a little to summon strength for a hard throw and strides quickly toward the line. He lets fly the axe, over-arm once more.

The axe leaves his hand and spins, handle over blade through the air, arcing. Wood pigeons scatter, frightened by the sharp blade that cuts through one of their number in flight. Those below gasp as the axe hurtles onward to shatter the bottom staves of the garth's wooden wall, beyond the sapling.

The jaw of Cormac's young helper drops as if on leather straps. Cormac himself turns white, and it is only with effort that he can bring himself to walk up to the line again with his axe. Sweat beads on his brow, not from effort but from fear. This is his third throw, his last. He must make *this* throw matter, but on seeing Saeward's second axe still buried in the chipped wall staves he lets his axe arm sag. He strides to the line – and falters. He stops to jeers from the thronging Dyflin Gaels. Their shouts in his own tongue strike him like arrows in his back, making him flinch.

'*Come*, Cormac', Ketilbeorn tries to hearten him.

'Aye, Cormac, *come*', Thored claps and his Danes clap – slowly - with him. Murchad follows their lead, and Diarmuid stands.

'Cormac', the king calls out to him and tells him something in his own tongue. The fellow turns to look at him, nods and smiles, and then readies himself for his throw.

An uncanny stillness fills the air in the garth as Cormac stands, head bowed as if in prayer. He raises his head, steps back and jolts forward.

A scream fills the air that sounds like a war cry as the axe flies, as if pulled by unseen gods, to fall short of the tree by half an arrow's length. A distraught Cormac wails and drops to his knees as if felled by one of his unseen Celtic gods. Groans from the folk gathered around tell even those of us who do not understand the Gaelic tongue that their hopes have been dashed, silver has been lost. Now they have to stand by and watch the Aenglish outsider beat their man.

Saeward strides slowly up to the line and looks back at Cormac who turns away, unable to watch. Again Saeward says nothing, nor does he smile. He stands ready, wiping the axe blade on his sleeve - backwards and forwards – spits on the blade and steps forward up to the now worn line. He roars,

'*Wotan!*' and lets fly the axe to it find its way home. Blade down it thumps against the trunk of the sapling and bounces off, splitting the shaft of Cormac's axe lying on the earth, pinning it down onto the earth.

Cormac throws himself forward onto the earth as if asking to be speared by his betters. Diarmuid pushes through his Danes and stands, towering over his underling. The king bends to rest on one knee and takes Cormac's right hand. Whatever he says stirs the fellow into sitting to look up at his king, who raises him to his feet.

'Let it be known that I will not hold this man's failings against him', Diarmuid tells us. He looks long and hard at Saeward, at me and asks, 'Will you join my household Saeward?'

'My Lord, King Diarmuid, if were free to choose, I should still wish to free my homeland from the Northman king. Tell your man, Cormac that I think him a skilled sportsman. Tell him also, however, that he should throw his axe over-arm to get the *best* from his skill'.

'I understand you', Cormac tells Saeward and passes his king to take my friend's hand. That Saeward did not gloat after winning struck a chord.

'Was that a god, *Wotan*, to whom you called for help?' Diarmuid asks him.

'Aye, he *was* one of the old gods. He was the high god my forbears looked to in times of war, the god of the slain. Tiw was the god of war, and Thunor the god of thunder. The Christian God, in whom I believe yet, does not stand for war-making as you know. To which god did Cormac pray before he threw his axe?'

'*Fionn mac Cumhaill* was no god, but was a Gael warrior of long ago with his band of men, the Fianna. Cormac called on him to summon the strength for his best throw –', Diarmuid sucks his teeth and closes his eyes briefly. Ketilbeorn behind him rests a hand on Cormac's shoulder, and pats it. Diarmuid turns in his tracks and walks very slowly back to his hall with his underlings following.

Thored comes up behind Cormac and growls,

'You lost me silver, Cormac. Can you can make it up?'

'My Lord –'Cormac begins to answer, but is cut short by Saeward.

'I did not win. You saw, Ivar, did I win?' Saeward stares hard at me, willing me to be at one with him.

'I can see what you mean, friend. Your last axe hit the tree, did not cut into it but cut into the handle of Cormac's axe. I would call that a draw, if anything...' I feel like kicking myself. More than that I feel like kicking Saeward, but I have my wound to think of.

Thored and Ketilbeorn look at one another and at me before their eyes rest once more on Saeward. Thored is first to speak,

'You say that was a *draw?*' His stare tells me he cannot grasp when his luck has not left him.

'If you wish we can still take your silver', I grin toothily at him, reaching for the bags. He draws them to his chest, out of my reach, and laughs. He has a belly-laugh that sounds as if it comes from below the earth.

'Should you say this was a draw, our silver stays with *us*. King Diarmuid gets his back when we seek him out in his hall. You can have your *own* silver back, however', Ketilbeorn offers and looks closely at the bags, 'here'.

He hands me my own bag and runs a finger under his great raven's beak of a nose to wipe away a 'dew-drop'.

Thored grins, shakes his head in unspeaking mirth and walks away in the king's wake with a much happier Ketilbeorn in tow. Ketilbeorn pushes Cormac ahead of him and lets out a throaty laugh at something Thored has told him.

'This will stand us in good stead, Ivar, you watch!' Saeward tells me behind one hand as Godwin and his brothers stride toward us,

'What was *that* all about, Saeward?' Eadmund asks, still unable to believe what had gone before. 'Shouting '*Wotan*' before you threw the axe was odd coming from you, was it not? Does being with Ivar bring out the heathen in you?'

'I wonder whether the heathen has ever left us East Seaxans, Lord Eadmund', Saeward answers smugly, only to be rewarded with a dark scowl from Godwin.

'Heathens notwithstanding, you should not show yourself to be at one with the Erse', Godwin scolds, after first making sure there are none around to overhear him. After all, he wants the help of Diarmuid to help claim his lands back in Sumorsaetan, or even the crown. If he let them know what he thinks of them, they might not be so eager to do as he wishes without asking for his silver before he was given a ship, let alone men.

Saeward says no more and Godwin sees no use in further chiding my friend. He beckons me to one side and asks,

'Is this the way to get Diarmuid's help, letting his man win?'

Do I have to tell my kinsman, who would be king, how to deal with underlings? I steer him away with a hand on his shoulder,

'He did not let Cormac win. The Gael thought he had lost and fell to earth, thinking he would be punished for failing his king. I think Saeward threw short'.

'He *threw* short?' Magnus' eyebrows rise. Godwin and Eadmund are as taken aback as is their younger brother.

'You *saw* the first axe dig into the bottom of the wall?' I ask. 'I can show you, if you like. Come with me and look for yourself, kinsman'.

'By all means, Ivar - I have to see this for myself. How many strides is that, by the way?'

As we make for the part of the wall behind the sapling Godwin sees the axe that Saeward threw first. He asks,

'Is this Saeward's own weapon?'

'Aye, it is', I answer as Saeward bends and picks it up, looks closely at the blade and walks along behind us, to where Cormac's axe lies, its shaft split by Saeward's third thrown axe.   Godwin stands and looks down, blows his lips and walks on. He is plainly stunned by the feat, but says nothing.

He has said nothing yet about what he thinks of Saeward's skill. Were I Godwin, I would acknowledge that skill before Saeward takes up Diarmuid's offer of a seat on his hall benches as a household warrior.

A yawning Hemming comes over to us from our sleeping quarters and – scratching his backside - asks,

'Have I missed something?'

Saeward shakes his head, pursing his lips. If he wishes Hemming not to know, we cannot enlighten him. He does think to ask,

'Did you win, Saeward? What will you do with all that silver?'

'We drew', is all Saeward wishes to tell him.

Hemming stands, mouth wide open as we walk on to the wall. When we stop at the wall he follows on and gapes at the axe mark in the bottom stave.

'Whose was this?' he asks when he gets over the shock.

'That was Saeward's second throw', I tell Hemming, trying to stop myself from laughing and giving away the riddle of Saeward's 'draw'.

'It must be at least three-score and ten strides –'

'My thought too', I agree, still stifling my mirth.

Hemming strains to see another axe on the earth nearby and asks – *demands*, rather,

'How far did Cormac throw his second axe?'

'You should find it in the short grass – somewhere the other side of the oak sapling behind you', Godwin answers warily, not wishing to give any more away, but Hemming will have it out of one of us before long.

'I can *not* understand this, Saeward', he scratches his head. 'Your axe reached *this* far and yet you say you *drew* the match. How *is* that?'

'He was thinking ahead', I tell Hemming. He stares at me as if I had sprouted a second head, so I feel I must tell him, 'Diarmuid will feel his man Cormac has not lost, so will be more likely to help Godwin. The way things were, we might have had to take on the Northmen near Brycgstoth by ourselves – *swimming* across the Seoferna I wonder?'

'What about your *winnings?*' he asks Saeward.

'Lord Godwin won', is the answer Saeward gives, to a blank look from Hemming.

'Your skill as a warrior is greater than your skill as a thinker. Fear not, we still need you', Godwin laughs.

We all laugh out aloud at that, even Hemming.

He may have understood, but I hardly think so. Godwin is right about one thing, we need his skills as a warrior, however lacking he is elsewhere.

'*Food*', Godwin turns Eadmund around as Saeward wipes his axe blade clean with grass plucked from around the roots of the sapling and we all follow him into the hall. We are now looking forward to drinking and the later feasting that will come when Diarmuid allows Ketilbeorn and Thored to take ships and bolster Godwin's claim over the west.

Allowing that we have a hard task ahead of us, and there will be months – *years* even, and that is very likely – of fighting before we can see our way straight to putting an Aenglishman on the throne, and it may very well not be Godwin in the end if Gospatric or Osulf have anything to do with it.

First things first, we must land on the Seoferna shore of Gleawanceaster shire and take on the Northmen. Hopefully the weather will be with us and we can catch them unaware, sheltered by a westerly sea mist. At worst we will take them full on with their lances – something that does *not* bear thinking of!

On a cold fore-year morning the thick mist that blankets us seems to be the answer to our prayers. Godwin drops from the steerboard quarter of Ketilbeorn's ship and splashes through the shallows. Behind him am I,

Eadmund, Magnus, Hemming and Saeward. Ketilbeorn is already ashore with a score of his Danes, and when we close on them, Ketilbeorn signals us to keep still.

The waves lap noisily on the shore with the wind chasing them, drowning the splashing of hundreds of men wading ashore through knee-deep, ice-cold water.

'*Where* are the men you say will flock to your banner?' Ketilbeorn asks when Godwin reaches him.

'They *will* come soon, fear not', Godwin answers. His long hair flaps about across his forehead in the freshening wind that threatens to blow away the mist, our shield. I look around, away from the wind to try to see what, or *who* is afoot – hopefully anything *but* Northmen.

There are shapes some way off, inland to the north, many of them. Godwin has been made aware of them too, and stands watching through the thinning greyness. He strides forward to meet them, only to be greeted by a spear that thuds into the sandy earth of the foreshore.

'What is the meaning –'Godwin begins to curse loudly and more spears hit the tussocks of long, dark marram grass around us.

'Form a shieldwall – *here!*' Godwin yells hoarsely as Thored and his men splash ashore through the surf. Thored calls on his men to do likewise and Ketilbeorn glowers at Godwin.

'*I was told*-', my kinsman begins.

'As of now *I* lead!' Ketilbeorn chides Godwin. 'Forget about what you were told, for now we must hold them off. We will be unable to set sail for Sumorsaetan with arrows flying – *fire* arrows, even – so we must fight them to a standstill here until they fall back. *Then* we can leave! Believe *me*, Aenglishman if I learn you have drawn us into a trap, you will pay for it with your life! Get behind that *shieldwall,* men!'

He yells over the wind at men who have just landed, waving at them with his sword to strengthen those at our northern flank. They are the men who will have to hold the line until these attackers spread out before us. Our attackers are *Aenglishmen!*

Oddly no more spears - or arrows – thump into our shields. I would be willing to bet one of the *fyrd* leaders means to speak before the attack gets underway again. Sure enough an elderly fellow, an *ealdorman*, comes forward through the mass of men that now blocks our way inland – *should* we wish to go that way.

'Thegn Aelfred', Godwin knows him, '*why* do you lead fellow West Seaxans against *me*, Godwin Haroldson?'

'I know who *you* are. I have known since your man rode into Brycgstoth burh, to raise *fyrdmen* to fight our king's law! *Go*, sail back to where you came from if you wish. Do not bring these Danish freebooters to fight against fellow –'Aelfred is not allowed to finish.

'Who are *you*, calling us Danish *freebooters*, you old scarecrow?!' Thored roars above the din of jeering from the West Seaxan ranks. He plainly knows the Seaxans' tongue, 'Take your rabble and flee before we turn you all into *carrion!*'

'Is this what *you* want, Godwin?' Aelfred's eyes narrow to slits against the cold wind that whips up his dragon banner.

'I want us to fight together, *side by side*, against the outlander king!' Godwin pleads, but his words fall on deaf ears. Behind us, Ketilbeorn's men bay for blood – Seaxan blood. Wishing to live up to his namesake, Thegn Aelfred has as good as called them out. He will pay dearly for his folly. Many will pay, needlessly. All they had to do was fall back toward their fields and Ketilbeorn's Danes would have sailed on for Sumorsaetan.

There are no Northmen in sight here, only scores of Aelfred's fyrdmen. This will be the first time they were ever called on to fight for *many* years, not even within the lifetime of their youngest!

Around me Ketilbeorn's Danes bay for blood still, hammering the backs of their shields with their axes and swords. Aelfred has not yet even formed a shieldwall. His bowmen loose off a hail of arrows, the sky darkening for a short time as their points drum fast into our shields.

Men drop to their knees, men who had not raised their shields in time and Thored howls like a madman,

'*Onward – slay* these sons of Seaxan bitches!' The middle part of the shieldwall presses forward like a hedgehog as throwing spears sail outward at Aelfred's *fyrdmen* over their heads. Ketilbeorn yells at his bowmen to unleash their willow wands into the ranks of the bowmen.

For the first time since Ubbi Ragnarsson stormed these shores over ten-score years ago Dane fights Seaxan. Only this time we have Seaxans with *us* – aside from Hemming and Saeward.

Spears soar into the grey heavens, down onto the massed Brycgstoth *fyrdmen*. Aelfred's men fall back northward, bleeding from wounds meted out by fellow West Seaxans attacking from the south. Who are the newcomers – are they likely to turn on *us* when they learn they have set about the wrong foe?

We shall find out soon enough. Some of these newcomers are looking at us...

'I want to see your shields – *up!*' Thored yells at his men before Ketilbeorn sees that our West Seaxan 'friends' are aiming at us now.

Some of Ketilbeorn's men had already seen where the arrows were being aimed before he calls out for the rest to withdraw to the ships.

Godwin, his brothers, Hemming, Saeward and I are in Thored's shieldwall and we must stand with him whilst Ketilbeorn's men form a three-deep ring at the head of the strand for us to fall back through and man the ships. Bowmen will stand at the prows to hold off Aelfred's fyrdmen when we are all aboard. Hopefully things will fall into line and we will not lose too many men, but men *will* be lost nonetheless.

As Aelfred's standard is at the head of his men, so will he be close by - easy for Thored's bowmen to aim at. Godwin has had the same thought and makes Thored aware of it. Straightaway Thored points out Aelfred for his bowmen, but before they can aim at him there is a wall of shields in front of him. How lucky can a man *be?!* We have to find another weakness within their ranks, draw him there and *then* finish him off.

Arrows fall amongst us again before we can make out the weakest part of their shieldwall. These have been aimed at us from the south, threatening to cut us off from Ketilbeorn and the Seoferna strand. Thored barks at his men on that side to use the arrows embedded in our shields against the West Seaxans.

Where on earth have they *come* from, though? Surely they are not Godwin's *own* men from Sumorsaetan?

'Do you know these men to our south-west, Godwin?' I ask.

'*Back*, men *fall back!*' Thored roars above the din of clattering shields before Godwin can answer, as the newcomers slowly press toward us. We shuffle sideways as the men to our fore filter through our rank and *we* now become the front row.

'Keep your shields *high*, to your shoulders', I warn my kinsmen.

Hemming needs no telling, and nudges Saeward to keep his guard up, higher than he has already raised it. Luckily an arrow that would have found his chest merely thuds into the top of his shield and splinters it. He looks away as some of the splinters fly toward his eyes – *very* luckily! One of the splinters embeds itself in his jaw and he cannot pull it.

'Saeward, come here', I call out. 'I will draw it out for you!'

He holds high his shield as he makes toward me, one of Thored's Danes sags to his knees beside him and he stops as if frozen to the grass.

'Come!' I call again and he shakes his head, the splinter waggling as he does so.

I cannot make my way toward him, but in the way we pull back we come together and he turns his left jaw to me. Sliding my axe into the loop at the back of my shield I take the splinter between two fingers and draw it sharply free. He hisses with the pain and I reach for my axe.

It slips from my grasp and drops to the blood-soaked grass at my feet. There is no way I can reach for it without letting arrows through the shieldwall and call out,

'Thored, *my axe –*'

'Draw your *sword*, fool!' he yells back.

I am loth to leaving my pride and joy to these fyrdmen, but I do not want him yelling at me like some fool beginner. He roars once more, *'Pull back again!'*

We do as bidden, and I see my axe on the grass between the shield walls. One of the Seaxans reaches out for it from beneath his comrades' shields and an arrow tears into his arm. His high-pitched screams pierce my eardrums and he falls forward to fall prey to a Danish arrow through his shoulder. As the Seaxan falls on top of the axe, hiding it from sight, another arrow tip buries itself into his back. He would soon have been dead anyway, from the soil on the tip of the second arrowhead. The third has sealed his *wyrd,* sending him to his god.

'Fall back!' Thored roars once again. *'Board the ships!'*

It is a shame my axe will have to stay there. I will never have another like it. One of Aelfred's fyrdmen will find it, maybe, after the corpses have been buried. He may yield it to his thegn, or keep it for himself – less likely. I am left with my grandfather's sword, and hope it still has years of use left in it. A weaponsmith in Sumorsaetan may make another, but I hold out no hope for that.

Somehow my thoughts stray to my horse in Wulfberht's stable. Will Braenda be safe there? Would *Wulfberht* be safe in Barnestapla, once the Northmen send word to their earl about him being saved from them by the Danes? They would know his ships, surely. Having allowed him to trade, Willelm fitzOsbern might then have second thoughts. Wulfberht will be known to have helped outlaws flee the long arm of his king's law.

Aboard Thored's ship again we watch the front of Aelfred's shieldwall close on the foreshore. His bowmen loose off another hail of arrows at us over our shield-tops, whilst Thored's cut down those foolish and foolhardy Seaxans unwise enough to show themselves above their shields.

'Show the fools how sharp are our arrow-tips!' I hear Ketilbeorn mock the unskilled West Seaxan fyrdmen – not *so* unskilled, however, that they could not push us back onto the ships!

Yet strength of numbers had as much to do with them seeing us off today. Will Godwin's faith in his followers in Sumorsaetan be borne out? He will be hard put to get Ketilbeorn and Thored to come back with him, unless Diarmuid can help him.

Time will tell... Meanwhile, we must test out the steadfastness of Eadnoth the *Stallari* along the coast.

The sun shines as we come into the mouth of the river north of Barnestapla after a half day sailing south-west, ships made fast in the lee of the headland. Whilst we eat with Ketilbeorn and Thored on deck, Godwin outlines his thoughts on how to go about summoning his followers from the hamlets around. Riders have been sent out with word for Eadnoth.

Now he calls on me to go with him as well as Eadmund, Magnus, Hemming and Saeward. On the eastern bank of the river now, Wulfberht's hamlet is in sight across the Pedride. This is the side of the river, he says, where we should find the men who will flock to his banner. I can only hope for his sake that he finds them this time.

'There is sun glinting on steel to our south', Hemming warns Godwin.

Harold's sons look to where Hemming's finger stretches.

'Could this be the *Stallari*?' Magnus asks.

'Would that it were', Godwin nods.

Ketilbeorn had been in talks with Thored some time before Godwin sat with them. Eadmund shields his eyes from the sun to our right.

The day is not yet over, but clouds threaten from the north-west behind us, the wind coming across the coast of Wealas.

If this is a welcome, then I am a bishop's whore!' Hemming swears under his breath to me.

'I think you *would* look fetching in long skirts', Eadmund tells him behind one hand and grins wickedly at Saeward and me.

'He has the *hair* of a woman', Saeward mocks Hemming, for which he is given a dark look. True Hemming looks womanly from behind, with his ash-blond locks, but Saeward only gets away with the jibe because they are friends – so far. I dare say Hemming would be much less than soft and yielding if an outsider had said it to *or* of him.

'They would not be *war* standards, that the leading men carry, would they?' Magnus ponders.

'As I said', Hemming sneers, 'this is no welcome'.

Godwin thumps his right palm onto his left fist and sourly tells us to turn about, back to the rivermouth at Barnestapla,

'We can outflank them', I offer.

'Outflank them – *how?*' Godwin stares sideways at me.

'Half the ships set out and land along the coast. The men march inland on Eadnoth, whilst the others seem to make a stand on the western riverbank. When the men come around Eadnoth's fyrdmen from the north and around their rear he will wish to talk', I answer.

'Can you put that to Ketilbeorn and Thored?' Godwin asks as we make back over the rise down to the riverbank at a trot.

'As long as I am not out of breath when we meet them', I crack. He looks heavenward as we stride across the bridge. His lack of wit may be down to being amongst the womenfolk for too long when he was a youth. Magnus is much like him in that way. Eadmund, however, is more like his father, or Tostig, quick-witted and better amongst menfolk.

'Ho, what gives?' Ketilbeorn looks up as we come into the main camp, set up near Wulfberht's hall.

'We think Eadnoth the *Stallari* is close by', Godwin answers first.

'Is that not what you wanted?' He can tell by looking at Godwin that all is not well.

'He has his war banners', I tell him, having finally got my breath back. 'From looking at the numbers of men he has with him, he is not here to talk. I had a thought'.

Ketilbeorn looks from me to Godwin, to Magnus and Eadmund, and back to me,

'You are a deep thinker, Ivar. What is it you have for me?'

'If either you or Thored takes half the ships around the point to the east', I draw in the dry earth at my feet with my sword-point. 'Put ashore and cross the land southward to behind Eadnoth's men –'

'The hammer strikes on the anvil', Thored smiles at me.

'It is a fine scheme', Ketilbeorn is at one with Thored.

'Can you take horses on your ships?' Saeward asks Ketilbeorn.

'We can take horses on our way overland', Thored tells him. 'There is a well-known steading to the east of here. We can drive the Seaxans onto you, and set the bowmen on this riverbank. Thored, will you take the men around Eadnoth?'

'That I can – *come*, Ivar, there would be no time to get horses aboard to do what we must', Thored beckons. 'Hemming and Saeward, come too!'

We take the track close by Wulfberht's garth at a run, before coming to a *karve* pulled up onto the stony foreshore. Thored barks at the crew, who come to life and push out the long boat into the river after we clamber aboard.

'Come on Saeward, *heave yourself over the wall!*' Thored laughs, pulling him hastily into the vessel by his rump as he gives word to the oarsmen to run their long oars out through the oar-holes.

We come to the steading, three hundred of us. As there are not enough horses, many would have to run. Thored knows this, and takes a tally of the horses. When he is done he asks me,

'How many mounts would you say, Ivar? I make the number three score and ten'.

'Give or take a half-dozen, I would say around that many', I answer. 'What are we doing?'

'As you said, Ivar, we will press on Eadnoth from behind, around thirty of us on horseback with others – the bowmen - on foot. The rest go back to the ships and land on the east bank of the river, to take the track there and catch the Seaxans off-guard!'

Three-score or more of us take the track that will bring us onto Eadnoth's rear. If they know to form a shieldwall the bowmen will pick them off and we ride around behind them to catch any out, who are reckless enough to try to stop us. My mount is not as surefooted as Braenda.

She stumbles on uneven ground where hummocks break up the land. There were trees here once, I would warrant, and the thegn has not yet had time to put his men to the task of turning it into growing land.

Hopefully the earth will be more even where Eadnoth and his fyrdmen march to meet Ketilbeorn, otherwise our outflanking trick could not be followed through. If our horses stumble we give the fyrdmen the day, and it is likely we shall forfeit our lives unless Eadnoth has us taken to give up to Earl Willelm. Then our goose *would* be cooked!

'There are armed men ahead!' Hemming reins in.

'Have they seen us, do you think?' I ask.

'Hard to say – no I do not think so', he waits for Thored and the rest to catch up to me, some way behind him. When Thored is with me I tell him there are scouts ahead.

'Is there a way around them?' Thored asks, craning his neck to look around. He nudges me to look where his sword points, 'Over there, to the south, is woodland. We can ride around them and let the men march through. By the time they see us riding them down it will be too late for them!'

'Very well', I nod. 'So be it'.

Hemming rides ahead of the marching bowmen, straight toward the Seaxan *fyrdmen,* whilst we ride around them.

They do not see us, riding at them out of the sun, as the bowmen have made inroads on their numbers even before we close on them. Saeward catches a youth trying to crawl away into a ditch, calling him,

'Hey, *young warrior* - where do you think you are going?'

'*Spare me!*' the youth cowers, throwing away his sling.

'Only if you stand and fight like a man. Here, take this', Saeward tosses his sword down at the lad's feet. In his right hand is his long-handled axe, made for him by the weaponsmith Thor in Lunden *burh*.

'I do not know what to do with this, *I am a slinger!*' The youth whines, baring his teeth in fear.

'*Finish him off!*' Thored snaps at Saeward, whose iron-hard grip pins the youth to the road bank. 'Either that or send him off with a flea in his ear – *scum of the earth!*'

'Slinger, you should have run faster!' Saeward tells him, bending to pick up his sword. Fear has the lad in its grip and, although he must know nothing good comes of lying there, he is powerless to stir himself. The axe blade falls swiftly onto his skull. He jerks back, dead in the twinkling of an eye.

Thored grunts and nods, neither time nor word wasted in the arching of his right eyebrow. He waves the men on and climbs back into the saddle.

'If you must toy with those you mean to kill, do not do it again with me', Thored tells Saeward under his breath. He has seen Saeward throw axes, and knows what he can do. He does *not* believe in wasting time. I have come to overlook Saeward's more irksome ways.

Saeward, for his part, merely nods and swings himself into the saddle to follow me. No more words pass between us as we press on towards where Eadnoth makes for Ketilbeorn's men, thinking they are all he has to beat. Eadnoth would have counted on his scouts to give warning of anyone around his flank. I will grant that Eadnoth is a foxy old fellow. The drawback was in choosing men who were unskilled in the task they were given.

We come to a rise that overlooks the river, to see Eadnoth's shieldwall going headlong at Ketilbeorn. The fyrdmen with their *stallari* seem at least knowledgeable in the way they keep their line from the southern end of the wooden bridge. They have been allowed to push back those of the Danes given the task of seeming to give way, but will find they have more behind them.

'Gudbrand has covered the ground well', Thored points to the north where the men on foot trot along the riverbank towards the bridge.

As yet Eadnoth does not seem to have seen them – or us – and wades into the fight at the head of his shieldwall. Many of his thegns and household warriors will be there with him, the others with their own *fyrdmen* along the line.

Eadnoth and his men ought to know the land and yet they push on almost to the sticky mud of a bog before they see they must break up their number and go round. This is where Gudbrand's men prove useful. They bring up the rear of Eadnoth's shieldwall, with us on our horses, and crash through the West Seaxans. Eadnoth himself, at the fore of his men, is still unaware anything is amiss until he turns and sees us bearing down on him. He barks at his household men and thegns to form a ring around him, lashing out at those of Thored's Danes who come near his sword point.

The going looks good. We are winning and Eadnoth's massed ranks thinning out when we hear a hunting horn behind us. When I turn I see there are *more* West Seaxans at our backs. Where did *they* come from – how is it we failed to see them?

Thored growls,

'Tricky, these Seaxans, are they not?' He grunts and wheels his mount in time to be missed by an arrow aimed at his back. A number of the other Danes who came on horseback are now on foot, their mounts shying, trying to get away from clashing sword and spear points. Axes fall, both ways, shields used to fend off attacks by fyrdmen with long spears and slings.

Saeward, still mounted, uses the butt of his axe to stun one of Eadnoth's thegns who threatens Thored with a stabbing spear. The thegn drops to his knees, Saeward's axe scything into his chest and blood spurts everywhere.

Thored's chain mail is spattered, but he does not mind. He has been saved. Eadnoth's men are now to fore and behind us, with Ketilbeorn's men struggling to bypass the boggy ground to help us.

With a troop of his Danes, Thored makes for Eadnoth, to catch him alive and use him to assure our safety. Yet somehow the *stallari* has reached the thick of the fighting and flails like a water mill with sword and spear. Despite Thored shouting at his men to spare the Seaxans' leader, Eadnoth is cut down. Men trying to sidestep weapon thrusts strike back. Thus it is that Harold's one-time friend in the west falls to a Danish axe.

Godwin will be saddened, but he is safe on the seaward side of this bog. We, meanwhile, must drag ourselves away from this mess. Thored is beset by fyrdmen led by a thegn and I am too far away to help. The last I see of him before he vanishes behind the forest of bodies his head has been hacked off by blows from a scramaseaxe.

Saeward and Hemming thrash away at others who get in their way, Saeward still mounted and Hemming on foot. Someone tries to pull Saeward down and is brought low by a sideswipe from his axe. Blade cuts into flesh and, being pulled back rips away a spear-bearing arm. With men all around striving to cut me down, I must keep my wits about me.

Ketilbeorn must be closer, surely! When I look up there are only more Seaxans all around, and my sword arm is tiring. Suddenly the fyrdmen clamouring to catch me are panic-stricken, in full flight, under attack by Godwin, Ketilbeorn and a body of Danes. Some of Eadnoth's men still try to spear me, but pull back when Saeward bears down on them from behind me.

'Ivar, *with us* -' Godwin yells over the din of sword and scramaseaxe hammering down on shield. More Danes fall around me as we fall back towards the river and struggle across broken ground towards Barnestapla. Men behind me fall to spear and slingshot as we cross a narrow bank of sand on a bend in the river, to flee the West Seaxans in full cry. Another shieldwall here opens and lets us through – Saeward last, trying to rid himself of a young thegn set on earning an early death – coming back together behind us. The young thegn roars as he is hewn from life.

Magnus and Eadmund are with the ships when we pass through Barnestapla, Godwin having ruled that they should be kept safe.

'I hope you are fulfilled now you have shown yourself the hero!' Magnus snaps, sullen.

Godwin stills his younger brother's outcry.

'There will be time yet for you to show your mettle'.

'Come, Magnus', Eadmund pats his back, only to be shaken off.

'Do not 'come Magnus' me, you who wish to keep your hide safe!' Magnus hisses, pulling an arm away from Godwin.

'Young Magnus', Ketilbeorn spins him round to look him in the eye, 'I lost a kinsman today, fighting these damned Seaxans! Were you to call *me* a coward – not knowing your brother – I would throw you off this ship and leave you to them!'

The Dane shows him the jeering Seaxans on the shore and warns him,

'There is *still* time for me to think again, with our bowmen keeping them back, about taking you back with me to Dyflin', Ketilbeorn ends and Magnus stands, downcast, biding his time.

7

The ships drift into Dyflin's shallows, oars raised, until we run onto the sandy foreshore. Murchad is there to greet us.

'How went the hunt?' he asks drolly, falling silent when he sees Thored is no longer with us. The mast count of Ketilbeorn's fleet should have told him. As it is, Ketilbeorn's dark looks ram the meaning home. There *will* be drinking this evening, but only to forget. Murchad waits for Godwin to come through the mass of men, but knows on seeing him that there is no need to ask him, either. To look at him, my kinsman could bring on a storm.

Magnus seems ready to talk to Murchad, but Eadmund grips his arm to keep him from doing so.

'Ivar, it is good to see you', Murchad tries with me.

'It is good to see you, too, Murchad', I answer, holding up my hand to keep him from further angering Ketilbeorn or Godwin. I add, to let him know it is not him we are not angry with. 'We will talk later'.

The usual banter is missing when we sit to drink in the evening, the men being sullen at the loss of friends and the lack of any gain whatsoever. Others glare at Godwin as he passes. They blame him for their ills, and not without good grounds. I do not know Ketilbeorn's thoughts, but will learn of them very shortly.

Diarmuid is elsewhere in Leinster, not to be back again for another week. On trying to cheer the men, Murchad learns slowly what happened. We listened to Wulfberht and found his knowledge lacking; now the old man may be called on to give his answers on why he thought the men of the west would flock to Godwin's banner.

'Is Wulfberht anywhere in your father's kingdom?' Godwin asks Murchad, nursing a cup of ale.

'I can ask – you wish to see him soon?'

'If not sooner –'Godwin answers flatly. 'I have a reckoning for him, as has Ketilbeorn if he cannot answer to his liking'.

'That sounds threatening', Murchad cocks his head to one side. 'Might I ask why?'

'I sought counsel from him, and he failed me'.

'Surely he did not tell you that you should test his counsel?' Murchad likes Godwin, but he has known Wulfberht for longer. He cannot believe the old man would wilfully lead Godwin astray and wishes to help.

'He knew *why* I asked for counsel. I told him why', Godwin is steadfast in this at least. This will make things hard for Murchad or his father if it comes to a trial of will.

Wulfberht is likely to agree with Murchad, and will hope for the king's son to shelter him from Godwin's anger. Whether Murchad can shelter him from Ketilbeorn's wrath is another matter. It will take all Murchad's or Diarmuid's wits to soothe Ketilbeorn's anger if he thinks Wulfberht has something to answer for. Having lost none of his men, to wit *us*, Godwin might be easier to deal with. However he will be held to answer for misleading my young kinsman, so far as to risk men's lives!

Godwin risks Diarmuid turning down another attack by his Danes as they have forfeited enough men already on a fool's errand. Would Ketilbeorn be happy with a settling of scores? After all, Eadnoth was slain in the day-long fight and Thegn Aelfred only ousted the Danes from his own lands. No outstanding matters have arisen from either raid, but for the lack of gain to make up for the losses.

Can Godwin sell another attack in the west to Ketilbeorn and Diarmuid at further risk to them? After all he kept his brothers back from the fighting near Barnestapla, Ketilbeorn will say, when many of his own warriors were of the same age as them. Both Eadmund and Magnus were willing to enter the fighting, they will tell him, but he is afraid of what Eadgytha – his mother – will say to him if his brothers fall. She may even deny him a meeting, not speak to him again.

'I will have Wulfberht sent here when he comes next', Murchad seems to read Godwin's thoughts, 'and ask what counsel he gave you, whether he should be held answerable for this letdown. Both you and Ketilbeorn may speak to him *after* he has seen me'.

'You cannot say fairer than that', Ketilbeorn shakes hands with Murchad and they now await Godwin's say-so.

He knows they are only waiting for him, but as Ketilbeorn has proved already that he will wait only a short time, *ever*. Godwin stands, arms crossed over his mailed chest, thumb pulling at his upper middle teeth. He nods and reaches out his right hand to Murchad first, who takes it, and to Ketilbeorn. The Dane keeps *him* waiting now, but not for long – not for as long as Godwin kept the pair of *them* waiting. He smiles thinly and takes Godwin's hand.

Now we only have Wulfberht to wait for.

'What did Godwin ask of you, before you brought him here on your ship?' Murchad asks Wulfberht.

Wulfberht hedges,

'You mean would I bring him to see your father?'

'*Before that*, when he asked whether the men in the west would rally to his banner and you answered that they would', Murchad steers the old fellow to what we want to hear.

'Before that... ', Wulfberht looks blankly back at him.

Godwin is about to take him to task when Murchad stifles his outburst, browbeats him.

'Look, Wulfberht, *did* you tell Godwin the thegns in West Seaxe would help him fight the Northmen?' Murchad could be no blunter with him.

'I *did*, my Lord', Wulfberht answers at last. Godwin breathes out, and Ketilbeorn sets his teeth.

'*Which* thegns did you mean by that?' Murchad asks next, watching the old man closely, 'Where would they have been when Godwin landed?'

'Thegn Aelfred in the shire of Gleawanceaster would stand with Godwin, I told him so – did I not, Godwin?' Wulfberht looks to my kinsman to bear him out. Godwin nods without taking his eyes away from the man he now knows sold him short.

'Thegn Aelfred *fought* us, near Brycgstoth!' Ketilbeorn roars, 'As did Eadnoth the *Stallari* and *his* thegns in Sumorsaetan! My kinsman Thored fell near *your* home *burh*!'

'Eadnoth told me only months ago that he would *never* send his thegns and *fyrdmen* against fellow Aenglishmen!' Wulfberht blurts. 'I do not recall ever asking Thegn Aelfred, but I was led to believe that he was true to his oath!'

'Did *he* last give his oath to the new king?' Godwin asks, looking up into the darkness of the rafters, pressing his eyes shut, as if seeking counsel from the Almighty. I wonder that is where his answer lies – not in the rafters, but in asking whether the thegns had given their oath to Willelm.

'So what *now* – do we let them think they can give their oath to the Northman bastard, or do we kick them in their soft parts to show them they have sworn an oath to a fool?' Ketilbeorn asks.

'He is no *fool*, I will give him that', I give them my insight.

'Aye, they do not follow fools', Saeward says half aloud, but Ketilbeorn catches his aside.

Then why does he keep slipping away back to Rouen whenever he thinks the kingdom is on an even keel?' Godwin snaps.

'Too true -' Ketilbeorn agrees, 'but he leaves his kingdom in good hands, I understand'.

'His namesake the Earl of Hereford and his half-brothers do well by him, guarding the southern and midland shires', I put in.

Godwin spits his answer,

'We showed them how well they guarded the kingdom! How else would Eadric and his Wealsh friends have dealt the earl a bloody nose at Hereford? Willelm had to come to Exanceaster from Lunden to deal

103

with us himself, so good his earls were! Were it not for some thegns fearful of losing their lands, the Northmen would have still been there. I say they *can* be beaten!'

'Aye, they are no better than we are!' Ketilbeorn nods briskly, 'However –'.

'It was the West Seaxans outnumbering us at Barnestapla, coming at us from the south that beat us', Eadmund blurts, breaking into what Ketilbeorn wished to add.

'The Northmen were nowhere in sight', Magnus agrees.

'What do you wish to do now, should my father give his blessing to attacking again?' Murchad knows Ketilbeorn wants a settling of scores, to make up for the loss of Thored and to try for gain elsewhere in the west. Having raided there before in his youth, he knows the land is rich in abbeys, churches and stows or storehouses for the king's tithes.

'We will do better next time!' Ketilbeorn thumps the post he stands beside and brings down a shower of cobwebs and dust. 'Someone is not doing their best in your hall, Lord Murchad!'

'I will see it is done', Murchad laughs, shielding his eyes from more dust that falls on Ketilbeorn.

Ketilbeorn bursts into thunderous laughter and we all join him as one of Diarmuid's alewives brings cups and pours her sweet-tasting gold for us.

'Now that I *call* ale', Saeward smacks his lips, setting us off into laughter again. Even Wulfberht has forgotten his ordeal in the cupful he downs, in such a short time as Murchad has barely tasted his.

'Now *there* is praise for your ale, Asa!'

'Lord Murchad, he is not the *first* who knows how good my ale is!' the woman answers, winking at the Seaxan trader.

'Nor will he be the last', Murchad answers. On seeing my friend playing with his cup he asks, 'Saeward, I take it you wish your cup to be filled again?'

Asa passes in front of Saeward, as if she had not heard her lord and then steps back to pour, rasping,

'If you want more, you had best hold your cup level!'

Saeward comes back with,

'You are not so great to look at, Asa, but you know a thing or two about what a man likes!'

'You mean aside from a sharp axe?' Asa points at one of Murchad's tall, strapping Danish guards. Her meaning is taken, and Saeward cheers himself with emptying his cup.

The guard smiles at his woman's ready wit, saying nothing.

Ketilbeorn says something into Murchad's ear, raising a laugh, and then asks Saeward loudly,

'Murchad wonders, if you wish to play at throwing axes with friend Frodhi there?'

'The only woman I take a liking to here in Dyflin has to be spoken for!' Saeward grumbles, to gales of laughter. He holds out his cup for Asa to fill, but is told there will be drink enough in the evening.

'What about *Cormac's* woman?' I ask, raising more laughter.

'At least that only cost me a little effort', Saeward answers sorrowfully, 'he would run me into the ground!'

'We must look for a young wench for you who is free', Murchad soothes my East Seaxan friend's woes with an arm on his shoulder, to which we all raise our cups and drain them.

'You do not *wish* a match with Frodhi?' Godwin teases. Hemming laughs. It was he who drew Saeward into throwing axes against Cormac for a bet. Could it be he is thinking of making good his losses? After all, there were *three* bags of silver at stake. Missing out on them may have rankled.

Saeward leaves the hall and puts up one finger to Hemming.

Diarmuid is back in Dyflin earlier than Murchad thought he would, and calls us in for talks. Godwin, Ketilbeorn, Murchad, Eadmund and Magnus and I are the only ones he wishes to be there. Saeward and Hemming are given leave to seek out their own pastimes in the stews near the river, with Frodhi to show them around. Asa must be an understanding woman, to let her man loose amongst loose women! Murchad's father quickly raises the matter of how we will spend the coming months,

'How will you make ready for your next raids, and when will you sail?'

'We must show Godwin and his brothers how we stand in the shieldwall', Ketilbeorn puts forward. 'I saw how brave you were when attacking, but you must be strict with yourselves, unhurried in weighing up the strengths and weaknesses of the foe. I shall take you under my wing. Learn from your kinsman Ivar by all means, but he also needs to look at the way he behaves in the shieldwall. All men in the shieldwall must stand as one and I think he knows that, yet I would guess he has not been in one since being with his kinsman – your father – against this Willelm on the south coast. How many years ago is that, now?'

'You are right, friend', I allow. 'However, we need someone or something to keep us sharp'.

Murchad assures me with a firm grin,

'Fear not, Ivar. *We* will keep you sharp! Speaking of which, I hear you lost your war axe fighting in Defna'.

'I have indeed my Lord. I was sorriest at its loss'.

'It is unlikely you will ever find it again. I can have a good one made for you', Diarmuid tells me, to which offer I nod and smile in answer. He tells of the tasks ahead, 'In the neighbouring kingdoms I have *many* foes. I need to make them heedful of how sharp my claws can be! Meanwhile, Godwin, we will talk over what you aim to do to stake your claim on your kingdom across the sea'.

In the following months, when not wearing down Diarmuid's neighbours with raids on their kingdoms, we lay down our plans for taking Defna shire with Ketilbeorn and Murchad. I understand he means to come with us, to take on the Defna fyrd or Northmen – *or both.*

At quieter times my thoughts stray again to Braenda, my woman. I say *my* woman, as it seems to me she sees me as the only man in her life now – if I could only bring myself to *believe* that. She *says* I am, so who am I to mistrust her? I should like to see her, to bolster myself and to feel she longs for my manhood.

Meanwhile my days are filled with weapon drill.   Ketilbeorn sees us all as raw beginners, to 'hammer us into shape', as he puts it. He truly tries us, bawling at us. Daily my kinsmen, Saeward, Hemming and I fall into our beds after these drill bouts before carousing at night. We look more and more like the Danes around us by the week, dressing as they do – the years I spent amongst Aenglishmen, I had almost forgotten how Danes speak and spend their time, even these who pair off with Gaelic women and give their sons Gaelic names as they do on Man.

'Ivar, you almost look like a *Dane!*' Saeward jokes one Sunday during a walk along the riverfront.

Hemming shakes his head, cackling at our friend's wit, adding,

'Were it not for the chipped teeth and ruddy cheeks I would take *you* for a Dane, Saeward'.

'*Hemming*, do not mock! The Aenglishmen's chipped teeth and ruddy cheeks are what drew Aenglish women to the Danes when we came', I tease. 'Since the Danes came to your kingdom, your men have had to smarten themselves *greatly* to find a woman!'

'*My kingdom*, eh', Hemming huffs, 'I will have you know *my* forefathers came with Svein Tvaeskegg, he of the forked beard!'

'You cannot win them all', Saeward rubs his nose, laughing at Hemming.

'*Friends*, you have struck lucky!'

'*What?*' I start, turning to find a short, fat fellow beaming up at me.

'What did you say?'

'You and your friends are the *lucky* owners – should you wish to gain from this fateful meeting – of a *karve* fit for a king', the fellow beckons us to a vessel that bobs at the end of a cable on the rising afternoon tide.

'She looks a trim vessel', Hemming answers, tongue-in- cheek, taking in the loose decking and flaking paint.

'*Very* kingly', Saeward adds, trying not to laugh.

'Could we bring a friend to look her over?' I ask. 'We shall be here again shortly, if that is all right with you'.

'By all means', our new-found 'friend' smiles welcomingly.

,   'Who shall we say offers this karve?' I ask, stretching out a hand to him. I have to make it look as if we are truly thankful to him.

He takes my hand to seal our friendship and answers,

'I am Hereward, and you are -?'

'Call me Eadweard', I lie, and leave with the other two.

'The less we see of him the better', Saeward laughs.

'And he calls himself *Hereward!*' Hemming chuckles and, shakes his head in disbelief.

'Of *all* names, eh - that was why I called myself Eadweard'. I look forward to our next meeting, with Murchad.

'There was the likelihood his name is Hereward', Hemming scratches his beard.

'Just as the likelihood of me being an Eadweard. Come, we will learn soon if that *is* Hereward's *karve*', I answer, striding back for Diarmuid's garth with Hemming and Saeward trying to match my strides.

'...There is a fellow who calls himself Hereward at the riverside', I am the first to lay eyes on Murchad in the yard.

'Indeed – *is* there?' Murchad yawns.

I walk back beside him,

'He says he has a karve for sale, fit for a king'.

'Fit for a king?' Murchad echoes my words. He stops dead. 'You said his name is Hereward?'

'I did, my Lord'. I think he knows the man.

'Show me where you met this – Hereward?'

When we take Murchad back to the riverfront Hereward is nowhere to be seen. Saeward mutters something about 'fools errand', and we are about to leave when the fellow calls out after us.

'Eadweard, I see you have brought your friend'.

'We have, Hereward. This is our friend Ulf. He knows about boats and when we told him of yours, we could not hold him'.

'You will *not* be disappointed, Ulf!' Hereward takes Murchad's elbow and almost pushes him along the riverbank.

'She *is* yours, is she?' Murchad hunches to look along the deck, noting the state of the planks and peeling paint I told him of. There is also water, I see, sloshing around beneath the deck planking. The boat rocks with the rising water pushing her stern upriver, and I think I see something untoward under sailcloth by the steerboard.

'She *is*, Ulf', Hereward follows Murchad closely around the unlucky vessel.

'I recall seeing this karve before. It *is* Hereward?'

'You do? Dyflin is not so great a *burh* that a man could miss her', Hereward ducks answering about his name.

'She looks like a vessel my friend Thored sold off not long ago. Do you know Thored?' Murchad asks, towering over Hereward, making the fellow look small.

'I cannot say I do. I bought her a little while ago from someone. Thored might like to look her over again, to see if she *was* his?' Hereward seems deep in thought when Murchad takes him by the arm and points out the poor state of the vessel over all.

'I would say she is taking water. Would you not say so?' Murchad smiles craftily, as if he has something in store for Hereward.

'*Really* – do you think so? She was almost new when I bought her', Hereward is still deep in thought, perhaps trying to recall when – he says – he bought the vessel, or does he know Murchad for who he is?

'Would you like to show us how she fares on the open water?' Murchad asks. 'You know how to handle her?'

'I would be glad to show you, Lord Ulf', Hereward begins. 'But I have no-one else to help float her from the foreshore. If you give me some time, I will gather some of my men to show you how she handles.

'I think *you* should show us', Murchad holds onto Hereward's right shoulder. '*We* will help you aboard'.

Before he can flee, we draw on the cable, bringing the vessel to shore and bundle him over the deck wall onto the vessel. He thumps onto the deck and struggles to his feet, flapping his hands as if he were trying to take flight from his plight. He wails loudly,

'What do I *do?*'

'Take yourself off to the stern and turn the steering oar hard right whilst we push you back into the river', Murchad points to the stern.

'He has no inkling!' Hemming sniggers behind one hand.

'You can stop that, or else you can help him crew this wreck!' Murchad snaps, winking at me. I have to do my utmost to stop myself laughing.

Hemming takes heed of Murchad's warning and we heave Hereward on his stinking *karve* out into the flow, getting our breeks wet up to the knees into the bargain. Hereward runs to the stern, clattering along the uneven decking, tripping twice before he reaches the steering oar.

Saeward has said nothing all this time. He has not needed to - the grin he wears says everything for him. The four of us stand at the waterfront, clapping and cheering him on, wondering if he will see an oncoming warship before one of the crew leans overboard at the prow and bellows at him,

'*Hey you* – do you know how to use that thing you have your hands on?' The fellow looks along his ship at the oncoming warship's oars rising and falling. One drops onto the deck wall of Hereward's vessel closest to the ship, splintering it. Another falls hard after it, a little further forward and hits another part of the deck wall. The *karve* tilts toward the bigger longship, its mast tree next to suffer under the weight of a third oar.

Hereward stands and wails, watching helplessly as another oar dips and cuts into his deck wall,

'Oh no, *no, no – help me!* I cannot swim!'

'Nor can we swim, sorry!' I yell back through cupped hands over gales of laughter from the riverside and the warship, now having passed clear. The karve sits low in the water, bubbles bursting around her as she settles and Hereward runs up and down the deck, waving his arms about, sobbing for dear life. 'Help me – *help me!*'

'We might as well throw a rope and *tow* him in!' Saeward giggles fit to bring on hiccoughs.

'He will be fine!' Murchad waves back. 'He will soon learn to swim – even if he has to paddle, *like a hearth hound!*'

'*I* have seen him try to swim – he has done this sort of thing before', one bystander tells us, 'and he *never* learns!'

True enough, as the vessel founders Hereward takes to the water like an old woman I once saw swimming in a Northanhymbran river – the Swalge I think – whose skirts billowed on the water around her. Hereward's coat billows and he kicks like a child to push his fat body forward. When he can swim no longer he puts his feet down on the riverbed – to stand up to his chest in freezing river water.

'Give him a hand', Murchad tells Hemming and Saeward, who stride forward and haul him to the riverbank.

Hereward pulls off his coat and makes to drop his breeks, but Murchad strides past me and stops him,

'*Not here!*' Murchad jerks his chin and shakes his head.

Laughter follows. Gael and Dane alike stop to look on at the bedraggled Hereward standing, shaking like a pup after its first wash. Some make cat-calls at him, making sure Murchad does not see, although his bark is worse than his bite when in a good mood.

'Come Hereward, follow us and we will give you warm clothing', Murchad seems to show a new side of himself.

'What are we to do with him?' I ask, taking care Hereward comes no nearer to me than arm's length. I would not care to catch a chill with another raid on Defna shire in the offing.

'We give him an earful and send him on his way', Murchad answers, eyeing Hereward.

'I know where you can make a good landing in Defna shire – 'Hereward is stopped there by Murchad, who turns in mid-stride and looms over him with one hand on Hereward's wet collar. The fool is not cowed, however, and goes on, 'Talk is that you are going to settle a score with them for the thrashing the fyrd wreaked on Ketilbeorn'.

'You know more than is good for you', Murchad tells Hereward under his breath as he snatches at the folds of Hereward's chins, making him flinch with pain. 'What have you to tell me that will stop me throttling you?'

Hereward thrashes, trying to loosen Murchad's iron grip.

'I think he wants to tell you something', I tell Murchad, pushing down on his iron-strong sword hand.

Murchad smiles thin-lipped at Hereward, and eases his grip, but does not let go of his collar. Shaking his head like a hound, Hereward summons the strength to talk, and begins with what he thinks may profit the Erse *aetheling,*

'Go on', Murchad glowers.

'In the south there is a river, the Tath, with a broad strand on its eastern bank where a long time past a Danish army landed to raid. They wreaked havoc on many abbeys and noble houses that are there still, waiting to be hit – like apples on the tree waiting to be picked', Hereward gabbles.

'*Slower*, fool – none of this makes sense! *Why* should we want to raid in the south?' I stare into his eyes, trying to see for myself what he will gain. If I overawe him, he may tell us what he wants from telling us this.

'There is a new lord in the south', Hereward begins anew.

'What would that have to do with *us?*' Murchad lifts him off his feet, almost choking him. Hereward's hands flail again like watermill wheels in a flood tide.

Hereward croaks, still white from being half-strangled,

'His tithes are due'.

'What of it? That is *their* king's headache, surely?'

Murchad seems maddened at the way Hereward feeds him the knowledge, instead of telling him everything at once.

'He will not have them taken to Wintunceaster if there is a threat from the sea'.

'Do *you* know anything of this?' Murchad stares at me, dark eyes seeming to burn like coals. He pulls Hereward to him and snarls, 'Again, *why* should we attack this new lord?'

'He is a *Bretlander*, Lord'.

Murchad's eyes gleam as he looks at me over Hereward's balding, shiny skull. It is as if Hereward had waved a magic wand over the aetheling.

'He is a *Bretlander*, Lord', Murchad echoes Hereward's words at us.

Laughter breaks out again and Murchad hoists Hereward to his feet. He toys with the fellow,

'Why would *I* want to know that?'

'His father's lands were raided by Thored and Ketilbeorn not fourteen months past. He might be worth fighting if he learns that Ketilbeorn wishes to raid his lands in *Defna* shire'. These last few words are gurgled as Murchad grabs his collar.

'How does he know *that*, I wonder?' Murchad asks Ketilbeorn, drawn by tidings of Hereward's bad luck on the *karve*.

'We can have it from him soon enough', Ketilbeorn takes hold of Hereward's wet coat and lets go of it again to wipe the palm of his hand on Hereward's jaw. '*Eeugh* - what *was* that?'

'It must have been something floating in the river', Hereward runs his own hand over his jaw and flicks away onto the shore path something that looks like a sea snail. Ketilbeorn glares at him.

'Where did you hear about me wanting to raid in Defna?' Ketilbeorn snatches Hereward to him. '*Were you eavesdropping?*'

'*No*', Hereward wheezes when Ketilbeorn lets go of him again. He gives a start when Ketilbeorn snarls and almost squeaks in fear, 'No, *Lord!*'

'I think he *must* have been listening in – or paid someone else to listen in for him', I gaze into Hereward's wash-water eyes and he flinches. Shaking his head he looks alarmed up at Murchad and Ketilbeorn who still tower over him.

'You *paid* someone to listen!' Ketilbeorn hisses loudly enough for someone behind him to jerk his head up as he passes.

'He was talking to a weaselly-looking outlander down here yesterday', the newcomer points at Hereward.

'Is he here anywhere, this weaselly fellow you speak of?' Hemming

111

asks, blocking the way.

The newcomer screws up his nose, trying to think.

'I have not seen him, before *or* since', he answers, sneering at Hereward. 'You have to be careful what you say with some folk around'.

Hemming steps aside and lets him pass, and all eyes are back on Hereward. He is sweating now, despite having been dragged out of the river like a herring. He looks up from one of us to another. Our scowls frighten him and he clutches his hands together, begging.

'*What?*' Murchad eyes him the way a hunter eyes a boar.

'I do not know what *he* was talking about', Hereward whines wretchedly, pulling back. 'That man is lying!'

'*Why* would he lie to me? He must know he would be found out and punished if he stayed here! Stand up *and speak to me like a man!*' Murchad towers over Hereward, now on his knees.

'He was talking to *me* yesterday!' Hereward almost sobs as Murchad lifts him bodily.

Hemming takes off after the bypasser who told us about the 'weaselly' fellow he said he saw Hereward talking to. When he looks back on hearing Hemming's footfalls he drops what he was carrying and hares off into the thronging folk in the market nearby.

'What is his name?' Ketilbeorn asks, looking from Hemming – now walking back to us - to Hereward.

'Where does he hail from?' I ask.

He did not sound the way Dyflin folk talk, Danes *or* Erse, nor did he sound like anyone I have heard from Defna shire.

'*I* do not know', Hereward whines. 'I have never set eyes on him before!'

'You know nothing of him, what his name is or where he stems from?' Hemming is back and stands beside me again, breathing hard from running.

'*Do* you know where he comes from?' Ketilbeorn asks Hereward again.

'*No*, I have said so, Lord', Hereward groans. He is told how close he is to learning the names of the fish in the river when Ketilbeorn shakes him by his arms.

'For someone in such a dire mess, your manners are sadly lacking, Hereward', I tell him, trying to think of where the outlander may stem from. 'You are not from Defna shire yourself?'

'My Lord, I have sailed around the shire on two coasts', he begins. 'I have been into the Tath rivermouth but no further. I am from East Aengla, but the Northmen made me homeless when they pulled down my home to build one of their strongholds in Grantaceaster'.

He shakes himself like a hound when Ketilbeorn lets go of him, and tells Murchad,

'I learned of Lord Ketilbeorn and his kinsman Thored –'

'*Where* did you learn about us?' Ketilbeorn asks Hereward under his breath, threatening.

'As I was about to tell you, Lord, over years of trading around the shores of Frankia and Aengla Land I have heard many things. I have learned of your raids in Bretland, such is your renown, and I have listened closely to what the Defna shire men say about their new masters. Word flies faster than birds, Lord. Some of those words are of the new lord in Defna known as Earl Breon. There is another lord there, known to them as Willelm *Gualdi*, of whom it is said that he relishes deflowering maidens in the south. He also relishes taking the Defna men's silver for his master the king'.

'It is true', Murchad nods. 'I too have heard'.

'What should we do, sail for Defna soon and take their tithes before they are passed along to their greed-ridden king, or do we wait until we are ready?' Ketilbeorn asks Murchad.

Murchad smiles and takes Ketilbeorn aside,

'We say we will go in the summer and then send him', he turns a thumb toward Hereward, 'off on his way to wherever he was going. We sail in the late fore-year'.

'Good thinking, my Lord', Ketilbeorn mumbles and turns back to Hereward.

Murchad beckons Hereward to him, smiles to show he means him no harm, and tells him,

'We shall need time to make ready. Therefore it will be unlikely we sail before the height of summer, as much as needs to be done. We will take your word about the fellow who fled to the market, that you do not know him', Murchad lets Hereward leave. He has had one soaking today. If we find him where we are going we shall know his game, and you can do with him what you will'.

'If I see him again, Lord, do I send word to you?' Hereward seems happier now. He looks back at Murchad as he leaves.

'Do that', Murchad answers, and turns with us to leave. The *karve* wallows in the river, more underwater than can be seen on it. Someone will have to tow it out of the channel before traders come to grief, either out to sea where it will sink, or out of the water altogether, to rot on the foreshore or to be taken for firewood.

'Are we to keep an eye on him, lest he meets the other fellow somewhere in the burh?' Hemming asks.

'His work will be done soon. Give him a few days – there is no way anyone could miss him – and then find somewhere dark. You understand?'

Hemming touches his forelock and we set off back for Diarmuid's garth. Murchad will urge his father to bring forward our sailing, and he seems to want to sail with us. How many men and ships will we have this time?

There will be long evenings before the sailing season is upon us again. Hereward will tell his 'friend', and the Northmen in Defna shire will learn of our coming.

Godwin is happy with sailing in the fore year. He will think he has waited far too long already, but must look back and see what little has been achieved with haste. Come Eastertide we will all be raring to go but the tides will even then not be right for us. These things cannot be rushed!

Hereward *was* seen not long after he was pulled from the river. Sure enough, it was with his 'friend' he was seen, the one who told us of the 'weaselly' fellow he saw Hereward talking to. The 'friend' was later seen aboard ship sailing east before we ourselves left, and Hereward was dealt with, found floating on his belly near the mouth of the river, and when asked we said we knew nothing of his whereabouts. No-one was going to ask any more about him. As Hemming said,

'He will not be missed - *anywhere*'.

Great things are afoot, ships readied with stores for the crossing stowed aboard. Dyflin is in a fever and no trader has lost out in our long-foreseen undertaking. They will speak to no-one about what is happening here, their oaths given to Diarmuid, and broken on pain of death.

We are in Diarmuid's hall again, drinking at the feast before we sail, when Wulfberht brings tidings of the *fyrd* in Defna shire being warned by their outlander lords against siding with outsiders, the wit not lost on Diarmuid. Fighting laughter he asks the old man,

'Who passed on this ruling to the *fyrdmen*? Could an Aenglishman ask this of his fellows without bursting into laughter?'

Ketilbeorn, cup of ale in hand, forgets the loss of his kinsman for long enough to relish the wit and almost throws his ale into Murchad's lap next to him. Fuming, Murchad stands and tries to wipe his breeks, only to upset his father's cup before Diarmuid can raise it to his lips.

The laughter echoes long and loud around us, those near enough to have seen the foolery laughing longest. Saeward almost chokes on the ale he slurped. Reddening, Murchad leans on the long table and asks his father's leave to go and find something else to wear.

In the din of laughter Diarmuid hears wrongly and tells Murchad,

'Aye, son, the ale reeks. You had best ask one of the maids to bring more rushes for the floor!'

Murchad clenches his teeth and clambers over the bench, only to miss his footing and land on soiled rushes behind him,

'In God's name pick me up!' he yells above the din. Diarmuid, having already emptied several cups of ale, looks over one shoulder and bursts out laughing again. A very much more reddened Murchad flaps about on the floor until helped to his feet by Hemming and me. Hemming holds his nose and looks away and Murchad roars loudly, 'Where are the damned hounds that did *this?*'

More laughter follows, and, failing to see the funny side Murchad storms out of the hall. Diarmuid's eyebrows dance on seeing his son leaving the table under a dark cloud, but he says nothing. No doubt he too will look to one of the maids to follow him to his bed – if he still has it in him after all this drinking before falling asleep.

Thinking about fulfilment strikes a chord. I sorely miss Braenda, not having seen her of late. Nightly I have seen my friends – all but Saeward, who has yet to understand their needs – leave the hall with maids or other womenfolk. True, *I* have taken one or other of these wenches, but I can hardly think any more which ones they were.

For a man soon to test his skill and strength in fighting, I seem to have spent too much time drinking these days.

During the daylight hours we have all been hard-wrought putting our skills to the test against one another. Men have been wounded - some badly with blood shed or sprains. Some have proved useless, and been sent away, unable or unwilling to knuckle under and take heed of their betters. There have been times when fight masters have lost their temper and beaten tried and tested warriors.

So hard has the burden been on them to give Ketilbeorn, Murchad and Godwin enough sturdy warriors who can take on many more than their own number if needed.

All a man can do after all that is drink and forget his day and his aches. No doubt he will sleep off the ale after bedding a woman and gone back, rested and ready, to be bullied and barked at much the same as the day before.

For the time being I have to put Braenda to the back of my thoughts if I am to see her again after fighting in southern Defna, and look forward to having her with me again one day. I would be no use to her if I were I lamed, would I?

On looking about me in this smoke-filled hall I think I see a flame-haired young woman busy gathering cups and beakers for washing. When she goes back to the kitchen I follow her, through moonlit darkness from the hall. In the kitchen she sets down the cups by a sink and looks for a cloth to wipe them with. As she begins I come up behind her and stroke her breasts.

She stands, stiffened, aroused. Hands seek my manhood and we begin to moan. When she turns her mouth opens and she begins to scream. When my hand goes up to her mouth and she bites me, my gut feeling is to quieten her but my fist hits her too hard and she falls to the floor, stunned. Hearing someone near I leave by the door out to the hall and go back to where I was seated. She was not Braenda; that much is plain.

No-one seems to know I have been away, and one of the alewives fills my cup, giving me the eye. I may have drunkenly bedded her, not that I know, but she plainly recalls and lingers.

'Asa, come fill my cup!' Ketilbeorn calls out. Asa – I am glad I let her go. I would not want to fall foul of her troll of a man!

I am a coward, I tell myself, knocking a poor maid off her feet. Looking about and seeing no-one will miss me, I leave the hall for the kitchen again and listen out for any maids that might be within. On hearing none I enter, but there is nothing where the flame-haired young woman lay.

Another of the maids enters and asks, grinning mischievously, what I am doing,

'You wish to help with the washing?' She giggles and tosses me a cloth, asking, 'You know how to use one of them?'

'I was looking for a young maid, a flame-haired –'   I am not allowed to finish,

'*Oh*, she left with a headache. She said she had *fallen*, tired out from the long day's work, having hit her head on the floor. Shall I tell her you came?'

'No, I shall find her again when she is well', I lie and make to leave.

'She lives near the river, if you want to know...' the maid tells me hopefully, 'in the same street as me, *if you want to know*'.

There is something in the way she tells me, hinting at offering herself to me, but I shall be rising early in the morning and shake my head, smiling.

The maid calls after me, laughing as I leave for the hall,

'*You know where I am, then*'.

Halfway there I think better on it, drink having already got the better of me, and make for my quarters to get as much sleep as I can. The hour is late and Saeward's snores guide me through the dark to my own door.

8

At long last we have the sea spray on our cheeks, the wind driving from the south-west as we are steered past the small islands to the west of West Wealas. To make the best of the wind, our steersman has called for the beitass to be added to the steerboard side of the sail. When we come about near the mouth of the Tath the beitass will be drawn in, he tells us. Ketilbeorn nods, his eyes on the sea to the north. The last thing he wants is for the Northmen to learn of our path through the western seas.

In anyone's eyes we could be heading for the Centish or Suth Seaxan shores, although our most likely landing would be in the south-west. Fighting *every* Northman, Fleming or Bretlander this side of Wintunceaster, as well as the West Seaxan *fyrd* would be taxing!

In true Viking manner we will steer well clear of the coast, so that we can veer in toward our landing shore under cover of mist or poor weather. There is an eyot a little north of the rivermouth, as I think back on it, where our ships can put in and anchor in the sound to the south of this eyot. Ketilbeorn knows this coast well, having passed it often on the way to raid around the Seine or Loire.

Saeward's is not the only nose to run during our crossing. Both Godwin and Magnus seem to suffer, and Magnus balks when Ketilbeorn offers Eadmund some fatty hogs-flesh and ale. A little teasing banter and light-hearted laughter follows on the lines of,

'Fear not, the flesh is well-salted, Magnus. Only the fat takes some chewing' and, 'The fat will sit well on the stomach, Eadmund – take care not to drink the ale too soon after eating or you will look as green as the sea out there!'

Ketilbeorn slaps Godwin's back before making his way forward between the rowing benches to the prow, the ship bucking and yawing with the waves crossing under us. Watching the Dane stride down the deck, Magnus looks fit to throw up – which he does soon after, much to Eadmund's and Hemming's glee. Godwin scowls at his brother who looks down at the deck, making out to be ashamed at tormenting his little brother. He looks sidelong at Hemming, who has to bite his lower lip to keep himself from laughing again.

Coughing from Ketilbeorn takes Godwin's thoughts off his sea sickness and he looks up.

'Godwin, you and your young brother will be happy to hear that your ills will soon be at an end! We should make landfall early this evening'. Ketilbeorn rests a hand on Godwin's back and tells him that for someone who has spent so much of his life on land, he has not done so badly. My kinsman smiles weakly at that, nods and leans overboard with one hand on the sheets, the other on the ship's deck wall.

A grinning Ketilbeorn winks back at me and walks back to the prow. Were I Godwin, I should take cheer in the Dane's words. I would say he keeps much to himself - what he does *not* say may be more telling.

Within the hour the Defna shire coast comes into sight in the north-east, West Wealas to the west of that. The sail is hauled in and the oars run out, to dip silently and bring us into the mist-enshrouded rivermouth overlooked by the hills of West Wealas. With a blood-red sky to the west that casts its red glow on our prow, two score and ten ships creep stealthily upriver to the tree-lined eyot near the mouth of the Tath upriver.

Glistening oars skim the dark waters, making a wide wake. Backward and forward, the oars rise and drop, kissing wavelets, sending me into a waking dream. As many longships again lie bobbing in the offshore swell. When their masters see a signal from Ketilbeorn's shipmaster they will follow between the points either side of the Tathemutha.

'What – or who are you thinking of?'

Saeward has come forward to stand beside me, with Eadmund leaning, looking over the side into the seemingly bottomless river. Has *he* begun to feel green about the gills and will not own up to it?

'I was being sent to sleep by the shift of the oars in the water', I answer lazily, still spellbound.

'I found that, by watching the oars being pushed and pulled, I got over my own sea-sickness', Saeward lets me know.

'It can do that to a man. How is Magnus now we are upriver?' I ask in turn, looking over one shoulder to see he is eating. 'Well done, that man!'

He grins sheepishly back at me and, still chewing hard, holds up the meat for me to see. In his other hand he holds a wooden cup. Whatever is in his cup agrees with him, from what I can see.   Godwin, on the other hand, still looks green at the gills.

'*Soon be ashore!*' Ketilbeorn pats him lightly on one shoulder before passing on to the steersman behind us. Murchad strides back along the deck, ducking under the mast-trees and bypassing the mast-partner toward us to ask of our wellbeing. He has been standing in the bow since leaving Leinster's shore, and seems to have been hiding his own ills. Godwin and Magnus need feel no shame. He greets Godwin for the first time since we rounded the islands,

'*You are well, I hope, Godwin!*

'To the best of my knowledge I am, aye', Godwin lies. If Murchad can hide *his* unease, so can my kinsman.

Magnus grins and finishes the last mouthful of his meat.

Behind him Saeward screws up his mouth and hastens to the deck wall to heave the last of his morning meal into the swirling river water. When Hemming chuckles Saeward throws out an arm at his head, and misses when Hemming ducks out of reach.

'*Children*, there will be enough time for sport when we meet the Seaxans – *if* we meet them!' Ketilbeorn chides, scowling.

Being called a child does not endear him to Saeward. Having slain many Northmen since first riding to the south coast with me, Saeward may think he is a match for *any* man here. Nevertheless he says nothing, over-awed as he is by a man at least two heads taller than he is, and a wrestler of high standing.

Our ship grounds on the gravel strand of the eyot and the men leap overboard into the shallows to heave her higher, away from the high tide that will surely follow us up to the banks of the Tath before evening.

Stores are taken off the ship and camp is set up when Ketilbeorn is happy that we have not been seen, still out of sight of anyone. Meanwhile the mist has cleared, driven further upriver by the wind channelled between the heights on either side of the river. We can now be seen and the other half of the fleet has yet to be anchored out of sight near the rivermouth.

'*Damn* this stupid mist!' Ketilbeorn curses. We are open to attack if anyone is watching. Although darkness is almost upon us, we can still be seen from the land.

Murchad orders men to stand guard with bows, to keep careful watch. Now we are here, we do not want to be taken off-guard. There are cattle drinking from an outward-flowing beck above the river north of us, no doubt anyone tending them may yet warn his thegn of incoming ships.

'*Watch that shore!*' Ketilbeorn tells some of his men to wade across shallows from the eyot to the mainland.

Darkness soon draws its long fingers over our fleet. Fires are made on the western side of the thickly wooded eyot, out of sight of any Defna scouts, the men told to keep the smoke thin and low. On the ships anchored mid-river in the Tameth lights are lit, swung out on hinged iron stays over the water. If a morning sea mist does not hide us from prying eyes, we shall need to be on our guard.

Morning comes, bright, warm and laden with threat. There are riders on the eastern riverbank of the Tameth, upriver of the Tath. Ketilbeorn has called in our guards from across the narrows, to watch from the eyot, and there are bowmen at the prows of the ships. Whilst Murchad, Ketilbeorn and Godwin talk earnestly in the camp, Eadmund and Magnus watch and listen.

'What gives?' I ask Eadmund, who puts a finger to his mouth and nods toward our leaders. With them, Saeward and Hemming behind me, I watch and listen. Stirrings from the eastern bank of the Tameth take my eye and I leave the talks to see what is amiss there.

'They have been coming and going all morning, Lord Ivar', one of the Danes tells me, pointing at more riders passing close by and halting to take in our ships.

'None has dared come within arrowshot', another of the Danes adds to what his comrade told me. 'They are wily, these Seaxans, I would give them that!'

'Being raided by Danes must have taught them something', I answer, tongue-in-cheek.

'You lived amongst them, Lord?' the first Dane asks, having possibly been told by those who have heard of me. I have become something of a shadowy noteworthy, a 'Lord' without land either in the homeland or on Aenglish soil.

I doubt any of these Danes has ever seen the homeland. Yet nor do they see themselves as Erse. They are not Gaels, but 'the black outlanders' as the Gaels call them, something to do with their black leather jerkins. They are *Ostmen* by their own lore, although some have Gaelic mothers and speak a sort of Gaelic tongue understood only by other *Ostmen*.

As to being called 'lord', that may help rather than hinder me should we have high losses amongst the leadership. These Dyflin Danes would not follow anyone they saw as unworthy.

Armed *fyrdmen* foregather on the riverbank. This is no welcome. Some of the riders are sent away by thegns, who then set about posting their men to guard the Tath on both banks whilst they await more men to strengthen their hand.

'So, tell me what is happening, Ivar?' I hear Ketilbeorn ask. When I turn to him I see Murchad is with him, Godwin behind with Eadmund and Magnus standing to the rear of them watching the riverbank.

'It seems to me the Defna *fyrd* has come to greet us'.

'This is a welcome I had not hoped to see', Godwin smiles ruefully at Ketilbeorn and comes forward around Murchad to stand by me.

'*Are* we welcome?' Murchad points at the armed men massing now on both banks of the Tath.

'I could not say, until I have spoken with whoever leads them', Godwin answers.

'Would you *need* to speak to him to weigh his answer?' Ketilbeorn looks askance at Godwin. 'From looking at these men, I would not say he will be willing to let us land'.

'There may be a Northman earl here since we left', I offer, 'and the thegn here may hope to strike him with his skill at leading his men'.

'We shall soon know', Ketilbeorn notes drily. He has been watching what is happening further back on land, and nudges Godwin to show him that there are Northmen amongst the *fyrdmen* now. They are on horseback, with long lances. Ketilbeorn and Murchad have seen them too, their dark looks tell me they do not wish to tangle with these Northmen if they have to leave their ships too far behind. Thwarted by the Danes' sudden lack of zeal to fight, Godwin swears and thumps his left palm. He lacks understanding of the way the Danes see Frankish horsemen, never having had to meet them on foot.

'The horses are afraid of fire', I tell Ketilbeorn. 'If our bowmen loose off fire arrows at them they will be affrighted'.

Ketilbeorn looks oddly at me, as does Murchad.

'It would not be long before we ran out of pitch to dip the arrowheads into', Murchad scornfully tells me.

'We carry the pitch with us, and burning torches to light the pitch from. The riders would not dare come too close, surely you must see that', I try to talk sense into him. Ketilbeorn should know better, but walks up and down on the strand before turning back to Godwin.

'We leave now, no-one loses', he thumps the ship wall.

'You have had second thoughts, I can see', Godwin tries to stir Ketilbeorn. 'You do not wish to go back to Diarmuid empty-handed, do you?'

'I would find it hard', Ketilbeorn agrees, looking sidelong at me, nodding slowly.

'They cannot stay there, can they?' Magnus asks me.

'The *fyrdmen* could, for as long as their food lasts. I do not know about the Northmen', I have to allow.

'They would have to ride back to where they are quartered, to an abbey, or to a nobleman's hall', Godwin knows the Northmen have the same rules to live by as our huscarls had. Each lord, earl or bishop, had so many each, although less than the king. A lord or the Church had to have land to let to the huscarls so they could pay for all their needs, whereas a Northman lord does not.

These Northman lords are greedy – or *greedier* than ours. They do not want to share out the land that the king grudgingly gives them. I say grudgingly because without *their* horses and sword-hands he would never have become king.

Without *him* they could not ride roughshod over the Aenglish. They must lean on one another to keep their kingdom safe. Take away the king's men and the *fyrdmen* would need to far outnumber the Danes to beat them.

'So – we turn away the horsemen with their long spears and we only have the fyrdmen to deal with', Murchad looks from Godwin to me and at Ketilbeorn. 'How *far* are these abbeys and halls from here, that we can strip them of their silver and gold?'

'Overland, *that* way', Godwin shows them, pointing northward to Tathestoche and then eastward, 'and not far, east of the river is the hall of one Anshelm, tithe gatherer for the church'.

'We only have to get past *them* if we rid ourselves of the Northmen?' Ketilbeorn points at the *fyrdmen*.

'That is all'. Godwin nods, adding, 'They will have no stomach for fighting if they lose their Northman friends'.

'You are sure of that?' Murchad asks.

'I *am* sure', Godwin nods again.

Murchad and Ketilbeorn fleetingly trade meaningful looks, then Ketilbeorn calls to the men on his ship,

'Make pitch – we need enough to fill a leather pail!'

Whilst some of his men are busy cutting wood, others make fires and set up spits to hang iron pots for stirring.

Meanwhile we follow the shore of the eyot to find slender, straight willow wands for arrows.

'The Wealsh had longer bows for warfare', Eadmund thinks back on our time with Bleddyn and Rhiwallon, when their bowmen fired burning arrows onto Willelm fitzOsbern's stronghold at Hereford. 'Their arrows flew further'.

There are ash trees on the eyot, and thickets grow on the side toward the mainland, but not so that the fyrdmen on watch could see what is happening when the Danes' bowmen cut it down for their use. We are pressing on, slowly but surely.

The oncoming dark masks our bustling, even if the sound of chopping echoes across the narrows between the woodlands. What they do not know is that we are taking steps to send their horsemen fleeing, and when the Seaxans are shorn of their better-armed friends, they will back way and give us room to land men who will truly teach them the skills of war-making!

Others build a high wall on the side of the eyot towards the mainland. By dawn there will be many fewer trees behind us.

Godwin and his brothers catch well-earned sleep within Ketilbeorn's stronghold, much in the same way as many Seaxans elsewhere found high-walled strongholds sprouting up around them in the days of King Aelfred. A double gate now guards the strand where the ships are drawn up, the only gap in the wall being on our western shore.

Should the Seaxans make headway against us, we can put up a fight before withdrawing to the ships and rowing to the far river bank. The West Wealsh will not help them against the Danes – they may even help *us* if needed. Indeed, there is a gathering of them on their side of the Tameth, watching closely.

'A wall has sprung up around us', Magnus wonders aloud to Eadmund as Godwin strides toward Ketilbeorn to hear about the outlook for the day ahead.

'The pitch is ready, Arnbeorn tells me, 'as much as we shall need'.

Ketil outlines what is ahead for us,

'The ships across the rivermouth will draw in to allow their men onto the land. My bowmen will begin loosing off their arrows soon. Have something to eat first, Godwin. Take what you wish of the salted fish, bran and ale. Apples there are, but not sweet ones'.

We seat ourselves around one of the fires and take from the pile of fish on a smoking grate. Warmed, the salted fish taste better after a bowl of bran and goat's milk.

'Where does the milk come from?' Godwin asks, chewing bran, awed by the plentiful supply of food and ale.

Ketilbeorn points downriver and grins.

'Some of these Defna women are not as fired-up about keeping out us Danes from their land. Ulf has his winning ways, after all. Their men seem to keep their women short when it comes to some things, if not for silver, then, well you know...' Ketilbeorn laughs heartily. His friend Ulf, nearby, wears the same smug look, like the cat that lapped the cream.

Ulf, in early middle age, is not tall like Ketilbeorn. He is well-made, however. What women like, I daresay. A friendly look from him would melt any woman's heart. Whatever the Seaxans think of Danes, as I have said before, their womenfolk are not nearly as steadfast.

Godwin looks across at Ulf, nods and goes back to his morning meal. Whether he agrees with Ketilbeorn about Ulf's looks I would not begin to second-guess him. He must have seen something in Ulf, however, because he beckons him over.

'I hear you have a way with women?' he asks Ulf. Is he looking to be counselled? His own looks turn heads, I have seen in Dyflin, so what does he need to know?

'If you say so, Lord', Ulf grins knowingly, 'I will take your word for that'.

'Here is silver for your task', Godwin adds.

Ulf turns my kinsman's silver away, telling him,

'My Lord, I have been paid well for my task already, as you put it. Both Ketilbeorn and Wulfrida paid me, one in silver and one in kind'.

'The woman, Wulfrida, paid you for taking her goats-milk?' Eadmund laughs as he spoons bran carelessly into an already full mouth, almost choking.

'No, Lord. I *offered* to pay her for the milk - she paid me *with* the milk for giving her something her husband had not, being away watching that we do not land on his riverbank. I told her we would soon make landfall. She said she hoped I would look in on her after we won'.

Laughter breaks out all around the fire, and cheering begins. One fellow calls out to Ulf,

'I hope she has a sister!'

'I took her *as well*, Ingiulf!'

More cheering follows, and Ulf's laughter is catching. Even Magnus laughs out aloud. Godwin has at last grasped the funny side of Ulf's tale, but he is more taken with something else. He beckons Ketilbeorn to him and asks,

'Has any thought been put to a *ruse?* Suppose we make it look as if we are attacking further downriver?'

'A ruse, you say?'

Ketilbeorn beckons Murchad and lively talking begins between them.

Ketilbeorn is keen on such an attack. We have enough men and ships after all. If it looked as if we were to make a landing near the mouth of the Tameth, the fyrd might follow. Murchad asks what we would do with the other ships,

'We cannot, after all, make the other ships vanish'. Murchad's reasoning is well-founded.

The Seaxans and their Northman masters would not fall for such a ruse if half the ships stayed put upriver. There needs to be more thought given to Godwin's ruse. He plainly did not think enough over it, and Ketilbeorn's eagerness marks him out a fool in Murchad's eyes, until Ketilbeorn raises another thought,

'A mist might hide them'.

'Are we to sit here until another mist comes in off the sea?' Murchad groans and makes to stand.

'We *make* one', Ketilbeorn proudly announces.

'How do we do *that?*' Murchad barks with laughter, shaking his head in disbelief at Ketilbeorn's muddle-headedness, as he must see it.

'The wind is from the south-west. Fires can be lit on the western shore of the Tameth –'Ketilbeorn begins.

'I can see these folk in the west allowing us to set fire to their land!' Murchad despairs of Ketilbeorn's seemingly woolly-headedness. The Dane seems to be grasping at straws. 'Let me know your thoughts when I am back from my walk'.

Murchad takes two of his men and sets off around the eyot. Ketilbeorn mulls over setting fire to the land here.

'Well?' Murchad demands when he strides back toward the campfire.

'We ask them', Ketilbeorn tells him, happy at finding the answer so soon.

'*We ask them*', Murchad echoes mockingly, I might add smugly.

'You are a king's son', Ketilbeorn tells him, not that he is likely to forget, 'Speak to them, Lord. They will think more of you than they would of me'.

'*I* should ask', Godwin stands, still fishing bones from his teeth. 'My father was, after all, the Earl of West Seaxe'.

'Will that weigh with *them?*' Murchad has been offered a way out of having to ask the West Wealsh, but disbelief creases his brow. 'Your father lost to the Northmen, after all'.

'As I said, he *was* Earl of West Seaxe. As earl he was looked up to by our neighbours in the west –'Godwin is halted by Murchad again.

'All but Gruffyd, I hear'.

Looking up from where I sit by the fire, I put in,

'All but Gruffyd, aye, and Aelfgar, but Gruffyd's followers slew him and handed his head to Earl Harold after we cornered him and his followers in the hills of Gwynedd'.

Murchad looks open-mouthed at me, not having been told the whole story through no fault of Diarmuid. He may even have been told another rendering by a Wealshman. Saeward nods beside me. He has been munching quietly on salt fish, thinking. Now he puts his thoughts across,

'If the grass on the headland we set fire to is damp, there should be enough smoke to hide half the ships. There would be no loss where a marsh west of the headland should stop fire spreading to their crops'.

Ketilbeorn sits, mulling over Saeward's words. Murchad leans over to ask something, but thinks better of it and Ketilbeorn asks instead, scratching his thick greying beard,

'Who would we ask?'

'There are men standing on the riverbank'.

Having told us of these fellows, Saeward waves toward them adding,

'They must know who or where their lord is'.

'We could send a boat across', I add, nodding. I pat Saeward's shoulder to show him I think he is right. Murchad seems to think the same, arching his brows at the still distrustful Ketilbeorn.

'What if they are friendly toward their Seaxan neighbours?' Ketilbeorn sniffs and wipes his nose on one finger, flicking the droplet to the earth by Murchad's foot. As it is, the *aetheling* has not seen and so all is well. He might easily have taken it as a slight and all would not have been well between our leaders.

'I will row across to them, if you are unsure whether to send one of your men', I tell him.

'*No*... No, I will send a few men with you. A man alone might not be safe there', Ketilbeorn looks down at the earth, up at me and shakes his head. 'I am sorry, Ivar. I am not shaking my head at you. Thoughts are gathering in my head that are not linked with the matter in hand. Take Ulf's ship and see what they say over there. Ask them if they will allow us to set the riverside weeds alight'.

Ulf salutes Ketilbeorn and we stride to his ship across the shingle, Saeward in tow behind me.

'Does he go *everywhere* with you?' Ulf asks, grinning.

'No, *not* everywhere – mostly he goes where he thinks he is needed', I answer, knowing full well where Ulf's thoughts were leading.

Ulf grins lopsidedly under Saeward's cold stare.

His best way out is in keeping any further thoughts to himself, and he takes it. We board his ship behind him and several of his men push us out before leaping back aboard to take the oars with their shipmates. The ship slides quietly across the river to its western bank and men ashore come down to meet us as we near them.

Ulf calls out in their own tongue, I would say, to ask for anyone who can speak for them all. This is handy, having a man who can speak to the West Wealsh without having to ask for another to speak for him.

'That one says their lord is close by, atop the hill', Ulf tells me, pointing at a spry fellow who hares off uphill to fetch him.

We wait on the riverbank for the lord, looking about us. Ulf's thoughts wander as a stout old fellow comes slowly down to speak to him. After some hand-shaking and nodding we await the outcome of the lord's pondering our wish. He speaks with his underlings and answers.

'He says he has to ask someone else, who lives near the ness we would set fire to', Ulf lets me know what is going on.

'Tell him we need not burn all the weed cover if we can make enough smoke. Damp weeds or grass should make for thicker smoke', I tell Ulf. He nods and tells me I still have to wait. *No* weeds will be burnt until the fellow comes, whatever the lord says.

A tall, handsome looking fellow rides downhill and along the riverbank toward us. He turns to Ulf, smiles brightly and alights from his horse to come to us. Talking begins again. Ulf asks the lord to allow us to set light to the riverside, but he does not seem keen. The talking sounds more pressing, Ulf waving his hands about.

The fellow asks me, using the Aenglish tongue,

'*Why* is it you wish to burn the headland?' He does not look straight at me, which I think is odd for a nobleman.

'We need to make a smoke screen so we can attack the Northmen up the Tath towards Tathestoche', I answer. His brow folds low over his eyes and he turns away from us to think, arms folded across his broad chest. He broods darkly for a while, and then turns back to Ulf.

'The wind will come around from the south-west in the morning', the fellow tells us without turning to look at us. 'Then it will be right for making smoke to your ends. If you do it today your smoke will be wasted'.

Why is he shy of showing himself to me?

'Come, Ivar we know now we can do it', Ulf tells me. 'We can come back in the morning – *are you sure* the wind will come around from the south-west then?'

Ulf turns back to the landowner to catch his answer.

'If I say it will', he answers, not finishing.

'Let us away to tell Ketilbeorn', Ulf tugs at my sleeve. He has what we came for and sees no use in asking for *or* about anything else. I have a sneaking feeling that there is more to this that we know nothing of, and should find out. Ulf snaps at me, 'Ivar, *come!*'

When we see Ketilbeorn and Murchad after landing on the eyot again, Ketilbeorn is eager to hear our news. When I say about the landowner speaking to me in the manner of an Aenglishman he too is wary.

'This fellow who gave us the right to use his land, what did he look like?' he asks.

Ulf shrugs and says only that the fellow was tall, ruddy, beard silver-grey and spoke to me in the way Godwin does. So Ketilbeorn asks me. Not being able to look the man straight on I cannot add much to what Ulf has told him. Saeward raises a hand to speak and all eyes are on him,

'He had a silver ring on this finger', my Seaxan friend shows him his second finger. 'Set in the silver was a garnet in the shape of a serpent – like the one you have on your *shield*, Lord'.

Ketilbeorn stares at Saeward, and then at me before asking me again,

'Are you sure you did not see him well enough to add any more than this that Saeward said about his ring?'

'As I said, when he spoke he did not look straight at me'.

'How is it *you* saw the ring?' Ketilbeorn asks Saeward.

'He stood pointing south-westerly, telling us about the way the wind will blow. When he lowered his hand to his side I saw he had a sword at his belt, and it was only when he rested his hand on the pommel that I saw the ring. He pulled his hand away, hiding it under his cloak when he saw me looking at it'.

'Odd, do you think?' Ketilbeorn asks Murchad. He then looks at Godwin fingering his beard and asks, 'Do you know him, Godwin – is he one of *your* men?'

'One of *my* thegns, do you think?' Godwin scratches the back of his head, thinking.

'What about Thegn Gudfrid?' Eadmund offers.

'Gudfrid, the one father outlawed for stealing land from the Church?' Godwin shakes his head very slowly, then stops and asks Saeward, 'A silver ring with a *serpent* garnet? Did it have a silver eye, the serpent?'

'I did not see any eyes on it', Saeward answers dully.

'I gave Gudfrid a ring, but at the time he was not a thegn. Father gave him land around the River Pared, eastward toward Glaestingabyrig, near Aethelney. He wanted more, and he had walls built around Church land close to the abbey', Godwin recalls, slowly. He thinks on, to when Harold held a trial,

'For that father outlawed him after a hearing, during which Abbot Thurstan bore damning witness to his bullying of a priest when the poor man saw what he was up to. He left West Seaxe, but no-one knows where he went afterward'.

'Now he owns land in West Wealas overlooking West Seaxe', I ponder the man's *wyrd*.

'What would he want from us as a reward?' Murchad knows the answer almost as soon as the words left his mouth, 'Land, I wonder?'

'He would not get it from *me*', Godwin thrusts out his chest and pouts.

'Then he would get it from *Willelm* for betraying us!' Eadmund swears under his breath. He looks up, to see Ketilbeorn staring at his brother.

'In betraying you he betrays *us*', Murchad swears, '*God, what* a mess we could find ourselves in if this goes against us!'.

'Does he know Godwin is with us?' Ketilbeorn looks at me now. Ulf shifts awkwardly, and his lord turns his eyes on him.

'*I* may have let slip', Ulf glowers at the ground at his feet.

When Ketilbeorn starts to snarl at his underling I help Ulf out, denying that he said anything about Godwin.

'You did not', Saeward tells Ulf, agreeing with me, reddening at being stared at by both Murchad and Ketilbeorn.

'Does he know *you?*' Godwin asks me.

'He may know me, I do not know. He *may* have seen me with others of your father's household'.

'Do we go on with this, or sail back to Dyflin?' Godwin asks Murchad. They are uneasy in one another's company of late, Diarmuid and Ketilbeorn being the ones who wish to gain something – *anything* - from our undertaking. As long as there is something to take from here that is worthy, or can be sold, I think Ketilbeorn would forsake Godwin's dreams.

He also wishes to get his own back for Thored against the West Seaxans.

'We go on', Ketilbeorn growls, '*and God help those who wrong us!*'

'We *will* even the score if Gudfrid steps out of line', Murchad adds icily.

'Then let us to it. We need to think of how we will do this in the morning', Godwin rubs his hands. He will gain renown, if nothing else, from this raid. What Ketilbeorn and Murchad get out of it is for them to see, and I pity any Northman – mounted or not – who tries to hold them off.

Throughout the night rushes burn around the camp as men ready themselves for the morning. A ship will land Ulf, Saeward and me on the western shore of the Tameth, on the strand below the headland. We will lay fire amongst the bushes and undergrowth and make as much smoke as we can to hide the ships that will bear down on the West Seaxans, letting them see only those ships that sail downriver. Hopefully the Northmen will think we seek to hide the ships withdrawing and stand down their men. What the West Seaxans will want to do is push us back to the ships, as they cannot hope to beat us.

The *fyrd* and the Danes are evenly matched – it will be like the old days when Ubbi and his brothers raided Aelfred's kingdom - but the *fyrd* leaders will try to bring their Northman friends back into the fray as quickly as they can. Once a gap can be made in their ranks it will be a sprint to the abbey, the thegn's hall and those churches near enough for plundering. There is only so much time before we have to pull back to the ships, yet it *can* be done.

That, too, is like the old days. My kindred knew their numbers were not enough to hold off the Seaxans forever, but they loved a good fight.

Morning dawns - thick with mist! We do not need to make smoke and Ketilbeorn is thrilled that we need send no-one to use Gudfrid's land and draw him into the fight ahead.

Murchad will take half the fleet downriver and land near the mouth of the Tameth on its eastern bank, Ketilbeorn to the mouth of the Tath to land upriver on its eastern slopes when they have rowed a couple of miles towards Tathestoche. Saeward and I will be with Ketilbeorn, my kinsmen with Murchad. Some of the ships are to hold the rivermouth clear, to stop any West Seaxans bringing in ships to block our leaving. They should hardly be needed, as the wind would be against them coming westward along Defna's coast.

'I want to hear only the oars dipping in the river', Ketilbeorn warns his men. 'Pass that on. Ivar and Saeward watch out at the prow for the Northmen or Seaxans – or both. Three ships will hold the mouth of the Tath, so as not to allow anyone to block our way out, to watch for the Northmen coming from Exanceaster. With all these hills in the way they will not be fast in coming, and I hope we will be out again before they can come to bother us. We want nothing untoward to happen, as it did to Thored. Understand?'

'Your word –'I begin. Ketilbeorn smirks, the smirk turning into a friendly grin. He thumps a big hand onto my right shoulder.

'As long as you know', he tells me, as if needed.

'It will be like old times?' Saeward asks.

'What does an East Seaxan know about that?' Ketilbeorn snaps gruffly, barely hiding a grin.

'*You would be staggered!*' Saeward laughs, to be hushed by Ketilbeorn, finger to mouth.

'As long as I am not the one who has to stagger away', I chortle. 'I have yet to get my horse back from Wulfberht's stable. Having lost my axe to these Seaxans, I do not wish to lose more'.

'What is he doing there?' Ketilbeorn asks.

'*She* – we were taken in Wulfberht's ship to Dyflin, when your ships frightened off the Northmen', I am about to add more when Ketilbeorn puts a finger to his lips again and jabs the air to our right.

'To the prow, Ivar', he waves us forward. As we make our way there I see the riverbank through gaps in the mist.

Someone on the shore sees us and points, yelling,

'*The Danes are here!*' Before he can speak up again an arrow finds his throat and he drops to his knees, ashen. The mist closes again and the ships skim forward like serpents on the water.

All is quiet again, the oars dipping, out of sight. No sound can be heard, so still do the oarsmen lower their oars onto the unseen river to push her forward. I hear a drumming on the earth of the riverbank. Horses!

Ketilbeorn is almost out of sight astern beside the steersman. He looks my way, worried at the sound. I wave my thumb downriver, showing him there is no need for alarm – *yet*. The Northmen would not have seen us in their haste. Murchad and he agreed, should one half of the fleet or the other need help they should loose off a fire arrow into the air. The men at the rivermouth have been told the same, and I look downriver to see if any flaming arrows show above the mist, hoping I *could* see if one were loosed off.

'Watch out to steerboard for any Seaxans', I tell Saeward.

'*I* am one!' he answers, scowling. 'You sound like one of these Danes here'. When he sees me beaming at him he cannot help grinning from ear to ear and thumps my back hard enough to hurl me forward on the deck. I have to step forward to stop myself flying head over heels at the prow, or over the side into the fast-flowing river.

'*You know my meaning!*' I scoff under my breath, having forgotten he *is* indeed one of them, albeit an *East* Seaxan. Righting myself again, with the rowers behind me cackling, I watch ahead to see if there are any gaps in the mist through which we might be seen.

Hearing Ketilbeorn's heavy tread on the deck planks behind me I half turn and let him come up to me.

Keeping a weather eye on the river bank – what I can see of it – I ask him where he means to pull in.

'Not long now', he answers.

He seems to be waiting and it is not long before he tells me why he has said nothing for so long,

'My spy tells me there is a wide strand on a river bend, where at least ten ships can be run up side by side. I have been counting the bends since we entered the Tath'.

'And the *rest* -'I wait to let him tell me more.

'The rest will put in at the riverbank. There will be men watching over the ships', he answers, waiting on the river- bank'.

'What of the horsemen?' I ask.

'*Horsemen* – oh, should any show my men have been told to pull back onto the ships. The bowmen are to keep an eye on them, should they look as if they might try to take us on'.

'The mist may clear before we reach the ships again', I begin, only to be told to be still. He scowls at Saeward when he looks to want to tell me something.

Saeward thinks better of whatever it is he wants to let me know and, looking sternward, stretches his right arm out for the steersman to turn the steerboard oar.

As the ships ground onto the strand men leap overboard, fully armed and form a line on the riverbank. Those still aboard stow the oars and arm themselves, ready to go ashore with their comrades. Ketilbeorn nods at Saeward to arm himself and asks me,

'Can you take a third of my men and march eastward to the abbey there?'

'How far is that?' I ask in turn.

'I have been told it is not far', Ketilbeorn looks me up and down. He smirks, 'You should have no bother with the monks'.

'I was not thinking of the Brothers, my friend. My thoughts were about the four-legged sort of bother, namely the riders', I begin to wonder whether Ketilbeorn has been hit on the head too often in fighting.

'Form a shieldwall if you are beset by them', he shrugs. 'You want wealth? Fight for it – I thought you were a *Dane!*'

'I am not a fool!'

Ketilbeorn hisses, reddening, shaking with anger,

'*Then stay here with the ships!* You think *I* am a fool?' The men nearest us look up, worried. This is not the right time to see their leaders arguing.

'*We should stay together,*' I snap back, *as one!* I do not know who your spy is, but the shire is crawling with *fyrdmen* and Northmen. If he did not tell you they are here, then he means us to walk into a trap!'

'*What* – we should walk rings, abbey to abbey and noble's hall and back again? *Foolish pup*, I ought to teach you –'

He says nothing more. Arrows rain on us. Shields raised, we weather the storm. Ketilbeorn's bowmen loose off their arrows at an unseen foe. I can only thank my maker the Northmen have not come with their crossbows.

'*Off the ships – form a shieldwall!*' he roars.

He looks to me and shrugs, 'You may be right about my spy. For now we must make this landing worthwhile'.

'Do we send up a fire arrow?' I ask.

'Would they see it from where they are, at the rivermouth? Besides, we need them to stay there. If we are foolish and bring them upriver we could easily be cut off from the sea', Ketilbeorn tells me, dropping down onto the pebbles, with Saeward and I close by on either side of him. We stride forward to take on the *fyrdmen*.

We link shields and push forward, our war chant drowning shouts from untried *fyrdmen*, breaking the heart of the Seaxan shieldwall. Men fall away on either side, those ahead trampled underfoot by scores of booted Danes as we slash and stab our way through them. Screams rend the air and all is mayhem once more.

Bones are crunched underfoot as we push on over their corpses, using the dead to raise us above the heads of the living, making the foe even more fearful of us.

Some are little more than children, here and there a thegn doing his best to stem our tide. But their efforts are wasted and they fall back, to be slain as they run amongst the 'herd'. Our way forward seems clear and the Defna men look to be overrun, but soon all goes awry.

9

To our cost, in the uproar of the slaughter, we have overlooked the line of shields ahead of us. Half-hidden by a thin mist, this new shieldwall begins to come toward us.

Ketilbeorn sees the new threat almost too late.

'*Stand fast and lock shields!*' he roars at the men around us. A few of his men are too far ahead to hear him, and fall to a new arrow-storm.

We hear, louder as they come nearer, what was yelled by the *fyrdmen* at the Northmen on Caldbec Beorg. I had hoped we would never have to learn at first hand that the likes of Godwin and his brothers were not wanted. Their time was gone and the new Northman masters would reap the harvest of West Seaxan steadfastness.

'*Ut! Ut! Ut!*' The clash of sword and axe on shield is meant to ram home their unmistakeable meaning that we are unwelcome here, the din deafening from only a sling's throw away.

'The others were sops', Ketilbeorn knows now.

'Sent against us to draw us in', Ulf adds.

It is too late to fall back to the ships now, with the fyrdmen on one side and horsemen on the other. We have to hope for a lull in the fighting before we can leave this lea.

The men around us gird their loins for a hard fight, not so much looking to come through this as to die well. A man who knows how to die well will live on, in tales of the slaughter told by lyre-plucking skalds to ale-swilling listeners. These men around me may hope, as I do, that we will be alive to hear songs about *our* pluck.

Ketilbeorn has told me he wishes for no more than to get even for Thored's slaying and, if allowed, to come away from this with something other than just his hide. His breathing is shallow as he gathers his strength, head and shoulders above the rim of his shield. I daresay their bowmen have been told to mark him as a leader, much in the same way as Northanhymbran bowmen sought out Harald Sigurdsson, and Flemish or Northman bowmen marked Harold.

I will thank my stars if I can walk away from this.

Eyes narrowed to slits in the glare of a strengthening sun, Saeward and Hemming to my right eye the oncoming *fyrdmen*.

Ulf, to Ketilbeorn's left, bares his teeth in a wild grin. He has no doubt seen many days like this. When everything begins his skill will be brought to bear on those foolish enough to come too near. We await the crush of shield on shield, the push and shove.

Well-aimed spearheads search out our legs under our shields. It is for us to swipe them aside, crush the spearmen's hands with our own shields if we can and pull their shields down. With the weight of our axes on their shields, they fall too far ahead of their bodies to keep them from harm. The shrieks, the screams and howls of pain rend the air. Men to either side of us drop, blood pouring from wounds to head, shoulders and chest.

Until now the horsemen have been kept back, but as horns blare along the length of their shieldwall the *fyrdmen* fall back to allow them through. These newcomers to the fight sit high in their saddles, lances held before them, shields on their left arms.

'You have had this before, Ivar. How do you fight these?' Ketilbeorn asks from the corner of his mouth.

'Tell your men to step back, keep their shields up and wait for your bowmen to bring some of them down', I answer, not looking at him but at the horsemen, 'before hurling their spears'.

'Did you hear that, Ulf?' Ketilbeorn asks.

'Aye, Lord', Ulf nods and looks over one shoulder. 'Bowmen, I want a hail of arrows from you – *aim high!*'

As the horsemen come forward at a trot, someone blows a trumpet behind them. Their horses break into a canter and the lances are held level under their arms. Arrows stream into the air over us and hiss down at the oncoming horsemen. Mounts and riders tumble head over heels or fetlocks. Several Northmen struggle to their feet, wave fists at us and limp back to beyond the *fyrdmen* to lick their wounds.

More shield-thumping follows and the *fyrdmen* strike out for our shieldwall, ahead of them a hail of arrows picks numbers of Danes and brings them to their knees. Ulf yells out, almost screaming,

'*Raise those shields!*' He blows out his cheeks and shakes his thick-maned head in disbelief. 'Time and again I have told them – *have I not, Ketil?* I have yelled into their ears, kicked their shields until my toes hurt!'

'You cannot mother them, Ulf!' Ketilbeorn growls back at him, setting his jaw, ready to dispatch some of the oncoming Seaxans.

'All the same –'Ulf begins afresh, only to be told by Ketilbeorn to keep his *own* shield up.

'- And tell our bowmen to send some of their arrows *back* at them! The Seaxans are not the only ones to bring their toys'.

Laughter breaks out amongst the Danes behind us as Ulf's bowmen leap around, picking arrows from the grassy earth to loose off back at the foe. It is hard for me to think of fellow Aenglishmen as the foe, having once fought alongside Harold's Seaxan *fyrdmen* against the Northmen. These are trying times indeed!

Fyrdmen and their thegns stride forward into a hail of arrows. Most

136

think on raising their shields over their heads, but some – fearful of arrows thumping into their chests – keep their shields neck-high and die all the same with arrows dropping onto their shoulders and necks.

Faltering, hoping to be called back, those still standing look over their shoulders. There are no horns, no trumpets to tell them to withdraw and it befalls Ketilbeorn's bowmen to send them back, reeling.

A loud cheer breaks out around us. Men wave their axes and spears high at arm's length and the cheering dies down again as more horsemen rally to attack us.

'*Shields up* -' Ketilbeorn roars again as more arrows fall onto us ahead of the horsemen. This time they want to keep our heads down until the horsemen reach our line. 'Bowmen on the right, let loose *across* the field!'

Arrows rain down on the horsemen again, felling oncoming riders whose shields are on their wrong arms to fend them off. Try as they might, the Northmen cannot pull round the great kite-shaped shields that they carry across their lances without blind-siding themselves. As they come up to us Hemming, Saeward and I, together with some of Ketilbeorn's Danes, leave the shieldwall and hew at their saddle straps with our axes. Cursing riders fall from their mounts, screaming as our weapons cut into them. Their lances useless whilst they tried to shield themselves against the Danes' arrows, the Northmen's feeble efforts to attack us work against them and they are called back by trumpet calls.

There is a short lull whilst someone out of sight of us thinks up a new way of breaking us. Water is passed along our line as we wait for the next onslaught. Some have brought bread and meat with them, and spend their waiting time munching through what is in their bags until Ketilbeorn calls on them to make ready for the fight again.

Ahead of us their bowmen are arrayed before their line, ready. We have been evenly matched so far, but now it seems more men flock to their lord's banner, whoever he is.

'Over there, to their right – what do you see?' Ketilbeorn has seen them, filling the ranks from the north. Their numbers swollen once more, they are set to push us back to the river. Our own dead have been carried to the back during the lull, wounded borne to the ships to be tended to. I nod, acknowledging this new threat and make my friends aware of it.

'I *have* been watching them', Saeward tells me.

Hemming rounds on him,

'*And you said nothing?*' I suck in my cheeks to show my bemusement and Ulf glowers darkly at him. Ketilbeorn does not bother saying anything.

'I thought *everyone* knew', Saeward snaps back at Hemming and stares dully at Ulf, now beside himself. 'There they were, plain as your nose, coming across open fields to be with their fellows. Who could have *missed* them?'

'Let there be an end to this!' Ketilbeorn growls at them both. 'They have *been* seen and that is an *end* to it! Be still *or be off!*'

Ulf reddens but stays still. We all watch as the West Seaxans raise their bows, and then raise our pockmarked shields to ward off the new threat. Arrows thud on my shield. It must look like a hedgehog, I tell myself. It seems to me I am carrying a *heavy* hedgehog.

Ketilbeorn raises his sword for his own bowmen to begin again once the arrowstorm has died down. The last arrows hit our shields and a trumpet calls ahead of us. I lower my shield to see another line of men on foot coming toward us, and a stone hits my helm on the crown.

'*They now have slingers!*' I warn the others and prod the air with a finger at a hail of small stones. Some of the men, not seeing the stones for the noseguards on their helms, are struck on the brow and their helms are pockmarked with shallow dents. Luckily everyone here wears a helm. The rest of us have our shields up and watch past them at the line of men passing on either side of the slingers. The din of stones on wooden shields is deafening, some of the arrows break off, making the shields feel lighter. Men flinch at the din but the slingers do not let up yet.

'*Aim at the slingers!*' Ketilbeorn calls to his bowmen. Without shields, the slingers have to withdraw beyond their own reach and our arrows drop on the nearing *fyrdmen* again.

With them are Northmen both on horseback and on foot, pushing. Shield slams hard on shield and the pushing begins. Men groan with the weight of the oncomers, our shields groan too, yet not as much as those who wish to press us onto the riverbank away from our ships.

Ketilbeorn roars over his shoulder at the men behind to hold their shields hard behind our own. The Danes to our rear pull back at the right to ease our withdrawal back to where the ships have been drawn up. It seems to me we will be going nowhere *but* back today. It is merely a matter of how many of us will be alive to *board* the ships!

'One step back – *give way!*' Ketilbeorn roars. As we pull back that much the *fyrdmen* fall over their own shields and we can hack at them as they sprawl helpless on the ground.   Saeward has not heard Ketilbeorn, nor does he know we have drawn back. He is out on his own to my right, flailing with his axe at fellow Seaxans and emboldened Northmen. Shield before me, my new axe tucked into its strap at the back of my shield, I pull hard on his belt. As he sprawls on his back between the two rows of men our shields lock back into line. The foe shall not find their way through.

'Next time Ketilbeorn calls on us to fall back one step *do so!*' Hemming yells against the din of clashing shields.

'*I heard nothing!*' Saeward snaps. He brushes the grass from his mailcoat and picks up his shield, and then pushes back into the line beside us to laughter from behind.

'*Listen out!*' Hemming yells above the clash of sword, axe and spear beneath and around our shields. Saeward either pays no heed or cannot hear, choosing instead to ask me,

'Next time, dig your elbow into my side!'

'If you wish', I answer, ramming my shield at a horse's flank as its rider veers.

The horse shies, and prances backward into the oncoming line. Screams of pain rend the air from those the horse tramples on and the men behind it push it forward again, only to be kicked at. The rider is thwarted in attacking our shieldwall, unable to rein in his frightened beast. Fighting on horseback the rider may gain in height, but hemmed in like this he is as much at risk from his comrades on foot as from us.

The *fyrdmen* make our task easier, the uproar they bring about as they come onto us unsettling the Northman's horse.

Finally man and horse fall, the nearness of the Seaxans to him blocking any help he must pray for. Before long Ketilbeorn calls for us to step back again, I thump Saeward's arm with the flat of my axe blade and we withdraw in line.

Once more men are left sprawling in front of us, those nearest to us and those who have fallen onto us are given short shrift. There are too many of them out of reach and this time they are not taken off guard as they were last time. Nevertheless they are wary of it happening again and the press eases.

War trumpets call them back again and we all look to Ketilbeorn, who scours the land behind us over one shoulder.

'When they have pulled far enough back we will pull back so get the river on our right', he tells Ulf, who jerks his chin up and down. He beckons me to him, 'I have not seen any use in summoning help, Ivar. We will fall back on the ships and withdraw downriver. Someone let them know we were coming!'

'I would not think it beyond Gudfrid to have told them through a rider', I offer. During the fighting it has dawned on me that the former thegn wished to reclaim his lands, and to do that he would have to toady to the Northman lord.

'You think so? I thought he might have been my spy'.

Ketilbeorn sighs. He lifts off his helm and presses his eyes tight shut, wiping a sweat-darkened beard. Opening his eyes wide, he stares up at the heavens and curses. When I say nothing in answer he tells me again,

'Sometimes I tell myself I should have been a *skald* in Diarmuid's household'.

'*You think so?*' I ask in turn, grinning widely.

'No, *not really* - forgive me, Ivar. I am tired, too old for this kind of trade. I wonder I *should* have been a skald, but they do not live long in Dyflin. When cuckolded husbands find them *bad things* happen! The Gaels are not as forgiving as us Danes'.

'*We* are forgiving?' I ask, bemused. I know our women are easier, but as husbands Danes are by no means forgiving, of all folk in the northlands, we will go a long way to sort things out, 'sorting' in our eyes meaning slaying as well. 'I hardly think so, Ketilbeorn. I would say it is the other way around'.

'You know the Gaels as well as I do, do you?' he raises an eyebrow.

'I thought they shared their women', I try pulling his leg. He does not buy my banter and scowls darkly at me.

'I do not think my father-in-law would see eye-to-eye with you, Ivar', he thunders with laughter.

'Why so?' Nothing is happening amongst the Seaxans and their Northman friends, so we may as well rest.

'He had a Gael's way of dealing with cuckolds when he came home from warring', Ketilbeorn tells me.

'Which was?' Saeward asks, and earns the darkest scowl I have yet seen Ketilbeorn give.

'*Mind your own affairs*, I was talking to Ivar!' the big man glares down at my friend. Saeward is not cowed, and looks back up at Ketilbeorn, who goes on coldly, 'He cut off his manhood and fed it to his hounds'.

Saeward swallows, saying nothing.

'What, you are not so brash any more?' Ketilbeorn notes Saeward's look and looks closer at him. 'You have gone white, my good man. Have you something to tell me?'

Men around us laugh to ease the strain of warfare, and wondering if they would come away alive. Blood cakes their chain mail and covers their boots where the foe came close enough to breathe on them before dying. Some have scratches on their foreheads or cheeks. Others have lost fingers or eyes and must wait until we gain the safety of the ships before their wounds can be treated.

Behind us are our dead and badly-wounded. These last might easily die if carried back to the ships and are helped into death with a friendly, soothing words. They are told their kinfolk will be cared for before they are smothered.

Our foes, either Seaxans or Northmen, are not known for their fair treatment of those taken alive after the fighting. Being left to die in pain is not unknown.

Three riders come across the field to us as the last few are smothered. One of the riders looks like a noble. He does not wear the chain mail or leather scales I would say to be Northman or Frankish. From what I recall of the Bretland defenders of Hereford, he is one of them.

'Who leads you?' he asks in understandable Aenglish.

'*I* lead them', Ketilbeorn answers calmly, turning to take in the newcomer.

'I come to offer a lull in the fighting', the rider tells Ketilbeorn, who screws up his eyes and looks at me, shaking his head.

'What does he mean?' Ketilbeorn asks me.

Not waiting for me to tell Ketilbeorn, the rider tells him what he means.

'I wish to take the time for our wounded and dying to be tended. If you like, the Brothers can see to your men, too'.

Ketilbeorn looks from him to me and Ulf before looking back at him. He asks,

'Who are you that you can offer this?'

'I am the earl, Breon by name, from Bretland'.

'How long do you need, to tend to your wounded?' Ketilbeorn asks, looking down at the foot-beaten grass at his feet, kicking at a molehill with the toe of one boot.

'My friend, the Northman Willelm *Gualdi* and I agree that we will give you until the shadows of the trees come around to point to our lines. We understand you have suffered many losses, as have we, and you must be given time to bury your dead', the Bretlander earl Breon tells us.

Ketilbeorn shrugs and gives the earl a half-smile.

'We have nothing to bury them with, save the swords and axes we fought with'.

'*You can have shovels –*'

Breon's offer is turned down flatly by the Dane, who shakes his head and laughs,

'Thank you, no'.

Breon stares. He cannot understand why Ketilbeorn is so loth to take his offer.

'Look, my men understand when they set out that not all will be home to share out any gains. This time we have nothing to show for our undertaking save our dead and wounded, so they have died in vain', Ketilbeorn tries to enlighten the Bretlander lord.

'I can do nothing for you there', Breon scowls suddenly and makes to ride off before Ketilbeorn catches his eye. 'What is it?'

'We will leave here soon. If you give us time to board our ships we will not bother you again'.

Earl Breon looks askance at me and asks,

'Is your friend in earnest?'

'We can do you more harm than you think', I bluff. 'There are as many ships at the rivermouth, with as many more men led by the *aetheling* Murchad from Leinster and my kinsman Godwin. If you bring us gold and silver from the abbey at Tathestoche, they will not be brought to bear on your hard-pressed men'.

Breon stares coldly at me, and then throws his head back to laugh throatily. The laugh sounds uncanny, seemingly to rise from the earth beneath our feet. He brings his head down again to look at me and there is a twinkle in his eyes when he tells me,

'Something tells me you have the makings of a bard in you. The tale you tell is the best I have ever heard by my hearth! *Murchad* is dead, your kinsman Godwin and his brothers withdrawn across the rivermouth to Gudfrid's land. My fellow Celts, the West Wealsh as these Seaxans call them, have told me they will not harm the men left to think back on why they undertook his raid of yours. I believe they wished to raid on Willelm *Gualdi's* lands and manor, is that so?'

Not knowing who this Willelm *Gualdi* is, I have nothing to say on that. I try to hide my feelings about the news on Murchad and Godwin, but he can tell his news has cut me as sure as a sword or axe.

'You look crestfallen, er –' He knows my name anyway,

'*Ivar*, I believe you are known as?'

'If you say so', I stifle a yawn.

He smiles again and notes,

'You are tired from this long day of fighting, as are we all. Very well, Dane', he looks back at Ketilbeorn, 'Ketilbeorn by name I believe, you can board your ships. Leave, Ketilbeorn, never to show yourself again on my land on pain of death. Do you *understand*, my friend? That goes for *you*, too, Ivar. My king knows *you* well. He knows you are still in the kingdom and warns, through me, that should you be caught you will suffer for the evil you and your kinsmen and friends have wrought!'

My lips curl back at his warning, a red rag to a steer. How dare he threaten *me*, this Bretland upstart, whose men ran from the untried Suth Seaxan *fyrd* on Caldbec Beorg! It was only because Willelm's horsemen cut down the brave – if foolhardy – thegn and his men at the bottom of the dale that the Bretlanders came away with their hides. I hope my sneering answer gives him something to take back to his king, for want of a better name,

'Tell your king, the bastard son of a tanner, that I will *not* leave this kingdom until *he* is thrown back into the sea he crawled from', I tell him to cheers from Saeward and Hemming.

Those Danes around us who heard and understood me jeer at the Bretlander earl and shake their weapons. Breon smiles thinly, turns his horse and whips it back toward his lines. He looks back once only and is almost thrown when his mount rears, frightened by the loud banging of swords, axes and spears on shields.

'We have little time to get back to our ships', Ketilbeorn tells his men. To me he merely says, 'I hope you are happy now. He may not be so keen on giving us time to board again, now he has let you know the truth'.

'He may be lying', is all I can be bothered to answer.

'I hope you are right, Ivar. Back to the ships, lads, *fast!*'

Now and then we look back to see we are not about to be run down by Breon's horsemen, speared from behind on our way. We are not long back at the strand, by the ships when I see horsemen coming after us over the rise, a line of them a score wide.

So much for Earl Breon giving us time to leave!

Ketilbeorn is warned and as many bowmen stand, arrows at the ready, heads into the earth, as there are horsemen we can see on their way. The earth shakes as the riders near us, the sound of arrows whirling into the air not as loud as the groans and screams that follow. Horses run forward and the bowmen let them through, some with their riders' boots stuck fast in one stirrup, heads bumping along on the grass tussocks. *A fine sight to gladden a man!*

No-one bothers us again as we board the ships. I feel much better now, standing by the steersman with the oars creaking together ahead of me.

Saeward is as yet untouched, hale and hearty as ever. It makes me bitter that as often as we have fought against these Northmen and their hangers-on, Saeward is unhurt! Am I bitter against him? No, it is *Urd* I hate, deeply! Urd, who spins our *wyrd* at the roots of Yggdrasil with her sisters Skuld and Verdandi, owes me much since she let that Northman fasten on me with his arrow at Exanceaster. For all I know he went on to drill many other unlucky souls before he met his maker.

I am pulled from my daydream by Hemming, who asks me if they will let him piss into the river over the ship wall.

'*What?*' I turn to see him laughing, with Saeward clutching himself behind.

Hemming laughs,

'I wondered whether you were still with us, Ivar'. He adds, 'Saeward asked if your wound still hurt. Does it?'

'To be truthful, these last hours I have had no time to think about it'. I have to be honest. It may be my wound has healed, not having brought me any grief for the past few days. The arrow wound had only just come into my thoughts.

'Hmm, whatever you say', Hemming is unmoved and goes back to talking with Saeward.

They have been told to watch for the earl's men. Horsemen can ride faster overland than our ships can pass downriver under oar, so it makes sense to keep up our guard. I keep watch with them over both banks, bowmen straddling the ship walls behind us eyes firmly fixed on the wooded banks where riders or *fyrdmen* with bows at the ready might lurk.

When we reach the mouth of the Tath, the sight of wrecked ships and dead Danes strewn on the lea pains Ketilbeorn so much he turns away from the sight. He stuffs his right fist between his teeth to keep from roaring out his grief and asks, when we are mid-river on the Tameth, whether we have passed them

'Aye, Ketil, we have left them well behind', Ulf lays a dish-sized, hairy hand on his friend's shoulder to ease his pain.

'We have nothing to show for our undertaking, and now I must tell Diarmuid his son has been slain!' Ketilbeorn groans.

'It must be done', Ulf tells him flatly.

Ketilbeorn groans again, stuffing his fist back between his teeth. Is there really nothing to be done but tackle our *wyrd* head on, hard as it will be?

The rest of the ships are lined along the foreshore, hauled fully out of the water on Gudfrid's land. There cannot be more than a score of them.

Ketilbeorn is truly grief-stricken. For the first time I have known him, he does not know what to do,

'So many *men lost* - so many *ships!*'

Ulf takes over running the ship whilst his close friend stands behind the steersman, out of sight and free to let loose with his feelings. We keep ourselves busy closing on the other ships.

I see Godwin and Eadmund on the strand. Magnus is nowhere to be seen. Murchad sits, legs stretched out, on a sea chest. Arms folded, pouting, he kicking at pebbles. Ketilbeorn has not seen him yet, being on the wrong side of the ship to be able to take in the men ashore. Ulf elbows him and guffaws,

'For a corpse your friend Murchad looks fairly healthy'.

'*What* –'Ketilbeorn spins around, letting go of the ship's side, almost falling on his steersman, '*Where?*'

'Murchad is there, seated on a chest, kicking stones', I tell him, showing him the *aetheling* amongst the others. Beaming with delight, Ketilbeorn leaps overboard when we reach shallower water and wades ashore without waiting for the oars to be drawn in. He hurtles up to Murchad, knocking Eadmund out of the way, and wraps him in a bear hug.

By the time I reach them Ulf has already told Murchad why Ketilbeorn almost smothered him,

'The lying Bretlander told us you had been laid low in fighting his men'.

'I *did* wonder', Murchad grins, slapping Ketilbeorn across the jaw with his palms. 'Aye, old man, I *am* alive. *Calm down!*'

'Well, what *could* I have told your father?' Ketilbeorn growls at Murchad. 'The Aenglishman here could *never* have gone back to Dyflin with me!'

'As it is the Aenglishman, as you call Godwin, has lost a brother – as good as. I doubt he will live much longer', Murchad tells his close friend.

'Magnus was clubbed by a horseman', Eadmund tells me, pulling me away from Godwin. He takes me to one of the ships and shows me the sad, huddled bundle that is my young kinsman. Wrapped in his cloak he looks childlike again, ashen, cheeks bloodied. His head sports streaks of dried blood, hair matted with the sweat of his helm – now *deeply* dented and lying on the ground beside his boots.

'The wounds are not as bad as they look', Saeward huddles beside Magnus, peering at the young fellow's scratches, dabbing the blood away with a clean cloth. He peels away the cloak from the worst wound and sucks in his cheeks and gives his finding on Magnus. 'A few days is as long as I give him'.

It was not a clubbing that brought my kinsman low, although by the graze on the back of his head that was nothing mild. What cut him down was a wound from a *lance*.

'Would you take Magnus to Bosanham to bury him?' I hear Godwin asking me. Eadmund standing beside him, head bowed.

145

'What will you tell your mother?' I ask as if in a dream. This is not happening, I tell myself.

'We will one day find ourselves at Count Baldwin's court', Godwin tells me. I keep my thoughts on Tostig and Judith to myself, not knowing what either Godwin or Eadmund would say if they knew I had kept from them the knowledge that he was alive. He says nothing about what he will tell her about Magnus.

Knowing Eadgytha would find the news hard to swallow I say nothing more.

'I will take him', I agree.

'We will both take him', Saeward puts in without being asked. Hemming, standing behind Saeward nods that he, too, will come.

'You will need a ship', Murchad tells me dully.

'Your Lordship is kind', Godwin thanks the *aetheling* for me before I can answer. Murchad looks from me to Godwin and again at me, eyebrows raised askance.

'Aye, my Lord, I would be thankful for a ship'.

I fear he would die on us, my young kinsman, were we to try and reach Bosanham overland. The ride would be fraught with hazards, taking a young fellow barely alive over hill and dale from western Defna shire across Thornsaetan and Hamtun shire to the western corner of Suth Seaxe. He has seen little fighting, but for taking Hereford with us, his knowledge of warfaring scant. Whilst his skills are not altogether lacking, I would say his sheltered life has worked against him. He should have been toughened before tackling our way of life.

Ketilbeorn offers one of his ships with a seasoned steersman, Ogmund, to take us through these hazardous waters. Bosanham's inlet will be hard enough for him to find if he has never been before, past Wiht, Suthsae and Haeglinga. The sand-bars off Haeglinga's eastern shore at low tide would have us aground with the wind pushing from the south-west at this time of year.

'Do you know Bosanham?' I ask Ogmund. He thinks, looking down past his steerboard oar at the swirling waters.

'Is that where the southern shore turns –' he stops and thinks briefly, trying to see it from past sailings, 'north-westward past what the Seaxans call Seolesigge?'

'It is indeed', I brighten. 'You have been that way before?'

'Many years ago', he tells me.

He chews his upper lip, deep in thought, adding,

'You will have to give me some time to think of the way, but we can sail as soon as you wish. Make the young fellow as snug as you can amidships. He will be better off there. Either aft or forward, the ship's rocking could make him worse. We can land once or twice, to build a fire –'

'*Build a fire?*' I cut in. 'We would be seen, surely?'

'We have done it here before without anyone seeing', Ogmund tells me with some forbearing, 'have we not, Toki?'

A hulking fellow lumbers sternward to where Ogmund and I stand, talking. He sports an eye patch, but other than that there is nothing about him that hints at Toki being a warrior. He is overweight, his gait clumsy, almost tripping over the last bench as he cuts the corner.

'*Aye, master*, what gives?'

'I said we have camped on the Seaxan shore without being seen', Ogmund says again.

'*Oh,* we have, *we have!*' Toki gurgles delightedly.

'And if anyone were to test us, you could see them off *single-handedly*, eh Toki?'

Toki gurgles again and grins toothily. He lumbers away forward when called by one of the crew to help shove away.

'He could see off *anyone* on his own!' Ogmund laughs. 'They would be scared stiff at the sight of *him!*'

'I *believe* you. He would give me the runs if I saw him coming after me!' I watch after Toki as he leaps over the side, almost squashing two of his shipmates.

Ulf has been told to come with us, to add one more sword hand to our strength. He cackles by my side at the sight of the two men sprawled out on the wet sand, swearing at Toki in a blend of Gaelic and Norse.

Ogmund grins and takes hold of the steering oar as the ship is heaved off the strand, into the shallows,

'His heart is set right'.

With one last heave the men are helped back aboard – all but Toki.

'He shall have to get *himself* back aboard!' Ulf laughs out loud as two of the crew try to heave him over the side. He almost pulls them overboard in their effort. The giant grips the ship wall with both hands and launches himself over, head-first onto the foredeck. Toki's landing brings laughter from all around, and from the many still ashore who have been watching.

'Think on this, Ivar', Ogmund tells me now the ship is well out to sea, 'that should we be seen by the Northmen we are on our own'.

'I *know*, friend. Taking Magnus to Bosanham must be done, nevertheless. He is dying and wishes to be where he spent his childhood. Who are we to deny him? You will be able to take shelter in the inlet nearby at Bosanham whilst we take him to Earl Godwin's hall there. I think someone can be found to tend to him and then we will be back with you', I tell Ogmund, watching the skyline ahead for sails.

'Very well, just as long as you know they will not take kindly to me, a Dyflin Dane bringing in outlaws', Ulf shrugs and Ogmund tends to his steering oar whilst I stride forward to look at Magnus. Saeward is with him, to see he is at ease. Hemming watches from the steerboard quarter by the prow, to guard against all comers, who would wish us to stay away.

The serpent's head has been taken down from the prow, to guard against Ketilbeorn's ship being taken for a raider, so hopefully we will be safe from prying eyes.

It is dark when we make landfall on the first evening. We are on Saint Aldhelm's Head, some way short of Wiht, and Ulf thinks we should head out to sea from here, around Wiht to steer clear of being seen when we pass the isle.

'How much longer would you say it will take sailing the long way around Wiht?' I hear Hemming ask him.

'Best ask Ogmund', Ulf answers.

Ogmund does not wait to be asked,

'From here around to the south of the isle would be most of a day's sailing, and making camp there is the best way to duck the Northmen prying around the east of Wiht. Their trading ships sail into Suth Hamtun and their warships into Portesmuth. They are the ones we should stay clear of. Taking the early high tide will be our best hope'.

'How do you know all this?' Hemming asks. Saeward looks up at me, staring across the fire at Ogmund. Toki looks closely at him, too. I would say by the way he cocks an ear to listen. He has little knowledge of sailing these waters or getting about West Seaxe to him.

'Aside from raiding, I have traded in these waters, and the road to Lunden is best from *both* these burhs', Ogmund is free with his knowledge at least. 'They were laid long ago for someone who *knew* about building. We must get some sleep now and I have set watches. No-one should see our fires beyond this bluff, so we can keep them burning. Come morning we will be well clear. Good night, rest well Ivar, Hemming, and a good night to you, too, Saeward'.

Ogmund pulls Toki from where he rests by the fire.

'You share first watch with Ingialf'.

Toki grumbles, but does as he is told and takes up his post after first easing himself against the rocks nearby.

'We must take turns in watching over Magnus', I tell Hemming and Saeward. They both nod and we draw straws. Mine is the shortest and I keep my kinsman company for the first part of the still long night.

'Ivar, am I dying?' Magnus suddenly asks.

'Do not think of it. Why do you ask?' I try to shield him from his *wyrd*.

'*Truly*, Ivar, do not lie to me', he bothers me.

'Are you afraid?' I ask. He reaches out a hand to me and I take it in both my own. 'I will try to help you over, Magnus, but you have to be steadfast. You must believe you are going somewhere good –'

'I believe one day I will go to the Lord', Magnus tries to overcome his fears and smiles up at me.

'*Good*. Stay true to your belief. Whilst you are amongst the living, whatever you want, just ask for it', I pat the top of his hand and he pulls it away to rest in the waning warmth of his body.

'I will sleep now, Ivar', he pulls the cloak over his eyes and I wrap it around him so that he can still turn if needs be.

'You know Bosanham well?' Magnus whispers hoarsely.

'It is where I first came to Godwin's hall with my uncle, Hunding'.

'Godwin's hall – I did not know my brother had a hall here?' Magnus asks.

'Your grandfather's hall', I enlighten him, smiling.

'*When* did you first come here, Ivar?'

'I first came when I was still a child. My uncle the king wished me to live with my aunt, your grandmother Gytha, some time after my father died', I tell him, seeing myself when very much younger.

'That was in Knut's days, was it?' he asks on – nothing if not dogged!

'You must have sleep', I tell him.

'If I am dying, how will not sleeping alter things?'

'You might *not* die', I lie. I wish I were right, but Saeward thinks he will not last out the week.

'Do *you* believe that?' Magnus pushes back the cloak and eyes me. He scratches the thickening beard he has been growing these past months. In his eyes the men around him seemed able to win over the women they wanted, and he wanted some of that.

There *is* something there that seems to want to snub death. He is not going to roll over and take his *wyrd* without at least a token fight. There is the spirit of his grandfather in him yet. He may *not* die after all!

'I believe you *will* live. Get some sleep, kinsman, and we will see in the morning how things are with you. You have the Viking in you from your grandmother, you know?'

Magnus chuckles and flinches with pain.

'*Rest*, Magnus!' I tell him and pull the cloak back over him. He nods weakly, but the spark is still there in his eye. I *saw* it!

Saeward wakes me with a cup of broth and bad news,

'Ivar, your kinsman died in the night'. I cannot hide the tears and put the cup down on the earth by the fire in a bid to stem the flow. My grief is driven home to me because I kept him believing he would live.

'If you wish, we will still sail on to Bosanham for a priest to bury him', Ogmund puts a hand on my back. I nod wearily, pick up my cup and stand.

Hemming and Saeward watch as I walk away from the fire. The crew pack away their belongings and stow them aboard. Saeward and I lift Magnus to where he had slept yesterday, this time covering him. The cold sea air will stop the smell of death spreading around the ship.

Ogmund swears his crew are willing to undergo the risk, easing my pain at the loss of a dear kinsman. Back in Dyflin with Godwin and Eadmund, I hope to ease their pain of losing a brother.

Telling their mother will still be an ordeal, there will be more tears and Gytha will stifle her sorrows again. However, Godwin and Eadmund do not mean to sail to Flanders yet, wishing instead to fight on for longer. It is another matter, whether anyone is willing to back them further. That is something only they can answer. Ketilbeorn will look elsewhere for gain, and neither Diarmuid nor Murchad will push him into doing the same against his wishes.

In a thin sea mist the ship noses eastward out from the long ness for Wiht.

'Ogmund seems to think this mist will shelter us as far as where we can safely rest for the night', Hemming tells me.

'The wind has dropped, though', I note from the sagging sail that only fills every now and then. 'The oars will need to be run out, I think'.

'You may be right', Ogmund agrees across the other side of the afterdeck, 'although I hope not. There may be more a full wind further out to sea'.

He looks up at the top of the sail where one of the crew keeps watch above the mist.

The fellow lowers himself suddenly and aims a finger northward. He tells us breathlessly,

'Ship to the north-east - coming our way',

Ogmund draws on the steering oar to bring the ship on a northward course, and waits. Ulf points to the mast top and the fellow pulls himself up unwillingly, hand over hand. We need him there to avoid a clash, not wishing to have to swim for shore. He slides down again and points easterly, giving bearings to a fellow crewman who passes on his news to the ship's master.

'There is a ship heading seaward ahead of us. From her path my lookout thinks she may be a trading vessel bound for Bretland. We will cut behind her and her master may well never know we are here!' Ogmund tells me, grinning lopsidedly.

He seems to relish the thought of outwitting the other ship's master. I just want to have my kinsman buried so that I can get back to Wulfberht's stable and take Braenda away. Somehow I feel I miss my horse more than my woman – *what am I thinking?* I miss them *both*, but I cannot say which of them I miss more!

We are blown past high cliffs on the south-west of the isle, around to the lower south-east where there are inlets we can put into. Whether the islanders will tell their new masters of our being here, I do not know. They may merely keep their own counsel and go about their daily lives as if we were not here.

Whichever way things are, we will soon know...

'Are we safe from prying eyes along here?' I ask Ogmund.

'There are prying eyes wherever we go, Ivar', he throws his head back and laughs.

'Not even on Groenland would we be safe from prying eyes!' Ulf claps me on my back. 'Ivar, just as there are folk anywhere who would not know we were here if we stood in front of them, we have to think of those who can see and whose tongues might wag'.

We find a fitting cove and make camp. There are trees here that will shelter us from much, but not any or all harm. Hemming and Saeward help find kindling for our cooking fires in the evening light. The days are lengthening now, so we have to be careful about how far from the shore we go.

I am talking with Ogmund and Ulf at the stern, looking idly at the strand beyond the prow when I see something stir behind the first mast-partner. The sail has not been spread over the mast to give us shelter on the still cold nights, and at first I think the wind has caught the canvas.

Then I hear wailing and walk forward to where we left Magnus trussed in a watertight sack behind the mast. The sack is jerking about and I have to undo the bindings to look inside. Is my kinsman *alive* after all? Both Ogmund and Ulf have seen what I am doing and hasten to help be unbind Magnus.

'*God*, I could hardly breathe in there!' Magnus sits up with a jerk and almost knocks Ulf off his feet.

'We – *Saeward told us you were dead!*' I yell, helping him from the sheet.

'It would not be the first time he was proved wrong', Magnus answers in quiet anger.

He is helped onto the nearest bench and rests his head in his hands.

'Shall I bring water?' Ogmund fusses.

'It was getting hot in there, stifling!' my young kinsman sounds as if he had been suffering for some time – since *yesterday?* 'I *would* like some water!'

'Well, we thought you were dead', Ulf seems to ask for forgiveness, but knowing him it may only be to defend himself from blame.

'You had gone cold', I tell Magnus. 'Saeward could hardly tell you were breathing, and he is only skilled one of us who knows these things. He will have a fit when he sees you are alive!'

'So he should! Should we put him in a bag?'

'I can only say I am glad you are alive', I steer him away from ordering Ulf or Ogmund to swaddle Saeward.

'Only just', Magnus shivers in the oncoming dusk.

'Get some broth for him, Ivar', Ulf asks and fusses over Magnus again. My kinsman could hardly stand his mother's fussing, so this outsider's 'mothering' will be even less welcome!

One of the crew has a pot of broth on the boil and sees me coming.

'Do I hear right? The young fellow, your kinsman' has come back to life?' he asks, half-laughing. He lowers a ladle into the broth and fills the cup I hold. 'Here, give him some bread to go with it'.

Although the bread is hardening – baked in camp the day before yesterday and kept in a cloth bag – the broth will soften it. I walk slowly back to the ship and hold it up for Ogmund to take, and climb back over the ship wall.

Godwin will be glad that his young brother has awakened from deep sleep. It will ease his meeting with Eadgytha. The earliest he will know will be when Ogmund steps ashore on the riverside in Dyflin. Meanwhile I think I will stay with him, keep him safe. Whether Saeward wishes to stay with us at Bosanham after Magnus threatened to have him bagged -?

I hope he and Hemming will stay with us, and ride north with me when Magnus is up and about again. Speaking of Saeward, I think I see him and Hemming with armfuls of dead branches. He will be taken aback when he sees the 'corpse' has come back to life!

'Lie down, Magnus', Ulf tells him with a wicked grin. I do not know whether the lad has seen Saeward, but he does Ulf's bidding just as the East Seaxan comes back to the ship.

'We have kindling enough, but I see the fire is burning well already', he tells the crewman by the boiling pot.

'Leave it there then', the fellow answers. 'I think you are wanted aboard'.

'Oh, indeed? What could this be about – what have I done wrong *this time?*' Saeward groans outwardly and plods back to the ship, hauls himself aboard and stands in front of me.

'*Now* what, *Master* -'he scowls, touching his forelock like a thrall.

'*Cheek*', I grin, letting him see there is something afoot. He then looks down at Magnus, speechless as he sits up.

'Like Lazarus, I *rise* before your unbelieving eyes', says Magnus, glaring darkly at Saeward as he speaks and tries to stand. Ulf takes one elbow, Ogmund the other but my young kinsman pulls away from them. Just for that short time he stands, unaided, but has to sit again with a thump on the bench.

'I – I really thought you were dead', Saeward mumbles, shaking his head. 'Truly, you seemed to have breathed your last'.

Smiling weakly, Magnus tells him,

'I may need your help a little longer, Saeward, as long as you do not write me off again like that'.

A grin spreads slowly on Saeward's broad mouth as he reaches down and lays a hand on Magnus' shoulder. Ogmund and Ulf both heave with laughter behind Saeward as if to say 'You have weathered your shock well'.

'We must all eat and rest, to be ready for the early tide', Ogmund tells us all. More men have come back to the ship, some standing up to their knees in the shallows looking up at Magnus by the deck wall, all grinning. Everyone loves to marvel at a man come back from the dead. The thought of cheating our *wyrd*, getting back at death, gives us feelings of hope. The young man has *luck*, they are telling themselves.

10

If anyone saw us in the inlet we will never find out. The islanders might not have been friendly toward the Northmen. Our crossing the following morning goes ahead without let or hindrance and we are soon out to sea, the prow carving through the waves.

With Ogmund's hands firm on the steering oar we are pushed by the surf past the sandbar over the falling tide, sail taken down, oars run out. Toki rows for two. His broad hands draw the oar on his own up to his chest in time as we head roughly northward into the narrows ahead past the bluff to our steerboard side.

As we come sliding into the shallows below Bosanham, ceorls, their women and offspring crowd the foreshore.

'Who are *you?*' An elderly priest pushes through between them and stands in the shallows to one side of the prow, staring up at me in disbelief when I go forward. His mouth opens, and closes quickly. When he finds the words I hear him ask,

'Are you Ivar Ulfsson?'

I nod, not knowing him.

'You do not know me?' he asks, echoing my thoughts. 'I am Aelfric. At one time I was meant to be a warrior –'

'Aelfric Herbaldson?' It comes flooding back to me where I saw him last. 'I thought you had left'.

'I did leave. I went to learn the priesthood. Lord Harold knew I was not set to follow the warrior's way. It was he who paid for my teaching'.

'And now you are back', I grin. Aelfric was a childhood friend, one of my first after getting to know my kin. Svein always saw him as a weakling, but as he said, Aelfric did not want to be the warrior his father wanted him to be. Herbald was a Frankish noble Earl Godwin brought with him from Thorney, a friend of King Eadweard's. Bitterly thwarted in his wish for a warrior, he was deeply upset at the son who wished for a cassock instead of chain mail.

'I have long been back. It is you who strayed', he grins. 'Welcome Ivar. Who have you brought?'

'I have two friends, warriors –'I begin.

'It always pays to have warriors as friends', Aelfric smiles up at me.

'And I have one wounded kinsman', I finish. Dumbfounded, he asks who the kinsman is. I tell him, 'Magnus'.

'Magnus – you mean Harold's son?'

'The same, aye', I answer, nodding.

'Where is he – where are Godwin and Eadmund?' Aelfric asks,

upset that Magnus has been wounded but baffled his brothers are not with him.

'Magnus is aboard Ketilbeorn's ship, behind me', I wave to where I last saw my kinsman. 'Godwin and Eadmund are on their way back to Dyflin, if they are not already there'.

'*Back* to Dyflin –'Aelfric wonders aloud.

'Aye, we landed in Defna with a fleet of Danish ships and men from Dyflin', I tell him.

'You know I think nothing comes of warfaring', Aelfric looks at me, the wagging finger in his words. Given short shrift by his father for his monkish ways, they parted the best of foes.

That was many years ago. He left Bosanham to learn to , be a priest at Wintunceaster and when he came back his father was gone – not dead, merely gone with Svein to fight the Wealsh in Hereford shire. He never came back, so they say, because he fell out with Svein. That, as well as killing my younger half-brother Earl Beorn, was why Svein left for the Holy Land to seek forgiveness. He did not feel he needed to ask forgiveness for begetting a child, young Hakon, on Eadgifu, abbess of Leominster. There was some wrangling with the king about that, but it died with Svein on his way back.

If I entrust Magnus into the care of Aelfric, will he take on the mantle of carer when he learns anyone could gain from turning Magnus over to the Northman earl Willelm on Magnus' head?

'He is another of my flock, Ivar. There is no need to ask', Aelfric tells me when I bring it up with him after much thought.

'You know you could be taken to task by the bishop of Wintunceaster, were he to know?' I may talk myself into caring for him myself, but Aelfric is a friend from long ago. He shakes his head and ushers me to his small church close to the hall built for Earl Godwin in the days before I first came here.

'I shall wrestle with my guilt in my own time', Aelfric smiles and leads me to his scriptorium. This is where the church rolls are kept, of baptisms, weddings and last rites – or hatches, matches and send-offs, as Godwin laughingly put it. His send-off, too, is down amongst the rolls here.

There is a musty, stale smell of old, dry calfskin and food leftovers nibbled at by small creatures. Crumbs on the desk betray Aelfric's keenness, his need to keep body and soul together into the small hours after his daytime ministries are dealt with.

'Hurry and bury them by daylight, worry about them by candle-light. I have everything about my flock here at hand, so I can read what has gone before I add my own jottings', Aelfric knows I have seen his earthly leftovers and grins broadly.

'Now – we must talk about how we hide Magnus from the outside world'.

'Surely', I agree. 'A man must eat, even a man of the cloth. God knows, your archbishops, bishops and abbots eat well enough, although they do their eating with two-legged guests'.

He laughs and strides to look at the rolls.

'This one', he holds one up, 'is Magnus' baptism. I do not want to have to write on his passing. Lord knows, Ivar, one day soon I may no longer be in this world and I would sooner be gone before your young kinsman'.

'Aelfric, you did not bring me here to look at Magnus' rolls, and I have things to do before I leave again'. I scratch my chin, the new beard growth on dry, salt-water-soaked skin irksome.

I should rub something in, but where am I to find such a salve here? Aelfric shuffles to a small shelf and brings forth a small flask. He holds it up to the weak candle light, nods and brings it to show me,

'This will help, I think. I suffer from dry skin in this sea air. Rub some in and tell me in the morning what you think before you sail. If it is any use to you I can let you have more'.

I thank my old friend and take the flask, asking,

'Was there something else you wished to tell me?'

'That was it', he smiles, points at the salve and blows out the candle as we leave, locking the door behind him.

'Would anyone else wish to see the rolls or have you something dear to you that you wish to keep from prying eyes?'

'I would say the rolls are dear enough. They are my flock, as I said', Aelfric leads me to the hall where everyone is being fed, along with Hemming, Saeward and the rest of the crew. Toki draws the eyes of the young women, sinew rippling on his wrists as he grips his cup tightly. I daresay these folk will not have seen such a show-off before in their lives!

'Toki, give the showing-off a rest and drink up!' Ulf scolds. 'We must be up early in the morning to catch the tide'.

Ulf laughs hoarsely, hunched across the table as I stride up to him, then sits up and asks,

'What is it, Ivar?'

'What is *what?*' I ask by turn. He shrugs and I look around. 'Where is Magnus?'

'Magnus is abed', Saeward tells me and goes back to eating.

'He looked ashen when we carried him in, straight to one of the rooms', Hemming looks up at me as I sit beside him. He goes on,

'Ordwulf said to take him as soon as he laid eyes on the lad'.

'Amen', Saeward says, looking up from his feasting.

'*Amen*', most of the Danes chorus, some crossing themselves as the Gaels do at home.

Ogmund belches and wipes his hands of chicken fat on a cloth and stands. As he stretches, the crew stand in their turn and nod their thanks to the maids. It is their cue to leave for the night. Ulf stays behind with us and helps himself to more food.

'You will get fat', I smirk.

'With the fighting *I* have been doing of late, I have *no* fear of putting on weight!' Ulf beams before laying into another chicken leg.

Saeward splutters and wipes his mouth. He looks up foolishly at the maids giggling behind their hands, reaches for his cup and knocks it away in the effort. He thumps the wood hard, rattles his bowl and horn spoon, and swears under his breath. A maid brings more ale as Ulf chides,

'Have you not had more than your fill, Saeward?'

Saeward's scowl is taken as an answer. Ulf knows about his axe-throwing and would be foolish to call him out, even though he would rank as a thegn here.

Hemming stands and yawns. He has had enough of Saeward, friend or not, but does not want to try the East Seaxan.

'*God, I am tired!*' He asks the way to his bed and leaves before Saeward knows he is gone. Saeward sits hunched over his cup, holding his chin in one hand. With the other he raises the cup, drains it, bids me good night without looking at me and trudges off in

He has hardly left the hall when someone nudges me and asks mournfully.

'Spare a thought for a poor ale-wife?'

Without looking up I push my empty cup to one side for the woman to take it, if she must. Next she thumps me on the shoulder and asks,

'Does the young Lord wish for more ale?'

'If you have more in that tun, I will have some more', I nod, still without looking at her. I have things to think about and the last thing I need is an ale-wife bothering me.

'You want more to eat?' she keeps on at me, and to crown it all pokes my side! It is only now that I look up at her. The woman is no old crone, as she sounds... I look up at Braenda.

She laughs when she sees my jaw drop, and sits beside me on the bench, stroking my neck with the back of her hand. With a kiss on my ear she stands again and asks,

'*Do* you want more ale, Lord?' On a nod from me she throws back her head and laughs throatily, like the old hag she made herself out to be. She is back before I can ask for any more. Sensing my wish for something more she asks, 'My Lord Ivar, what *else* would you like?'

'I think you *know* the answer, but for now I will make do with a bowl of hazelnuts', I chuckle. With a sly wink she leaves my side again, and is again seated beside me within the blink of an eye.

'Would you sooner have the nuts or *me*, Lord?'

'Is this some sort of test, wench?' I ask, reaching for the bowl.

She snatches it away from me and asks again, laughing,

'Nuts – *or me?*' I reach around her and she leans back, the bowl in her outstretched right hand. She picks a nut from the bowl and prises it past my closed lips into my mouth, telling me, 'Bring them with you'.

Braenda sets the bowl down beside my ale and stands. Putting her left foot on the bench, she pulls up her long dress to show a pair of creamy, smooth legs, and then she is away again. I look around, but no-one in the hall seems to have seen us at play, scoop a handful of nuts from the wooden bowl, ale cup in hand, and leave for my bed.

'I would not keep *her* waiting', someone says from the shadows. Whoever he is, I cannot see in the poor, flickering golden light. I answer that I do not mean to keep her waiting and press on.

'Someone said not to keep you waiting, so here I am', I say before closing the door to my quarters.

'You do not listen to many, but when you *do* listen you are quick on the uptake!' Braenda laughs lightly and raises the covers to show she is stark naked, her full breasts aglow in the candle light. She beams up at me and beckons. 'Can you undress yourself yet, Ivar?'

My breeks fall to the floor, showing her my manhood.

'If you want me to pull off your shirt, you had best kneel in front of me – stretch out your arms, Dane, and you shall be rewarded!'

When I open my eyes she is still beside me, nestling against me, right arm across my chest. Her long red tresses rest in a tangle over her harm. It is light outside and someone thumps on the door. Half awake I call out,

'What is it?'

'Will you sail back to Dyflin with Ulf and Ogmund, or do you mean to stay?' Saeward asks through the door.

'I think Magnus would like me to stay', I answer.

Wrapping my right arm around Braenda's shoulder, I pull her to me. A lazy smile comes to her lips but she keeps her eyes closed.

'I shall let Hemming know we are staying'. Saeward clears his throat, and adds, 'It is not often you see your woman'.

'I wish I had friends like that', Braenda whispers into my right ear and presses her lips to it. 'Did you *want* to go back to Diarmuid's court?'

I shake my head and doze off again. With Braenda still here with me, I should make the most of her company. Magnus may know little of what is happening around him in the next days. Nevertheless, soon I will make my way north with Saeward. Hemming may well stay, too, for the time being. He is free to do what he will.

Would he have been happier around me, were Guthfrith alive? I think they *were* both ready to come with us when Eadwig, Saeward and I were on their side of Exanceaster's walls, but Saeward was too hasty with his dagger before I could stay his hand. I think he was aware of my anger at his rashness, but mulling over it will not bring back Guthfrith.

When I open my eyes again Braenda has gone. As I pull on my clothes I wonder whether she is still in Bosanham and ask about her in the hall whilst I take my morning meal.

'Your woman is making herself useful', Hemming tells me when I sit across from him. She *is* still about. This is worthy of note!

I hear Aelfric say behind me,

'I am glad she feels at home here'. He even *sounds* glad. 'Where do you know her from?' he asks next. Should I be honest with him and risk his Christian wrath? He may have become a priest with a burning wish to stamp out un-Christian thoughts within his flock, as Godwin's priest Father Cutha was, or he may understand a man's needs come before his beliefs.

I tell him half,

'I met her a long time ago'. It is the truth, after all, and I have hurt no-one.

'I asked where you met her', Aelfric presses.

'He first met me in Wealas, after Earl Harold and Tostig crushed Gruffyd in Gwynedd', Braenda tells him. How long has she been standing there behind me, listening in? 'We met again in Eoferwic after King Harold won at Staenfordes Brycg'.

'You are a bird of good omen, then?'

Aelfric's smile is open, childlike. He will take the first answer he is given. I feel foolish about holding back.

'If you wish, *I am*', Braenda smiles brightly, bends low over me, showing her ample bosom to one and all, and kisses my cheek warmly. Aelfric reddens, Hemming's eyes are out on stalks and Saeward grins slyly.

'That was well done', Saeward says to me under his breath after both Aelfric and Braenda have gone elsewhere in the hall.

'Better than I could have answered', I laugh hollowly and start crunching an apple.

'Were you going to fib your way through your answer to that poor priest?' Saeward asks. The way he puts his questions is much like a wife or a mother-in-law.

'*I* thought I did well enough', I lie. He knows I would have been uneasy answering Aelfric.

'Hah, you *did*, did you indeed? What is there to eat?' The break is timelessly Saeward's manner. He will quiz you and when he thinks you are stuck for an answer he will switch to talking about something else altogether. Like a mother-in-law.

'*Your* mother-in-law would never talk to you in that way', Braenda whispers in my ear, and bites it. When I jerk away she chuckles and tells my friend, 'You can have porridge, Saeward'.

'Good, I *will* have porridge', he nods and winks at me.

'See how my woman looks after you?' I grin at him as Braenda makes her way to find someone with the pot.

'It is almost like being wedded to her. How do you do it? I gather she was with you when I knocked on your door', Saeward looks up at Braenda and the young maid with her, who thumps the pot down and ladles the porridge into a wooden bowl for him. 'She reads your thoughts, too'.

'Ivar -'she begins, but I have no stomach for it.

I shake my head and ask instead for smoked fish. Why were we given teeth if we were to shovel porridge into our mouths?

I catch sight of the discthegn weaving his way between the benches toward me and look up at him as he stops beside me,

'Lord Magnus wishes to speak with you. Could you see him now?' He hovers like a fly, in sight but out of reach. 'It cannot wait, Lord Ivar. He may not last the day'.

Last time someone said he was dead he came wondrously back to life. Now I am told again of his fading, and it is not Saeward who gives me word of Magnus' looming death. It may be Bosanham's Brothers know more of wounds than Saeward learned from Wealtham.

Someone else will have my fish, I am sure.

'Ivar, come here and sit by me'. Magnus has been propped up in his bed. A pitcher of water rests on a low table beside a cup within his reach, and he has a silver cross on a rosary at his bed-head. Whether he has eaten I do not know.

'You are resting well, I hope?' I ask him.

160

'Well enough, I thank you for asking, kinsman. I need to ask a good turn of you, which is why I asked Osberht to find you and send you to me'.

'Ask, Magnus, and it shall be done', I bow in the manner of a household underling.

'You still have Saeward and Hemming with you, I understand?' I nod. Magnus sinks deep into his thoughts, his next words hard to find I think. 'Can you let my brothers know I have not died?'

'I think Ulf will tell them when he sees them, if he has not already done so', I swear to him. He sinks into thought again, as if brooding over something.

'Where will you go from here, Ivar?' he asks.

'I was thinking of riding to Barnestapla to get my horse from Wulfberht's stable', I smile at the thought of seeing her again.

'What if the Northmen have her? The horses we left with him, he could not hope to feed them all no matter how wealthy he is!'

'Nevertheless I shall seek him out and ask for a ship to carry us across the Seoferna to Wealas. That way we will not have to ride through Thegn Aelfred's lands. I daresay the Northmen have found someone amongst their own ranks to fill Eadnoth's shoes'.

'You have thought this out', Magnus looks from me to the floor. He would sooner we stayed with him, at least until he died I think. 'Can you wait until I am gone?'

'You will not die for *years* yet – you may even outlive *me!*' I laugh. But he can do no more than smile. He may know more than I.

'Saeward also thinks I will live longer', Magnus looks up at me again. My eyes meet his, and on my winking he brightens a little. Saeward's knowledge is as good as that of any healer. It was he who tended my kinsman's wounds, after all. He has seen men wounded much more grievously who lived on, for how much longer I would not know. Magnus' wounds have not bled for days now. He has rested well, as both Saeward and Aelfric have told him to. And he has eaten the meat broth made for him, made with fruits of the earth.

'Do you feel your strength coming back to you?' I ask, trying not to stand over him so that he can look at me without craning his neck, but I feel the need to walk about. My own wound is playing up again now, standing talking to Magnus.

He nods, smiling again, and tells me,

'I do feel a little better, 'thanks to your friend, and with Aelfric's help. He not only heals the soul, he knows how to mend a man's flesh.

'Very well, Magnus, you need your rest –'I begin again, but Magnus cuts me short.

'Stay - talk to me. Tell me about your woman. I understand she came here?'

'She *did* come, aye', I grin widely. 'She is still here'.

'I wish I had a woman like that. When I am well, I shall have one of the hall maids come to me', he grins, thinking about it.

'You *should* have a woman, kinsman', I cheer him.

'Have you seen one here who would have me in her bed?' His look is full of mischief, like a child who has found something sweet that his mother kept from him. I rest a hand on his shoulder and chuckle,

'I would say there are a few who would suit, but you must get better first before you go looking for that kind of thing'.

'You are right Ivar. First I must find my strength again. Talk to me of other things', he yawns and I sit at the side of his bed to tell him of Aethel's home in the woods near the Hvarfe. He is soon asleep and I ruffle his hair. One day, I hope, I will have a son of my own like him, a son I can teach to handle sword and axe. With luck Magnus will outlive me and sow the seed of his kinship. One day, hopefully, our offspring will live in a land free of this Northman king's clutches.

Saeward looks up at me as I walk slowly back through the door into the hall. He smiles when I tell him and Hemming that Magnus is asleep.

'He breathes well?'

'Like a babe-in-arms, Saeward'.

'Aye, thanks to you and Aelfric he is well, I say to myself. My thoughts run to Godwin and Eadmund. Will I see them again, and where? Gytha and Eadgytha, her daughters Gytha and Gunnhild and son Ulf should be safe with Baldwin – they may even have met with Tostig and Judith and their sons. Ketil and Skuli will be young men now, like Magnus and his brothers, learning from their father to be leaders of men.

'You have fallen silent, Ivar. Is there something ailing you?' Hemming asks. Saeward beside him drains his cup and holds it up to be filled.

'I am alone in my thoughts', I sit on the bench across from him and a wench comes to give me a new cup.

'You wish for ale?' she asks, and on my nod sets down a wooden cup. Before she leaves to bring a pitcher of ale Saeward catches her hand. This is so unlike him! The woman does not pull her hand away, but looks down at him and smiles before telling him, 'Another time, old man'.

He lets go of her with a scowl and a heavy sigh,

'Did you *hear* that, Ivar? *Old man*, she said – *me*, an old man!'

'Do not take on so', I tell my friend. 'There are others here who would have you at the drop of a cap'.

'Aye, Ivar, like toothless old hags and the likes, eh?'

'*Fool!*' Hemming tells him. 'You give up too easily! Try again, and again. She may like you, and is testing you to see what you are made of!'

'He is right', I nod and raise my cup to the wench as she walks away again, with a look over one shoulder at Saeward. 'Faint heart wins no fair woman'.

'I would bet you missed *that*'. Hemming chortles beside Saeward, cuffing him over his head as he rises.

'Where are *you* headed?' Saeward asks after him.

'I should stand on the bench and shout out to *everyone* that I need to answer the call!' Hemming snaps back, leaving Saeward reddening. There are no holes deep enough for him to crawl into and laughter follows him as he chases Hemming out through the door into the oncoming night. What would I give to hear what Hemming has to say to him now!

'Where has your friend gone?' asks the wench on her way around the hall to gather empty cups.

'I would say he has had to take some air', I answer, trying hard not to laugh.

'How is that so funny?' The look she gives me as she leans on the corner of the table tells me she wants to dally, but not to give her feet a rest.

'It was the way he followed Hemming', I have to laugh.

'Where would *you* go, to rid yourself of all that ale you have put away?' The woman is tiresome, staring at me as I sit gaping into my cup. She presses a hand onto mine, 'Do not take on so, Ivar. I only want to know how you look without that tunic or those breeks'

'*Slut*, - you have not met me before, have you?' Braenda stands fiery-eyed behind the wench, arms by her side, fists clenched.

'I cannot see a brand to show he belongs to you', the wench laughs and throws her hair back over her shoulders in the manner of a dare.

'The marks *I* leave are on the women who cross me', Braenda glowers, eyes like burning coals.

'Wretched woman you do not know *me!*'

The wench cackles,

'I am *Rhonwen*. Men and women fear me between here and the western marches. When I am done your bones will *rattle!*'

I have never had this before, two grown women, two *spay-wives* fighting over me. Those around slowly draw back, some to the corners of the hall. Others around us draw back to the doorway and vanish into

163

the night.

'Try leaving the ring of water I have left around you, Rhonwen', Braenda's laugh is so loud it seems her echo runs through me. Rhonwen does indeed try to cross an unseen ring. I look around her but see nothing. Could Braenda have sprinkled water around Rhonwen before she was aware of it?

'*Hag*, what do you think you are doing?' Rhonwen cackles suddenly and kicks out at Braenda. There is a sound like stone hitting wood and Rhonwen bends to tend to her foot. She glares at me and makes to snatch at my sleeve, yet she cannot reach me. 'I will *shred* your liver on the kitchen bench, you –'

'The only liver *you* will ever shred will be that of a hog in Uffen, *scurvy slut!* Your eyes shall rot in their skull-bowls, your heart catch fire in the arms of your dark master!' Braenda seems to be getting into her stride and Rhonwen laughs frenziedly as she struggles to leave the 'ring' that no-one could see but her and Braenda. This is all beyond me, but I cannot bring myself to leave.

It is as if I were riveted to the bench!

'Let me *out* of this ring, hag, lest I shrink your head on your shoulders when I get free!' Rhonwen's eyes bulge with pent-up fury, her brows arch and her eyes light up like hot coals in a smith's hearth. But for all the cursing she can go nowhere. There is suddenly a smell of scorching wood in the air and all eyes are on Rhonwen – there is only a handful of us left within the hall.

Aelfric is one. He is lost, out of his depth, yet drawn to the now screaming Rhonwen.

'Ivar, *hold fast onto the priest!*' Braenda warns before Aelfric comes too near.

I reach out to my old friend, not wishing him to come to harm. He has a silver cross on a rosary that swings to and fro as he tries to get free of my grip. Rhonwen has *some* strength left, and with it she tries to wrest Aelfric away from me – *but why?* Is she not afraid of his cross?

'Have you holy water in your chapel, priest?' Braenda asks Aelfric, to awaken him and break the hold Rhonwen has over him.

Her words pull him back from the brink and he jerks his head up and down.

'Bring some here, to me', Braenda smiles at him.

He almost runs from the hall, the silver cross whipping him as it leaps about his midriff.

'Dare to throw that washing water over me and I shall drag you down with me, *whore-hag!*' Rhonwen howls, but Aelfric is gone. Will he dare to come back again with the holy water? Will it even shorten the odds in this fight to hold the woman?

Aelfric comes back, panting into the hall. In one hand he has a beaker, and in the other he has a pestle. Braenda beckons him, Rhonwen glares, eyes like an adder's. She seems to wrestle against unseen bindings and stretches a hand out to catch Aelfric, but he slowly, timidly, walks wide of her to Braenda's side.

'Sprinkle water on Rhonwen. Do not stand so *close!* Do it from here! She can still reach you', Braenda pulls him back.

I pull away. If she could reach Aelfric, then *I* am still too close to her. Rhonwen's adder eyes light on me. They seem to dance, trying to draw me to her. Her mouth opens in a gruesome leer when she thinks she has me, and then she begins to writhe as Aelfric's pestle splashes the water onto her. Screams and loud groans fill the hall. Those still in here hold hands over ears, but I am spellbound, unable to do anything further. The handsome wench I thought wished to take me to her bed has turned into a twisted, scab-ridden old hag!

More howling and groaning follows as Aelfric sprinkles the water onto Rhonwen, the eyes rolling up into their sockets.

Braenda stands uttering spells, unheard over the shrieking and groaning, and Rhonwen buckles. Her back sprouts scabs each time more water is sprinkled on her, and bends outward. The earth groans with her as Rhonwen shrinks within her clothes, blackening and twisting, writhing.

Even as the hunched, blackened back cracks and settles on the charred floor beneath Rhonwen, Braenda holds Aelfric back in safety. She will not risk her rival sapping the priest's strength.

Foul smoke fills the room, the stench of rotten flesh hanging on the air, and a dark stain spreads across the floor from where Rhonwen stood. Braenda pulls Aelfric back and tells him to throw the rest of the water down onto the creeping black rim. Smoke rises where his holy water splashed and the rim stops spreading. Charred ashes are all that is left of Rhonwen, until a stiff wind sweeps them through the hall. Someone about to enter the hall steps back quickly as the ashes are whipped up through the doorway by a stiff, cold breeze, out into the moonless night.

I find the strength to speak after a long stillness,

'You did not speak Aelfric's name, why?'

'If it was known to her, Rhonwen might have spoken it to draw him to her bosom. She would have become his mother, anything he loved, to steal his soul. With that she might seem to die, but it would be Aelfric who died and Rhonwen would have become him'.

She does not smile yet, there is something that still bothers her.

'She knew *your* name, Ivar'.

'What do I do to save myself?' I ask, 'She is no more, surely? We all saw her life end'.

'That was only her worldly self. She is not dead, Ivar. She could come back to life through you', Braenda tells me, gazing as if she were telling me 'farewell'.

This is worrying. I thought she had begun light-heartedly, but now I wonder how Rhonwen could come back through *me*. I must look forlorn, because Braenda smiles and tells me she will do all within her to save me from the dark master.

By this time we are seated either side of the long table.

Saeward walks back, stares at me and sits a little way along on the bench away from me, crosses his fingers and clutches the small wooden cross that hangs on a length of cord around his neck. Hemming enters after him, gives Braenda a sidelong look and nods. Something is happening, but no-one tells *me* what.

'Do you feel well, Ivar?' Braenda asks, strengthening my fear, but I try not to show it.

'I feel fine', I lie. From their looks I must have sprouted three heads, and I have a creeping sense of foreboding.

Aelfric comes toward me as if nothing has happened. At least this is heartening. Then he walks around me with a look that could sink a ship.

'Do you feel you would like to lie down?' Saeward asks, but does not undertake to help.

'What *is* this?' I ask finally, fed up with their jape.

'Shall I *tell* him?' Braenda seems to beg the others to let her free me from my burden. Hemming and Saeward nod gravely. Aelfric merely looks dully at me and shrugs. 'You have fallen prey to a prank being played on you by your friends here. They were taken aback with Rhonwen, but needed to let go the great strain they were under'.

'Putting *me* under more strain in doing so?' I snap, glaring at the three of them.

Aelfric was a pawn in their game, so I hold nothing against him. Braenda should know better. I will get even with them, fear not!

'Tell me this was not *all* a game!' I thump the boards, sending cups and bowls leaping into the air.

'Oh *no*', Braenda comes and stands beside me to ruffle my hair as a mother would do to a wayward son. She puts a hand around my shoulders and tells me, looking at the others, 'Rhonwen *did* go up in smoke because she could not leave the ring of water I splattered around her. That much is true. She tried to flee by drawing Aelfric to her, as she would have used him against you, my love'.

'I thank my maker *you* were here, Braenda', Saeward reaches behind me, having slid back along the bench to sit by my side. I elbow him in the chest and he presses his eyes tightly as in pain. 'Ivar, let bygones be –'

'That was for your childish prank!' I shall make Hemming suffer as well, make no mistake, but not enough to turn him against me. *That* would be a mistake!

As for Braenda – how could I get even with *her?* I need to think about that. I owe her for setting us free from the evil of Rhonwen, as we *all* do here at Bosanham. Would Magnus have fallen prey to her when she had dealt with us? I dread to think how this could have ended but for my woman...

My woman – it seems odd that I think of her as my woman. How could a free spirit such as hers belong to *anyone,* and how could I even think of getting even with her? For now she is mine. In the morning she could be away again.

She is gone when I rise. I go to see Magnus, to see how he fared. Had he been told of Rhonwen?

'Aye, Ivar, I was told by Osberht. He could not stop crossing himself. Even now he still crosses himself when I ask about her. He will say no more, but that your woman Braenda saved us all. He is *deeply* in awe of her! I thank you on behalf of all here for befriending her –'

'I also have her to thank', I stop him. I cannot take thanks for someone I have no hold over but who has a firm hold over me!

'You will be away soon', he says. A nod from me lets him know I have to leave but wish him well. He says no more and lies back, eyes fixed on the cross that hangs on the wall before him.

Aelfric will look after him, bring him back to health.   This kinsman of mine would have been better suited to the Church, if only he knew. He is not made for war, as are Godwin and Eadmund.

I find some words of comfort to give him,

'Aelfric tells me you will be on your feet soon'.

'I hope so', he answers without taking his eyes from the cross..

Should I tell him what we are about? He may be made to tell the Northmen about us, but then the Northmen may not know who he is. This shire is part of either Odo's or Willelm fitzOsbern's earldom, I do not know.

'We, Hemming, Saeward and I, must talk over what is open to us'. The less he knows, the better it is for him. I *can* tell him something, however,

'We are agreed that we should make for the north'.

'That may be your best way forward. Osberht tells me we are in the earldom of Bishop Odo. I understand you and he are not the best of friends', Magnus grins cheekily, still not looking at me.

'You could say that', I cannot help smiling. To think that it was only days ago we all thought Magnus was dead... He is very much alive! 'He has tried to catch me ever since he was berated by his half-brother in front of his own men for trying to hang me'.

'He was trying to *hang* you?' His eyes are wide open as he looks at me. I thought that spree with Thorfinn was widely known.

'It is a long saga', I laugh. I should tell him one day when this struggle against King Willelm is over and done with.

'You could tell me the bare bones', he presses.

'Well, it happened this way...' I tell of Thorfinn, whom he knew, and of our sea crossing from here, being shipwrecked and taken hostage by Guy of Pointhieu. Lastly I tell him of our bid to let Wulfnoth taste some freedom, lie with a woman even? However Thorfinn's trial of strength with an axe had led to the bishop having us taken back to his brother's stronghold of Falaise to be hanged for trying to free Harold's youngest brother – uncle to Magnus.

'I should like to meet Wulfnoth one day', Magnus looks far away. My telling seems to have worn him out. By the time I leave his room after pulling the fleece up over his chest he is asleep. I close the door quietly and tip-toe back to the hall.

Late the following morning a small ship, a *karve*, shows around the bluff in the morning. From its sail it has to be Aenglish, from Defna. Folk throng the foreshore to see who it is has come to see us.

I make my way forward through the gathering, to meet her shipmaster, whoever he may be. Shipping their oars, the seamen leap over either side into the shallows to run the *karve* up onto the strand. A stout, elderly fellow astern beside the steersman makes his way forward along the vessel toward the prow, to be helped onto the sandy strand by the young men with him. He beams brightly on seeing me push between the foremost men.

'Ivar, I am glad you are still here!'

'*Wulfberht*, what gives in Defna shire?' I ask.

'*Northmen* - the land is crawling with them, they are *everywhere,* I have never seen so *many!*

When I ask,

'Is anyone looking after your stable?' I think he knows why.

'Your horses are safe - at Rhosgoch, with Bleddyn and Rhiwallon.

Ralf, you recall I spoke of my Danish shipmaster, took Godwin's horses to Dyflin but the brothers were elsewhere and Diarmuid took them into his stables. Murchad told him you were here with Magnus. He thought you would sooner sail from here to Wealas anyway, rather than ride across shires infested with Northmen and Bretlanders to be a part of the uprising'.

'Uprising, *what* uprising do you mean?'

'Eadric says he has heard of unrest everywhere, in West Mierca, Defna and West Wealas', Wulfberht tells me. 'The Northman earl Willelm does not know *which* way to turn. There is talk of fines on *burhs* and hamlets alike for the killing of Northmen, Flemings and Bretlanders'.

'How *is* that?' Hemming asks from behind me.

'It is the *Murdrum Fine*, levied on those fellows of the slayers who are still about after the outlanders have been found dead. Corpses are being found everywhere, in woodlands, underwater in ponds and ditches, in fields, in the rivers. It is only in their *strongholds* they have not been found dead!' Wulfberht laughs along with those closest to us who have heard. 'Have you seen any Northmen *here* yet?'

I think back on what I have been told by my kinsman and tell him,

'Osberht, discthegn to Magnus here, has seen none lately, not since we have been here. However he thinks we may be in the earldom of Odo of Bayeux'.

'It will not be long before *he* pokes his nose in here', Saeward grunts and burrows around in his nose with a small finger.

'I daresay he might leave it to you if you make your talents known to him', I chide. Saeward looks closely at his fingertip, flicks something to the ground and flashes a brief smile. The corners of Wulfberht's mouth drop at Saeward's lack of manners.

He looks pained at me and shakes his head. Looking back at me, he tells me behind one hand.

'Well, whatever, you can take this as a warning. If they have not been yet, it does not mean they never will. Time, friend, give them time and they will bring the door down looking for you'.

'I shall heed your warning', I tell him. This is our cue to leave. 'Have you time whilst we pack our things?'

'By all means, Ivar, I will take my farewell of Magnus. He is in good hands here?' Wulfberht clearly knows his way around and strides toward the hall.

'Magnus is not in the hall', Hemming tells Wulfberht.

'Oh, *where* is he then?' Wulfberht half turns.

I show him the smaller building nearby,

'He is in the small dwelling, *over there*'.

'Very well, when you are ready, I shall await you on the foreshore', Wulfberht nods and takes the path to where I told him my kinsman dwells.

We have little enough time before we sail, but long enough to pack and eat. Braenda is still here, I learn. I make my way to where I was told she is and find her scrubbing clothes. I have never seen her work hard like this before and she sees me stop dead in my tracks.

'You have never seen a woman work before?'

She sounds gruff, almost like a man.

'I have never before seen you work hard like this', I laugh uneasily.

'What is it you wish, anyway?' She looks up at me from the work, her hand against her forehead clutching the brush. 'Come, tell me – you can *see* I am busy!'

'Wulfberht has come to take us to Wealas where –'

'To Wealas - what is *there?*' she frowns.

'My horse is there, for one thing', I tell her.

'Your horse is there, the one you named after *me?*'

Braenda bends down and begins scrubbing again. 'At least you will be near *one* of us, one of your two Braendas. I hope you will be happy together'.

'I was hoping you would sail with us', I am losing time here. I should be packing my things, she packing hers.

'So I could meet my *namesake?*' Braenda shakes her head and picks up the garment, wringing it as she does so. Is she making things hard for me, testing me, or is this a show of wit. This is the wrong time for wit.

'Well?' I ask.

'Well what?' she asks by turn, then looks up at me and laughs.

'You should *see* yourself. You look like a lost child - I thought you would never ask!' She throws the garment down and strides over a washing basket to usher me away.

'What about the washing?' I nod back at the clothes.

'What *about* the washing?' she almost echoes. 'We must pack, and eat! Shall we have a bet? Last one back to the hall undresses you when we next make love!'

'What if I win -?'

'Then I undress you, as ever'.

Her mouth turns down in the corners in mock anger, and she hurtles back to the hall ahead of me, shouting, laughing,

'*I* won!'

'Ah well, I shall have to pull my own clothes off!' I put on a look of gloom.

'It will be well worth my while waiting for!' she bubbles and ducks under my grasping hand.

We are soon ready, fed and have taken our farewells from Magnus, Aelfric and Osberht. As Odo does not know Magnus, they can easily say my kinsman is a sick ceorl. His room is sparsely furnished, so as long as Osberht thinks on burying his bloodied mailcoat and weapons, no one would think they were lying. Magnus is unlikely to need them any more, after all.

Wulfberht leads the way back to the *karve* with Braenda close behind and we follow, laden with our war gear. With the weight of our mailcoats and weapons Hemming, Saeward and I sink into the soft sand by the prow. The steersman helps us into the vessel and the crew heaves Wulfberht's karve into the water as another ship comes into sight past the bluff.

'Who is this?' I ask the steersman.

'God, the Northmen are here!' Wulfberht snaps and yells at the ten oarsmen, '*Heave for your life on those oars!*'

The steersman hisses through clenched teeth,

'At least *their* ship is heavier!' He pushes hard on the steering oar, past the oncoming ship, almost under her prow.

Try as they might, the Northmen are unable to cut us off from the channel that links the inlet with the sea, and our oarsmen heave the *karve* over the sandbar just as the water falls, The Northmen are trapped! Arrows follow us out, but fall harmlessly onto stern post and on the sandbar behind us. They must have been half-asleep when they saw us leave Bosanham.

'*Free!*' Braenda laughs out loudly and breathes in the salt air by the carved prow. I watch astern as the Northmen shake clenched fists and weapons at our fleeing stern and Wulfberht's crew unfurl the sail.

'There is something else leaving Portesmuth', Hemming calls loudly from the steerboard side amidships.

'Where, what -' Wulfberht stares. '*Where is it?*'

Hemming shows him, and Wulfberht breathes out,

'She is a trader's vessel, harmless to us, or to *anyone* for that matter!'

'That *is* cheering news!' Hemming knows little about ships, but then he has spent most of his life in East Seaxe or Middil seaxe. He and Saeward are useful, nevertheless, as lookouts.

We follow the seaway Ogmund used around the south of Wiht, putting in at the south-west of the isle where we overnighted on our way here. There is no call to risk bad luck by sailing under the

Northmen's noses around the north shore! No-one is about when we put in, hidden as we are by trees and bushes from the nearest homes.

11

'So *this* is the woman Braenda?' Rhiwallon clicks his tongue as he walks slowly around her, his own woman standing nearby scowling darkly.

'I *am* the woman Braenda', she answers tartly. 'Who might *you* be?'

His woman chokes, trying to keep herself from laughing out aloud that there is someone here who does not know him. She hurries away to find something to do, knowing Rhiwallon is in 'safe hands'.

'I am Rhiwallon', he answers, longing to woo her but upset by her put-down.

'I know now as much as I did before', Braenda smirks openly, making Rhiwallon squirm. I daresay he feels smaller still than he already does; cheerless.

'Rhiwallon is an *aetheling*, brother to Bleddyn ap Gruffyd', I tell her.

'I have heard of *him*', she answers, turning on her toes to follow Saeward to the hall.

I turn and shrug at Rhiwallon, who waves me away glibly and goes back to whatever it was he was doing when we entered the stronghold. Men and women stand staring at her as she passes. Do they know who she is, and has her name ever been on their tongues?

'There will be a feast', one of Bleddyn's household underlings tells me, 'in the name of Dewi Sant'.

'Who –'Hemming is about to ask 'who is that?' when Saeward hisses the answer in his ear. 'That *tickled*, fool!'

'Your name would be mud if it got out that you did not know who Dewi Sant was', Saeward tells him, holding in the itch to cuff him over the ears for calling him a fool. He also holds in the need to laugh.

We come to the hall, where we will stay for the short time it takes to toady to Bleddyn. I recall the last time he spoke to me was not friendly by any means.

Hopefully passing time has made him milder, although I do not hold out any hopes. He must know he has something I wish to take, namely my horse. He could make life awkward for me, unless he wishes to be rid of me quickly.

'You are back then, Dane?' Bleddyn comes by the doorway from the other side and bars the way with his right arm.

'Bleddyn, seeing you cheers me!' I lie, and he knows I am lying. His smile does not mean happiness at seeing me. His gaze lights on Braenda and the smile becomes a leer.

'This is the one you named your horse after?' He chortles, thinking

Braenda is unaware of the link.

'The horse is a fine mount', Braenda's answer takes the wind from his sail and he is left clearing his throat, trying to think of something else to put me – or her – down with. What she says next reddens him, 'As also am I - and I am well aware you would like to see how well I ride'.

Bleddyn splutters and turns away from her, not wishing to show his awkwardness. Braenda has to bite her bottom lip to stop her laughter. Hemming and Saeward both look fit to drop. Understanding their feelings, I would dearly love to be miles from here to laugh openly, freely. But we are here at Rhosgoch and only Braenda has the upper hand. They are afraid of her. If they ever learned of Rhonwen's doom they would be even more afraid.

'Ivar, I would say you wish for your horses to be given back to you', Bleddyn begins anew, 'yours and theirs'.

He looks at both Hemming and Saeward. They nod.

'Will Braenda ride with you?'

'I shall ride north with them', Braenda tells him, nodding. What she does not say is that she can come and go at will. She needs no horse to find her way around the kingdom. Telling him that would only make things worse for us, I think. He might even hand us over to the Northmen through a go-between. Earl Willelm would be deeply grateful to him after what Saeward and I have meted out on his kind. Hemming would be dealt with in another way, having merely left the king's host to come with us.

'Very well, I shall have a horse readied for you – *after* the feast. I will let you sit at my long table this once, and then we will take our farewells', Bleddyn smiles coldly. What is he up to?

When we are on our own again, the four of us, we talk over Bleddyn's wish to have us at their feast.

'He is trying to be friendly, whatever his feelings toward you, Ivar', Saeward tells me. Hemming shrugs.

Braenda looks from Saeward to Hemming and asks,

'What do *you* say?'

'It could be a trap', he agrees with me.

'On the other hand we should see it as a act of goodwill. He may wish to show kindness toward us before we are out into the wilds', he finishes.

'You may be right, yet on the other hand we must be on our guard. Bleddyn threatened Ivar the last time he was here, is that not so?'

'He did indeed', Saeward thinks back, 'because he thought Ivar had taken something from Hereford he thought should be his. I have it in my saddlebag still'.

'What is it?' Hemming wants to know, and Braenda looks hopefully at Saeward. He is willing enough to tell them after first looking to see if I think it warranted. On a nod from me he goes on,

'A scrap of calfskin from a small wooden chest that came was found with the help of a key found on the fat Frankish priest, Earnald who spoke for the Aetheling Eadgar at Lunden Brycg. The king does not know the Aenglish tongue, and needed a go-between. Earnald came forward. Afterward Theorvard plied him with drink at the 'Eel Trap' so that he did not run to Willelm to tell him what Eadgar had in store for him. We found Earnald on the road to Centland and thought he could listen in on the outlanders' talking amongst themselves. Earnald died first, on the road east and we took him on for burying somewhere away from prying eyes. A bear found his corpse before we could bury him'.

Hemming's jaw drops and Braenda grins when Saeward adds the gruesome ending,

'All there was left to plant were a few bones after the bear was done with him. It came for us, too, but someone else killed him with an arrow to the head'.

He tells them of the Centishmen who threatened us, and of their wyrd after we saw them being driven before Northman riders. Hemming's eyebrows rise and fall, Braenda looks at me and draws a soft hand around my bearded jaw, telling me,

'You have been sore-tested since we first met in Gwynedd, poor man'.

'Not as poor as some folk we came across, eh Saeward?' I answer truthfully. 'Many are the dead Seaxans and Centishmen Odo left behind him in a swathe across the southern shires. We met a number of them, one a fellow whose tongue had been torn out by the Northmen for answering back!'

Braenda cringes at the thought. Hemming stares bleakly at me. Thinking back on it, Saeward is bitter,

'Make no mistake, friend', he laughs hollowly. 'We sent *many* a Northman to his maker for the sins they wrought on this fair land!'

'So I should hope', Hemming's jaw tightens as he nods at Saeward. I think he may have something to add.

He may have something to say about the time he, Guthfrith and the others of Ansgar's household rode west with Willelm, about what the Northmen got up to on their long road west to Defna shire.

'We were riding through one hamlet when one of Willelm's crossbowmen brought down a hog. The ceorl whose creature it was ran, out from his dwelling to deal with the killer. He was bundled to the

175

muddy earth, his wife dragged out and raped before his eyes. Then they slew him, dumped his corpse into a mud pool and put a rope around the woman's neck to pull her behind them. Children inside the dwelling screamed as their home was set on fire, the woman screamed, fought with her tethers and was pulled off her feet. When they stopped to make camp not long after someone cut the rope and left her for dead by the roadside. We could say nothing –'

'You said nothing?' Braenda fumes at Hemming. Saeward says nothing, but stares sullenly at him – wishing, I wonder, that he had killed him *as well as* Guthfrith. Braenda snaps at me, 'Have you nothing to say, Ivar?'

'Saying anything would have brought down Willelm's wrath on Ansgar's men, but would have gained nothing. I know you both think of him as being craven, but think on this. He and his comrades were a small part of Willelm's host. Ansgar would have paid dearly along with them'.

'They would have seen what Aenglishmen thought!'

'And then *what?*'

I round on Braenda for the first time since I have known her and she is rightly taken aback. 'They would have been hanged there and then! They were on a war footing, and mutiny brings with it death in war. By not taking part in the deed they showed themselves better men. I do not know whether Willelm knew what had happened unless these men boasted of their dark deed'.

Braenda's mouth is clamped shut. She seethes, keeping her thoughts to herself. I will know soon what I have earned by my outburst. For the time being she bides her time.

The feast is noisy. Drunkenness and shamelessness abounds – and that is just Bleddyn and Rhiwallon! Much of the food goes to waste, being scoffed by the hall hounds. When the ale and mead runs low, men are sent out to bring more from neighbouring strongholds. In the morning there are men and women strewn around the hall, over bench and table, spent, bared from the waist down.

Neither Bleddyn nor Rhiwallon is to be seen, Braenda has gone and I can only think of finding the stable to take my horse.

'Best take a fourth horse', I say to Saeward before we leave.

He nods and one of the few household men still about brings a saddle. Hemming frowns, wondering why we should need a saddle for a horse that has no rider.

'It will look right', I tell him. 'No woman would ride a horse for such a long way without a saddle – would *you?*'

176

'Aye', Saeward is at one with me, 'it must look right, for her if nothing else. We may need to come back here'.

'I *hope* not!' I chortle at the thought of having to put up with Gruffyd's sons.

'You never can tell', Saeward smirks. 'I hope I never see those two, ever again, but they *might be* needed again one day!'

'You know what they say, you cannot pick your kin, but you can your friends', Hemming swings himself into the saddle and digs his knees into his horse's flanks.

It feels good to be back with Braenda my horse, and she trots on as ever before when I click my tongue. Saeward follows on with the fourth horse in tow. Men on watch pull open the gate for us and stare after us as we take the road north. It will soon be summer, the trees and flowers put on a show in blossom and the lambs are already grazing away from their mothers.

Somewhere on the western side of Scrobbe shire, clouds gather to the west and night is on its way from the east. A last glimmer of the reddening sun finds its way through the trees to our left... and we are a long way from anywhere.

'What are we doing for somewhere to rest this night?' Hemming asks from behind. He and Saeward have been riding side by side these past miles, 'Braenda's mount' trotting behind Saeward on a long rope. They have left me to my own thoughts and I am thankful for that.

Braenda, 'my woman', left suddenly without saying anything to me, without bidding us farewell. I miss her again, sorely, but I must think of the now.

'Look for lights', I tell them.

'Would they be to the east or to the west of us?' Saeward calls out.

'More likely to the east', I answer. 'We must be somewhere near where Scrobbe shire meets Ceaster shire. These will be Eadwin's lands'.

'Is that Eadwin the earl of Mierca?' Hemming asks, whether from idle nosiness or a wish to glean knowledge I could not say. He should have an answer,

'He is the same', I nod, looking over one shoulder.

'Not much of an earl, if you ask me', Saeward sniffs loudly. 'I would say he will be earl only until Willelm finds one of his own to fill his shoes'.

'That could be soon', I would say not before time, but I keep that to myself. It is not for me to say who is worthy, and I would sooner an Aenglishman held the earldom than a Northman or any other of

Willelm's underlings.

'Will they be is Ceaster, he and Morkere?' Hemming asks. Again he asks from a need to know.

'Who can tell where they are?' I throw up my hands. 'Who can even tell where *we* are, for that matter?'

'You are in Ceaster shire', says someone from the shelter of the trees to our right.

Being ahead of us, Hemming drags the reins of his horse around to see where the man is. Saeward stares into the half-darkness, I think I see whoever it is leaning back against an ash tree. This still being the fore-year, many of the trees here have still not gained all their leaves, a dying daylight shaft of light almost points to him.

'Look this way, my friends', the fellow calls out to Hemming and Saeward. He then says to me, 'You can see me, am I right, Ivar Ulfsson?'

'It is Eirik!' Saeward whoops.

'*Quiet*, there may be those around who do not wish us well!' Eirik waves him down. 'Get down off your horses and come here'.

We do his bidding, and lead our mounts to the trees.

'Look down there', Eirik tells us.

There is a gap in the trees through which we can see a score, at least, of Northman horsemen below us. Some are mounted, most are on their feet, helms in their hands, watching something. What they are watching is out of sight behind the wall of chain mail and leather.

'Would you say we could scatter and rout them if we took them unawares?' Saeward asks.

'I think a *score* is a few too many', I answer.

'Could we get *closer* –'Saeward offers.

'*Still* too many', I say. 'There are as many mounted as we are, we have no bowmen and their mounted men have lances'.

'We *have* a bowman', I hear someone say close by.

'Oh, I forgot to tell you, Theodolf came away from Rhosgoch with me when your Northanhymbran friends went home', Eirik says off-handedly.

Theodolf walks into what light there is left.

Our getting-together might be merry later, when we have dealt with the Northmen, if we are still able to lift a cup of ale.

'There are six of us now', I grin at Theodolf and hug him. Eirik is happier, now we are at one about taking on the horsemen below and I can Saeward already looks forward to the fray.

We must think quickly about we hope to pull off, lest whatever finishes below before we can make our attack, and we go our ways through the trees. Theodolf will use several arrows on those horsemen still mounted before we tear through them and send them scurrying for dear life! Whilst Eirik, Saeward and Theodolf will ride one way into their number once most of the horsemen have been laid out, Hemming and I will come the other way at them.

All the way down through the trees Hemming and I guide our own mounts away from broken branches that litter the track. None of us makes a sound and we come to the clearing. To our right I see the flash of an axe blade in the moonlight. This is our time!

We wait until Theodolf unleashes his arrows, three finding their mark straight away. One man ducks one arrow, the back of his neck catching the next. There is only one man left mounted, who wheels his horse around to see who has taken them on. Saeward's thrown axe pushes the man back over his saddle, and even if the axe did not kill him, the sickening crack of his backbone against the raised back of his saddle would.

'On your right –'Saeward warns. I duck as a crossbow is aimed at me, and Hemming brings his sword across the Northman's shoulder from behind.

'*I owe you both!*' I yell as I bring my axe in an upward cut on the midriff of one of their riders trying to mount beside me. He was the one I had aimed for when Saeward warned me. Seeing me duck his comrade's aim must have led him to think he was safe.

There are only seven left standing after our first rush. Theodolf has cut others down with a lance he uprooted, the pennon now deep red with the blood of a few more of Willelm fitzOsbern's horsemen. They stubbornly fight their corner, three back-to-back with their sword arms flailing at each of us. Before long, being the only ones alive, they throw their weapons one by one to the ground in a heap and raise their arms to show they yield.

'What will you do with us?' one asks in halting Aenglish.

'What were you *doing* here – what was it that held you all so rapt that you did not hear or see us coming?' I ask.

The one who asked me what was to happen to him and his comrades shrugs. He looks to the others to tell him, then turns and tells me,

'I think the ones who were rapt, as you say, are now dead', he tells me. I think not.

I think whoever they were watching is still very much alive and close by. The three shrug in turn when prodded with swords, and raise their arms when Saeward tips their elbows with the flat of his axe – now pulled from the rider it cut down so quickly. They do not waver to throw up their hands when he glares at them. They must have seen the way his axe hurtled, spinning through the evening air.

We do not have to wait long to learn what it was they would not own up to watching. A muffled scream comes from the darkness of the bushes. Our three Northmen make a start for their horses when they think our eyes are no longer on them. Eirik trips one with his right boot, sending him cart wheeling into Saeward's blade point. The other two stand stock still, looking sullenly down at him. If he is the only one who knew the Aenglish tongue, then now what?

'Tie them together by their hands', I tell Eirik. 'They cannot mount a horse that way'.

'I can tie them to this stout sapling', he offers, one hand on a young oak beside him.

'Very well, do that. Theodolf aim an arrow at this one', I kick one of them in the backside, 'whilst Eirik binds them'.

That done, leaving Theodolf threatening these two with his bow, the other three and I stride toward where the trees are bunched together.

Before we come amongst the trees, Hemming leaves us to turn left into the bushes. Eirik, Saeward and I walk on. Whimpering draws us to an ash tree, where a young woman in a white shift shivers in the clutches of an ugly wretch in black leather. With her shielding him, the wretch watches as we close on him, a dagger blade in his right hand held against her bosom. His left hand has the maid's wrist gripped tight across her full belly. She is plainly with child. Where has she been brought here from, where the nearest dwellings seem at least a mile or so away?

The wretch is afraid. His threat to kill her is empty. If she dies he will not live long if caught. He cannot flee, as the only way he has of reaching his horse is through us. We close on him and the maid wails to us to stay away,

'Oh God in Heaven, do you *want* me to die?'

'He will not kill you. Has he hurt you at all?' I ask, still closing on them. The wretch presses his blade on her, draws blood and she squeals for pity and tries to wrest herself away from his grip. In doing so she bites his hand and he roars like some underworld demon, cuffs her across her forehead and she falls to the ground.

The wretch is unaware of Hemming behind him as he reaches down to drag the maid to her feet. Before he can reach her Hemming's right hand comes up under his chin, his jaw in the grip of a well-taught huscarl. His cry of strangulation frightens away nesting birds, and then his neck is broken in an echoing crack.

The corpse is left to drop onto a rain-dampened bed of last year's mottled brown leaves, onto his hostage. The maid screeches fitfully when the head falls into her lap and Saeward lifts her clear. He stands her on her feet and gives her a stern ticking-off,

'Your screeching makes me flinch, young woman! Be quiet before *I* give you something to scream about!'

When we come back to our horses Theodolf is on his knees, clutching his stomach. The two Northmen look on, worried.

'What is amiss, Theodolf?' Saeward kneels beside him. 'They have not harmed you, have they?'

'No, Saeward. Neither of them has hurt me. There was another of them close by. I did not see him come and I put up a hard fight before he drove in his blade. He ran as you came back. Their comrades will be here soon, I am afraid!'

Saeward looks at the deep wound in Theodolf's belly. To me it seems the outlander shoved in the blade and drew it upward. There is blood everywhere and Saeward hastens to the pack on his saddle, from which he pulls a long cloth strip and wool. Blue spirit is poured freely onto the wool and pressed onto the wound, bringing forth first a loud roar and then groans.

The cloth is wound around Theodolf's waist, the end torn in two to tie around him and tied tightly, bringing a hiss through clenched teeth and a long groan.

'Will he be able to *ride?*' Eirik asks, eyes wide open at what he has witnessed.

'He has done before, and hopefully this time will not have to do so long. Are we far from a hospitium?' Saeward asks Eirik.

'A *hospitium*', Saeward snaps, 'where his wound can be tended hopefully by a monk who knows what he is doing'.

'There is an abbey nearby, where I work in the kitchens', the young woman steps forward to tell Saeward.

'Have they a hospitium there?' Saeward looks down at the slight creature. Her eyes are reddened from weeping, and she holds her own belly in fear of losing the child.

'They have, Lord'.

Saeward grins broadly and ruffles her hair, telling her,

'I am no lord, child. I am the same as you – or was, until this one came along and led me into the warmongering I do now', he elbows me.

'You *love* the life!' I laugh, and he pushes me away.

Hemming laughs hoarsely and adds,

'I daresay he does not know which world he wishes to be in, that of killing *or* healing!'

'I daresay I have been thrown into both worlds, *head-first!*' Saeward answers grumpily.

'*And* you love it!' Hemming echoes my words.

'I *must* love it, to put up with the likes of you and him', Saeward rumbles and thumps me in the chest again.

'Meanwhile, if the wench would like to show us the way to this nunnery', I grin at Saeward, to be upbraided by the maid.

'*I am no wench!*' she screeches up into my left ear and begins pummelling my chest.

'Very well, you are no wench', I wriggle a finger in my ear to restore my hearing and tell Eirik to put her on his saddle.

'My name is Eadburga!'

'Very well', I snap, 'Eirik put Eadburga onto your saddle and we will follow you'.

Saeward has to ride beside Theodolf to keep him in his saddle. Our young friend has lost a lot of blood and might very well fall asleep riding.

'The nunnery is in the dale below', Eadburga tells Eirik, pointing to way.

We take the track after Eirik. Hemming and I are the only ones who would be able to fight off any attackers.

I ask Eadburga if there are many Northmen about.

'*Northmen* – what are *they?*' she turns to look up at Eirik behind her.

'He means outlanders', Eirik answers and she looks back at me over one shoulder.

'These outlanders were the first I have seen. I was told there are many of them in Scrobbe shire. They must have come from there', Eadburga tells me loudly.

'*Shh*, child - not so loud, or you will bring more onto our heads!' I tell her, looking over my shoulder at Hemming. He in turn looks over one shoulder 'There may be some of them on their way already after that one fled'.

'None behind yet', Hemming tells me after pressing his horse on to catch up.

'I take nothing for granted. Do you think there could be only this score of them in the shire?' I shudder to think that the whole dale might ring with their shouts as they scour the woods for us. 'How is Theodolf, Saeward?'

'He will live', I hear my friend give his word. 'There is blood on his dressing, but he will not bleed to death'.

We ride on through the night in stillness with only the footfalls of our mounts and from time to time their snorts to be heard.

On reaching Eadburga's nunnery late in the evening, a fuss is made of Theodolf as he is taken to a bed, but we cannot stay. They abbey is the home of *nuns*. I think many years have passed since men and women were allowed under the same roof here. A crusty old abbess looks scornfully up at me when I ask for beds for the night for Saeward, Eirik, Hemming and myself.

'You should stay at the inn, if you are so worried about your young friend', she waggles a finger at me. 'I am sorry, but that is how it must be. I know I should be thankful that you helped Eadburga, but I will send her to show you the way from our gate'.

'How was it she was taken by the Northmen?' I ask, wondering whether she had the abbess to thank for being taken by them.

'Eadburga has the freedom to look after her widowed mother near the inn', she answers, unworried that the maid might fall into the wrong hands on her way there or back. .

It is not for me to fret over her. Eadburga is the abbey's ward, after all. We have brought her to safety and that is the end of that, I know. Eadburga sees us to the gate and lets us know how we find the inn. I nod, look down and she is gone, back into the darkness of the abbey.

'There is nothing for it then, but to find this inn', Eirik sighs as he mounts first, easing himself into his saddle, shuffling his backside around to find the best way of sitting for these – hopefully – last few miles.

'At least we know Theodolf is in good hands', I heave my aching body into my saddle and the other two follow suit. Saeward groans. I cackle, 'What have you to moan about? You are not the one who had an arrow in his rump, are you?'

'What is this about an arrow in your arse?' Eirik laughs out and turns his horse about.

'In short, we went to spy on the Northmen around the walls of Exanceaster. On being hoisted back over the wall one of Willelm's bowmen sent a keepsake after me. Saeward tended to my wound, and I was in the care of the abbess of a small nunnery near the burh's walls but even now I feel the aftermath', I finish, nudging Braenda into a walk.

Eirik says nothing, but looks past me at Saeward and flashes a smile. We press our mounts into a trot and soon find ourselves in the nearby hamlet.

'Do you know this god-forsaken rat-hole?' Hemming asks Eirik. '*Is* there an inn?'

'The old woman said there is, and Eadburga told us the way. Why would they lie?'

Eirik reins in and waits for an old fellow to come level with him before asking,

'We have been told there is an inn –'

'Down on the left there', the fellow does not wait for Eirik to finish. He raises a hand to show us, keeping hold of a gnarled walking stick with the other.

We ride on, Eirik still to the fore, and alight at what might be an inn. He bangs on the door and someone within rasps,

'Who is that at *this* time? *Go away!*'

'We need shelter for a night or two', Eirik tries again.

'Sleep in the woods and come back in the morning!' comes the answer.

Tired from the long day's ride and angered by the abbess, Saeward snarls,

'If you do not open this door I shall kick it off its hinges. I shall give you to five –'

'*Dimwit* –', someone yells back from within, 'do not think *I* am shivering in fear!'

'Right then – *five!*' Saeward takes a step back brings a boot up, ready to kick when the door creaks open. He has to be held from falling backward by Hemming, who pushes him forward and growls,

'We are *in*, go ahead and see what this innkeeper says to us now'.

Past the threshold, we look around within. Only one rush light burns near a stairway, showing benches and boards but no one about. I turn in the doorway and push the door to. Only then do I see someone with what looks to be a club, ready to bring it down onto my head.

'*Ivar* –'

I do not need the warning from Hemming, having already sensed the fellow attack me. In sidestepping my attacker I put out my left leg and catch him as he trips, my right hand grasping his. His wrist seems thin for a man who could shout so loudly and as he flails, trying to stay on his feet, he falls against Saeward.

'The fool is drunk on his own ale!' Saeward takes hold of the fellow's shoulders to steady him and Eirik takes the rush light from its socket on the wall to see what ails with the innkeeper.

'What is it with you, master innkeeper? Do you not wish to fill your pockets with our silver?' I ask, trying to stop the fellow thumping me hard on my chest. What I see takes me aback, 'Wait – this is no *man!*'

'Hold still woman, what do you think you are doing?' Saeward grips her wrists so hard she shuts her eyes in pain. He lets go of her and she stands sobbing, rubbing her reddened wrists.

'*Beast* – what are you?!' She whimpers.

'Where is the innkeeper?' I ask. She bursts into tears and sobs fitfully. I cannot wait until she calms down and take hold of her shoulders, 'Take a hold of yourself, woman! What is there that is *wrong* here? We need beds for a night or two, *is that too much to ask?*'

She sniffs and blows her nose on her apron before looking up at Saeward to tell him,

'You will have to find your own beds, do what you will to find food and ale'.

Saeward turns her to look up at me and tells her,

'That man there, Ivar, is who you should speak to'.

She looks up at me, bewildered and wild-eyed, and throws up her arms,

'What do I care who you want me to speak to. Find your beds, find your food and *leave me be!*' These last few words are sobbed, rather than spoken.

'What is your name, child?' I ask, putting my hands on her shoulders to calm her, but she shakes me off again.

'I am not a *child!* I am a *woman*, wife of the innkeeper!' she howls and runs into the darkness, thumping against benches in a bid to flee us.

'Best leave her be', Saeward turns me by one elbow toward him and the others.

'Aye', Hemming grunts.

'She has as good as told us we can do what we want. All we have to do is *find* the food and drink'.   .

'I could eat a horse', Eirik laughs.

'We may well have to if we can find nothing else to eat', Hemming tells him. 'Stop moaning or we shall start with yours!'

'You would never –'

'*Try me*', Hemming squares up to him.

We all laugh, Eirik as loudly as Hemming, but I am not sure Hemming's words were mere banter. I have a feeling Eirik is *not* willing to try him. Each of us pokes around in corners, lifts bags, scours and roots through the kitchen. Rush lights do not last long, and we have gone through all of those we found at the front of the inn, when Saeward laughs at finding what looks to be a hidden store at the back of the kitchen floor.

Hemming and Eirik take their time reaching Saeward, whilst I look further.

Eirik looks down at the bags of food Saeward has unearthed and quips,

'All we need now is something to drink with this food'.

'The bread is stale', is all Hemming says drily at the sight of the baked goods that Saeward has brought forth.

'Is there any meat', I ask, 'or fruit?'

'Where would we find fruit - at *this* time of year?' Saeward looks up from his find.

'Are there any barrels of apples at the back of the inn?' I ask. 'Sometimes innkeepers also pickle plums for passing trade'.

'*You* thought of it, you look', Hemming tells me flatly.

'Anyone else -' Heads are down, searching through the bags, so I go looking for a back door. I am in luck. There *is* a door that leads onto a patch of land on which a sty is sited by trees. Closer to the back of the inn a goat lies beside a hen house, safe from foxes. The goat looks up at me and struggles to its feet whilst I search on around the back of the main building for what might be a barrel or store of apples. The goat, being tethered to a stake, strains to follow me but yields to fate and wanders back to where it lay before I woke it.

Kicking barrels tells me they are empty, until the last one thuds at my kick. Is there some way I can prise off the lid? There is an iron bar with a thin wedge at its head, which when pushed down rewards me with a creak and the lid drops onto the earth. Within are indeed small russet apples that have not rotted over winter, and I pull out a couple of fistfuls of the fruit to show the others.

Back inside the inn, I look about in the stillness. No-one stirs. It is as if I had been the only one to come this way. A short walk back through the inn, as still as death, tells me there is something wrong.

'Where *is* everyone?' I call out loudly. 'I have *apples!*'

Someone tells me from behind,

'You have apples, we have your friends!'

My hand goes to my sword before I turn, but men come from the darkness on either side of me and grip my arms before my sword can be pulled free of its sheath. *Where* did I leave my axe?

'Tell me your name, and I will tell you who I am', the fellow has men bring rush lights, and the young innkeeper's wife.

'Where are my friends?' I ask. My tone does not seem to go down well with him and one of his men cuffs me across the back of my head with a mailed hand.

'I shall do the asking for the time being', the man speaks the Aenglish tongue well, yet he is plainly an outlander, not a Northman. 'Again, what is your name? Do not forget, we hold your friends and if you do not behave yourself they might suffer'.

'I am Ivar', I tell him.

'Ivar – is that all, nothing else?' he tests, and beckons one of his other men forward.

He tells his underling something in a tongue I do not know, and turns back to me,

'Well, Ivar, can you tell me about yourself – what are you doing here?'

'My friends and I were on our way to Ceaster, to seek Earl Eadmund', is all I will offer, and it is a lie. I do not think he is anywhere near Ceaster, but more likely further north in Northanhymbra or with King Maelcolm. He thinks about this, looks down at the floor, kicks at a bench and knocks it against a table leg, and looks back up at me. The bench leans against the table and the outlander kicks away at a bench leg, sending the whole thing clattering to the stone floor.

The outlander's men bring in Saeward, bound and looking wretched. He is pushed to the middle of the floor to look at me and told to kneel. Still standing stubbornly, Saeward is kicked in the back of his leg and drops to his knees.

'Your friend here', the outlander speaks to Saeward, 'tells me you are here to look for an earl. What did *you* tell me?'

Saeward says nothing and one of the nobleman's underlings kicks his back, pushing him, helpless, to the floor.

'What did you *tell* me?'

Saeward is dragged up onto his knees by two of the outlanders and thumped on the jaw.

He looks a mess, with straw and dirt down his front, bloodied and sullen. He also has dark red and blue rims under his eyes from being hit.

Feeling sorry for him, I tell Saeward,

'For your own sake, tell this fellow what you told him before. It cannot harm'

Saeward smarts from the wounds meted out to him. He fixes me with his good eye and turns to the outlander. Jerking his head brings the nobleman forward, hoping to hear something whispered. Saeward head-butts him, and sends him reeling back against the upturned bench to fall backwards over it.

Three of the outlanders rush at Saeward, who rises to his feet and elbows the first in his stomach. A second comes close to me and I stretch out one leg to trip him. He lands sideways onto his lord and the third outlander stops still beside his lord to keep him from harm – or else he is wary of the East Seaxan and will not close on him. His lord is still on the floor, unable to rise, nursing his brow with both hands.

The innkeeper's wife pulls a dagger from its sheath on the belt of one of the fallen outlanders, and cuts Saeward's bindings before coming to me Saeward wrings his wrists to get the blood flowing again. I rub my wrists and slide the sword from the scabbard of the nearest of the outlanders.

The last outlander looks fearfully at us both and down at his lord. He bolts, straight onto the blade the innkeeper's wife holds in front of her. She does not know what she has done and shivers with fright at the sight of the young outlander clutching his stomach. The thump of mailed feet outside the room tells me there is at least one more of the outlanders and wave Saeward to stand behind the door. I wave the woman away from me after taking the knife from her, and push the young outlander to the floor behind the table.

In the poorly lit room, no-one can see the nobleman on the floor from the door. He is still unable to say anything, cannot even moan after being head-butted by a man with the skull of a bull! The thumping stops and whoever it is raps on the door. Luckily the man does not wait to be told to enter and pushes the door open. He sees me standing with my hands behind me, as if still bound, looks from left to right, still in the doorway with the door almost wide open. The man is about to step through when Saeward slams the door onto him, throwing him back. More thumping is heard beyond the door and Saeward opens it again to see what has become of the outlander.

Framed by the door, I see Saeward lift him with both hands and dash his head on the door frame. I am the first to say anything after all this time,

'Where are the other two?'

'Hemming is in the next room', he shows with his right thumb.

'What about Eirik – where is *he?*' I am beginning to wonder. Was our friend waiting for us, and if so how did he know we were on our way north? It did seem odd that he should be at the trackside and knew it was us passing in the light of the setting sun.

'I thought he followed you out, at least that was how it seemed', Saeward scratches his beard and then smoothes it, thinking hard.

'We must go and free Hemming and ride away, back to the abbey'. I am at a loss. After riding north with us and Harding, riding back and fighting by our side against Earl Willelm and Hrothgar de Montgomerie, has he gone over to them? As unlikely as it sounds, I still have to think of the likelihood. Should we stumble upon him again, there will be some earnest talking ahead.

'I do not know about you, but I am tired... and hungry! Hemming will be, too, I daresay', Saeward growls.

I have to own up to him,

'I am at a loss'.

'You cannot know everything, all the time', Saeward walks over to the groaning outlander whose head he drove into the door frame and looks down at him. The look he then gives me seems to ask, 'Shall I finish him off?' At a nod from me he draws the fellow's sword and thrusts it into his stomach.

All I hear is a deep sigh and then all is still again.

'What about the others, the noble and his three dimwits?' Saeward asks.

'We can slit their gizzards, but these folk here in the hamlet will have to pay. I recall being told it was something called a Murdrum fine'.

'Too late, I would say! I have already killed him', Saeward kicks the man's feet and pulls out the wickedly long blade from one of the benches that their lord must have rammed in before I came back into the inn. He had not had the time to claim it back before wrong-siding Saeward.

When I tell him,

'Very well then, finish them off', it seems a weight has been lifted from his shoulders and whilst I free Hemming, he sets about ridding the kingdom of a few more unwanted foes.

'Wait', I tell him as he hovers over the nobleman, axe at the ready. 'Not that one'.

'Why do we want hostages? Think on when you and Harding had the two Northmen –'Saeward sounds let down.

'That was Harding trying to show them he was a great fighter', I tell him. 'When this one has outlived his usefulness you can have him'.

Saeward smiles thinly and quips,

'That was Harding letting them know that they were that much brighter they were than he. Shall I bind him, then? Otherwise he will only bring us woes'.

'Go ahead', I nod.

Hemming grunts,

'I would like to know what Eirik is doing right now –'

'What *should* I be doing?' Eirik asks from the doorway out to the road – such as it is.

Hemming makes a start towards him, his right fist balled, ready to fell Eirik. But before he can reach Eirik I stand in his way.

'*Let me teach him a lesson!*' Hemming bawls.

'Teach me a lesson – *what in?*' Eirik is nonplussed.

'Hemming – and indeed so do we *all three* – believes you brought these outlanders here', I tell the baffled Eirik.

'*Which* outlanders did I bring here?' Eirik is ready to push me aside

189

and set to with Hemming.

'The ones in the other room, on the floor', Hemming scowls darkly and steps aside, his fist still balled. 'See for yourself'.

Eirik passes an angry Hemming, looks over his shoulder lest he be taken unawares and strides slowly forward. He side-steps Saeward with his axe, and looks about on the floor.

'Who *are* they?'

'We thought you would know', Saeward shrugs, takes his axe in one hand and brings it down on the outlander who kicked him in the back of his legs. He lets go of the weapon, spits on his hands and wrenches the axe out of the man's backbone. 'He will bother no-one else'.

'Are you killing them all?' Eirik asks Saeward.

'Not the nobleman', Saeward answers, snorting.

'He wants to know from him who told him we are here', Hemming grins, his right hand now open, tapping the seam on one leg of his breeks.

'*I* could tell you the answer to that!' Eirik snaps back.

'Oh, and who would *that* be?' Hemming squares himself up to look Eirik in the eyes.

'We all did, when we let that youngster ride free!' Eirik thumps the door frame, bringing dust and cobwebs down onto his shoulders. Saeward laughs out and bends to bind the outlander nobleman's hands.

'*Go on*, think back on it. When Theodolf was wounded there was a young fellow there, ready to meet his maker and we turned our backs on him. Some fools we were, to miss him. If I had been closer, I would have brought him down!'

'Are we now straight on that?' I ask Hemming.

'But how would he know where to come?' Hemming is still unmoved.

'*He* is not with them. *This* one', Eirik kicks the nobleman's feet, 'would have gone to the nunnery and asked there. You do not need to be a wise man to know the rest'.

'Hopefully Theodolf is safe with the nuns', I steer the talking away from our mistake – *my* mistake. Am I getting too old for this life? There may be years before this is all behind us.

I owe Theodolf much, and now he is wounded – again. It is for me to ensure he does not fall into the hands of Willelm fitzOsbern or the like. He would never live a day locked up by them, and I could never again look Aethel in the eye. I know she is not of his blood, but she raised him together with Hrothulf in her home. She was distraught when Theodolf told his father about her once being Copsig's lover, not because she wanted to keep it from Hrothulf – although she knew he would be hurt knowing that - but because she saw Theodolf as her son, now her own had been killed by the Norsemen at Skarthiburh.

12

'When he wakes', I tell Saeward, pointing down at the nobleman, 'I want to speak to him'.

He nods and kicks the now bound outlander's backside. The man stirs, shakes his head and looks up at Saeward.

'Give me some water'.

'I am no man's thrall', Saeward answers. 'If you want water, being the nobleman you are, you should know how to ask'.

'Can I have some water?' the nobleman asks hoarsely. 'My throat is burning!'

Saeward looks about the room. Although outside the darkness is being chased away by the grey fingers of dawn, in here we still need rush lights. I look around me for unlit rushes and find a bundle, take it to a lit one and hold up the burning light at arm's length.

'Ah –'I see something in one corner that looks like a water butt and look inside. It is half-full of cold water and a ladle hangs on its edge under the back of the loosely-fitting lid. A scoop should be enough for what he needs. I tell Eirik, 'Sit him up'.

Propped against the upturned bench, the nobleman takes a draught of water and gargles, then spits it out on the floor, over Hemming's left boot. Hemming growls like a hall hound.

'I am sorry!' the outlander snivels, looking up at me instead of Hemming. He then smiles, why I cannot fathom. I scowl back at him and he looks away. With a besom shaft, Eirik turns the fellow's head up to look at me.

'If you like, we can begin where we left off', I tell him.

'I know *your* name, Ivar Ulfsson', he smirks.

'Ah, but I do not know yours, do I?' I smile. He smiles back, thinking I will be easy on him, so I bend low and clip his ear as I would an unruly child. 'So what do I do to hear what I want to know? Will you give me an answer, or do I have to squeeze it from you, like a blackhead?'

'What is a blackhead?' he asks, frowning.

Hemming coughs and enlightens the outlander,

'It is a worm with a black head that lives in men's dirt-ridden skin, like your kind'.

'Well, what do you call yourself?' I ask again.

'As a nobleman of the king, I should be freed from my bindings before I answer', he smirks again. He will be a poor learner.

'As a nobleman of this bastard you call a king, you will answer him', Saeward cuffs the nobleman across his right ear and we stand back to await the answer.

'When we catch you –'he begins.

He is almost throttled by Hemming, who tells him only,

'*Wrong answer*, my friend – what is your name? Answer, *or else*', a dagger blade is brought forward sharply, and almost slits one of the nobleman's nostrils.

'I am –'he holds back and Hemming snarls into his ear.

'You are... *who?*' I smile bleakly, knowing I have two friends eager to part this fellow from his life, and I will be no wiser about who my foe is, where he has come from and what he is doing this far north from Scrobbe shire. I know Hrothgar de Montgomerie has a stronghold close to Scrobbesbyrig, and that his overlord Willelm fitzOsbern has one of his strongholds at Hereford. I also know of the Bretlander Breon in Defna, but which others there are this side of Lunden might be useful, if not to me then others who wish to fight the outlanders.

'I am Hubert de Mesnil', he licks his lips, 'and I am thirsty again. Can I have more water?'

'You want to wash away the bad taste?' I laugh.

'We all have to say things we would sooner not', Saeward grins and carefully draws the blade of his axe across a blood-soaked white rag torn from a dead outlander's shirt. Our friend Hubert sees the rag and starts back. Saeward sees his mouth downturned and looks up at Hemming, telling him, 'Show him that rag *you* have'.

'You mean *this* thing?' Hemming glares into Hubert's eyes, 'It was taken from the undershirt of one of your men. I found him not far from here, shitting his dear life away. Standing over him I could smell his fear – rank, it was. *Where* do you get these children from? You cannot call them men. The aetheling Eadgar is more of a man, even for his lack of years, and he led the Middil Seaxe *fyrd* together with Lord Ansgar at Lunden Brycg! Do you know what happened there, friend Hubert, in Suthgeweorce? I will be willing to bet you were not told by your beloved king!'

The nobleman can find no answer. Now *I* need another one from him, now that Hemming has loosened his tongue a little with his threats,

'Where have you come from, Hubert?' I ask

'I am from the Cotentin –'Hubert begins.

My long sigh should let him know I am not happy with him. I ask again, using other words,

'I mean, where have you come from *here,* in *this* kingdom – how far away did you begin your day?'

'I came from not far to the south here, from somewhere called

Haordine', Hubert tells me, looking sideward at Hemming with his dagger. He shrugs when we look blankly at him.

'*Hawardene* is in Clwyd', Eirik butts in, 'on Bleddyn's lands. I wonder, does he know these outlanders are there?'

'You are wrong, are you not?' Hemming snarls, his eyes glint at the thought of seeing the Northman into the afterlife.

'Hawardene is in Wealas, you know that?' I ask Hubert.

He throws up his hands and groans,

'Of course, you are right and I know nothing. I am the outlander - is that your word?'

'Not knowing any other word for it, I have to agree you are an outlander. As far as I know, Northmandige is no part of this kingdom', I tell him.

'For once it is you who is wrong!' Hubert risks his life this way, quicker than he could bargain for, 'The Northmandige *is* part of this kingdom – *now!*'

'*How is that?*' Saeward is on his feet now, ready with axe in hand to do my bidding.

'Your king is our *duc!*' Hubert almost spits.

'Saeward, sit down and let him finish!' I tell my friend, who is ready to gut the outlander like a fish.

'Aye, *then* you can finish him', Hemming drools and Hubert pushes back at the bench.

'*This man is mad!*' Hubert's fear overcomes him and he pushes the bench back toward the table. 'I am telling you what you should know and you let this madman *dribble* over me!'

'There are some things I need to know, and others I do *not*', I smile. 'You keep telling me useless things'.

'Hearing you babbling about '*our king*' and your '*duc*' does not help', Eirik hunches beside Hubert across from Hemming. 'Tell me, do you know the lord who owns the stronghold at Hawardene?'

'You mean the *Comte* Hugo?'

'No I do not mean him, whoever he is!' Eirik stands again and I try my luck with Hubert.

'Have you seen or heard of either Bleddyn or Rhiwallon, the sons of Gruffyd?'

He stares at me and it is my turn to shrug.

'Take him outside and finish with him', I tell Saeward, before turning to my Danelaw friend, 'Eirik I need to know something about the lie of the land from you'.

'What is it you need to know, Ivar?' Eirik passes behind Hemming and Saeward as they manhandle Hubert de Mesnil to his feet. The

Northman shivers, no longer the masterful lord I met earlier when I came back into the inn.

'Which way is Ceaster from here?' I ask, to the din of Hemming and Saeward scuffling with the Northman between the benches. He keeps trying to dig his heels in on upturned flagstones to hold back the two East Seaxans from their task. I wait until he is taken outside before telling Eirik to go on, but before he is pushed and dragged through the open door he yells out,

'I can get you through our lines!'

What does he mean by '*our lines*'?'

'Do not listen to him, Ivar. He is only trying to save his own skin', Saeward grunts as he pushes Hubert through the doorway.

'Wait. *Stop there*, I have had a thought. When he tells me what he is talking about you can gag him. What do you mean by '*our lines*', Hubert?' .

'There are men from the Northmandige, men from Bretagne and men from Flanders all around here, almost to Ceaster', Hubert smirks, thinking he is safe for now.

He does not know Hemming or Saeward.

'Is that likely?' I ask Eirik.

He answers with raised eyebrows, 'Who knows?' Before I look back to the Northman Eirik feels he has to add,

'I have been in Wealas until of late. The first I saw of this shire was the day before you showed'.

'You say you can get us through your *lines*, whatever that means', I begin. 'Think on this, however. My friends here are keen to see you back to your maker. You may *try* to cheat them, but you will not cheat your *wyrd*'

'What is that, *my weird?*' Thinking to belittle us, Hubert smiles, I think too cock-sure. We shall see.

I merely smile back and tell him,

'We live and learn. Fear not, you will know soon enough'.

The Northman's smile freezes and turns into a sort of leer when Hemming grins toothily and runs his dagger up and down his mailed sleeve to sharpen the blade.

'Your turn to learn your *wyrd* will come soon. Just think, before you die you will have at least learned one new word of our tongue', Saeward tells him. 'Never let it be said we let our foes leave this world without at least *some* new wisdom'.

Hubert is no longer so cock-sure of himself when he pushed down hard onto the now righted bench and gagged. Bound and unable to speak for now, he can only watch as I share out the apples and ale to wash them down with before we ride on. I think the innkeeper's wife will be glad to see our backs. She mopes about in the dark, mopping up the mess of blood, not looking at any of us.

Not long later I pick up my leather gloves, my sword belt, axe and helm. The others do likewise and follow out to our horses. Saeward has a thought,

'When we rode into Hrofesceaster you wore Northman war gear and I a Benedictine brother's robe. I still have that robe in my pack. You can ride as Northmen, with *their* lances and shields, and then throw them away when we are safe, far away from their crossbowmen. We can leave *him* for the wolves', when he says this last Hubert looks wide-eyed at me, as if pleading.

I have a fleeting thought, but if I am wrong about it this Northman can easily point me out if we have to come this way again. He is best dead but for now he is a tool, a weapon against his own kind.

After going back to the abbey to ask after Theodolf's wellbeing, and on being told he is as well as he can be, we ride north through the woods toward Earl Eadmund's home burh. Happy at knowing our young friend is well, this leaves us with no worries.

Between the tall beeches are bushes, thickets through which I can barely see. It would seem, from looking around, that we are the only souls here. Or are we? Why is it I feel we are being followed?

'Would you say something is afoot?' I ask the others.

'How do you mean?' Hemming answers from behind.

He has our guest Hubert, riding alongside, safely bound by his hands to the pommel of his saddle. His legs are bound together beneath his tall horse's belly.

I see a shadow, a man on horseback flitting between the trees to our right.

'He has been there, keeping up with us ever since we left the inn', Saeward tells me. 'I should have said earlier, but I think we might put on a burst of speed to see whether our shadow does likewise'.

I nudge Braenda into a fast trot, the others follow and so does our shadow. Further along, where the trees thin out he will be out in the open. We can close on him by then if we head for that side of the track and break into a canter to chase him off – or down. There will be somewhere to corner our shadow in these woods, surely, a rock wall or deep gully across which his horse will not leap.

When we near a gap in the trees the rider kicks his mount into a gallop. We give chase and the air rushes through our lungs. The ground beneath us rushes up at us and everything around melts into a whirr of light and darkness. Saeward breaks off to our right and Eirik to our left where the track widens, Hemming and I keeping to the middle ground with the Northman in tow.

Saeward and Eirik are almost level with our shadow, Hemming and I have made ground and there is a steep river bank ahead. The hooded rider ahead draws on the reins and Saeward overshoots, Eirik cuts to the right in front of our shadow to turn him back.

Riding at us, our quarry tries to pass close by me when I pull my left boot out from the stirrup, kick out and catch the horse's shoulder, grazing it with my boot. The creature rolls over, eyes lolling, its rider thrown clear, sprawling on the grass.

'Lucky fall, friend', I tell him, leap out of my saddle and cross the ground before he can scramble to his feet.

'Aye, friend, it is *very* lucky - luckier for *us* than for you! You would not have wanted to be caught by Saeward there', Hemming agrees with me, nodding at his fellow East Seaxan, 'he eats men like you – grinds their bones into mush and eats it as porridge next morning. He is an *ogre!*'

Eirik laughs and looks up at Saeward as he slides down to the earth.

'What tales are you telling of me now, trouble-maker?'

'Oh, here is the ogre now!' I laugh. Hemming feigns fright and stands behind me, as if hiding.

'I heard that bit about me being an ogre', Saeward bends down and prods our shadow. 'Not very shadowy now, though, is he?'

'I say we look under that cowl', I step forward and bend, he backs away. Eirik, standing behind stops him pulling further away. I step forward again and push back the cowl. I brush aide the wavy chestnut hair that has fallen over a woman's brow.

'*Eadburga*', I am taken aback at seeing her, '*why* were you following us?'

'I wanted to get away from there. This land will be crawling with the outlanders and that crusty old abbess would sell me to keep her draughty old nunnery!'

'What about your sick mother?' Saeward asks.

'She told *you* that one?' Eadburga scoffs and looks away. She then looks up at me when I ask about the Northmen we saved her from, 'Having seen me from the gateway earlier, they borrowed me from the nunnery'.

'Have you seen this man before?' Hemming asks now.

'Which man?' She stands and hobbles to look up at Hubert. '*Him* – he like as not sent them here from Scrobbe shire'.

Saeward is nonplussed,

'They came all that way -?'

'No, fool, they would have camped nearby!' Hemming snaps and watches her from behind, smoothing his lip hair.

'Were you camped around here?' I ask Hubert, Eadburga not having seen him before.

'On the other side of the river', he mumbles.

'Well into Ceaster shire', Eirik's eyebrows lift.

'You did not think they were this far north?' I ask him. 'And he said he came over the hills from Wealas'.

From the way he shrugs and looks back over his shoulder at Hubert, he did not. Now we have two we would never have dreamed riding with us. Hubert is our way through any of his more northerly spread landsmen. If we meet none before we cross the Deag, then he can be dealt with in the way they would with any of ours.

'Are you well enough to ride?' I ask Eadburga. Her horse is now on his feet, happily cropping the grass despite the bruise I gave him.

'You will let me ride with you?' She is open-mouthed that I would even think of allowing her.

I smile, helping her mount,

'I see no other way'.

'You have no thoughts of using me?' She pushes her hair back with the bone comb that fell to the ground when I pulled her cowl back, and pulls the heavy cloth forward over her forehead.

I would not say Hemming or Eirik had no thoughts of bedding her, but Saeward would keep an eye on them when Hubert was out of the way. She may not be as worried about them as much as would be about our Northman friend.

'You ride well', I tell her as I mount, 'not like a maid from the hamlet'.

'I am *not* a maid from the hamlet, as you put it so well', Eadburga presses her lips into a beaming smile.

'Oh, what *are* you?' Eirik is on her other side, sharp as a hawk dropping onto a hare.

'I am the youngest daughter of Earl Aelfgar'. Her answer almost has Eirik out of his saddle in a faint. Hubert, on the other hand, looks craftily across at her behind Hemming. He sees me eyeing him and looks away, back to the woods.

'Why were you at that nunnery?' I ask.

'I was meant to learn something, reading, writing... how to behave like a young woman of my standing. My brothers would sooner I were still there, I think. I knew little enough of what went on, without being stuffed away with all those boil-infested old hags. They may have asked about me, I may never know, but they would have been fed a pack of lies by her', she throws a thumb back, meaning the abbess. 'When she dies the gates of hell will open to gobble her up!'

When Hubert laughs she turns in her saddle and asks,

'What does he have to laugh about? When you get to Ceaster, what then, you throw him into the river as food for fish?'

'Now that is food for thought', I look back. The smile he wore has turned into a frown. Or is it fear?

Eadburga throws her head back and laughs. Her head shakes from side to side and she has to put one hand up to her mouth to stop her laughter.

'What is amiss?' Saeward asks, having eyed up the lie of the land.

'*Nothing* is amiss, Saeward. The Lady Eadburga here put forward her thoughts about what to do with Hubert'.

'The *Lady* Eadburga is it? I thought *she* was a frosty old bitch at Cingheford'. He winks at her and tells me, I have been hanging on your every word. Do they have carp at Ceaster?'

'We have a carp lake big enough to take him', Eadburga snorts and looks back, puts her tongue out and turns back to look at me. 'That should fettle him, cocky outlander! What do they think they are doing, carving up our earldoms?'

Hemming growls in answer, his horse brushing against Hubert's,

'*Hear, hear!*'

Not finished, he goes on,

'First, however, I thought we would take turns trailing him around', he pushes Hubert's horse away and glares at its rider.

'Why - does he have bad breath?' Eirik scoffs.

'He does, as it happens, and his horse is getting frisky with mine!'

'We could have a horse wedding in the stables once he has gone', Eirik sniggers. 'Who will be best man?'

'Who could we get to wed two horses', Saeward adds, 'a short-sighted bishop?'

'Archbishop Ealdred might do it, being as he was short-sighted enough to put the old king's crown on the bastard's head'.

Eadburga giggles at our banter and puts in,

'We have a bishop of Ceaster who would not know the day of the week if you asked him, nor the back end of a horse from its head!'

'*Have* you – asked him, I mean', Saeward asks.

'More than once, I fear. He was found wandering the cathedral, scribbling his speech before someone let him know it was still midweek!' Eadburga cackles in a very un-ladylike manner.

'Where are we headed?' I ask Eirik, to which the answer comes,

'I know of a river-crossing not far from here'. He answers and waves us ahead.

On we ride. When I am abreast of him I tell him he takes the rope to Hubert's horse when we reach the far bank.

'I would have offered', Eirik avows.

'I hope so', I answer, and wave him forward. He rides on, past Hemming, Saeward and Eadburga, and prods the air eastward.

'How far do we ride now, to when someone takes this fart off my hands?' Hemming asks as I draw close to Hubert's horse. The creature grunts and bucks, giving Hemming a hard time. It pulls away from Hemming and bumps against Braenda, almost sending me flying.

'It is that time of the year, my friend', Hubert laughs, but takes his eyes off me at the sight of my dark scowl.

On seeing my look of scorn at almost being unhorsed Hemming offers,

'I can take her around my other side Ivar'.

I shake my head,

'He is where he can be kept in sight'.

I look across to see Hubert trying to rub his eyes and ask whether he has something in them.

'It is something that flew into them - a little of the Aenglish wildlife, I wonder? Could my hands be unbound?'

'Press your eyelids together, blink a few times, then look downward and do the same again, like this', I tell him, batting my eyelids. 'It works all the time. Whatever has caught your eyes will drop downward'.

He does so a few times but shrugs,

'I am not as good at it as you are', he wheedles, pursing his mouth like a child.

'Press harder, do it a few times', I tell him. 'We need to keep going, so I shall not have your bindings loosened *or* undone. You will have to do better than *that* in a bid for freedom!'

He looks at me, still childishly, from beneath his eyebrows. I have never met a man less worthy of being a lord – Morkere perhaps. At least his betters, Willelm fitzOsbern and Hrothgar de Montgomerie gave Harding and me a better show.

Eadburga pulls back and waits for me to catch up with her. She asks,

'Did he try to pull a ruse on you?'

'How do you mean?' I ask by way of an answer.

'Did he look as though he had something in his eyes?'

'He did, as it happens', I nod and look at him as he passes with Hemming. How did she know?

'It may be they do not have much woodland where they come from, but I have seen many of them doing that – you know, rub their eyes. It goes without saying that gets them nowhere. They may make themselves blind before they learn', she looks into my eyes. 'Has anyone told you, you have lovely grey eyes?'

'Your brothers would not be happy to learn you made a pass at me', I tease her.

'Even *were* it a pass, what would it have to do with *them?* I am a woman now, not a child. If I wanted you in my bed at Ceaster, they could do nothing!'

'Your brothers and I have an understanding. The more land there is between us, the better', I let her know of my time in Jorvik after the fight at Staenfordes Brycg – less the hours spent with Braenda – and Morkere's plain dislike of me shown after the killing of Saeward's brother Beorhtwulf.

'They both need to be cut down to size, like overgrowing reeds or vines', she laughs. This is a new insight into the clan from one of their own! 'Although no-one I have spoken to seems to know what became of them after the fight on Lunden Brycg'.

'You do not know they were at this king's crowning?'

'I cannot think what they would have done there. Any Miercan lord worth his salt would have fought him to a standstill!'

'I watched them all give their oaths, Eadmund, Morkere, Waltheof – even Eadgar the aetheling had to', I let her know all the kingdom's nobles felt lost, unable to come together with their thoughts about how they would fight him. 'Some, thegns such as Eadric 'Cild' were dealt badly with by the outlanders and fought alongside the Wealsh *aethelings* Bleddyn and Rhiwallon at Hereford'.

'You were at the abbey?' she asks, looking closely at me. 'How did *you* come to be there?'

'Saeward and I went as Brothers'.

'I can think of *no* men less like Brothers of the cloth', she almost screams with laughter.

'I think we must have passed muster', Saeward sniffs, 'otherwise the Northmen would have seen us through our robes for what we were'.

'You might be right, Saeward', Eadburga rests a small hand on his, dish-like in breadth and depth, and yet he does not withdraw his hand from beneath hers. Is it that she is a child to him?

Or does he feel something stirring deep within?   His hands tell of long hours spent in fields and in the mill, and I think she knows that. Many Brothers of the cloth stem from land workers, amongst the men who work on the threshing floors.

Eadburga, on the other hand, is the daughter of an earl. Her brothers may be in Ceaster, or further north even. Will her older sister be here? Aelfgifu could well still be in Mierca with her son Harold, my kinsman's heir at least in name.

'After we have been to Ceaster, what then?' Eirik asks next, unaware Hubert's eyes may be on him, ears no doubt flapping like those of a hound on the hunt.

'I think we should be past Ceaster before we take the next road', I put him off, bending one thumb backward over one shoulder to let him know we should keep such things from our hostage.

He looks back and shakes his head,

'He must be asleep in the saddle', Eirik taps my free arm and points.

'He will be well aware of what is happening around him, mark my words', I tell Eirik under my breath. 'I think he is a master at the art of listening in. Watch him whilst I speak'.

'Very well, go on', Eirik answers and turns in his saddle to watch what I mean.

'We shall ride north, on to Cardeol, and turn for Maelcolm's court in the east of his kingdom. The *aetheling* Eadgar may be there already, with his sisters Margarethe and Christina -'

I stop when Eirik taps my elbow.

'You *were* right', he chuckles. 'The Northman's ears were surely flapping, like those of a horse or as though there was a strong gale pushing on them!'

Hemming, next to Hubert plainly thinks the Northman has fallen asleep in the saddle and elbows him fit to unsaddle him. It is as much as Hubert can do to stay upright when his horse shies, his hands still tightly bound to the pommel of his saddle.

'*Careful* Hemming', I warn. My hostage may be useless to me with a broken back if his topples backwards from his mount.

'Are we *keeping* him, then, after we reach Ceaster?' Hemming asks.

'We may hand him to the thegns there, for them to have something to bargain with the Northmen', I answer, looking Hubert in the eye. If he thinks there is hope for him, he may not try to flee. On the other hand, if they have met before on less friendly terms, he may not be keen to yield himself to them. His gaze is steady as he rasps,

'Why should I help you into Ceaster if you are going to hand me over to that pack of wolves? If we cross paths with my fellows, I might yield *you* up'.

'That is for you to think over', I shrug.

Hemming feels he has to make Hubert aware of what will happen to him before his fellows, as he calls them, set about us on our way in to Ceaster,

'And it is for me to push my blade into your waist *before* we fight them off'.

'Do we have something like a white cloth?' I ask Saeward.

'I can soon find one', he answers askance.

'We may need one soon', I tell him. 'Think about it'.

'Half of us are wearing Northman war-gear', Eirik makes him heedful. He nods and half-closes his eyes to show he knows what I mean and pulls his saddlebag around to fumble through what he has in there.

A lightly soiled cloth is pulled out. On a nod from me he stuffs it back and ties down the flap again. I hope he has more in there, as I would not wish to see him bind our wounds with that one!

When I sight the walls of Ceaster I rein in.

'Can any of you see riders ahead?' I ask my friends.

'Would they be out in the open, to be seen?' Eirik scans the land ahead.

'Granted', I allow. Why did I not think of that?

'You cannot think of everything', Saeward reads my thoughts.

There is woodland, north to south, and behind it on the low hills to either side are wildwoods. The trees have been cut back from the roadside, the northernmost stretch of Watling Straet, the old road from Lunden, to keep wayfarers from being fallen upon by outlaws.

'Something glimmers ahead', Hemming warns, showing us with the point of his spear where the lowering sun catches glistening weaponry somewhere ahead to our right.

'We should go through the woods, *behind* them'.

'*What* –'I see Eadburga looking at me from my right.

'I said we should go through the woods – behind the outlanders', she says again. 'My father and brothers used to hunt these woods and Aelfgar my father brought me to show where they rode to find boar and deer amongst the thickets. I know a way we can stay out of their sight until we are almost at the walls of the *burh*'.

This earl's daughter is no wilting lily.

'By all means, *lead on*', I tell her. 'But not before we make sure he cannot shout. Hemming, have you his gag ready?' Hemming holds the strap high that he used when we first had Hubert under our wing, so to speak. The Northman swears, but with Saeward to one side, Hemming to the other he can do nothing to stop them.

Thus readied, we set off into the trees. The track we follow drops down into a narrow wooded dale, out of sight behind thickets and heavy bushes. Oak and beech soar heavenward, our way becoming darker as we ride on. There is rustling to our left and Saeward eyes the close-set undergrowth. He may be looking for boar, but only a lone hart staggers into sight from its hide, still half-asleep. The deer vanishes from sight, back to safety, thankful we were no hunting party.

Light streams from our left, through the lush green crown of the woodland, onto Eadburga's smooth, youthful forehead. She rides with her eyes closed, long eyelashes resting on high cheeks. Hundreds of years of breeding rest on her narrow shoulders; the blood of Leofric may not be that of a king, but counts for as much in this earldom.

Of the five of us, a Miercan Lady, a Danish kinsman of King Harold, a former thegn from the Danelaw and two East Seaxans, only Eadburga is homeward bound here. Thankfully we have proved to be friends to her, having freed her from the grasp of one young Northman noble and bringing with us another as a safeguard against any foreseeable attacks.

'Eadburga, where does this track leave the woods?' I ask her.

She puts a finger to her lips and points upward to where the light from the streaming sun has turned golden yellow.

'Your words carry well in these woods', she scolds. I try speaking in a hoarse whisper and she giggles, 'Somewhere between will do'.

'Well, Eadburga', I try again, 'where does this track leave the woods.

'Better', she answers and tells me the track rises again within a mile of the burh walls. As I thought, a white cloth will be needed to stop us being drilled by arrows from within Ceaster.

Saeward has what we need, and pats his saddlebag to show me he can still read my thoughts. Having ridden for so long together, he knows what I am thinking of even before I begin. My East Seaxan friend is a gift, but has a testy side I would not wish on anyone. He can kill easily, but how he squares this within himself he will not say, nor do I burden him with asking. Hubert may think the threat to his life comes from Hemming, but life is never so simple.

Woodcocks take off from either side as we pass through a thwait. We stop, lest we have been seen through the trees, then ride on, eyes searching the western rim of the trees now bathed in the deep copper light of evening.

'If we wait a little longer, might we not reach Ceaster under cover of darkness?' Saeward wonders aloud.

'We must be at the gates before sunset', Eadburga tells him, 'or arrows will find you as easily as any outlander'.

'They need to see our white cloth', I shrug. 'For that we must risk the last mile or so in what is left of the daylight'.

'Fear not, Saeward. We will not break cover much before we reach the gates', Eadburga rests her hand on his again and any thoughts he may have had of being skewered by a Northman's lance seem to be put at rest.

At last it is time to break cover. Saeward ties his white cloth to the lance he took from one of the outlanders' horsemen, and raises it to its full height. We ready ourselves and, with Hemming and Hubert in the middle, burst forth from the trees towards Ceaster's welcoming walls. I hope they are welcoming, and we are not caught between evils.

Saeward is behind Hemming, our hostage now having had his gag taken from his mouth and been given water. Eirik is between Hemming and Eadburga, and I lead this odd troop dressed in a Northman hauberk and helm with my own breeks and leggings.

Men gather atop the walls, watching us near. Saeward has the lance with its white cloth flapping briskly in a freshening north-westerly wind from the sea, and there are Northmen closing on us from behind, by the look of them the strength of a *conroi* – over a score with their eager young nobles pounding the earth after us.

They may be wondering ahead who is chasing whom.

Eadburga rides well, as if on the hunt. Hubert struggles manfully to stay in his saddle, Saeward behind him with his lance close to the Northman's back. Should his horse stumble, it will be the end of him.

We are not yet within hailing when arrows thud into the earth track around us. Eadburga waves with one arm, yet arrows still fall. It is only when we are almost under the walls that the arrows stop. Someone above us must know who she is, even if they cannot make *us* out on the land bridge below them.

The thud of hooves behind us is louder, and I turn to see lance heads closing. Hubert turns in his saddle and yells something. Whatever it is he shouted, it seems to have slowed them down, but Saeward in his wisdom brings down the lance he carries and skewers the Northman from behind. The gates have not yet been opened, and he has angered our foe. Having slewed their horses, the Northmen now press them hard to catch us before we vanish from their eyes with their dead landsman.

With a loud crack bolts are pulled back within and the gates part. Eadburga screams,

'Let us in Aelfric, *quickly!*'

A gap opens between the gates, wide enough for one horse at a time to pass through. I let Eadburga lead, followed by Eirik and Hemming, Hubert sagging low over the pommel of his saddle.

Saeward is behind me with his lance topped by the white rag, as if set in stone. A rider I take to be the noble who gives the orders crouches low over the neck of his horse, making headlong for me, the thunder of his horse's hooves growing as he nears, onto the wooden land bridge. Saeward gives a start, wakes from his dream and sees the Northman,

'Get yourself *in* there, Ivar!' He barks at me and grips the lance.

'Come on, Saeward, who do you think you are?' I try to push him toward the gate but he will have none of it.

'Are you coming *in*, you two?' someone snaps from above. 'We have to shut the gates against them!'

'Saeward, get your body behind these gates!' I bark at him just as the young nobleman thunders over the wooden bridge that crosses the wide, deep ditch on this side of the burh.

'Ivar – *get down!*' he yells back at me and hews downward with his axe at the Northman's lance. The wood splinters, sending shards of ash flying, some my way. One I feel cuts across my right ear. Another flips into the nobleman's left eye. As he screams in anguish Saeward pulls me through the still open gates and we are chased by crossbow bolts. I still have Braenda's reins in my hands and she follows, luckily unhurt in the trade of arrows between angered Northmen and Ceaster's bowmen.

The gates crash to behind us and Saeward is hailed as a hero by those around the gateway. When the iron bar is pushed into its slots we all breathe out as one.

Beyond the gates, from what we hear, the nobleman and his following are seen off with a shower of arrows. Jeers follow them back along Watling Straet until they are beyond the Miercan arrows.

Men gather around Saeward, shaking his hand, slapping his back. He swells with pride until Hemming tells him,

'Grow up, Saeward. You nearly cost Ivar his life, trying to pull you to safety!'

'The one time I have men thronging around me to shake my hand, you have to go and prick me down to size! What *is* it with you?'

'You have *been* a hero, time and time again, if you but *knew* it!' Hemming reddens. Nevertheless the well-wishers throng around Saeward and Eirik pulls Hemming away to keep him from blowing off.

'Let him have this', Eirik laughs, Eadburga beside him cupping her hands around her mouth.

Hemming makes as if to 'throw away' the unbearable Saeward and follows us as we weave our way through the streets of Ceaster to Mierca's own *earlsburh* in the south of the burh.

This was where, in their time, Leofric and Aelfgar came when they were not needed by King Eadward. To the south or east they hunted, following deer and boar down narrow gullies between trees and undergrowth, or loosed off their hawks to strike at smaller prey.

The buildings are much as those of the *Earlsburh* in Jorvik, and added to over the years as needed. Outer gates swing open to show a yard with stables and outhouses. A smith makes horseshoes, tools and weaponry for the *fyrd*. Finer goods would be made elsewhere by a weaponsmith entrusted by the earl.

Eadburga takes us to the hall, to slake our thirsts and fill our bellies. She also sends one of her household back to the *burh* gates to guide Saeward here when he has had enough of the Miercans' back-slapping.

'He will not need to eat or drink', Hemming smirks. 'He can live off all that worship! What *are* we doing anyway, Ivar? I mean, when we leave here'.

'You are not thinking of leaving yet?' Eadburga teases.

'*When* we leave here, I said', Hemming forgets himself.

When he begs her forgiveness she laughs, boxes his big ears and comes to my side to look at my wounded ear.

'I have been amongst folk long and often enough to know when they mean to anger me and when not', she tells him. 'You will have to have that sliver of wood taken out, Ivar, *soon!* I can do it for you, if you will let me'.

'Well, mostly it is Saeward who tends to us. He learned his art at Wealtham, and watched as my kinsman saw to men's wounds', I tell her, nursing my ale cup.

'Your kinsman was a man of the cloth?' she asks, round-eyed.

'My kinsman was king after Eadweard's death', I answer, waiting for some sort of mockery about Harold taking Eadgar's throne. But nothing of the like comes. Instead she smiles and rests a hand on my shoulder.

'For all that my brothers say, I believe Aelfgifu when she says King Harold was well served by a loyal kinsman such as you are. She is far away from Ceaster, somewhere across the sea with her young son. He is a dear, sweet child, not beset by fits of temper as is my brother Morkere. Yet he *was* once kinder. I blame Eadwin for that, as Morkere did not want to take Tostig's earldom. More often than not I was sent to bed with my brothers yelling at one another until the deed was done. Tostig was your kinsman, too?'

I nod and take a mouthful of ale, saying nothing.

She goes on,

'I cannot believe - could he be as bad as is said of him?' she asks.

'He was badly counselled and allowed himself to be drawn into a squabble between landed Northanhymbran kindred north of the Tese, and Copsig had his hands on the tithes'. I would sooner not go into this, but as Eadburga has raised the matter, I must answer as best I can.

'What became of your kinsman, Tostig?'

'Did your brothers not tell you? He was slain at Staenfordes Brycg alongside King Harald', I lie.

'Something tells me that is not so', she presses, and takes a mouthful of her own drink.

'You alone do not believe what is taken by so many to be the truth?' I ask in turn. 'There is no man here who can say otherwise'.

'You can'. She upends her cup, empties it and holds it up for one of the wenches to fill.

'Is it so hard to believe Tostig is dead?' I ask again, looking her in the eye. 'Why is it you will not believe, when all others think it to be true?'

'Because you know it to be otherwise', she wipes her mouth with her arm like a man and belches. 'By the way, what became of Copsig?'

I tell her of our ride north, our meeting with Gospatric and his kinsman Osulf and how they had first been more for killing me as Tostig's kinsman than for dealing with Copsig. I go on to speak of our breaking into Copsig's welcome feast in the hall at Nyburna and chasing him into the church. Lastly I tell of burning the church to bring Copsig and his paid men out into the night.

'So, what happened then?' Eadburga stares open-mouthed as I tell of Osulf cutting off Copsig's head with his war axe. On hearing that last she says flatly, 'Good – *serve him right!*'

She drains her cup again and rises. We rise with her, Saeward having been led to us whilst I spoke of us chasing – and being chased – along the backbone of the kingdom into Deira and northward. Waving us to be seated again, she tells us,

'I must see to your having beds for the night, if not for longer. All that riding from Rhiwallon's stronghold must have left you saddle-sore. Bide awhile with us, will you. I will make amends for my brothers' shortcomings, if you will let me? Godgifu, I need your help', she catches a young woman as she passes and vanishes with her into the smoke-filled darkness at the back of the hall.

We settle down to eating and drinking, unfettered by outsiders – however good-looking Eadburga is – and play games such as Nine Men's Morris to let the food go down. Eadburga shows again in the bright torchlight and sits between Saeward and me.

'You all have beds for as long as you wish – where my brothers' huscarls would sleep, but for them being elsewhere whilst their lords are away', she links arms with us both and beams brightly at each of us in turn.

'I wish Theodolf had not been wounded', I say aloud, although not to anyone in the main.

'I can send for him to be brought here and looked after', Eadburga answers.

'The Northmen will be thirsting for our blood now. I would say they are scouring the shire right now for anyone they think may have helped us reach here', I groan inwardly at the thought of Theodolf being made to suffer because of us.

'He is safe where he is, for now'. She puts a hand on mine, 'Whatever you think of the abbess, she would never give him away to the Northmen. We can bring him, if you still so wish. My brothers' men could bring them, who know their way around the woods and would drive off any who came too close!'

'Fine', I nod, and put my other hand on top of Eadburga's to seal a friendship.

'We shall still need to know where next', Eirik tells me. 'I have nothing against waiting here for the Second Coming – whenever that may be – but idleness will not suit us in the long run'.

'Fear not, Eirik, I had not thought of taking root here', I swear. I would not want to waste a good sword-hand such as he could prove to be in the thick of fighting. My thoughts go to Osgod and Harding. Where did they go from Rhosgoch?

Talk turns to what is happening around the kingdom, and having been out of the way for so long it is good to catch up. Eadburga listens closely to what her brothers' men tell us. There have been risings in West Mierca, Defna and West Wealas. Exanceaster was attacked again, this time the men of the burh staying true to the man they now see as king and it was *Comte* Breon with Willelm fitzOsbern who broke through the West Seaxans. The king's brother Rodberht of Mortain was pinned fast in *his* East Sumorsaetan stronghold until another of Willelm's friends Geoffroi of Coutances with *fyrdmen* from Wintunceaster, Salesbyrig and Lunden chased away the attackers.

There are too many Church men putting their weight behind this king, and as men will not fight the Church lest their souls be damned into the hereafter, we have an uphill task ahead of us.

Who do we know who is unafraid of Mother Church in this kingdom? One tale that draws me is that told by a Wilfred of Stibenhede close to the east of Aldgata.

Some way astray of his home stamping grounds, this fellow tells us of a rising against Willelm in the old *burh* of Lunden. This must have been at the time we rode south into Centland, as by the time we came back to the 'Crooked Billet' everything had blown over.

'After Harold was killed on Caldbec Beorg and Willelm came with his horsemen, the Northmen beset the *burh* from the west. The old, patched-up walls run to here from the river before turning in at Lud Gata, from where they run north-eastward to Eadred's Gata', Wilfred tells us.

'We were taken that way by the Northmen after being caught near Hamstede', I tell him, nodding.

'I was told of the unrest the haughty Rodberht de Bruis raised when you were brought that way, aye', he answers. 'However, before we could gird ourselves for a long fight some craven Brother let them in by a postern gate by Lud Gata Bar. They were everywhere before we could stop them, but there *was* a fight below the Church of Saint Paul. The Northmen were given a mauling, losing many men before we were overcome. Aside from me, hundreds of others fell back into the shadows to get away from that rat's nest, never to be found'.

And now you are here in the north of Mierca', Saeward smiles thinly, 'an outsider'.

'No so', Wilfred waggles a finger at him. 'I have been welcomed here by all and sundry. I could make my home here'.

Saeward's brow rises.

He seems taken back by what Wilfred tells him. It should be nothing new to him, after all Hrothulf and Aethel made *him* welcome before he was hauled away by Osgod and his huscarls back to Jorvik.

'So what do you aim to do with yourselves, if it is not too much to ask?' Wilfred looks in turn at me, Saeward, Hemming and Eirik.

'We await news from the east, from Eoferwic', Saeward answers.

'*What* news? Is anything happening there?' Wilfred takes a swallow of ale before setting his cup down to help himself to food.

'Well, for one thing, *I* should like to know where Godwin and Eadmund went after the crushing blow *Comte* Breon dealt us in Defna', I empty my cup and hold it up. One of the wenches comes my way. Winking, she fills my cup and brushes against me before knocking Eadburga forward, spilling her ale.

'What was *that* about?' Eadburga splutters angrily and I look up at the woman.

She wears a cap tied around the back of her head, from which a rich mane of reddish hair pushes forward.

'Braenda – I would never have known you'.   I look long and hard at her, and pluck up the nerve to ask,

'Since when did you wear that little cap?'

'Since when was it anything to do with you what I wear, Ivar Ulfsson?' she snaps back.

'Nothing –'I begin anew.

'Well then, as long as you understand. Where is your *room* in all this...?' Her eyes follow the building around.

'You *know* this woman?' Eadburga wonders, eyes wide open in wonder.

'Aye, *he* knows me', Braenda smiles. 'I would be grateful of your keeping that in your thoughts'.

'Do you have anything to say, Ivar?' Eadburga looks from Braenda to me.

'Not if I do not wish to rock the boat, so to speak', I grin up at Braenda. 'It does not do to test out Braenda too much'.

Braenda leaves my side and walks away, hips swinging, leaving Eadburga to ask again,

'Surely you have something to say?' On seeing me shrug she shakes her head forlornly and asks the next wench for more ale. Whatever she has aforethought, if she wishes to risk Braenda's wrath I can do nothing. She will learn.

'She will learn', Saeward echoes my thoughts and goes back to his chicken leg.

'What will she learn?' Wilfred asks, nonplussed, to which I tap one side of my nose and he laughs, 'It is like that?'

'Very much so', Hemming laughs. He too taps his nose and goes back to eating. Wilfred throws his hands up in dismay and chuckles. Only Eirik is forthcoming,

'The russet-haired woman Braenda is a close friend of Ivar's. She is the one he named his horse after'.

'This is some kind of game – *is it?*' Wilfred booms and throws his head back in laughter. 'I think I may have heard about that along the way!'

'This must be all over the kingdom', I yawn and scratch my beard.

'They must know it all over Wealas by now –'Eirik shrugs. 'Did you not want anybody else to know?

'It is something I would sooner not have to hear everywhere. Think on this, Eirik, everywhere I go men will say of me that I saddle my mare and ride my woman. Nothing will be said of my fighting spirit. Do you think *I* want that?'

Eirik looks shamed. He does not know where to put himself. Wilfred stares from Eirik to me, and asks,

'That goes for me as well, does it?'

'Suit yourself', is all I say to that.

'It is out now, and what has been said cannot be unsaid', Saeward puts an arm around my shoulders, as if I were a young maiden. I elbow him off and he laughs. 'You could call out every man who raises the matter, but you would soon be tired out!'

'I would only have to call out one man', I gaze at Eirik, 'and beat him into yielding'.

'You mean word would get about', Saeward raises an eyebrow and also looks at Eirik. The fellow is edgy now, not sure of what to do. His eyes dart from Saeward to Hemming. 'He would soon get over it, but he would no longer be a friend to you. He might even yield you up to the outlanders'.

'*Would* you?' I ask Eirik.

'*God*, no, I would *never* do that!' Eirik is flustered now, unsure of himself. Wilfred looks him up and down and says something behind his hand to Hemming, as if not wishing Eirik to hear but loud enough to be heard as far afield as Jorvik.

I beckon him closer. He dithers and looks as if he would run from the hall. I beckon him again, no hint of what I feel or will do when he does come.

'Sit beside me', I tell Eirik.

Saeward shuffles away, along the bench to make way for him. I can see Eirik shaking like a leaf, but he comes and sits beside me.

'Eirik, how long have we known one another, off an on?' I ask.

Eirik scratches his head and thinks – hard. He looks up, squinting across the smoky hall, and at me.

'It must be a year or so now', he seems more sure in answering.

'Two, as it happens', I put him right. 'In those years have I ever threatened you, or did you feel threatened by me?'

'*Er*, no you have not', he shrugs.

'Can you think *why* I would threaten you?'

He shrugs again and empties his ale cup, holding it up for one of the women to fill it.

'*However*', I add, '*should* you go telling others again about the name of my horse being the same as that of my woman, I might think again, understand? Do not think of this as a threat, Eirik. It is a *hint*'.

I push my cup up against Eirik's and empty it.

'For now I wish to find my bed. Where has Eadburga got to?'

'I will take you there', says someone behind me. When I look up I see an aged fellow, a discthegn?'

'I will see you all in the morning', I use Eirik's and Hemming's shoulders to push myself up from the bench. 'Think on it, Eirik, you are a good friend. Were it not for you Harding and I would have been caught by Willelm fitzOsbern. I shall think back on that and hope our friendship lasts. Good night'.

'Sweet dreams' they chorus. I think I heard Eirik mumble a good night. I soon catch up with the discthegn and follow him along endless walkways. This is so unlike the rambling *Earlsburh* in Jorvik. I thought the *Earlsburh* was odd after Godwin's hall in Suth Seaxe. This is something more akin to a riddle. At last we reach my room.

'What is your name, friend?' I ask before opening the door.

'I am Earnwin', he nods and touches his forelock.

'Can I gift you with a silver coin?'

'You may, my Lord, if you think you can spare it', Earnwin answers, a little cheekily. I overlook the slight and press a silver penny into his palm. He touches his forelock again and takes me aback with the speed at which he leaves. I think no more of it and open my door wider.

A rush light burns jerkily until I shut the door.   There is a bowl of water on a stand in the corner, the light from the burning rush jumping from time to time as I cross the small room. I only need a bed and unbroken sleep until morning, but am I likely to get it?

'You took your time', a woman tells me – not Braenda but Eadburga.

'Do you think this wise?' I ask.

'This is my home. The russet-haired woman Braenda who sees you as hers was key-keeper to my sister, Aelfgifu. She went with her to Wealas all those years ago before wedding your kinsman. She should know where not to tread', Eadburga pats the bed beside her.

'Eadburga you do not understand. I cannot afford to lose her as a friend', I sit on the bed. 'She is more than a lover –'

'Very well, *be* a fool! *Stay* until Theodolf is brought here, but then you must go! I will not have men in my home who do not do my bidding!'

She storms out of the room, having first clothed herself. She is a good-looking young woman, and will soon forget the likes of me. Meanwhile I must hope Braenda comes soon, as I need to let her know my feelings for her.

'Theodolf is here', Saeward tells me a few days later. 'He is still badly in need of care, but he will live- *just about'*.

'I shall look in on him', I vow.

'Do that', Saeward nods, 'he is looking forward to seeing you again, I cannot think why'.

'Meaning –', I stand over him but he goes on eating his porridge.

'Sit down, fill your belly! Have some of this', he finishes the bowl and stops another woman on her way past. 'Any more of this – how do you make it so *creamy?*'

She smiles and ladles another few spoonfuls into his bowl.

'I wish *everyone* liked it as much as you! You see so many leave theirs'.

'If they had to ride the length of Wealas and the shire of Ceaster they would *not* leave it!'

'Saeward here leaves only the squeak when he has hog meat!' I elbow him.

'Give *me* some of that. If he says it is good, who am I to gainsay him?'

Eadburga strides past just then, looking over my head at Earnwin. She speaks to him and he nods, comes to my side to tell me,

'My Lady says you should eat, say your farewell to Theodolf and leave'.

I take in what he has said, and ask where my friend is, so that I might see him before leaving.

'When you have finished eating, I will take you there'.

13

'Well, well – *Ivar!* What brings you here? I was led to believe you would be on your way sooner,' Theodolf struggles to right himself in the bed given him here in Eadmund's *earlsburh*.

'We - Saeward, Hemming Eirik and I - must be on our way again today. I thought I would look in on you to bid you farewell for the time being. If when you are well again you make your way across the kingdom to Aethel's home, we will try to look in on you again'.

'You fell out with Eadburga. How on earth could *anyone* fall out with her?'

'It had something to do with her waiting in my bed for me. I told her of Braenda – they met one evening before you came, and sparks almost flew! I could smell the brimstone again that I came across when Harding and I met his woman Aethelhun at Aethel's steading! Braenda was almost overcome by Aethelhun -'

'That was when I was still at Rhosgoch, right?'

'Aye, it was. You missed nothing. If Aethelhun had fixed on you she could have made you hers – not for the better, mind!' I tell him. 'How is your wound?'

'I was told I will live, by no less than Saeward', Theodolf chortles.

'When did he come to see you?'

'This morning – he said he slipped away before the morning meal, as soon as he heard I was here. I see you waited until you had filled that hole in your jaw!'

'How is that?' I ask.

'You have porridge in your beard! You are a messy eater in your old age, are you not?'

'I am getting too old for this criss-crossing of the kingdom', I allow, nodding and add, 'I was hungry, young friend!'

'And I am too young to die', he adds, his mouth twisting with the pain of a laugh he has to keep in'.

'*You* will not die', I tell him, cupping his shaven jaw in my right hand.

'What if I *did* die?' he groans, not trying hard enough to sound hopeful.

'Where would you want to be buried?' I go along with this mad line of thought, the wit of which passes over my head..

'I should like to die with my bow in my hand and my father's amulet, Mjoellnir on its leather strap around my neck', he shows me where it is.

'Do you want it now? Would the Sister not take it from you if she

saw it? It would be seen under the shirt –'

'If you will not do that for me, I can find someone who will!' he tells me huffily, and holds in his side in pain. Is it real pain, or is he trying to milk pity?

'Very well, but if your carer takes it from you then I cannot say –'

'Aye, *aye,* I cannot say I was not warned!' he shakes his head and hisses, trying to hide the pain.

I reach for the talisman and look closely at it. I ask,

'Did Hrothulf ever tell you what the runes were?'

'Runes – I hardly think he could read them himself, could he?' Theodolf holds up the talisman to the light and squints.

'Where are they?' he holds it out to me. I take it from him and run his forefinger over the carved lines that once meant so much to our forebears. His eyes open wide and he looks up at me, 'He gave me this before the fighting began in King Harold's shieldwall'.

'Which is why you are alive yet', I tell him.

'Do you *mean* that?' he asks and stares open-mouthed at me

'Your father knew what the runes meant. His father and his father's father knew, and long before that. As long as you hold onto this, you will live long and live well!' I wish I could believe that, but if it gives him hope I have put him on the right path. 'But do not try to come fighting with us again, or your luck will run out'.

'I thought you said I would live long and well', Theodolf stares askance at me.

'I *did,* and you *will,* but you have to forsake fighting – ever again. Go to Wealtham, or Rhosgoch where you have a woman and offspring, who will give you warmth when you grow old'.

'Would Gerda even look at me any more? She may have given me up for dead. Brihtwin would be angry with me – understandably – at my leaving his mother. As for Sigrid, she must also think I am no longer alive'.

'Then go back and show her you *are* alive. There will be Wealshmen who would shelter you from the Northmen. Take your time. Ride slowly or at a trot, west from here over the boundary and then ride south. They will take you in with open arms at Rhosgoch. It is only against me that Bleddyn feels ill will. Fare well, and one day we will meet again – God willing'.

'God willing – *are you sure about that?*' Theodolf eyes me and tries to laugh.

'Being around Saeward does things to a man's thinking', I grin broadly, pointing at Mjoellnir on its cord around Theodolf's neck. 'Live well and do what your carers tell you, that way they may overlook your

drawbacks'.

'I shall try, *very hard* Ivar', he smiles and reaches out his left hand. 'Grasping my right hand will give me untold pain! Forgive me'.

'You are forgiven. Farewell Theodolf', I leave his bedside as footfalls beyond the door tell me Earnwin is on his way to take me to my horse.

On looking around the door I see Eadburga's discthegn stop and crook a finger at me,

'I was looking for you, Lord Ivar. You make a man's hard-won life harder. The Lady Eadburga told me to see you out of Ceaster with *all* your friends. It took much talking for me to point out the foolishness of her sending *Theodolf* on his way with you when he had helped save her!'

As we thump along on the uneven floor stones back to the hall I offer him silver, but he wants nothing of it,

'I did not do it for you, Lord Ivar. I did it for all good Aenglishmen, whether Miercan, Northanhymbran or East Seaxan. Raise your sword to the Northmen, chase them back over their sea and wash out the mouth of that fool Eadric 'Cild'!'

'*Why* – what harm has he done you?'

'I have heard he has sold his sword to the man who calls himself king now. They have come to a 'friendship', whatever that means. Ask no help from him, Lord, and you will not be let down'.

'So there you are, at last! Do you know how long we have been waiting here?' Saeward grumbles with a wide grin that seems to make his lower jaw look odd. Hemming chides him for moaning and Eirik shrugs.

We have come to the yard, where my friends await me with our horses. I mount as Braenda trots on to the gates ahead of us, the others already through by the time I get there. Hemming half-turns and beckons me on, 'I am told there is a side-gate ahead in the *burh* wall where we can pass through to cross the Deag, on towa

rd Northanhymbra –'

'Aye, Hemming, I know. We came this way to teach Gruffyd all those years ago, passing close to these walls'.

'Why did we not ask Thegn Eadric for help?' Eirik asks, not having been told about Eadric's new 'friend'.

'Earnwin tells me he is friendly with Willelm', I answer. He and Hemming stare open-mouthed, Saeward merely sniggers.

'What is so funny *now?*' Hemming snaps almost fit to bite his head off.

'I am laughing at what some would do to keep the earth under their

217

feet!' Saeward growls back. 'Talk like that to me again and we will soon see what could be funnier!'

'The pair of you can get down off your fat arses and fight it out like men – *with your fists!* First man down yields! Well, *how about it?*' I shout them both down just as riders show to the south-east - twelve riders, two with broad pennons on their lances.

'First we should put some earth between us and *them!*' Eirik prods at the air with one, long bony finger.

'God, where did *they* come from?' Hemming looks away from me and digs his knees into his horse's flanks, heading north.

'*Not that way*', I yell across a strengthening breeze and wave to woodland I know will shelter us for some way!

He digs his boots into his mare's flanks and is almost thrown off again when she rears. By the time we catch him up he has calmed her again and sets off at a canter ahead of us. Another look back tells me that, in trying to cut us off, the Northmen must have been hampered by the deep river and they are now chasing after us along the far river bank. They may still be trying to head us off at the next ford.

There are two hamlets to the west of us, Helsby and Frodhisham, where the Danelaw once met Mierca. That way would be a hard ride for us along the coastal levels. Our task is to find a track that will let us vanish northward into the trees.

'Ivar, look over *there*!' Saeward yells, slapping my right arm with the flat of his hand. I look back over one shoulder for the Northmen and see no-one. Where have they gone? Just as I have waved them on and followed closely, out of the corner of my right eye I see the flash of red and black on white – a pennon! They have almost caught us up!

'Ivar, *quick* – these boughs seem to be trying to close!' Eirik almost yelps. Whose doing could this be?

Ducking under swishing boughs and struggling past groaning bushes, I draw up with the others and stare in awe with them as the woodland seems to shut out the outlanders, like great wooden doors. Oak and beech, wild yew and holly almost seem to slide across our way here. This is uncanny!

'Ride on', I tell the others, thanking the wildwood in my thoughts for its help. Whoever – *whatever* – the eerie being that brought this about, I thank from the pit of my unbelieving soul.

A track shows itself, arrow-like through the tall trees. What little undergrowth there is in the way almost seems to slither out of our way as we ride. Briars there are none, the bracken yet to spread.

'Is your woman behind this?' Eirik is first to ask.

Hemming chuckles,

'Aye, she may have had words with the tree spirits'.

'Do not mock!' I warn. This is all too much for me, and I am trying my best to keep my head.

'*Heathens all*, say I!' Saeward laughingly chides, no longer sure what to believe.

'Say as little as you can', is all I can tell them, 'as we may need our strength for hard riding when we come into Northanhymbra. We have to cross the high hills, and they may yet be snow-clad, even now'.

'What about stopping to eat?' Hemming asks.

'When we come to a thwait', I answer, forgetting he has never been this way before.

'What is that – a *thwait*?' Hemming wrinkles his nose.

'A thwait is a clearing', Eirik tells Hemming, jerking his helmed head my way. 'Never ask *him*, he will only stare holes in you'.

'How am I meant to know?' Hemming throws up his arms and roars as loud as he can. A dry leaf flutters down from a high branch somewhere, unshed since the afteryear in the shelter of this welcoming woodland. It drops into his wide-open mouth and he almost chokes. Spitting out the half-chewed dead leaf his lips curl back, he spits out whatever else is left and rolls his tongue in loathing.

'God, what was *that?*'

'If you ride with your mouth wide open, do it looking ahead, not up', I laugh and sneak an upward look. Having chided him about being a woodland midden, I would not want to fall prey to a passing fowl when it passes one of its bundles.

Eirik catches sight of me looking up warily and cackles,

'Aye, Ivar, you would not want fall foul of the woodland fowl!'

Nudging Braenda into a canter, I grin cheesily. We have come to an old track through the trees, not used for many a year, the drumming of our horses' hooves muffled where the crowns of trees meet along this lucky 'find'. Many years' leaf cover dulls our passing as we ride for the high ground we passed through not long ago, following Copsig to his home ground of Jorvik.

This time we should not have to struggle against deepening drifts. There may still *be* snow about, but nowhere near as bad as in the late winter days.

'Shall we make a halt soon?' Hemming asks. 'My backside feels as hard as the saddle I am riding on!'

'I do not see why not', I answer. Before I can warn about any Northmen who may still be shadowing us he has dismounted and strides around rubbing his tender backside.

'You would not have wanted to be with us when we last came this way', Saeward tells him.

Eirik adds, piling on the woe,

'Aye, we spent half our time leading our mounts on foot, and in blizzards through knee-deep snow drifts'. Not wishing to make a meal of a forgettable time in my life I say nothing. Hemming shivers and rubs his chest. Is there an edge to the air I missed? I wonder how high we have climbed between the trees before we drop down to the roadway, leaving Braenda to roam in search of fresh grass shoots.

'We may be not far from the western slopes of the high hills', Eirik answers my thoughts, lifts one leg high and slides from his saddle. Saeward is last to do the same. It cannot still be awkward for him, alighting after all this time, surely?

'My bones are stiffening', he flinches. 'I felt well enough in the saddle, though'.

'You could have stayed mounted', I try to fight down the laughter, 'but it would have been even more awkward if you had slid badly off your saddle in a shit-bedecked inn yard'.

'You would have been both cursing *and* cursed then!' Hemming whoops. In years he is most likely a score younger than Saeward, and they have come to blows over this before. I should step in, but before I can I see shadows across the sun – the shadows of horsemen, they seem to me to number eighteen all told.

'Stand by your mounts', I rasp hoarsely, pointing at the shadows. How far off can they be? The sun makes them look bigger, throwing up their backlit shadows against the leafy rim of the woods.

'They are going the wrong way, if they are following us', Saeward notes.

'Is it likely they are looking for a way in?' I caution the others against talking too loudly.

'What became of the charm we were under when we entered these woods?' Eirik asks, raising thoughts of my woman.

'Surely your woman would shield us from our foes whilst we were in here?' Hemming asks cheekily. 'Think back on the way the boughs were bent back for us to enter'.

'I would not take her sheltering us for granted', I counsel, 'or forever'.

'Like that, is it?' Hemming sniffs and winks at Eirik. He elbows me and guffaws.

Mounting again, I warn them to stop talking,

'Keep it down!' Hemming mumbles something under his breath but not loud enough for me to make out. When the shadows have passed we ride the other way for a while, northward.

The wildwood thins as we begin to climb in earnest, scrub and undergrowth taking over from the tall trees. This land is fit only for raising goats - even sheep would turn up their noses at the poor grass! We are climbing steeply on this old road that crosses the landscape in an unforgiving straight line.

Just as I think of dismounting and calling on the others to do the same the hill levels off.

A track crosses the road we were following and I sense we have been this way before.

'Aye, this is the road we followed', Eirik answers after some thought. Saeward nods to my right. Hemming bides his time. This is all new to him.

'Which way was the inn?' I ask Eirik.

He levels his right arm and hand downhill to our right and shakes his head when asked if it is worth going there before taking up the road into Northanhymbra.

'Too far down for us to go and come back this way again', he adds, looking northward for landmarks.

Shrugging my shoulders and putting any thoughts aside about settling down to food, ale and a warm bed, I wave the others on with a heavy sigh,

'There is nothing else for it than to go on'.

'Never a truer word', Eirik digs his knees into his horse's flanks to get her going again.

'From what I know, chasing after Copsig, there was an inn we passed in the snow some way along here where we rode out of the Danelaw into Deira', I say out aloud.

I must sound hopeful, because Saeward and Hemming both look up smiling – or else they think I am a foolish old no-hoper. We shall soon see. Our road climbs again, some snow still clinging to old stone walls, and the air takes on an iron chill as we pass the tree line to the high tops where the road thankfully drops down to the next dale. More snow clings to the roadside grasses and stone walling that looks as old as the road. We pass between earthworks and downhill once more, past where stones have been taken for building. Thus pitted, the way is hard for the horses to pick their way.

I call to the others, who seem to find the going hard,

'It might be best we lead our horses for some way, at least until we reach a stretch where the road is still whole'.

Saeward grumbles, but as Eirik, Hemming and I drop down to the road he does likewise and clutches at the reins of his mare as much for his own safety as to ease her way forward. It is darkening below in the dale to which we find ourselves dropping fairly steeply. How this road's early users made their way down this road with waggons, pack beasts and men at arms without crashing to their backsides is beyond me! The hillside may have been more even.

'There it is!' I laugh out aloud, jabbing the air with my forefinger. 'I knew there was an inn around here'.

'So there is!' Hemming chuckles and nudges Saeward beside him, almost sending him flying on mist greased, damp stones.

'Hey, fool, I nearly went all the way back downhill on my arse!' Saeward scowls and purses his lips at his fellow East Seaxan. Eirik, only just able to stop laughing, steadies Saeward with his free hand.

'I thank you, fellow'. When Saeward turns in his stride and musters a grin for his helper he is almost pulled off his feet by his panicking mount. He yells at the beast, her eyes rolling, *'Whoa!'*

She grunts and whinnies, he pulls back on her and almost wins before she pulls him off his feet and drags him some way downhill on his backside. Saeward tries to dig his heels into the uneven road, to slow her, but the mare has been spooked by something. At last, almost out of sight a good few horse-strides on, she stops and begins cropping the grass beside the road as if nothing had happened.

'She thinks first of her stomach, just like her rider!' Hemming mocks and we see Saeward making a fist at him in the half-dark.

'Better stay out of his reach until he has filled his own belly!' I counsel Hemming.

'Naa-' he shakes his head. 'For all that din he makes he has a heart of gold! He would hardly do anything foolish to one of us that he would wish he had not done'.

'Let it not be said you were not warned', I lead the others downhill and help Saeward to his feet. Eirik holds the reins to his mare and Hemming puts a hand under Saeward's elbow.

Saeward lets fly a thump with a well-aimed fist at Hemming's stomach and the younger man doubles, retching.

'God, what was *that* for?' Hemming groans and wipes his mouth with the back of his leather glove when he his breath comes back.

'I think you know', is all Saeward offers by way of an answer, straightens his jerkin and mailcoat and steadies himself.

When Hemming looks to me I give him a look that tells him he was warned. No more is needed and we make our way in the gathering mist to the one light that shines at the front of a long, low inn.

Someone pushes a door open, letting out a shaft of light onto the broken old road we have been following. A thin, slightly bent old man closes the door behind him and rubs gnarled hands,

'You need rooms for the night and stabling for your mounts?'

Eirik answers for the four of us,

'You might say, aye'. He smirks, adding, 'You are quick on the uptake, old man. Are you the innkeeper?'

'I am not', the old man takes the reins of our horses and leads them into the darkness behind the inn. 'Go in, she is within'.

'I like the sound of *that*', Hemming rubs his upper lip and strides to the door, '*she* is within!'

'*Come in and be quick about it!*' The harsh croak belies the woman's looks. She laughs, throwing her head back, her neck bulging with the rasp of hoarse laughter.

The men within share her wit and raise their cups in salute to her harsh welcome. She stands, hands on hips, looking at us as we make our way between the benches. When we make to sit, she laughs out loudly, asking,

'Well, what are you about, the four of you? If you were hoping for hot food all I have left is lamb stew and rye bread. There is cheese, and I can have turnips put into the stew if you like? Ale for the thirsty wayfarers, I think?'

'Aye', I answer, grinning. The woman looks like a much fuller Braenda, a flowing red mane seeming to grow from her headwear.

'You like what you see?' She laughs, her breasts shaking under a heavy, green shift.

Eyes glitter like ice in the half-light of the fire in its broad hearth.

'I like the welcome', I answer truthfully. 'When I have slaked my thirst and eaten I shall be much more open to offers'.

Her laughter in answer to my wit comes like a crack of thunder. She folds her ham-like arms across a pair of breasts that make the hills we crossed look like pimples in the earth. She heaves and shakes with mirth.

'I think you understood wrongly, friend. I was not offering myself, although the thought is tempting. No, I would crush the life from you. You make a woman come to life, what is your name?'

'I am Ivar Ulfsson, kinsman of King Harold and his ilk. My friends are Saeward, the thickset fellow, his younger friend Hemming –'

'Less of a friend', Saeward grumbles, still sore from being dragged along the old road, 'more a pain in the arse!'

'All right, his fellow East Seaxan Hemming and the youngest one is Eirik', I finish.

'You look a likely bunch indeed!' The innkeeper bellows with laughter. 'Bristling with weapons, like hedgehogs on the road. Where are you hoping to go, got up like that?'

'We are headed first for Jorvik', I answer, forgetting Saeward, who soon makes me aware of my error.

'That is Eoferwic!' Saeward snaps, grinning at me.

The innkeeper quickly puts him right,

'That *is* Jorvik in these parts!' She beams brightly and Saeward bridles, but says nothing. In these parts the old ways of the Danelaw demand the name to be spoken as Jorvik.

'*My* name, Ivar Ulfsson, is Thyrig. When you speak to me, use my given name', she rasps, then flashes a bright smile and winks. 'You never know your luck, Dane!'

A much younger, wan woman breezes between the benches and sets bowls down before us, passes along between the next benches and does the same for other guests. Behind her comes an older child with baskets of cut bread. She reaches one of the baskets out to Saeward, who nods and smiles, and follows the young woman.

One of the men there leers and reaches out a foot to trip the child. Saeward stands and strides ahead of the child, kicks the man's boot away and hoists him to his feet.

'What if *I* tripped over that over-sized lump of flesh you call a foot?' Saeward glowers, brows beetling. The man's leer vanishes. He tries to work loose from Saeward's iron grip and gurgles for help from those seated on the other benches. No help is forthcoming from that quarter, nor from any other quarter.

There can be no help here for a fool.

'Hey, you', Thyrig comes back into the room from her kitchen with a pot of stew in either hand and sets them down with some strength onto the table before us. She stands four-square in front of Saeward and snarls, 'What are you doing with Ceolswein?'

'He was about to trip up the child with the bread baskets. In my eyes a man who torments children is unworthy!'

'Leofa can look after herself. She hops over his boot like a magpie and laughs at him! Ceolswein is a little simple, they all are here. It is something to do with their fathers taking their kinswomen to wife', Thyrig pulls the fool Ceolswein from Saeward's grip and pushes him to his bench. '*You*, East Seaxan, sit yourself down and slurp your stew before it turns cold! I want to hear nothing but champing jaws and slurping from you and your friends. Then we will all get along, do you hear me?'

'Aye, I hear you', Saeward sighs, gives Ceolswein a farewell stare and comes back to my bench to take his share of the fine stew Thyrig has put before us.

'Do you *heed* me?' Thyrig hovers threateningly.

Without looking over his shoulder Saeward stuffs bread into his mouth and nods, slowly. Thyrig demands an answer,

'I asked you, do you *heed* me? *Look* at me when you speak to me, or do you not know how to behave?'

Saeward shakes his head, stuffs more bread into his mouth and almost chokes when Thyrig grips the back of his thick neck with one dish-like hand.

'Answer, *oaf* -'

'Very well, I heed you', Saeward wheezes his answer and tries to catch his breath. I thump his back to help him breathe as he rests his head in his hands. 'What does a man *do* around here to earn a rest?'

'You can rest in your *grave!*' Thyrig snaps. 'Eat before it cools – I do not waste my time cooking when men cannot behave as if they were thankful for it!'

When Thyrig vanishes into the kitchen Saeward asks me under his breath,

'How does a woman get to be like that?'

'When the men around her are fools, like Ceolswein there', the young woman has been eavesdropping behind us without our knowing. She adds, pointing over one shoulder, 'Fear not, I will not tell her. In the morning you will be gone again, on your way, whereas *he* will be here until he falls off the bench with old age!'

'For which we will forever owe you', I tell her. What is your name?'

'I am –'

'*Ecgfrida*, where are you?' Thyrig roars. Ecgfrida answers the call and hurries away after gathering our bowls.

'At least now you know her name', Eirik grins.

'Much good it does me', I suck in air through my teeth and reach out for one of the chunks of bread left.

'Keep that ogre of yours on a chain if ever you come again', Thyrig has come from the kitchen and stands behind me now. 'I could take a liking to you, were it not for those you ride with!'

'I hear *and heed* you, Thyrig', I answer, at which she chuckles, rests a meaty hand on my left shoulder and runs it through my hair as she leaves for the kitchen once more.

'Now *that* is a woman I would not cross!' Hemming splutters and slaps a hand down on the bench beside him.

'What would your woman do if she found her in your bed, I wonder? I think the whole inn would shake asunder between them!'

'There would be nothing left of the inn in the morning!' Saeward offers a pearl of wisdom.

'Nor of me, I think!' I laugh and finish off the bread. 'Is there any ale to wash this down with?'

Ecgfrida comes back into the room with a pitcher of ale, as if she knew I needed it. An uncanny feeling comes over me again, in this hamlet where the men are fools and the women read our thoughts as easily as the spoken word. I shall be thankful of finding the road to Jorvik in the morning, away from these high hills.

Sleep overcomes me easily when I lay my head down at last. Whatever happens in the night, I think I shall be dead to the world come what may until the cock crows. All I hear is Thyrig singing out 'Sweet dreams' to me when I leave the main room of the inn.

Thankfully nothing does happen in the night that I was aware of, and that alone sends a shiver down my back. I sit with the others, awaiting the morning meal, talking of the day ahead. We should reach Jorvik before the day is out and, save for the unlikely meeting of Copsig's or Garwulf's kin, learn of what is afoot there.

'Is there anyone amongst you, who does not want porridge?' Ecgfrida asks. How long she has been standing there behind me, listening in to us, is anyone's guess. None of us stretches out an arm to turn down the offer, so she ambles back to the kitchen and closes the door noisily behind her.

We begin talking again. Never having been this way, Hemming is unable to add anything. He merely nods whenever I look his way. I am in the midst of outlining our way into Jorvik when Hemming tugs at my sleeve and jerks his head toward Ecgfrida, struggling with a wooden platter stacked with bowls and a steaming pot of porridge. Saeward rises to his feet, strides across the stone flags and holds open the kitchen door for her, for which he is given a cheeky kiss on his right cheek.

Above our laughter I hear an earth-shattering crash and the kitchen door is wrenched open. Thyrig stands there, clothes tattered and torn into shreds around her neckline so that her breasts hang loose. It should be enough to put a man off his porridge, all but Hemming, who lays into his bowl like a man starved.

Sweating like a man in the shieldwall on a summer's day, she howls at me,

'Ivar Ulfsson, I want you out of here as soon as you have eaten and saddled your horse! I never want to see you here *ever* again!' That said she slams the door again, bringing down cobwebs and soot from the roof timbers above.

'What brought that on?' Saeward raises his wooden spoon and

points it at the still shaking door. Still flustered and reddened from Ecgfrida's thanks for his help, he tries to take our eyes from him to the now unseen Thyrig by asking me whether I know anything about why the innkeeper is so messed up.

'Heaven alone knows', Eirik shrugs and finishes his porridge. 'Is there any left?'

Hemming answers, blowing on the spoon he holds up to his mouth,

'Help yourself, if there is any left, go on by all means'. He is about to push the spoonful into his mouth when the kitchen door opens again.

Thyrig stands there, tattered clothing half-covered by an apron. Her forehead is still wet and her apron front splashed from washing. Her mouth is drawn down at the corners and she looks grief-stricken. She almost sobs,

'Do not think I came to your door last night with any more than your welfare at heart!'

I am dumbstruck. Shaking my head slowly I absently blow on my porridge, not that I need to as it has cooled anyway. My bowl is hardly empty when Ecgfrida pulls it away and sets down a wooden platter laden with bread, cold fish and meats. She asks,

'What have you been *up* to?'

'Nothing *I* know of', I look up at her, but her eyes are on Saeward, who reddens again and leans away from her when she brushes past him on her way back to the kitchen.

'When you have finished you must go', she tells me again, looking back over one shoulder, 'you and your friends'.

My mouth feels oddly dry, even after drinking my ale.

'Are we ready?' I ask when I have eaten. 'Then we should pay for our beds and fare. *Ecgfrida,* where are you?'

She shows at the kitchen door,

'You called?'

'We wish to pay for our food, ale and beds', I tell her, jiggle my pouch with the few silver coins I have left, and wait for her to dry her hands.

'What *did* you do?' she asks again as I hand over a few silver coins.

'I have done nothing. I slept through the night until cock-crow this morning. One day I think you will learn the truth, but we will be far from here by then, no better off for knowing. Give my greetings to Thyrig and tell her I have done nothing knowingly'.

We are well on our way to the Hvarfe, to look in first on Aethel's steading before crossing the river – *if* we can cross the river for the Jorvik road. Winter may be behind us, but upland rain still swells the rivers that flow down to the Hymbra, and some of the snow will still be melting high up on the moors and mountains.

The steading looks forlorn, the dwelling house empty but for the woodland spirits I think may be there, unseen by us. I push open the door and almost breathe my last with fright. Braenda stands there, naked but for her hair spread across her breasts.

'Ivar –'

'Braenda, what did you get up to last night?' I ask straight out. 'The innkeeper Thyrig looked as if she had been attacked by ravens!'

'She came to your room, glistening with scented oils under her clothing, fit to wreak havoc on you in your drunken daze! Did you not know your ale had been tampered with? I had to teach her a lesson, Ivar – I was thinking of *you*'. Braenda seems to glide across the leaf-strewn dirt floor to me and puts her arms around my waist.

'So you did come?' I hold her to me. 'I was dead to the world - you know that anyway'.

She asks under her breath,

'Have you time?'

'I must first tell my friends to make themselves at home. Where did Aethel and Hrothulf sleep?'

'I will show you', Braenda smiles warmly and leads me to a dark room with a broad bed.

'First things first', I tell her.

I pull away from her and she lets her arms drop idly to her side in mock anguish.

'... I have a few things to do here', I tell the others, 'not least of which is to see that Theodolf's bed is ready for him when he comes home'..

'Braenda would not be here, would she?' Hemming asks, tongue-in-cheek. He nods and half-closes his eyes. 'Well, we will make ourselves at home as much as we are able to. Is there any food, or anything to drink here?'

'You are welcome to root about, as long as you leave everything else as you found it', I warn, eager to get back to Braenda.

'Go then, fill her with your seed and we shall see one another later, God willing', Eirik waves me away. Saeward and Hemming stand idly, watching. They grin wryly as I vanish through a door behind them.

Braenda snores as I snuggle up to her, making out she has waited too long, but comes alive when I cup my hands around her breasts and kiss her neck. We writhe around in the bed Aethel shared with my friend, her thighs wrapped around my midriff, her teeth nipping my chest playfully.

228

We become one, and time stands still whilst we sate our hunger for one another. When we are spent I fall back onto the head bolster behind me. Braenda lies across my manhood, her deep copper hair covering my chest. The long fingers of her right hand play with her tresses whilst her left hand wanders, spider-like across my lower midriff.

'I would never let another man spend his seed in me now that I am with child again', she murmurs, '*your* child, Ivar'.

'Did you not have a child by me after we first met in Menai?' I ask idly.

'She was fostered by friends in Mierca'.

'Does she look like you – or me?' I press. 'I should like to see her one day, whilst she is still young – in the flower of her youth, so to speak'.

'She has your eyes, and like you she can be testy –'

'I wonder where she gets that from', I joke. Braenda thumps me, whether in play or in earnest I do not know.

'What is her name?' I ask.

To me it is an everyday thing, knowing what your own child's name is. But on hearing from Braenda, I am not sure I do want to know after all.

'Her name is Eadburga. She thinks she is the younger sister of Aelfgifu, your kinsman's bride. I had to set her right when she took a liking to you at Ceaster', Braenda sits up and begins to pull on her skirts. When I stroke her she shakes me off and tells me my friends await me, 'Time is on the march, Ivar, as are the Northmen. You must be away from here before they come'.

I pull on my breeks as she leaves the room, and don my tunic just as Saeward raps on the wicker door.

'We should be on our way, friend. Your woman thinks the Northmen are on their way. Knowing her, I would not argue'.

'Tell the others to saddle the horses and have them brought to the front of the steading here', I point to where I think is the front of the dwelling. He laughs and points the other way.

'After such a short time with your woman you are out of sorts! Come, pull on your mailcoat and get your weapons. We will wait outside for you', Saeward snorts with silent laughter and leaves the room.

Braenda has gone, it seems. Her leaving is so sudden, as if she does not wish to talk further about Eadburga.

The child has grown so quickly! How could the wilful Eadburga be *my* child, when Braenda and I only met after Harold and Tostig had cornered Gruffyd in Gwynedd after the death of Aelfgar? Why would

Braenda tell me this, to hurt me or stop me asking more about our child?

We take shelter amongst trees nearby as a score or so Northmen enter the thwait. Their leader kicks open the outer door and enters, vanishing from sight in the gloom. Not long afterward he shows in the doorway and barks something at the mounted men outside. One of them, I think he must be a man of the same rank, wrinkles his nose and shakes his head. The young noble who had entered Aethel's dwelling draws himself to his full height before taking the few steps to mount his horse and the *conroi* rides off again, toward Jorvik.

I would say the young noble had thought of burning the steading but was over-ruled by a wiser fellow. They may be back, but by then we will be miles from here.

'We will shadow them', I tell the others. 'They may lead us to a river crossing'.

Keeping the Northmen in sight is easily said.   Our way takes us through deep dales and over becks that empty into the river, and it is only by listening for them crashing through the undergrowth that we keep them safely out of sight but within hearing – until we hear them fording the river Hvarfe well to the north of the steading.

'So this is the way they came', Eirik wonders aloud, standing in his stirrups when we come to the river bank.

Allowing time to cross after the Northmen, we stay out of their sight and hearing, and then take another road. I would say they do not know their way about too well, but well enough to have found this crossing. It could be useful to us in times to come.

The land is hilly between us and Jorvik, I know. It is also fairly hilly between the road the Northmen took and the way we will take. Thickly wooded as it is, there is no way they could stumble upon us on their way east. Are they headed for Jorvik, and if so where can they be housed there that they would not fall foul of the many who may well wish them ill?

Eirik is first to make a halt when we can be no more than a few miles from the *burh*.

'*This* is where their road crosses ours going into Jorvik', he tells me, holding back a tall sapling to show the Northmen passing below us.

'Follow the track that leads left to Tolentun', I answer.

When he looks askance at me I hold my right arm up, one finger showing a way that will take us well to the north.

'There is bound to be an inn not far ahead, where traders and craftsmen drive their waggons and carts into the *burh* from Treske and further afield'.

The Northmen are soon out of sight on the road to Jorvik and we cross well behind them. Beyond these low hills are the higher ridges that mark the moorland around Helmsleag. There lies safety, but we are not here for our wellbeing. We have a task, to spy out the land. To what end will become clear when we find someone who knows the whereabouts of the earls and the *aetheling* Eadgar.

14

We find an inn nestling amongst trees at a crossroad by Tolentun, one of the hamlets that lie abreast of a by-road to Treske. To look at the inn from outside there is nothing untoward. To be safe I ease myself from my saddle and ask Saeward to take Braenda's reins then make my way forward on foot to look around the stables. If there are Northmen in Jorvik, they could just as easily be out this way, close as it is to the north of the great *burh*.

To begin with I stride easily between the trees, ducking low branches, slipping between bushes and the few outbuildings. Where the gap is greater I inch forward doubled up, and finally come to the stable. Hemming is close behind me and almost comes to grief, stumbling on a molehill.

I wait for him to catch up before passing the wattle and daub wall of the stable to peer through a partly open wicker door on its western side. We enter and look around, to see what we might learn here.

There are several horses, and lances have been stacked together against the low hay loft, one bearing a lord's war pennon. A thought runs through my head, a little far-fetched, too outlandish perhaps to waste my time on. What if we bind the lances together against the main pillar, and I let the outlanders chase me into the stable for my friends to fall on them from the hay loft. They are six to our four, but we can overcome them when they try to free their weapons.

Hemming is for that, and offers more,

'We can hobble their horses, too, Ivar'.

'*Good* - can you ask Eirik here?' I send him back to fetch our Danelaw friend. 'Ask Saeward to come, too. He can bring the horses and tie them to one of the outbuildings there. His sword arm will come in handy when we do meet the outlanders'.

He touches his forelock in the manner of a ceorl, and vanishes, leaving me on my own by the stable. Not wishing to stir the foe into an untimely skirmish I stay out of sight, should any of the Northmen come to look over their horses. I want to take them wholly unaware. As it is, when Hemming and Eirik show from behind the nearest of the outbuildings no-one has stirred within the inn. Saeward comes next, puffing, out of breath.

'You might eat less', Eirik tells him thoughtlessly.

'And you might talk less', Saeward growls in answer.

'Hush, *both of you!*' I snap. Someone stirs at the back of the inn and it sounds as if they are coming our way. Pressing myself against the stable wall I hiss at my friends, '*Pull back!*'

They pull back, out of sight, and I follow the wall away from the wicker door. Only the birds can be heard. Luckily our own horses keep quiet and the Northman who comes to the stable is no wiser when he peers into the gloom, shrugs and strides back to the inn again.

I breathe out again and Hemming comes back with Eirik and Saeward in tow.

'Eirik, can you hobble their mounts, and Saeward bind the lances tightly together against the pillar?' I busy myself binding the shields together, the loose end tied taut against the rails that their horses have been tethered to. Saeward watches for anyone coming back.

'Can the three of you climb up there, into the hay loft whilst I enter the inn', I smack my hands together to rid myself of hay that has become stuck to them by my sweat. We have to work fast, so as not to be taken off guard.

Now I have the hard task, of rousing the Northmen from their slumbers enough to make them want to chase after me. I push the inn door open and stand there against the light,

'Do any of you numbskulls understand Aenglish?'

'What are you talking about, fool, calling *us* numbskulls?' one of them answers. The others laugh. One of the seated men blows into his ale and almost chokes as he demands from me,

'Who are *you* that you come here talking in this way to us? What do you take us for, Northmen?'

This raises more laughter and one of the seated men throws a raw turnip at me, narrowly missing my right ear. It is time for me to ask,

'Then who are you, with Northman lances and pennon in the stables?'

'We have been sent by Lord Gospatric to spy out the land in Eoferwic, to see what is happening there', one tells me. 'We have been told they have built a stronghold near the east bank of the river, and that all the homes and workshops between there and the river have been razed and flooded. There is a Northman shire reeve and what they call a *castellan* who oversees the stronghold itself. Maerleswein and Lord Eadgar are with the aetheling's sister Margarethe and King Maelcolm, so these outlanders must have taken it upon themselves to carve up the earldom between them. Who are *you*, anyway?'

'I am Ivar Ulfsson', I tell him.

'I have heard of you! So, *you* are Ivar Ulfsson? I must say I thought you were younger', the fellow smiles warily, 'and fitter'.

I answer wryly, drawing grins from those around me.

'I have my days'.

'I am Thegn Leodmaer by the way. Are you not a bit long in the tooth for the antics I heard you get up to?'

'What *have* you heard about me?' I fold my arms and stand, feet apart, ready for what may yet come, but then Saeward thumps into the inn behind me.

'*What* is happening in here? We have been waiting out there, ready to take on these Northmen with our blades and you are in here nattering with them like an old woman- '

'Old *women*, you say?' Leodmaer laughs fitfully, almost crashing to the floor when he leans back on the bench. One of his men reaches out and hauls him back by the scruff of the neck, just in time. 'Thanks, Eadmer. Answer me this, newcomer is the man Ivar a friend of yours?'

Saeward grins wickedly and waits before answering to loud laughter and slow hand-clapping,

'Well, I would not go as far as that. It is enough that I know him!'

'I thank you, Saeward', my answer is made through a thin smile. 'One day I shall put in a good word for you, too'.

'Your friend Saeward has a ready wit, Ivar',　　　Leodmaer tells me drily, stands and strides toward me. He takes first my hand and then Saeward's,

'What say you to our riding into Eoferwic dressed as Northmen, Ivar?'

'Do you speak their tongue -' I ask, 'any one of you?'

'Well, *no*', Leodmaer shrugs. 'Why do you ask?'

'What if you are tested?' Saeward asks next. 'One of their lords might ask or tell you to do something, and you may be ringed by many. Best if two or three of you enter the burh as Brothers. The outlanders do not bother men of the cloth, and you would not have to say anything save say 'bless you' to folk in the streets'.

'You have done this yourself?' Leodmaer squints at Saeward, trying to test him.

'We have both done it, at the great abbey church of the West Mynster when Willelm was crowned by Ealdred', Saeward answers for us both. Leodmaer's eyes widen and his jaw drops. He turns back to the bench and gulps down a mouthful of his ale.

Leodmaer quietens his men and asks where they might find monks' habits.

'There is a house of God near the Earlsburh, where we could ask for such clothing –'one of his men answers.

'What about getting there?' Leodmaer asks.

He squints at Saeward before asking anew,

'What about getting there - and who would we ask when we reach there? These Brothers are not likely just to hand out habits to any

234

passers-by'.

'I still have mine', Saeward tells Leodmaer.

'Would you be willing to risk your necks on *our* behalf?' Leodmaer gapes at us both. 'Are - *were* you ever a Brother?'

'Let me say only this. I came by the robe by cunning, but with the best aims at heart', Saeward grins to laughter from Leodmaer's men.

'It will be *your* necks at risk, if you can call it a risk, when you enter Eoferwic as Brothers', I tell Leodmaer.

He brightens and sits back down on the bench between his men. Swilling ale around in his mouth he looks up at Saeward. The East Seaxan reads Leodmaer's thoughts and tells him he will take two of his men,

'One should be as big as you, Thegn Leodmaer'.

'You think I should go?'

'If you wish to spy out the land, aye', I speak up for Saeward as Eirik and Hemming enter. Leodmaer stands and makes to draw his sword but Saeward stays his hand.

'They are friends', Saeward tells him.

'How many more are there of you?' Leodmaer asks.

He stares uneasily at the 'newcomers' and at me.

'These are my three friends who ride with me. There are no others', I swear.

'Not that I am afraid, you understand', Leodmaer drains his cup and bellows for someone to come and fill it. An old fellow opens a door to my left, peers out and shuts the door again. Muffled talking goes on behind the door and a young woman shows.

'My mother has brewed more ale, Lord', she squeaks with fright, half-hidden by the heavy, studded wooden door. I wonder where it came from, not being the usual sort of door you might find in an inn.

'*God*, we could be here forever - what are we doing waiting *here?*' Leodmaer grunts. He sighs and throws up his hands.

'Nothing worthwhile comes from rushing', Hemming sits on one end of a bench beside some of Leodmaer's Northanhymbrans.

'Well said', one of them yawns and stretches, bumping one of his friends across the back of his head. A tussle begins and Leodmaer roars at them both. The tussle stops and the men sit like children at the long table.

'Is he always like this?' Saeward asks one man.

Nodding toward Leodmaer he asks further,

'Is he always this heavy-handed?'

Leodmaer glares at me and then at Saeward,

'Who asked *you?*'

'What he means is that your men seem cowed by you', I tell the thegn. 'We are all going to have to fight the outlanders soon. Your men should have some fighting spirit'.

'Fighting spirit is not the same as being unruly, as King Harold would have told you, Dane. I am all for my men throwing themselves into the fight, but I will not have them behaving like fools - *or children!*'

'However you want it, Thegn Leodmaer', I nod. He sits fiddling with the pommel of his sword as a buxom woman struggles through the door with a pot of ale in either hand. Saeward is across the room before anyone can even bring themselves to stand and takes one of the ale pots from her.

'*Bless* you, young man!' she pulls his head toward hers and plants a wet kiss on his forehead.

'Saeward, my man, you seem to have a *knack* with women!' Hemming laughs out aloud. 'Only beware she is no witch, like the last one who took a liking to you!'

'Uncouth wretch, what was that about a witch?'

She rounds on Hemming, slaps him on one ear with a well-aimed open left hand and stands before him, threatening more.

'Well – *what?*'

'I think that was uncalled for, fool!' Saeward also rounds on Hemming and thumps him on his right shoulder.

'*Oaf* – have a care! That was my sword arm!' Hemming swears at his fellow East Seaxan, nursing his shoulder. 'Is it not enough her belting me without you rounding on me?'

'You will live', I laugh. 'It is not as if you were likely soon to be beset by the outlanders. *Worse than a babe in arms!*'

Hemming purses his lips and takes the cup of ale the innkeeper offers. She pinches his cheeks with both hands and plants a kiss on his beak-like nose.

'What was that for?' Hemming splutters, a mouthful of the ale dribbling over his chin.

'*Worse than a babe!*' she echoes my words and vanishes behind the heavy door to the kitchen or whatever it hides. We are left to talk about what we think Leodmaer should do to learn what he needs to know in the great *burh*.

Saeward asks out of turn,

'What is her name?'

'What is whose name?' Leodmaer snaps, rightly annoyed by my friend's aside, out of turn as it is whilst we are looking for a way of entering Jorvik without being taken and caged.

It is whilst we chide Saeward for sidetracking that I hear a rider draw up outside the inn. Leodmaer looks up, as do Hemming and Eirik. Saeward is still in a world of his own, like as not dreaming about having the innkeeper for his buxom lover. The outer door crashes open, a breathless rider thumps into the inn and makes for the nearest bench.

'What is amiss?' Leodmaer asks first, before I can open my mouth. We ring the fellow, agog for news he must be bringing.

'We need men, *armed* men and many of them to help fight the outlanders!' the fellow blurts out, mopping his forehead with a dirty rag from his belt. 'Our rising is doomed, lest men come to swell our ranks!'

'You see at least half a score here, armed to the teeth and ready to pitch in! *Lead the way!*' I set my cup down on the table as the innkeeper shows again with platters of food.

She sees us standing around the newcomer, buckling our sword belts and reaching for our helms, and yells above the hubbub,

'You have asked for food, sit and eat or my maids and I shall have wasted our time readying it. Go, throw your lives away *after* you have eaten and paid for it all! *Sit!*'

We all dutifully sit and wait for her to put out our food, all but Saeward.

'What is your name, woman? I wish you were mine, strong-willed that you are, and big-armed!'

'Why, what a wonderful man you are!' she gushes. It seems suddenly altogether unlike her, this new turn. 'I am Cuthfrida, what is *your* good name?'

'Good woman', he begins, and she reddens like a young maid, 'good woman I am Saeward the *'Northman-slayer''*

Northmen he has slain, true, but this is the first time he has ever called himself as such. Hemming and Eirik look at one another, smirking. Leodmaer looks fit to burst. This is so unlike Saeward. It is as if he were throwing himself at Cuthfrida - a willing husband?

'Saeward *the Northman-slayer*, you call yourself eh?' Leodmaer slaps the East Seaxan on his back hard enough to launch his teeth into the broth and earns a dark scowl.

'I have *earned* the name. What have you done of late, besides broadening your backside whilst the Northmen empty your coffers and take your women?'

Leodmaer gapes as Saeward draws his sword and shows him the dents along its blade.

'Friend, whilst you have been slopping your ale Ivar, Hemming and myself, have been cutting them down in swathes. We have been doing so since before the bastard king was crowned by the old fool Ealdred at the West Mynster! You have lived a charmed life here in Northanhymbra since Harald Sigurdsson was beaten roundly, *and* King Harold had to come north to do that! Earl Morkere and his fool brother were unable to thwart the Norsemen and Ivar, here, has been fighting since then – at both ends of the kingdom!' Saeward is getting into his stride now, and Leodmaer sits gaping up at him. 'Had your earl and his brother been able to throw back the Norsemen, King Harold would still have been alive today!'

'Well said, Saeward', Cuthfrida stands at the half-open studded door, arms folded, 'now sit down and eat, for God's sake. I would *never* have a husband who stood wasting hot air when good, hot food sat before him!'

Saeward slides his sword back into its sheath and sits, abashed. *Husband* – did I hear right?

We sit, ladling broth into our mouths, trying to stop ourselves from laughing and spraying the broth at one another. Saeward looks about but only sees bobbing heads as we all bend our backs trying hard to finish eating without collapsing in silent mirth.

'You will never know what a narrow scrape you had there', Saeward', I tell him as we head our horses onto the road for Jorvik.

Leodmaer and his men are ahead and behind us. Some grin at me as I catch their eyes, so I wink by way of an answer. We are about to do what we came here for.

Saeward, now to be known as the *'Northman-slayer'*, rides alongside Hemming, behind me. Eirik rides to my right. Leodmaer is well to the fore. The rider has passed on to the next hamlet with the tidings, happy that he has brought our number into the struggle.

Having ridden this way before, I know we are within an hour's hard ride of Bootham on the north side of Jorvik once we reach the broad road that runs between Jorvik and Treske. We shall soon see others, hopefully, riding to take on the Northmen.

'Soon', Hemming breathes out, 'soon we shall be doing what we set out to do'.

'See only that you redden your blade with the outlanders' blood!' Saeward growls behind me.

So that Hemming understands his meaning, Saeward adds,

'You very nearly shed good Aenglish blood at Exanceaster'.

'It would never have come to that', Hemming answers. He would sooner Saeward did not raise the matter again, lest others hear wrongly. 'I was looking for a way out when I met you two. I wish I knew what happened to Guthfrith – he would have relished reddening *his* sword with Northman blood!'

Saeward falls silent at Hemming raising his friend's name. Slaying Guthfrith was the worst thing he could have done and I know it will haunt him long after, if not to his dying day.

There are more men at the crossroads, milling around, waiting for a leader to take them onward. Leodmaer presses his horse through the throng and calls for them to lend an ear. At first no-one seems to listen, so when he roars like a bull on heat they all fall silent,

'Now I have your ears and eyes, can anyone tell me what they know?'

This sounds too much of a risk to me. When after only a short time of waiting Leodmaer hears nothing, and it takes me aback as well, he points at one of the young thegns at the head of his fyrdmen and asks,

'What do you know, friend?'

'Aside from hearing of unrest in Eoferwic, I know nothing. What I think is –'

'I will come to what anyone thinks', Leodmaer breaks in high-handedly. He stares at those around him on foot and on horseback. 'Those of you who are mounted come with me. The men on foot can follow Ivar here'.

'I would sooner follow Ivar Ulfsson than you anyway!' the man closest to me says under his breath and draws a baleful stare.

'Who is this Ivar, that we must follow him?' another asks.

'Aye, as he is kin to Earl Tostig we might be better off taking someone's horses', yet another cackles.

'What – he is one of *Tostig's* ilk?' Angry eyes burn into me. I did not need this now.

'He is a good leader!' Saeward barks angrily at them. 'Being also King Harold's ilk he has my backing!'

'They were as bad as one another!' I hear the fyrdman snap back who told everyone I was Tostig's ilk. 'We are better off with Thegn Eyvind!'

Yet another booms loudly, like a thunder-clap,

'You will follow behind Ivar Ulfsson!'

Who is this fellow – I think I should know him, if I could see –

'*Osgod*, where have *you* been?' Eirik yells gleefully.

'Eirik, I am glad to see you are with a trusted friend – and Saeward! Who is the other fellow?' Osgod strides easily through the press of men who part to let him through.

'I should have known you would be about in this corner of the shire!' Lifting my left leg over Braenda's saddle, I slide down her right flank and drop to the stony road. I pump his hand and slap his back when he comes close enough. 'It is good to see *you* again, friend! Is

Harding with you?'

No sooner have I asked than Harding growls his way past the nearest fyrdmen.

'You *missed* me, Dane?'

Harding scowls, and then the lines around his jaw crease deeply as he grins broadly at me, takes my sword hand and pumps it with both his great hands. When he is done I have to rub my hand to get the blood running through once more.

He next shakes Saeward by the shoulders, cuffs his right ear and glares at Eirik – before laughing hollowly and telling the fellow not to fear,

'Annoying cuss that you are, I like you!'

Eirik comes back with,

'Well, it helps'.

'Aye, *it helps!*' Harding gives him a friendly slap on one cheek and laughs deeply. '*Come*, Eirik, we shall slay a few more Northmen between us!'

'I thought we had beaten the Northmen', one of Thegn Eyvind's fyrdmen throws up his arms, his spear narrowly missing Harding's right ear.

'*You* will be beaten if you do that again, fool! We fought Harald Sigurdsson's Norsemen the other year. You have had time to put on some fat around your arse since then. These are Northmen sent by this new king Willelm to put us down! Are we going to *let* them put us down?' Harding clenches his fists and punches the air, bringing a roar from everyone around him.

'Who is your lord, Thegn Leodmaer?' Osgod asks loudly, trying to be heard above the din.

'Earl Gospatric sent me ahead from King Maelcolm's stronghold near Beruwic to learn more about the Northmen in Eoferwic', Leodmaer tells him.

'Will Lord Gospatric himself come south to help us?' Osgod asks further, knowing full well what the answer to that will be.

Leodmaer is stumped. He has been told no more than what Gospatric wanted him to know. It is the mark of a born leader. Should Leodmaer have fallen into the hands of the Northmen in Jorvik, they would have used all their means – short of killing him – to learn his master's wishes or aims. Only when they knew he could tell them nothing would they quietly do away with him.

'Very well, Leodmaer, as Eyvind, Ivar and I know the land we will ride on into Eoferwic. *You* will bring the men on foot with you. When you are in the burh, we will fight side by side and that is how you will learn what you need to know for your lord, Gospatric'.

'What of his kinsman Osulf?' I ask. 'Is he at Baebbanburh or is he also with Maelcolm?'

'Lord Osulf is with his kinsman', Leodmaer stares unblinking at me, as though I had no right to know, 'and so are the *aetheling* Eadgar, Earl Waltheof, Earl Eadmund and Earl Morkere'.

I wonder how it feels for Eadgar to be under one roof with those who sold him out to Willelm. It must be like suffering from a bad stomach ache, whatever they tell him now!

His young earls may have seen how their new master used them, showed them off at Falaise. In the same way he laid out the new-found finery he took without asking from the West Mynster and left for all his underlings there to gape at.

It is a sobering thought, even for someone who thought the grass might be greener on the Northman side of the hill that he might not have been worth as much to Willelm as he led them to believe. Now they are fawning on both Maelcolm and Eadgar, which one will see through them first, or will they awaken one day knowing they have been another man's tools? I would not want to be in their shoes when that happens, God no! Where would they go *then*, overseas?

The Danes would want no such fickle friends. My uncle Knut left his new underlings in no doubt about how he meant to go on when he took the crown here two score years or so ago. He had Eadric '*Streona*' beheaded with the sword for going back on his oath to both himself and Aethelred's eldest son Eadmund '*Ironside*', not once but twice - *each*. In that way he showed that no man crossed him and lived. That was something I already knew when I came here, not long after my father Jarl Ulf was slain at the altar of Roskilde's church. As I think back on it, my half-brother Svein is no easier to fool.

Olaf Haraldsson and his brother Magnus would be *no* more welcoming, since the young earls had helped my kinsman end *their* father's dream of taking Northanhymbra at Staenfordes Brycg

That leaves Count Baldwin in Flanders, whose kinsman Tostig was also beaten near Jorvik. Would Tostig put *his* trust in them? I think not.

They would have to sink or swim with Eadgar, show themselves to be his stalwarts. And if the *aetheling* asks me, 'should *I* trust them?' will he take my unwillingness to answer with them around as fair warning? Or should I speak openly and risk their wrath?

'Ivar, are you brooding again?' Saeward pulls me back from the realms of deep thought.

'I was thinking, my friend', I answer, not wishing to tell him *what* my thoughts were.

He does not press me further, having shown he can read my thoughts, my wishes and dreams - even when I miss my woman?

'I was wondering how Eadgar can stand having the likes of Eadwin, Morkere or Waltheof around him', I allow him so far into my thoughts. He nods, knowing that is as much as I shall tell him for now. He will learn more another time.

'There was a time when I might have asked if you were looking forward to fighting the Northmen in Eoferwic', Saeward winks and stirs his mare forward after Osgod and Harding. A few score others follow on, eager to cross swords with the outlanders. Before clashing, however, we must see what we are at. Has any of them seen what the foe's strongholds look like, inside and out, and how they lie? If so, will they share their knowledge before we go wasting men's lives?

I press Braenda forward, to ride between Osgod and Harding.

'How do the Northmen sit in Jorvik?' I ask them.

Harding looks at me, shrugs and nods toward Osgod,

'Ask him. He knows the lie of the land south of Treske. I am here to make up our strength'.

'They have two wooden strongholds, one near either river bank', Osgod enlightens me. 'When we stop near Bootham I shall show you what they look like. One of their builders drew the outlines before putting them up'.

'I take it these scrapings look like what is there?' I ask. It may seem odd to ask this, but men often alter their plans before they build something as weighty as the walls they need to hide behind when they are afraid of attack. Osgod stares into the air before answering.

'Some of my men were there when they were built, Ivar', he answers almost as if talking to a testy child.

'My friends in Jorvik-' He looks over one shoulder at Saeward and grins at me. 'Why is it I always look at Saeward when I say 'Jorvik' for Eoferwic? What was I saying? Ah - my friends in Jorvik watched them going up when I was away in Wealas, and they told me the stockades were true to the drawn outline. Since coming back I have seen them for myself and will vouch for my friends' knowledge'.

'As long as you are happy', I draw Braenda's reins and let them pass whilst I wait for my friends to catch up.

'What have you learned?' Hemming asks first.

'I have learned that the outlanders have built their rat-holes on either side of the river', I smile bleakly.

'Can we make them suffer?' Eirik asks, grinning.

'All I can say is, from what we know we may not suffer as many losses as if we went in blindfold', I answer, yawning. 'I am tired. Let us

242

hope we can rest in Jorvik before we take on the foe'.

Tongue-in-cheek he offers,

'I should think we can grant you that, old man. Once a man passes two score years and ten, he needs all the rest he can seize on'.

'*Young pup*, even asleep I could take you on and win!' I slap my left hand on his back.

He coughs and laughs,

'You may be right, Ivar, whatever you say. I have always taken my share of the fighting in a shieldwall, but I would never step forward out of line to take on a foe. I am no hero!'

'Who would you say had the makings of a hero, Eirik?' I ask as we ride side by side at a trot.

He thinks long and hard, I can see he feels awkward about answering, but cannot think of an answer and looks down at the road under his horse's hooves. Just as I think he has thought of something he shakes his head and presses his lips together, hopelessly at odds with himself.

'When standing in the shieldwall, how would *anyone* know a hero from the rest of us?' I try to help him out but he can only shrug and look away.

I suck in the cool air of an early summer's evening and tell him. It is unlikely he believes me now, but there will come a day.

Braenda trots dutifully side by side with Eirik's mount as I try to think of another way of raising his hopes. He wants to be seen as a warrior, and my kinsman made him a thegn because he saw in Eirik a man of his word, a man into whose hands he could entrust one corner of his kingdom.

'I think you, as much as anyone, could be a hero. You will not know until the time comes, and then it will dawn on you. It is a foolhardy man who steps out of line in the shieldwall, believe me. I have seen them, un-schooled in the ways of warriors. A king lost his crown having put his trust in such men, only through not waiting long enough for those who would have kept his crown on his head'.

He looks away again – *overwhelmed?* It is for him now to fulfil my faith in him, shine and show how my faith in him is warranted. As hounds we will hunt together for the outlanders, with Osgod and Harding at the head of our pack.

The smell of burning reaches my nose. Others among us may well know what it means, but we will see for ourselves soon enough. I will not come by any rest if we are to attack by night, yet a night-time foray could bring the Northmen low. It would be as well that Jorvik could sleep again, safe in the knowledge that their would-be masters have been shown to be mere men, as are we.

'What is it that burns?' Hemming sniffs the air, the last to know.

'Homes and workshops are afire, friend', one of Osgod's men tells him tartly. Hemming stares at me and shrugs.

'The fellow has kin in the *burh*?'

'If you were not so unfeeling, Hemming, you would not have to ask', Saeward groans. He is a man of the earth, a friend of men, understanding in many ways. This is the new Saeward we see now, not the oaf I first met at Wealtham all those years ago. I hope he lives long and well, to ride by my side against the outlanders.

'Very well, then, he has kin in the burh. He will get nowhere if he loses his head to thoughts of settling scores. Best we let them think they will get away with it – lull them into false hopes of living long in the bosom of their God'.

'Surely, he is *your* God too?' Saeward tries to stare him down.

Hemming is unabashed,

'Our kingdom comes first. Only then, when we have rooted out the outlanders like weevils from bread can we think of worship. That was the mistake King Aelfred made, withdrawing to Cipanham at the Yuletide before dealing with Guthrum'.

'Your forefathers came with Guthrum', I tell the fellow.

'I am an Aenglishman, Ivar. With you it may be otherwise. I is true my forefathers came with Guthrum. My mother's folk were Celts. What does that make *me*, if we can not see ourselves as of this land?' He smiles and digs his knees into his mare's flanks.

'That sets you right, Ivar', Saeward smiles too, but stays beside me. 'We are all Aenglishmen here, wherever our fore-elders hailed from, even you – or do you not see it that way?'

'You are right as usual these days', I have to laugh, and Saeward laughs with me.

'I sometimes wonder, though', Eirik puts in. 'I mean wherever I went in Mierca they made sure of telling me I was one of Harold's Danelaw thegns'.

'They still bear a grudge against the West Seaxans for selling out their kinsmen in the east, and against *us* for being of Guthrum's or Haesten's ilk', one of Osgod's men tells us.

Another rider adds from behind me to my right,

'Aye, Morkere kept calling us 'his Danes'. I ask you! *My* kin came in the deep, long rowing ships from the old lands to the south of the Jutes, well before the Danes, as did those of Wulfram here, eh?'

'Aye, true Ordmaer. True enough, in the old rowing ships like our Jutish neighbours'.

With much nodding of heads, those around us avow their Aenglishness. There will be no quarter for the outlanders when they are cornered within their wooden walls. Fire puts paid to all men's hopes of holding onto stockaded strongholds against those set on razing them to the ground.

'It is as we feared', a rider comes down the line from telling Osgod what he needed to know.

One asks from close behind Eirik

'What – *homes* have been burnt?'

'More, *worse,* the great church of Saint Peter is *also* afire!'

'*Wha-a-t -*' everyone seems to yell at once. Those few nearest me swear.

'*That* is unheard of! Who do they think they *are*, these outlanders?!'

A loud crack comes from the great church, like thunder. At Bootham we see the blazing roof fall in behind the church walls, crashing down in a shower of sparks.

'God be forgiving!' Saeward mumbles.

'They have gone too far for that! The bones of our great earl, Siward lie within – what would Waltheof say?' asks one of the thegns.

'Waltheof made his bed in the bosom of the new king. Now he and his brother earls toady to Eadgar. What he would think has no bearing on us, unless he makes good his oath to King Eadweard!' another spits. He looks toward me, shaking his head in disbelief.

'The youth has much to make good, to his late king – Harold above all!' I let him know. 'He fled before the fight against the Northman duke. Although he fought well enough at Lunden Brycg, that makes for little in my eyes. He would not look me in the eyes when I saw him together with the *aetheling* at Thorney'.

'You outlived King Harold?'

'Much to my shame, aye', I nod slowly. 'I was knocked on the head when I sought to take the fight to the outlanders. We might yet have won, and men still showed on the hill from the Andredes Leag even as the Northmen beset Harold'.

'He died a hero, *the usurper*?' another thegn asks. I make out not to have heard this last insult on my kinsman's head.

'He did indeed die a hero, wounded by an arrow. Even with his wound bound he fought on and was set on by three of the outlanders. It was then that I was hit on the head'.

The first thegn sucks on his teeth,

'Just as well for you then', he tells me. I am asked next, '*How* were you able to flee?'

'I came to before they came along the hilltop to spear those who still stirred, and donned the helm from one of their dead. Friends helped me away. I have no knowledge of how Hakon Sveinson reached Lunden, but he was in the shieldwall that met the duke and some few hundred of his horsemen. Since then I have neither seen nor heard of him. Our bowmen saw them off, some of whom were friends and only one still lives – as far as I know'.

'You do not *know?*'

I cast my thoughts back on where I saw him last, in the earls burh at Ceaster

'He was wounded fighting off a mounted Northman near Ceaster. The rider and his friends were making sport of a young woman'.

The thegn fingers his thick, curling grey beard, telling me,

'The lad has the makings of a warrior hero. In the world as it is now, he will not last long'.

'I keep telling him that', I answer.

'How did you help?'

'We laid into them, sent them packing did we not?'

This last I say to Eirik, Saeward and Hemming having by now ridden some way ahead.

'Oh aye, we *did*. We caught another one almost with his breeks around his ankles not far away. Theodolf was left at a nunnery, and was later brought to us at Ceaster'.

'Where he is now', I nod.

'This Theodolf - was his father's name Hrothulf?' another thegn asks, having been listening in for the past half mile as we neared the Earlsburh. 'When I think back I knew a Hrothulf who had a son, but he was backward'.

After a little thought I put him right,

'Hrothulf thought so, too. We were all taken back, Hrothulf, his woman Aethel and me, over the following days, when he showed us otherwise! He was with us on Caldbec Beorg, his and his father's bows making up for the lack of numbers amongst the bowmen but Hrothulf fell before the king'.

'*So* - he was *well* worth taking south with you', the thegn purses his lips in wonder.

'Aye *and* he saved the life of Ansgar the stallari with a timely arrow', Saeward tells the thegn. Having hung back at the Earlsburh gates to let us catch up, he has heard some of what was said between the thegn and me.

'Listening in, were you?' I chide. He pays no heed to me and lauds Theodolf's skill with the bow to all and sundry until someone roars out aloud from within the earl's dwelling.

'*Scum of the earth* – would you believe the outlanders have gutted the hall of everything they could carry?'

Osgod shows in the doorway of the great hall and bears out what his underling has already let the world and his wife know,

'It is true. There is not a bed, nor any bedding, in the building! These outlanders must the worst thieves I have come across. There will be no easy rest for us this night, and we will have to find what rest we can, *wherever* we can'.

Groans fill the yard. I think many more than I looked forward to a good rest before taking on the Northmen. There is worse to come,

'Ivar we need to talk, you, I, Harding, Wulfrum and a few others', Osgod hails me before I can find somewhere to rest my bones.

Like as not there will be little enough sleep for me after the talking is over.

'This *is* a weighty matter', Harding coaxes me toward where Osgod stands.

Osgod calls out from the doorway,

'I would not ask of you what I would not do myself', he ushers us into the hall, the thegns entering ahead of me. 'I know you must be tired, but this will not wait. We must know ahead of the morning what we are to do'.

The night wears on. Thegns squabble about who leads against the Northmen and how, nay-say one another's offerings and before long Osgod sees there is no way we can attack as one.

'Ivar, will you share your thoughts?' he asks me to take the floor.

'Who is this Ivar that he can overrule us?' one thegn snaps. 'He is no thegn, not one of us! He is one of Tostig's ilk, *I* know him. He and Copsig rode out together to grind the *geld* from our neighbours'.

I raise my eyes to the darkness of the hall's roof as I tell him,

'I am not here to overrule you, Thegn Wigod'.

'Tell him your thoughts, Wigod', Wulfrum groans. He too wishes to rest his head before the forthcoming slaughter. He stands threateningly close to Wigod and the fellow thumps back down on the bench he rose from.

Leodmaer has reached us and been told by one of Morkere's huscarls to join us in the hall. He jumps up from the bench closest to Osgod and yells at Wigod,

'*Old fool* - how you were ever made a thegn is beyond me! The fellow has done this sort of thing before; his bloodline is shared with Danish kings and King Harold. You would be better off listening, sooner than showing off your own foolishness!'

And so the evening goes on, into the small hours. Those who do not wish to listen catcall those who have the forthrightness of their beliefs or understanding. The night wears on and I give up any hope of resting. This is too much like the days before we rode through the Andredes Leag almost two years ago, when some could barely stand for tiredness after the long march south from Staenfordes Brycg.

At last, the meeting over, we find our way back to where we long ago hoped to be at rest.

'Was there any outcome?' Saeward asks from the shadows. He stirs to sit and listen to me just as Hemming looks up.

'What I have to say can wait, but not for too long. Sleep now and you will learn in the morning what is awaited from us', I tell them. The morning comes soon enough.

15

The morning dawns grey as we leave the *Earlsburh*. Horsemen line the yard as Osgod shows from the darkness of the hall, looks them over, smiles bleakly and tells them the worst,

'We shall all leave here *on foot*, that our coming should not be heard by the outlanders', Osgod tells them, to groans from the mounted men. The rest laugh when the stable lads come back out into the yard to take their mounts and they drop heavily down from their saddles.

Stilling the laughter by thumping the shaft of his axe on one of the stone slabs by the doorway, he outlines what he sees us doing this morning, and how. There are more groans as the thegns are told they must make their way amongst their men, so that if the outlanders see us cannot tell who are the leaders, who the followers.

'I shall be amongst my own men, with Harding', Osgod adds for them to know where they can find him.

The thegns mumble, their unrest unsettling the men. In their eyes his manner of tackling the Northmen does not meet with their liking. I think they would sooner try to take the foe by storm and fall to the outlanders' arrows than 'sneak' up on them. Osgod snarls, their foolishness testing him sorely,

'We should all seem to be of low standing until we are close enough to make our attack, then the thegns can tell their men what we want from them'. He chides the few still mounted, unwilling to yield their mounts. 'Down, off your horses, or forget fighting beside me!'

They look at one another, frowning darkly and slide down from their saddles to let the lads take their horses back to the stables. Osgod is now ready to take them on through the *burh*. He lets some of his men pass and steps in amongst the others. We, Saeward, Hemming, Eirik and I, follow him into the line. When I turn to look along them, Harding slips into the throng and the other thegns do likewise.

In this manner we snake eastward through the dark streets to the stronghold, the stillness of the early fore-dawn morning unbroken yet but for the calling of birds. The eaves of dwellings are alive with feeding nestlings, cock-birds warning off others. A red glow now streaks the high cloud ahead of us, heralding the rising sun. The outlanders seem to be *asleep* still.

Osgod halts his men, the stronghold ahead dark against the grey clouds behind. Some birds fly out from behind the palisade, and I have a thought.

'I was told that when Harald Sigurdsson blooded his men at Skarthiburh he had his men catch some of the nesting birds', I tell him.

'They fixed Greek fire to the birds' wings and let them loose again. When the birds flew back to their nests they set fire to the rooves'.

'How do we catch the birds?' Osgod asks, following them with his eyes. 'For that matter, how do we make Greek fire, whatever that is?'

I tell him what it is made from, and who would have the means to make it,

'Silversmiths would know where to find wherewithal for cleaning their metals, how to fix it to the birds and how to make sure of it flaring when the birds reach their nests'.

'Do we have any silver craftsmen here?' Osgod asks, and again a little louder lest those at the back could not hear. A few men have what is needed and leave for their workshops. When they have gone he lets his men know what else we need.

'Is there anyone here who can catch nesting birds?'

'My brother and I have nets', one answers.

'You live nearby?' Osgod cocks an ear to hear the answer.

'We do, aye. Which birds do you want catching?'

'You see the small birds flying out from behind the outlanders' lower stockade?' Osgod asks, the fellow nods and gives a low whistle to let his brother, elsewhere amongst Osgod's men, know he is needed.

The two of them set off into the darkness between the dwellings and workshops behind us, and the rest of us are left waiting. Not for long do we have to stand, however. The silversmiths are back with a small iron pail and hogs-hair brushes.

'Who are we waiting for?' one asks.

'The bird catchers –'Harding begins.

'Gudbrand and Tokig Herjolfsson live near Monk Bar. They will be some time yet, you know?' one of the craftsmen breaks in. 'I should think that by the time they get back and we have the birds the Northmen in there will be wide awake!'

'What is it you think we should do?' Osgod puts to the fellow.

'Someone could go to their gates in a monk's or priest's robe, looking like a man of the church', he answers and all eyes turn to Saeward and me. He asks, 'Have I said something odd?'

I nod to the thegn, and looking to my right at Saeward tell him why the men turned our way,

'Fear not, friend. It is what Saeward put to Leodmaer yesterday at Tolentun. He and his men were about to ride into the burh as Northmen'.

'What was wrong with that?' another thegn calls, unaware of Osgod glaring at him.

'To begin with, how would he answer to one of them asking in his own tongue what they were doing here? Leodmaer himself told me he did not know their tongue', I look the thegn straight in the eye and he looks away, put out at his own short-sightedness.

'Going as a man of the cloth might be a much better way in', Osgod brightens. I think he sees waiting for the craftsmen to come back *would* take too long.

'I have a monk's robe', Saeward offers, 'and can take two or three men close behind me –'

'Aye and more can follow, out of sight', adds the thegn who put forward using someone in a monk's robe. There, at least is one man thinking right. Osgod nods, happy with the way things are going. Morkere should be here to see him lead his underlings!

'Very well, Saeward. Who would you take with you up to the gates?' Osgod asks, looking at me.

I can very well guess whose names Saeward will put forward, and am not let down when he tells Osgod,

'I would take Ivar, Hemming and Eirik, my Lord'.

'I see nothing wrong with that', Osgod beams, looking back at me.

I can see much wrong with that. None of *us* speaks their tongue either, that I could think of. Did he think of that?'

'Do you know any of their words, Saeward?' Osgod *has* thought of that, after all.

'I would call out, 'Open the gates, I want to speak to the castellan on behalf of Eadgar *aetheling*', Saeward answers baldly. 'They all know who he is'.

'They do?' Osgod squints and shakes his head. He cannot believe what he has heard and, for my part, nor can I. 'Would your friends wear Aenglish or Northman mailcoats?'

'As we have some of their helms, mailcoats and weapons we could be Northmen *or* Aengle', I offer. Somehow I think I am looking forward to this undertaking now – I would not say I am wholeheartedly keen on what he has thinking of, but I could warm to it, I really *could*.

'Eadgar is more likely to send his own men than entrust his life to the outlanders, surely?'

'Would an Aenglish priest lead Northman men-at-arms anyway?' Leodmaer asks glibly.

'Why not, as long as it takes their eyes from the rest of us?' Osgod sniffs at the put-down.

Saeward dons the robe with help from one of Osgod's men, pulling it down over his mailcoat. Our knee-length mailcoats are much like theirs anyway, so in the half light they would not know us for not being Northmen, and unlike our huscarls the outlanders do not carry the long shields when they are on foot. We leave ours with Osgod's men and hope to have them when Osgod storms the gate after us.

With Saeward ahead of us, Hemming, Eirik and I stride out of the shadows, the dawn light creeping across the rooves around us. The earth ramp, built on top of rubble from the homes they pulled down, has been packed hard by horses' hooves and feels like rock beneath our feet as we scuff the road up to the gates.

One of the Northmen on guard calls down to Saeward when we reach their lift bridge, and my friend answers as he said he would. Crossbow bolts thud into the earth ahead of us, but I think not aimed at us. They are a warning not to go further until bidden, and anyway we are still short of the bridge.

Before long a head shows above the staves beside the gate house. In fair Aenglish someone asks hurriedly,

'What is it you *want?*' He must have something better to do, by the way he asks. He may have a woman waiting in his bed.

'My Lord Eadgar is here in the *burh*, and wishes to speak with the castellan about meeting with the king', Saeward lies, at one time unable to lie so well.

He has come a long way since meeting me. I find it hard not to laugh, and Hemming beside me seems to jump on hearing Saeward's brazen lie. Eirik grins, his teeth set. Is he afraid? There is the sound of men talking heatedly above, but I could never understand them. What I do understand by the loudness of the wrangling is that the lord of this stronghold is being counselled by an underling against opening up.

Saeward stands a little way ahead of us, looking up at the bobbing heads, hands clasped together as if in prayer, fingers twiddling. He is a wonderful player, like the skalds of old who hammered out their verses on Bragi's anvil.

After what seems a long wait someone above calls out and the gates groan a little way open. This is when we should hear men behind us edging forward, but nothing stirs. *Where is everyone* – has Osgod fallen asleep for lack of rest in the night? Just as someone with a brightly burning torch looks around the gate we are caught in a rush.

Men storm forward waving axes, swords, spears, every weapon you could think of around their heads. The Northmen behind the gates are overcome before they can heave the iron-sheaved oak gates to stem our flow. Men scream in pain, blood runs around the gateway, arrows fly both ways and we are hard put to shield ourselves. Osgod throws me my shield for me to hold aloft against arrows and crossbow bolts that fly from the wall at the bottom of the hill upon which stands the tower, the *keep,* as I have heard it called.

Osgod bellows under the withering hail of arrows from the inner wall,

'Where are the men with the fire for our arrows? Come on, *before* we are all cut down!' He has to draw his shield above head height, against being skewered by the murderous bolts loosed off by the Northman crossbowmen. Even then they still split his shield near the shield boss and he has to throw down one split shield before Leodmaer comes in through the gates, followed by a two men carrying an iron pot of seething pitch.

'Leodmaer, *get those fire arrows into the air!*' Osgod roars again

Almost as soon as he says it, arrow after arrow dipped in burning pitch shoots skyward, finding their mark on the walls ahead. Foe and friend alike clash screaming with fury, the crack of axe on shield sounding like whiplash. Swords skim chain mail, hauberks shear under the onslaught and spears are driven into men's flesh like hammer blows. Nowhere here is safe for the Northmen, from iron blade or shaft.

I am taken back to when we stormed Willelm fitzOsbern's stronghold at Hereford, but as I wrest my thoughts back to the here and now a Northman has his axe set to come down onto my head. From my right a spear is thrust upward, at the outlander's broad chest.

'*Die*, hogs-breath!' I hear one of Osgod's men yell.

The axe drops, almost cutting into my shoulder as it falls to the blood-soaked stones that line the road up to the higher staves ahead and above us. Many of these tall staves are charred from our arrows, some afire, and the castellan's men pull back to the inner gate before the burning wall falls onto them from behind. Here and there gaps open between the staves and the outlanders leap through the flames over their dead to seek the safety of a half-built inner wall beyond.

As quickly as the fighting began it seems to stop. No arrows or bolts come down at us and a tall fellow picks his way carefully through mounds of dead men, many his own, and waves his hands above his head.

'Weapons *down!*' Osgod calls out. He has to yell out louder, '*No more arrows!*' as some threaten to cut down the lone Northman.

'Can we hold off from fighting for a time, whilst we tend to the wounded and pull back our dead?'

'Very well', Osgod nods. 'What is your name, good fellow? You are a brave man'.

'I thank you for your kind words. My name is Willelm Malet, and I am the shire reeve here, south of the Tese'.

'Very well, Willelm', Osgod begins, 'how long do you think your men will need to clear away your dead and see to the wounded?'

'My castellan, Rodberht fitzRicard tells me we need only as much time as it takes the sun to climb over the keep. Would that be well with you...*Ahm*? Can I ask your name?'

'I am Thegn Osgod –'

'I am speaking with a *thegn?* I thought that, by the way you led your men you must have been an earl before Rodberht de Commines was chosen by the king. Is there a man here who ranks higher than a thegn?'

'There is not, my Lord Willelm Malet. There are many thegns from around the wapentake, who will have no truck with your taxes. Your friend in Dunelm, Rodberht de Commines, will find himself in deep water soon enough by the way he lets his men loose on folk north of the Tese. I should not want to be around when Lord Gospatric and Maerleswein come back with the *aetheling* Eadgar'.

'They wish harm on our Flemish brothers in Dunelm?' Willelm Malet asks, somewhat foolishly after Osgod's warning.

'You might say that they *do*', Osgod gives me a sideward grin, as if answering a child.

Malet grunts an acknowledgement to Osgod's warning, reaching out his right hand. Osgod spurns this token of friendship and turns his back on him. The Northman stares at his back and murmurs,

'Until midday, then -'

Osgod turns and snaps,

'Aye, until midday *and no longer,* mind you!' The tiresome shire reeve chosen by Willelm turns after a few strides and tells Osgod,

'I ought to tell you, thegn, a rider is on his way south to the king in Wintunceaster'.

Is this a warning or a threat?

'How long do you think we have before the Bastard shows here with his red crop?' Harding asks me behind one hand.

'*I* saw no-one leave before we attacked. Anyway, with all the outlaws in the wildwoods, the muddy roads along the way – who knows, he might not get there. The rivers to the west are not easy to ford, either, since the last rains in the high hills. For these Northmen, a week might be looking on the bright side. We could wipe the floor with them and be gone before their beloved king sees this side of the Hvarfe!' I answer for the shire reeve to hear.

'He left on foot, through a side gate', Malet tells us, having overheard me, and takes his leave, picking his way back to the keep.

'Your king could still be a week away', I call after him, 'As long as it took King Harold to reach here from Wealtham'.

Looking back at me as he struggles through the gap in the upper wall he gives no answer, barking orders instead.

254

There is a tall young fellow at the foot of the hill, who has been watching all the time his master talked with Osgod. Is he the castellan Rodberht fitzRicard? He will soon learn to fear the width of our blades, when his men run low on crossbow bolts. Then there will be no hiding from the wrath of these men around me.

Above us, the Northmen carry the dead to their last rest, and the wounded up to the keep to be cared for. I do not know why they bother. They will soon all be dead, barring the two leaders whom we will keep, to be traded for silver – or to warrant our safety should the worst comes to the worst. If this king lives up to his name, we would be sore pressed without Willelm Malet amongst us to guard our backs. The other one, fitzRicard, can be left here to tell the king we have his shire reeve, and that if they build another stronghold we will burn that down, too!

The day wears on, the sun climbs high above the keep. Osgod and Harding watch from beneath their outstretched hands, and I thump one hand into the other before growling at Osgod to finish with the outlanders,

'What are we waiting for? Unleash the arrows on them! They are trying to make us look fools!'

'Very well, Ivar. I would say there are many of us who think as you do. Leodmaer, Harding, tell the bowmen to gather here', Osgod says, digging a line in the earth ahead of us with his boot heel to show where he wants them, 'in line abreast. Their crossbows do not have the same reach as our bows'.

Someone waves something white from the tower.

'*Now* what is going on?' Harding asks, shielding his eyes. He points to where a square of cloth has been tied to a post and Osgod lets out a string of oaths.

'More time-wasting, that is what is happening!' Leodmaer snaps. He wants to end this as much as I, as do we all. He yells out aloud, 'Bowmen make ready, aim for within the inner wall and pay no heed to that rag!'

'For a silver coin, can anyone reach it from here with a fire arrow?' Harding asks, hinting that there might be something for a man who can render the 'rag' to flame.

'Who are your best bowmen?' I ask Osgod.

He in turn looks at Leodmaer, Wigod and Wulfrum.

'Well -?' Osgod grunts, waving them on.

The three thegns each pick out their best man, as does Harding and Osgod himself. The five men spread their feet at the line, shove arrows into the earth and take their stand. Osgod looks back at Harding, who takes his nod as a signal to call the men to order.

'A silver penny goes to the bowman who can set fire to that dirty rag up there'.

'If you made that three pennies it would be more worthwhile for us', one answers.

'Can you *do* it?' Harding tests the fellow. 'What is your name that I know who to call for when another such task arises?'

'I am Sigewulf, Thegn Harding. You know me, I tend your horses at Rudby', the fellow answers tartly to laughter from all around.

'Come, come, Harding. You should know your own ostler, surely?' Leodmaer laughs.

Harding scowls and snarls at his man to make ready. Sigewulf spits on his hands and pulls an arrow from the earth beside him. He sets the arrow against the thin cord that he has already drawn to the top of his bow, and tests its strength. The cord stretches taut and one of Leodmaer's men smears pitch onto the arrow.

Another of Leodmaer's men touches a burning torch to its tip, and Sigewulf lets it fly, to sing through the air and skim off the top pales of the keep. When the arrow falls onto the idly fluttering rag it is rendered quickly into a flaming ball of cloth.

We all roar and Sigewulf catches his coins in one hand as they arc through the air. Words being useless in the drawn out cheering, he mouths his thanks. Harding brims with pride at one of *his* men showing the way for the other bowmen.

I thump Harding on the back and yell out,

'Where have you been hiding your man?'

The outlanders fall back from the upper gatehouse, into the path of falling arrows that drill some of them like stakes in the earth. Leodmaer, suddenly hurtling past us to win his share of the spoils, grins wickedly as he yells,

'Catch yourself some of their silver!'

'And catch one of their crossbow bolts. I am sure they have not used them all!' Saeward cackles on his way forward, raising thunderous laughter from those near enough to hear. Osgod and I launch ourselves onward, past the upper gatehouse and up the track with our shields carried over our heads against the Northmen's crossbow bolts.

Some of our arrows bounce off the keep wall, falling onto unlucky shield-less souls attacking Rodberht fitzRicard's underlings. We have to deafen ourselves to the screams and groans of men with arrows buried deep into skulls, shoulder blades or backs, and batter down the doors to the outlanders' last post.

We have Willelm Malet and his castellan cornered in the great hall, with their last and ablest warriors standing between us and their lords.

Swords and axes, though chipped or blunted, are still good for killing. The Northmen await us – sweating in the muggy heat under their heavy hauberks. One or two wipe their foreheads with the backs of their un-gloved hands, staring at us, daring us to close on them. They have nowhere to go, and their lords cower behind the thin line.

'We will give you and your men quarter if you ride away from here, Willelm Malet', Osgod offers, 'and *never* come back'.

Malet shakes his head, laughing. Beside him the tall young castellan fitzRicard only stares sullenly down at his shire reeve, unable to understand what Osgod has offered his master? A door opens behind him and a fair-skinned, dark-haired young woman looks out from the darkness. She and Malet talk, he not taking his eyes off us. When she falls silent, I would say his answers did not fill her heart with glad tidings, he walks slowly forward between his men.

He says something to them and they stand at ease, swords and other weapons held at their sides whilst their lord strides forward to speak to Osgod,

'We may talk, but understand I cannot swear to anything', Malet tells him. 'There is nothing I can offer that our king will not undo'.

'Tell me *your* thoughts, on how you think to come away from here alive', Osgod answers.

'What do you mean?' Malet's eyes narrow.

Osgod enlightens him,

'It is not altogether up to me what happens to you, your kin and those of your men still alive now. They had best lay down their weapons now, before they and you meet an untimely end. You may kill some of us, but there are many more of us than of you. Before the red mist comes over these men, tell yours to yield'.

After some thought Malet turns and mumbles to his men, something in his own tongue, the nearest passing his words to the others who stand behind him. There is anger amongst them, heads shake. He tells them again, adding to Osgod,

'They do not understand how close they are to dying needlessly. Some do not care'.

'Is not their task to guard you and your kin?' Osgod snaps, to which Malet nods sagely. 'Then put it to them that they will have failed in their task if they die and are unable to keep you alive. *Go on*, tell them. I cannot hold my men back for long, and the others will not listen once the blood is up!'

Malet turns and barks at them, his order booming around the walls of the hall. This time they heed his words. They throw their weapons to crash loudly in a heap on the wooden floor behind the shire reeve.

Where FitzRicard looked worried before, now he looks frightened for his life. He has a lot to learn about the Aenglish, that they will not kill if the threat is taken away. Neither Osgod nor his men will kill for the sake of it.

'Now – what have you to offer?' Malet asks Osgod.

'You will be taken, your kin and your men, to a ford on the Tadceaster road. There you will be given back your weapons and you can ride south to meet your king', Osgod tells him.

'Very well', Malet nods, looking a little happier, 'I would not say otherwise'.

He turns and puts Osgod's offer to his men. They seem thankful, as does fitzRicard, and then Osgod gives Malet news he will find hard to pass on,

'The castellan stays - to safeguard our men against attack from your crowned tanner's bastard'.

Malet does not look straight at the young fellow, instead glaring at me – why, I do not know. Only when he is beside fitzRicard does he give him the news that renders the fellow dumb.

The Northmen file silently past Osgod, through the high doors of the hall, on down the wooden stairway between Leodmaer's men. Behind Saeward, Hemming, Eirik and me they pass other Jorvik men, clattering down the stairs to the ground, where they await their lord. The stillness is eerie as the few Northmen eye the *fyrdmen* and their thegns. The hatred is plain in their eyes, but for now the Northmen leave with their tails between their legs, *shamed*.

Rodberht fitzRicard bravely takes his farewell from Malet and his wife. The shire reeve's offspring stand looking bewildered, clutching their belongings, overshadowed by thegns Osgod, Harding and Wulfrum.

Saeward and I, together with Hemming and Eirik are to ride for the Hvarfe with Malet, his kin and his men. Behind us trot four saddled horses carrying the Northmen's weapons. Osgod has given me two of his men, Osleif and Aelfheard, armed with bows. These two will take either flank, threatening any of the outlanders who either stray from their single file or hold back. They relish their task, grinning widely as the outlanders yelp at the tips being pressed into their backs.

Aside from the yelps of pain, we pass wordlessly through the hilly woodlands to the Hvarfe. My thoughts go back to when Saeward and I rode this way less than two years ago, to find Brother Aethelnoth in his soiled habit by the river.

Saeward nods at me, reading my thoughts again. He has grounds to think badly of the aftermath of our coming here, of slaying Garwulf in the woodland and being taken back to Jorvik by Osgod. He will think back on being teased by Theodolf as he swung from the tree, feet caught in a rope trap laid by my old friend Hrothulf.

When we reach the ford the river is up, the water running fast, but not so deep Malet's men could not cross. His womenfolk – wife, maid, and his offspring – may balk at having to ford here. We halt the outlanders at the top of the bank whilst Osgod's men pass them with the laden horses to struggle across the flow. Once across, on the western river bank Osleif and Aelfheard tether the pack mounts to trees and struggle back across the strong flow again.

Osleif's horse panics mid-stream, almost throwing her rider into the ice-cold. Aelfheard takes hold of the frightened mare's bridle and steadies her, allowing Osleif to take the reins of his mount again.

Back on our side, Aelfheard undergoes some back-slapping from Saeward and Eirik. One or two of the Northmen seem stricken by Aelfheard's feat and stare disbelievingly. Malet claps his hands and calls out,

'Well ridden, good fellow!'

Osleif scowls as he rides up to us. Aelfheard beams broadly at first, grunts and looks away from him at me. I wink and tell him,

'The Northman is right insofar as you kept Osleif and his mare from drowning. Acknowledge his esteem, whatever you think of him. It is the mark of a man to take tribute from friend *or* foe'.

Unwillingly Aelfheard bows his head at Malet and passes, up to the head of the bank to await me.

'Your man will learn', Malet reaches a hand to me. 'A warrior –'

'I know, Northman', I break in and take his hand. 'A warrior will allow praise from friend or foe. It is time you left, before the river rises yet more. This river takes its water from the hills to the west, and when the rain comes, this flow rages wild. Go get your weapons before outlaws take them'.

His offspring are taken onto the saddles of two of his men, his wife rides behind him on his taller horse, her arms wrapped around his waist, hanging on for dear life even though she is nowhere near the river yet.

'There are outlaws - *here?*' Malet's eyes suddenly open wide and he shouts at his men to follow him across the Hvarfe. We watch them struggle across.

'*Whose* are these horses?' Malet calls across, his men untying the laden mounts behind him.

'*Yours* - their riders are now dead. It is of no matter whether the riders were your men or ours. Go before we unleash our arrows on you'.

Malet stares open-mouthed, so I add,

'Your master will not want to see you alone, shire reeve. Best go before you lose any more of your men. They have done well to live through our attack, do not let them down', I wave and press my knees into Braenda's left flank to turn her. When I look back he and his men have vanished, gone into the thickly wooded hills.

'All went well?' Osgod asks when we ride back into what was once Morkere's garth at the Earlsburh.

'All went well', I answer. 'Malet and his men have gone to meet their king'.

If Aelfheard wishes to tell of saving his friend in the Hvarfe, it will be for him to choose. Coming from me it might make him feel awkward amongst his peers. On the other hand, Osleif might bring it up. Would it be any less awkward for him coming from a friend?

'We had best look for what might be of use to us before we melt away, back to our homes or elsewhere', Osgod counsels his and the other thegns' men at arms and fyrdmen.

Harding adds, for the good of his younger f*yrdmen*, those barely growing their first beards,

'When your mothers ask what you have been doing these past days, tell them only that you have been working your thegns' lands. Thus, when the Northmen ask them they will be none the wiser, whatever they may think otherwise'.

These lads help bury their fellows, and those the Northmen were unable to, along with their older comrades - Morkere's huscarls that he has not seen for almost two years. There are no great gains amongst the smoking ruins of the stronghold we have sacked. Game aplenty is found in a store room of the keep's kitchen, and taken eagerly by those who know how good it can taste cooked well. Weapons there are enough of to choose from, crossbows wrenched from the hands of the dead unable to set their next bolts – and thrown away. As one of Harding's men shouted laughingly,

'Some of the outlanders were too slow loading these weapons, so what use will they be to *us?* By God, we would fill the earth with our own had we had these to fight with!'

The hated crossbows are piled and set fire to in the upper gateway to show our scorn for their weaponry. Would Willelm *understand* what we are telling him by this? It is said he is thick-skinned enough not to know how hated he is even amongst his own, so whether our meaning gets through his thick skull is for anyone to wonder at.

Hemming passes behind me and stops to watch the burning weapons, handles sticking out of the fast charring heap. Saeward turns to him and asks,

'Does the Bastard know what we are trying to tell him by this, do you think?'

'If he does not know yet that he, his underlings and all they stand for are not wanted, then you would have to drop a rock onto his rusty crophead before he understood. All I can say is, it is only a waste of good wood', Hemming answers with a guffaw. Saeward shrugs and wanders off to see what there is for him to take from here.

'Hey, you lot, look what they left in here!' One of the *fyrdmen* has reached the open door of the building and stands, laughing in the doorway. Others crowd around him, Hemming being unable to look over the tallest men's shoulders. He pushes through and yells at the last man to get out of his way.

As if no-one already knew there was something worth looking at in there, he crows like an old fish-wife,

'*Hello*, what do we have here?!' Hemming has more men pushing around him now, agog at what they see. He calls us to him, but Osgod is there first, barking at those nearest to make way,

'*What is it? God*, never in my born days have I seen anything like this!' Osgod stops and laughs. Weak with laughter, he coughs and splutters, staggering back toward me, 'Ivar, you have to see *this!*'

I stride across the grass and pull the nearest men back. Some of the others see me and stand back to let me through, elbow their friends and finally I am at the doorway. In one of the further corners lies a heavy fellow, barely into his hauberk, breeks around his ankles and an even bigger woman on her knees with her back to him. She looks over her shoulders at me, begging with her eyes, sorry for herself.

'Pull him off me, will you?' she whines. A woman from around here, by the way she talks, she must have been in here with him when we launched our attack. 'He is dead, *see?!*'

What I overlooked when I first saw them was the arrow in the Northman's lower back, just above his backside. I see it now, in the pale shaft of late afternoon sunlight that shines from a hole in the thatched roof like a long ash shafted spear.

I ask the men in the doorway, still staring,

'Have you *all* led such sheltered lives?' My laughter seems to shock some of them, and the younger ones redden when I add, 'You must have seen your hounds from time to time - or any of your livestock in the after-year? Hold fast, woman, while I pull him back!'

The arrow shaft stands away from the old hog's backside, quivering when I try to haul him off her. He is too heavy for me on my own, so I call out for the nearest men to help. One of the huscarls comes forward and holds the dead man by his shoulders. We heave the outlander off the woman and he falls onto his rump, breaking the arrow shaft, his manhood still stiff. Everyone around me cheers as she scrambles to her feet, trying to hide her lower half.

'Leave him as he is', I tell them. 'His fellows can have a laugh when they come back. Who knows, even their master might see the funny side?'

'Who knows?' my helpmate answers, brushes straw and dirt from his hands and mailcoat and leaves ahead of me. The men outside fall back and let us through to where Osgod stands, chuckling with Saeward and Eirik.

'Where were you?' I ask them. 'You missed a sight for sore eyes here. Someone will tell you what it was if they can stop laughing!'

'Why can *you* not tell us?' Eirik asks, wide-eyed.

'I might miss something out in the telling', I laugh and go back to Osgod.

'Thorstein told me you said to leave the hog's backside where he fell?' he asks, 'Is that right?'

'Unless you had something else aforethought', I rub dirt off my hands and stand looking him up and down. '*Had you?*'

'No, you were right. As he told me, you said their king might see the wit in it. I *have* met him, once only mind you, and that was enough. He seemed to me to have the slow wit of a backward child, laughing at the most foolish things his priest told him on behalf of Eadwin and Morkere. Neither of my *Miercan* lords understands real wit either, so I learned long ago'.

'They would have got on well together at Falaise', I tell him under my breath as Harding strides up to us, beaming broadly as if he had found something in the ruins worthy of him. 'What gives, Harding my friend?'

'You would never believe –'

Saeward breaks in and laughs hoarsely at his own wit,

'What, not *another* fat Northman with an arrow in his arse?' He quietens when neither of us laughs with him.

'You were saying?' I ask Harding to begin again.

Harding glares at Saeward and begins anew,

'There is a store of apple ale in the smoking ruins of the last store room along the wall there', he jabs a finger that way and beckons. 'You might as well come, Saeward. It might quieten you down with some of that in you! Where are Eirik and Hemming?'

He sees Eirik behind Osgod and waves, '

'Eirik, get yourself here. We are going to drink ourselves into a deep, happy sleep tonight! Bring Hemming with you if you can find him'.

'Where shall we find you?' Eirik asks.

'The last of the burnt-out store rooms along the wall here - that is where we will be. Come, Ivar. I cannot carry it all!' With that Harding lurches away again. He must have helped himself to enough already. I think he wants to make sure he will sleep well this evening, wherever it is we will be.

Skins and glass flasks of apple ale have been piled in a corner. Half burnt rafters and roof straw lies around everywhere, and rubble from God knows where is heaped beside the open doorway. Saeward trips on the rubble and falls against Harding's back, bringing loud curses from the thegn,

'*Christ in his heaven*, are you drunk already?' He turns and cuffs Saeward across the top of his now bared head, then stares at me in the failing light. 'Ivar, pull your friend to his feet and then we can gather these skins of apple ale together'.

I hoist Saeward from the rubble and he dusts himself down before taking skins from Harding to pass back to me. Between us, Harding, Saeward, Eirik and me, we pile a score of these skins beside the doorway before Osgod nears. He takes in our booty and his brow furrows deeply,

'What are you doing with these, Ivar?'

'Ask Harding. He is here, in front of me', I show Osgod. He peers into the half-darkness and laughs.

'Harding, I might have known you would get up to no good! What do you mean to do with all these skins – what is *in* them?'

Saeward does not wait for Harding to answer,

'Harding says they are full of *apple* ale'.

'*I can answer for myself!*' Harding snaps, and looks over Saeward's shoulders at his friend to avow what Saeward foolishly blurted out. He was plainly not going to tell Osgod, but there was no way of hiding his booty now. Bending a thumb toward Saeward, he says, 'As he said, these are skins of apple ale that I thought we should share out'.

'You *are* a thoughtful fellow, Harding!' Osgod smiles and slaps Saeward's back, telling him, 'I thank you, friend'.

Harding scowls at Saeward, thrusts another pair of skins at him and growls,

'These are the last'.

'What is that under the bag – *there?*' Saeward points to another heap behind Harding.

'They are nothing to do with *you*, East Seaxan!' the thegn scowls darkly and I pull Saeward toward the door before any harm can come to him. He can be a big-mouthed fool at times, but he is a friend and a good warrior. I still want him by my side.

'*Hush*, Saeward', I tell him. 'Wait there until we know where we are to take these skins. You will rest well after emptying one of *these* skins, mark my word!'

'*Half* a skin would do it, Ivar', he sniffs.

'What are the odds against my getting a bellyful *here?!* I may as well dream of getting riches. Are you listening?'

If he must know, I am only half listening. My eyes are on something to the south, beyond Mickel Gata.

Thick, black smoke billows from somewhere on the Saelgeby road.

'Where is Osgod?' I ask.

'He has gone down to the main gateway, *why?*' Eirik asks. When I point to the smoke he stares.

'What is amiss?' Saeward asks. He also stares when Eirik shows him, and stands on Harding's left foot in trying to see better over the wall nearest the river, only to be shoved out of the way roughly. '*Hey*, what-'

'I will give you hey, what! You stood on my foot, *oaf!* I hope whatever it is you tried to see is worth being boxed on the ear!'

'Something else is afoot to the south of the burh!' I tell Harding. 'We will need to know what it is'.

'Your fool friend was afoot – *my* damned foot!' Harding curses roundly.

'I think our outlander king is close at hand', Hemming mutters behind me, watching, as the smoke seems to blow westward.

'You might be right', I answer under my breath. He *is* right, never mind *might* be.

The black smoke spreads westward even as we watch. I catch sight of Osgod strolling with one of his huscarls and wave for him to look that way. He looks and hurries uphill our way, to see better where the smoke is coming from but the land toward the walls at the end of Mickel Gata is a little higher than we are.

Osgod picks up one of the skins to take a draught.

'*God*, we need to leave here before they ring the burh with fire!' he growls at us, telling us to stow the skins on a small cart beside on of the outbuildings and hitch a couple of horses to it. 'Pile on anything else we have found, weapons, hauberks – you name it, we can take it. We will have something, at least, from throwing out Willelm Malet'.

'We still have the *castellan*', Harding makes Osgod aware that we took Rodberht fitzRicard to bargain with.

'*So we do*, Harding, so we do. If the worst comes to the worst, we can slit his throat and feed him to the wolves in the wildwood when we are done with him', Osgod snorts, grinning at the hapless Northman, now some way off. Ringed by his *fyrdmen*, the fellow's hands have been bound and one of them has the loose end of the rope in hand, awaiting his thegn's order to leave. He knows the Northman can understand no Aenglish – *or can he?*

I counsel Osgod as we make for the gateway,

'We had best not talk about where we are going'.

'Why is that?' His eyes open wide and he looks askance at Harding, at Eirik and the others. 'He does not know our tongue, or why would the shire reeve have told him in his own tongue what we were saying earlier?'

'To fool us into talking freely around him, likely',

Harding is at one with me. 'When he and his castellan are together again, Malet can tell their king what we are about, and use the folk here to smoke us out, so to speak'.

'*You* think so too?' Osgod looks from me to Harding. If two of us say the same thing, there may be wisdom in our thinking. We follow Osgod downhill and he stands close to one of his men, whispering to him. The *fyrdman* nods and stands looking at fitzRicard whilst we talk.

'Would you say we follow the Foss eastward from here and strike north?' he asks Harding.

A little slow on the uptake, yet nevertheless sharp of wit Harding answers,

'Aye, that way we can cross to the Deorewent and eastward over the hills to Holdernaes'. Harding goes on to talk about some kinsman of his, one of the landholders of Danish forebears. 'He will put us up until the hue and cry dies down. We are as good as unseen there amongst the long corn'.

Osgod nods and takes his *fyrdman* to one side,

'Well, *did* he bite?'

'Like a pike, Thegn Osgod, he did', the fellow answers. 'He hung on every word Harding told you. I could see his eyes flicker when he knew I was still looking at him!'

'So much for him not understanding us', I hiss, and watch him lest he guesses we know what he is up to.

'Slit his throat now!' Saeward snaps, sliding his dagger from its sheath. FitzRicard flinches at the sight of Saeward's blade held ready, but Osgod pushes my friend's hand down to his side.

'*Fool*, we can use him to our own ends!' Osgod swears and takes us out of hearing. 'By talking openly around him, he will think we do not know he understands and his king will send his men on a fool's errand east to the sea. Out there you have to know what you are about, or you come to grief in the mire'.

Saeward shoves his dagger back down and grunts. He would sooner kill the Northman, we all know. We might let him have his way – *yet*.

'Get this man a horse, and for God's sake *bind* him to the saddle!' Osgod calls out as we walk hurriedly back to the gateway. We must make our way quickly back to the Earlsburh for our own mounts and head for the Monk Gata bar. It will seem to the outlander that we are after all heading for the Foss, from there the Deorewent and so forth. If we are put to the test we can use him to get past his fellows.

It is dark by the time we reach the *Earlsburh* again, and our mounts. Food is at hand in the feasting hall, but we have no time to eat.

'Can you good women pack it for us to eat along the way?' Osgod asks the women from the kitchen. They hasten back and forth through the garth again with good things to fill our saddle bags, cold meats, bread, cheese and fruit. By evening, well after sunset and like as not amongst the hills to the east, we may be able to stop and eat.

He has told on the way, with fitzRicard well ahead of us that we shall set out for the Helmsleag road once we are out of sight of Jorvik and any of his fellows who may have been sent to follow us. They do not know the fords as he does.

The crossing I made long ago on my way to Staenfordes Brycg could be in flood from all the smaller rivers north and west of the Deorewent, such as the long, winding Seofena through Helmsleag. Heavy rains of late might easily swell the river and I am no longer sure about the best river crossings, having been in the south at my kinsman Harold's side. The rivers do not stay the same for long in these parts, with the flow grinding away their banks.

If I am unsure of the rivers, it is fair to guess the outlanders know as little, or less.

We are soon out of the gates, with Osgod leading. Morkere's huscarls – now his followers – are with us, the *fyrdmen* having left to find their own way home around the *burh*. Rodberht fitzRicard rides between four of the huscarls some way ahead of us, Saeward, Hemming, Eirik, Harding and me.

What is left standing of the great church of Saint Peter stands skeleton-like against the red of the sky to the west, burnt to ashes on its southern side from the many dwellings and workshops around. The Northmen had the houses between the stronghold and the river set on fire so that any attackers could not use them to hide amongst before attacking. From what I heard, the fire spread north-westward with a warm south-easterly wind behind it, and took Earl Siward's great church with it. Archbishop Eadred can not have been happy with the new worshippers. I should not wonder he will bend the king's ear when he comes to stay with him at Biscopthorp.

The gateway at the end of Monk Gata looms ahead in the darkness. A worried gatekeeper asks from within,

'*Halt*, who goes there?'

'Is that you, Eadulf?' Osgod answers. 'It is Thegn Osgod riding for the Deorewent road'.

Eadulf waves us through from his cramped gatehouse.

'Pass, friends, and good luck on your way!'

'Poor man', Osgod says as we ride out of his sight. 'Eadulf lost his wife and offspring when Harald Sigurdsson stormed the *burh*. Now he lives here, alone with his thoughts. I wanted to give him somewhere to live, but he would not hear of it – he said he would be forever looking out for his wife coming home from seeing her sister'.

Harding growls, his words lost as our horses' hooves clack on the stone setts as we leave Jorvik for the road north.

'Osgod', I call out.

'*Whoa!*' he reins in his mare. 'What is it, Ivar?'

'Horses – *see*, over there to the east, near where the Foss bends to the north!'

We all halt. When the Northman fitzRicard cranes his neck to see Hemming draws the rope tight that binds him to his saddle, pulling him down sharply. Hemming is awarded with a dark scowl that raises a laugh from men close to them who could see. He slaps fitzRicard's mare on the rump, making her skittish, but is warned by Osgod to hold back from teasing our hostage further,

'*Keep still!* We do not know who they are, ours or theirs'.

Saeward bravely sides with his fellow East Seaxan,

'*Would* there be any of the outlanders here this late?'

'That makes sense, surely', I add.

'All the same, there are no others I know of who may be about on horseback in these parts', Osgod counsels.

Harding raises a warning hand and halts his mount suddenly. We all rein in and wait. Cold air from the Foss crosses the land and turns our breath into clouds that might be seen. Snorting horses are quietened, and all is still.

Men and horses follow the nearside Foss bank, from time to time plainly seen, hidden just as suddenly by bushes and small trees. A mist creeps across the land from the river towards us, hiding us better, and we feel safer. These riders might easily have others close by on the same side as us, or to our left coming from around the crumbling old wall to the west.

We hear talking, but not loud enough to know what tongue it is they use. Some of what they say to one another is carried across in the still air, jarring words that are neither Aenglish nor Northman.

Harding cocks an ear, and has to press his reins down on the mare's neck to hear when it shifts its weight, so that what is being said comes across better in the still night air.

The talking ends whilst these newcomers come onto the road ahead that we have been following. One of them speaks up, asking about the way ahead. I know who that is, but I listen a little longer lest I am wrong. I would be a fool if I took these men as friends and we were drawn into a fight against greater odds!

Harding knows who is talking and calls out through the thickening river mist,

'Earl Morkere, is that you?'

'Were it not, you would be well counselled to flee!'

Osgod asks, when Morkere comes through the mist,

'My Lord Morkere, what brings you here?'

'I might ask the same. Who have you with you?'

Morkere leads a score or more riders, amongst whom are his brother Eadwin and Osulf. Gospatric is not with them, so may still be north of Beruwic. More come into sight behind him, one of whom I know very well, and greet him,

'*My Lord Eadgar,* I am glad you are well. I hope your mother and sisters are safe and well'.

'*Ivar*, we are well met!' he greets me as a friend and reaches across to take my outstretched hand in both his, as he has often done before. Beside him, Morkere eyes me warily. Eadwin is too taken with talking to Osgod to pay me any heed. Osulf merely gives me a blank stare, choosing not to come any closer.

'We had heard there was unrest in Deira', I hear Eadwin say to Osgod and Harding, both of whom he knows better than he knows me. He either still does not trust me, or is ashamed of the way he sold out to Willelm. Still, Eadgar seems to have forgiven him, so it is not for me to treat him as a foe.

'The Northman king is close at hand', Osgod warns.

'Aye, Lord, the sky was dark with smoke to the south-west. We let Willelm Malet leave with his wife and offspring and what few of his men were still alive when he yielded their stronghold to us', Harding tells Morkere.

'We came away with his castellan, Rodberht fitzRicard', Osgod finishes, 'for us to use to bargain with, should we meet a band of their horsemen greater than our own'.

'It is as well you met with us, then', Eadwin answers with a nod, and looks around at the rest of us to see who he might know. Seeing me beside Harding he glowers and his gaze next lands on Saeward. My friend does not know he is being stared at until I elbow him and jerk my chin toward Eadwin.

'I thought I told you not to come this way any more', Eadwin hisses at Saeward.

The East Seaxan stares coldly back and tells him he no longer has any standing here,

'Neither you, nor your brother are earls, from what I have gleaned', Saeward's bluntness makes Morkere flinch, yet earns a sharp scolding from Eadwin.

'*You* might be wise to think forward on what you say, Saeward. There may come a day when this kingdom is not big enough for you to hide from me!'

'Eadwin still your tongue!' Eadgar snaps.

'We would do well not to make threats here', Morkere, oddly enough, wisely counsels his brother. 'We may need everyone's help who would grant us it'.

Eadwin nevertheless fixes Saeward with a cold stare, unmoved by his brother's warning. Morkere adds in the hope his brother will heed him,

'Think on this, too, he has the ear of the *aetheling,* and the skill and eyes of a killer. You saw the way he threw those axes at Thorney –'

'He has also brought down a few of the outlanders with that skill', Eirik adds, but Eadwin is unabashed.

He may have to learn the hard way.

16

'So, my Lord, what do we do with the outlander?' Osgod asks Morkere. He knows what Eadwin would say, but this was not Eadwin's earldom. There may be some thought in Osgod's manner toward Morkere, looking ahead to the day when we hope Eadgar will be king in Willelm's stead. Morkere may well be the earl here again.

'*How far* are we from Eoferwic?' Morkere uses the Aengle name for the *burh* he knew as his own for too short a time.

'In daylight you would see the ruins of the great church from here', Osgod answers. 'Two of the men could take him part of the way back before morning, and let him make his own way back to tell the king himself how his master the shire reeve was duped'.

Morkere grins, relishing the king's anger at Malet.

I doubt this king would be overjoyed to see *him* again, as little as Willelm Malet gladdening him with news of the loss of their stronghold. Where might the burden of blame rest without his *castellan* around, I wonder?

The one-time earl looks to Eadwin for counsel. His brother's eyes light up at the thought of us being taken,

'Send Ivar, with his friends', Eadwin's eyes light up at the thought of us being taken.

'Would you do that, Ivar?' Eadgar asks, handing me an opening to turn Morkere down.

'I do not see why not', I answer, looking Eadwin up and down. He holds my gaze, the bolder of Aelfgar's two sons now alive, but I can see from his eyes that he is taken aback at my taking on the task.

'You have no fear of being seen?' Eadgar asks me. He knows the answer even before asking, but feels he must make sure. Morkere offers a hand and I take it in the spirit it was offered. If I show that I hold nothing against Morkere or Eadwin, then neither will look out for me if my errand goes wrong. I, or one of my friends for me, will strike them down when time allows.

Having eaten we mount, Saeward, Eirik, Hemming, Rodberht fitzRicard and I, and make our way back across the ford toward the Jorvik road.

Hemming has the rope we keep on fitzRicard's horse. This brings me back to when we led the other Northman lord, Hubert, past the Miercan wildwood to Ceaster. How long ago was that now, a week? It seems a lifetime ago since I left Ceaster under a cloud, thrown out by Eadburga because I would not bed her lest Braenda showed. Thrown to the tender kindness of the waiting Northmen, with Hubert de Mesnil keen – it is likely - to see me brought low in the eyes of his fellows.

I shall not let *this* Northman lull me into riding further into the burh than I mean to. When the skeleton of the church of Saint Peter comes into sight above the trees is where we send him back, *no later!*

Mist still cloaks much of the land, making the woodlands look like balls of wool, and the River Foss seems to be afire with the cold air rising from its ripples as it wends slowly toward the Ose.

'We are to make toward the Deorewent as soon as we are rid of this one', I tell my friends, loud enough for fitzRicard to hear behind me. 'Thegn Osgod and the others will meet us on the road to Beoferleag'.

Eirik looks back at the outlander.

When he taps my left elbow this is to let me know the Northman was listening in. Good, half my task has been done.   Not long later I see the high, bare roof of the church above the drifting mist and rein in. Hemming draws up beside me. FitzRicard on his other side stares in the cold fore-dawn light at me, fearing what is to happen to him I should not wonder. When Hemming draws a dagger he gives a start and looks about, hoping to be saved from a bloody end. The East Seaxan grins sideways at me before bringing up the blade through the long rope.

FitzRicard looks in wonder at me, at the others, and at Hemming, who hands him the reins. When it dawns on him that we mean him to ride away he digs his heels into his mare's flanks and presses her into a canter. As we turn to ride back to the others we hear her galloping away, out of sight in the damp greyness. We shall be out of reach by the time he finds any of his masters to tell them where he thinks to find us.

'Do you think we could hope for kindness from him if ever we were taken?' Hemming asks.

'I should not think so', I answer. 'With us out of the way, his life will be easier!'

'He has too much to make up for', Saeward adds. 'Having belittled him he will suffer the wrath of his king before his peers. Malet will not be as keen to see him, but kindness or pity is one thing neither would show *us!*'

Eirik chortles behind me,

'Not if the Bastard sends his men out the wrong way to find us, he would not!'

So there it is. We stand to gain from fitzRicard's bad luck. Such is life,

'Back to Strenshalge it is then', Eirik booms and Saeward leans over in his saddle to cup a hand over Eirik's big mouth.

'Not *so loud*, fool!' I hiss. Saeward takes his hand away from his

271

mouth and clips Eirik across his ear as a father would do to a wayward son. I go on in a rasping whisper, 'There could be *any* number of Northmen around in this thick mist, without us being able to see them. Who knows, fitzRicard could even have doubled back to make sure we were going where we *said* we were!'

'Is it that *likely?*' Hemming asks, throwing his weight behind Eirik.

'Who are we to say otherwise?' I answer and nudge Braenda into a walk with my knees. A mistake could cost us our freedom – *our lives.*

The Deorewent has risen since we last came this way in the early morning and now, with the mist clearing and the sun's warmth growing, we have to cross the river again to reach the road north past Strenshalge.

As luck would have it, there are riders to the west behind us, and with their lances they are surely Northman or Frankish. The leading rider has a pennon near the tip of his and they must have seen us, as they put on a burst of speed across the lea.

It is time for us to put on a burst of speed. Fast running river or not, we must cross, and the sooner the better.

'Make for the river bank – *there!*' I show them with the head of my axe. This is where I crossed with Harald Sigurdsson's man, Arngrim. I nearly lost him through my own foolishness in crossing with him too close behind me. Unbeknown to me he had loosened his bindings. Now there are the four of us with twelve or thirteen well armed Northmen behind us. There is nothing for it but to risk a crossing, with all the weight of a river in flood pulling at our horses. Would *they* risk a crossing? Eirik and Hemming look sideways at me but Saeward has done this before, across the river near Leagatun – *and in winter!*

'*Make haste!*' I call over one shoulder, the horsemen closing behind us. I can see three have lowered their lances, hoping to catch any stragglers.

Saeward takes up the cry, having looked over my back,

'Hurry - *hurry*, the Northmen are closing behind you, Eirik!' He looks over one shoulder, and is almost run through by the first rider.

When the Northman passes him closely he swings his axe around his head and brings it into the luckless man's back. I can see the blood spray, spattering Eirik, but our friend takes his *wyrd* into his own hands and follows us down to the riverbank. Another horseman throws a shorter spear and I yell as loudly as I can to Eirik,

'*Down*, Eirik – *bend down!*' I do as I want him to, to show him what he needs to do. He has either not heard or understood. The lance strikes from behind, skewering him, the reddened tip raking Eirik's chest. His mare slows to a trot and stands at the riverbank, dead still, to drink from the river.

Wide-eyed, Eirik does not seem to understand what has happened to him. Blood pumps through the wound in his chest, and trickles down his jaw. His copper beard glistens with the streaks of dripping red and he lifts his arms as if asking why we are not beside him. And then one of the horsemen behind him rides up, pulls the lance from him and lets him drop backward out of his saddle, jerking in his death throes to the grass. The Northman sneers, raises his lance as if in greeting, and rides back to his comrades.

'If only we had Theodolf with us!' I swear and press Braenda up the far bank.

'If only we could bury Eirik!' Saeward thinks more of the man's rights as a fallen warrior. 'Should we wait for them to leave and then go back for him?'

Hemming adds his feelings, showing he is on Saeward's side,

'We *should* go back, Ivar'.

I think so too, but for how long will the outlanders keep watch on Eirik's dead body? We can only wait so long before Morkere and Eadwin take us for dead and talk Eadgar into leaving for the north. Osulf would lose no sleep over me, either.

'Do you think you could ride to where we left Osgod and the others, and let them know what has happened?' I ask Hemming. 'Tell them we will stay a while longer. If the Northmen leave we can bring his corpse to be buried along the way somewhere'.

I think back to a church in the woods, named for Saint Gregory, to the east of Helmsleag. Eirik would be taken care of by the Brothers, and would rest well there.

Hemming gives a wave as he turns his horse, turning again to nod when I call after him,

'You know the way?'

The sound of hoofbeats dies and we turn our horses, Saeward and I, to watch the other riverbank. Some way off to the west of the lea the horsemen sit in their saddles, eyeing us. They must know what we wish to do, so they are in no rush to make our task easier.

'How long shall we wait?' Saeward asks. He has no need to whisper, as the foe is far enough away not to be able even to hear us talking loudly, but he holds Eirik dear. For all Eirik seemed to poke fun at Saeward they were brothers in arms and fought side by side. I have to think long and hard about how I am to answer him.

'They may become bored and leave', I tell him hopefully, just as one of them rides south, back to the *burh*.

'You saw that', he nods his head sideward, after the rider.

273

'Aye, they may have sent him back to tell their masters what has become of them. They may be told to forget us', I answer, more in hope than from knowledge. FitzRicard and Malet may have told their king that I am here, within his grasp. I know he wants me taken, but not *how much*. Saeward is as much at risk as I am, having come with us to Hrofesceaster, and Hemming may be a wanted man since leaving Willelm's camp at Exanceaster. Lord Ansgar may have already been held answerable for Hemming's insulting the king by forsaking his camp.

'You take this too much to heart', Saeward tells me, smiling. 'You are as bad as I am'.

'It is because of me he rode with us, my friend. He saved us from the Northmen nobles Willelm fitzOsbern and young Hrothgar Montgomerie after they fled, and as you know he rode north with us to Baebbanburh and Nyburna. He was like a little brother, *testing*'.

Saeward grins and falls silent again. We lost touch with Eirik after leaving Hereford for Defna shire and Dyflin, only seeing him again when we crossed from Wealas into Mierca.

'Where are we to bury Eirik?' Saeward asks next.

I have to gather my thoughts before answering. We have lost a good friend in Eirik, and I believe we need to go back soon and bring him with us to Osgod's camp.

'There is a small church in the woods to the north, named for Saint Gregory. That is where he should lie, in the lee of Gamal's church. It would be a fitting last home for a warrior'.

'Who is – or *was* Gamal?' Saeward is not asking to pass the time, I know. He wishes to know of the man whose church we will stop at, not that I can tell him much. Gamal's death was bounded in dark deeds, and the land around these parts went to Tostig. It was at Tostig's feet that the blame was laid for Gamal's death, amongst others.

'Gamal was a well-known landowner, well liked by those who knew him, a fair man so I heard and dealt well with those who abided by the law'.

'A likeable man, then', Saeward says, looking across the river. 'Speaking of likeable men, I think we will soon be able to save Eirik's body. These Northmen have become fed up with waiting. Although it might be a trap', Saeward thinks aloud.

'Wait', I tell him. I add, 'It will soon be dark. Before long we can cross without anyone seeing, and bring him back from under their noses'.

My eyes tell me the Northmen have left.

My wits tell me something is amiss. Yet Saeward presses his knees in to his mare's flanks and I follow. Saeward and I cross together and heave Eirik over his horse, all the time looking over our shoulders – lest they *do* come back. We bind Eirik tightly to his saddle, his ground blanket drawn across his back to soften the cords on his skin so that he is not badly marked.

'Let us away, then', I tell Saeward.

There is a gnawing in the pit of my stomach, but it is not from hunger. One by one my friends become fewer. Our ride allows my thoughts to wander back to Theodolf, my hope being that he is getting better, and is safe from further harm. Is he still in Ceaster, I wonder, or has he been thrown to the wolves by Eadburga as we were?

With Eirik's horse between mine and Saeward's, I follow a track northward through the woods at a steady canter. It is not as easy to find the right track as I thought it might be, and twice we take a wrong turning. In the end we stop and look around, to look for such as flattened grass at crossroads, and broken branches between trees.

'*There!*' Saeward points at horse dung to our right.

'It could be anyone who followed that track in the last few hours', I answer, sniffing, looking for something else – *anything* else.

'The grass over that way looks well trampled', he shows me. 'The horse droppings are not as new. Shall I look further?'

'We will wait here', I nod and he turns his mare left.

'I thought you knew your way around here', Saeward asks witheringly.

'It is dark, Saeward. When you have not been this way for years everything looks alike in the dark. Do not forget, we were riding behind Osgod earlier'.

He grunts, but says nothing. Am I to suffer the burden of Saeward's scorn on top of everything else? He catches my arm when Hemming shows between the trees to our left and stops to wave.

'At least *someone* knows the way', Saeward snorts. Is he laughing at me? Come what may, we have some miles to cover and I shall not waste my time thinking about any ill will he bears me.

Soon the smell of smoke from camp fires drifts toward us through the trees as we close on the river, now to our left.   Not long after I see pinpricks of light through the darkness, and soon one of Osgod's lookouts calls out,

'Halt, *who goes there?*'

I answer, not faltering,

'It is Ivar with Saeward and Hemming'.

'Walk forward, that I can see you', he orders. We drop down gratefully from our saddles and when we are nearer he raises his spear and barks, 'There are *four* horses!'

'The fourth man is bound to his saddle, friend', I tell the lookout, lifting the blanket to show Eirik's head to one side of his mare.

'What *is* it, Arnwulf?' Osgod strides toward us from where a number of men lie sleeping around one of the fires. 'Ivar, what ails you?'

I rub my eyes, tiredness threatening even now to overcome me, and give him my best answer,

'Nothing ails *me*, Osgod. Eirik was speared by one of the outlanders near the river. We had long to wait before they left, which is why we have taken so long to reach here'.

'As well as losing our way through the woods', Saeward casts a scornful look at me as we make our way to the nearest fireside.

'That cannot be helped, Saeward. You did well to find us in the darkness, the three of you', Osgod grasps my hand as we pass close to where Eadgar, Eadmund and Morkere rest against their saddles, talking quietly.

Morkere looks up and grins mockingly at me. He almost laughs, telling me,

'You found your way back'.

'I told him he did well to find us in the dark', Osgod tries to dampen Morkere's scorn.

'All the same you took a long time. It will be dawn soon, and we must take ourselves off to the moors before this king of ours sends men after us', Morkere sneers. He looks at Hemming and Saeward before staring back at me. He tells me smugly, 'You are missing one'.

'No, Morkere, he is on his horse. Look behind me', I thumb the air over my right shoulder toward Eirik's mare.

Eadwin gazes past me at our friend, bundled over his saddle,

'You are not going to trail your friend around the wapentake, I hope? You have somewhere aforethought to have him buried, I would guess. Tell me we are not going to have him with us all the way to the Tese'.

Osgod chuckles and crouches beside Eadwin,

'Worry not, my Lord. Ivar has thought of that. On our way north we will stop at the church of Saint Gregory to ask of the Brothers that we can leave Eirik's body to their care'.

'Thank goodness for that!' Morkere breathes out.

'Amen', Eadgar adds to laughter from Saeward. Looking up he asks, 'You laugh, friend Saeward. Why is that?'

'I had worried, with that self-same thought of Eirik's smell following us beyond the moors before Ivar told me we had not far to take him'.

'We are at one then', Eadgar raises his eyebrows to heaven and nods at me. 'What is he like to ride with?'

'*He* is no worse than some I could name', Saeward smiles and looks down at his mud-spattered boots. If he thought otherwise, would have told the *aetheling*?

The deep rumble of Harding's laughter can be heard from where he stands tending to his horse, setting off others within hearing, and before long the whole camp rocks with laughter. Morkere seems to redden, his older brother standing then to shake his shoulders from behind.

'They are not talking about you, little brother – at least, I should not think so', Eadwin cackles and Morkere's reddening deepens.

'Why would I think they were talking about *me?*' Morkere brushes off the slur gruffly, although with the last word almost a squeak. His effort might be more believable if he did not shake with righteous anger.

'True, why *would* we be talking about you?' Eadgar tries to smother his laughter, sparking another outbreak of laughter around the campfire. Although at least a half-score years younger than Morkere, Eadgar's wit is sharper. He has had to grow up fast these last years, what with losing the crown first to Harold and then to Willelm.

He will no doubt see much suffering before the Northmen are done with us.

On breaking camp before the dawn chorus begins, bed rolls are stuffed behind saddles, fires are kicked over and anything that might show we had overnighted here is broken up and buried or thrown into the river nearby. We ride north-eastward in a long line, two abreast toward Staenfordes Brycg and cross to the other bank before striking out northward for the moorland ahead. We should be at the church well before midday.

If Willelm sent anyone to find us in the east he will be angered when he sees them ride empty-handed back into Jorvik. He may call Archbishop Eadred to him and claim hostages.

Eadred may have the skill to calm this king, on whose head he set the crown before witnesses. It will be on Eadred's shoulders that any blame rests, therefore, if his king behaves unwisely toward the folk of Jorvik. It was the Church, after all, who wanted Willelm crowned, so they must live with the outcome.

At last, through the trees, we see the church of Saint Gregory, the church Gamal endowed with gold and silver gilding and a richly adorned sun dial above the main door. Tostig gave much else, more gilding undertaken on the church.

I know my kinsman felt badly about his forerunner's sudden end, because he knew the men behind the slaying. He will have to live with it, wherever he finds himself.

With the butt of my axe I hammer on the great iron-bossed oak door, and wait for someone to show. The echoes of my hammering die away but no-one stirs, so I hammer again - longer.

The creaking of a door hinge in a smaller building behind me makes me jump in my skin and I turn to see an elderly Brother shuffle along the narrow path toward me, his hood pushed back from his head. A thick white beard frames a ruddy, bald head, a long, spare frame hidden by the thick folds of his dark, dun-hued robe. He wears leather-thonged sandals on broad-spread feet. Whilst I take him in someone behind me steps forward and threatens him. It is Morkere, taking on himself the mantle of a lord angered at being made to wait.

'Behave, Morkere!' Eadwin chides, and steps forward to greet the fellow.

The Brother answers calmly,

'He is young yet. Who am I blessed with greeting this fine morning?'

'I have a kindness to ask'. I touch my forehead.

'Which is –'

I wave Saeward forward with Eirik's mare, answering,

'I have a friend who needs your blessing and care in death. He is behind us'.

Saeward shows the Brother Eirik's lifeless, sorry body and hands over the reins when the old man reaches out and asks me,

'Do you have a name for your friend?'

'His name, Brother, is Eirik', I pat Eirik's back as he passes, slung over his mare's saddle. 'He was a brave warrior'.

Eadgar and Eadwin bow their heads. Morkere has his head pushed forward by his brother and he has the wit to keep it bowed. The Brother frowns, clears his throat and looks sideward at me. In raising my brow I hope not to have to add anything in words and he understands,

'We will take care of your friend, my son. Will you say a prayer for him?'

'We will indeed, Brother –'

'I am Brother Godwin'. He hands the reins to a youth who has come from another building close by, and puts his hands together. 'Before we pray for Eirik, will you want his horse back?'

'I think not, Brother Godwin', I smile and clasp my hands together at my waist. Saeward puts his hands together in the way of a church man, and Hemming merely bows his head. Beside me Osgod and Eadgar clasp their hands together across their chests. The others, behind me, murmur the words after Brother Godwin and all end with the same loud 'Amen'.

'Will you take bread with us this fine morning?' Brother Godwin asks, looking closely at Eadgar. It seems to me he knows to whom he is talking. A shake of the head from the *aetheling* brings a nod of acknowledgement from the church man and we walk slowly back to our mounts.

We are on our way again, having taken our farewells from Eirik and Brother Godwin. The high moorland beckons. One of Osgod's men leads us through leafy dales and up onto broad, wild, treeless moorland. Sheep graze to left and right, paying no heed to us as they crop the short grass between outcrops of heather. Older lambs look up and make way for us, and the youngest flee to their dams' sides.

Upward still we climb, through Bransdale and onto a higher moor to where we can see, from left to right, other dales running north-to-south to either side below us. To the right is the northernmost horseshoe rim of Hroarsdale and ahead, out of sight the young river Aesc dashes over and between rocks, east to the sea at Hviteby. That much I know from riding with Hrothulf and Tostig.

'Where are we?' Eadgar asks.

'We are high up on Blekingey, my Lord', Osgod answers.

'Why are we stopping here?' Eadwin stands in his stirrups and is almost thrown by his mount as it panics.

'Calm your mount, Eadwin. We have stopped to take ale and anything the old crone can offer to eat', Osgod answers, trying hard not to laugh. Eadwin strokes the horse's nose, pats its neck. A wizened old woman comes out to see what the fuss is about, goes back inside again, and shows again.

'How many are you? I need to know - for feeding'.

Eadwin looks her up and down, but cannot think of what to say. He has been taken unaware by her coming back out again. Eadgar answers for us,

'I should say there are a good score of us'.

'*Good?* What is *good* about it?' she grunts.

Eadgar's hapless look is no help to her.

She scowls up at him, mumbles about having to send a lad with an ass for more brewing barley, and vanishes into the darkness of the dwelling-cum-alehouse before showing again to ask,   'I only have seating for half of you. The rest will have to wait out here. Hands up,

279

who wants sheep's broth?'

Most men's hands shoot up.

This riding makes men hungry! These fellows look eagerly at her at the thought of something warm in their bellies, and then sigh again when she tells them gruffly that they will have to take turns with the bowls.

'Draw lots', I offer. 'There may be spare rush lights'.

'Fine', one man says, asking, 'Who will ask *her*?'

'Afraid of a little old woman, are you?' Beorn-Ulf   teases his friend.

'She is a spay-wife, I am sure of it!' the answer comes, and the fellow spits on the grass at his feet.

'Then watch I do not turn you into a toad!' Having come out again behind him she hisses, making him jump. 'Who wants bread with his broth?'

Hands are raised, uneasily this time. She counts them and goes back indoors again, wary eyes following her.

I laugh, throwing my head back,

'She will not turn you into toads before she gets her silver for the food and ale'.

'All very well for you to talk, Ivar, with your spay wife looking in one you now and then to see to your comfort', Hemming rasps. The men eye *me* oddly now, thanks to him.

'Do not listen to the fool', Saeward swears and clips Hemming over his head. His fellow East Seaxan glowers back at him but he out-stares his friend and goes on, 'He wishes *he* had a woman to warm his blanket for him'

Laughter eases everyone's thoughts. Talk of spay-wives or witches up here leads to bad dreams at night. Folk in these dales are more gullible than in the lowlands, what with the darkness on moonless nights being blacker and dark thoughts running through all men's heads at talk of things that crawl or crash about in the night.

With the warm broth inside us, and the sun on its way back down again in the west, we are ready to ride on. Men struggle to their feet after dozing on sheep-grazed short grass and Osgod comes back out into the weak sunlight. Stretching, he looks about and seeing me mounted, yawns and scratches his beard,

'Oh, what it is to be young and keen!' he jokes. He must be at least a half-score and five years younger than me, and takes his standing these days with a pinch of salt, a thegn in name only.

The Northmen in Jorvik have not acknowledged his standing, I would guess. He is therefore footloose and free to go where he will, without owing anyone anything in the way of loyalty. So now we are together, an *aetheling*, two earls, an ealdorman and several thegns amongst our number.

'Are we ready?' Eadgar asks as he swings onto his saddle and everyone answers with a loud '*aye*'. When he looks our way we nod. He nods and jerks his head to the left to follow him, behind Beorn-Ulf. Our way leads downhill, where Beorn-Ulf waves his left arm for us to leave the main track.

'This way takes us through Westerdale', he calls out, 'and from there through the hamlet of Kjelldale to Aigetun. We can overnight there.'

'As you see fit', Osgod answers without looking at him, and belches.

'We are in *your* hands good fellow', Eadgar adds to the hum of thankful mumbling from the others. By the time we reach our beds most of my riding fellows will be saddle-sore. Saeward looks my way and winks, elbowing Hemming at the same time.

'What –'

'Are you still awake there?' Saeward snorts.

Laughter underlies this seeming worry about Hemming's well-being. I can see the man's tongue pushed hard against the inside of his thickly bearded cheek. When will he learn about trimming the thing? Women might see something in him then, I am sure.

'Nothing you need fear!' Hemming answers gruffly. 'If I fall off my horse my feet will still be in the stirrups and she will drag me along!'

'It might be a bit bumpy around here, friend', Saeward can no longer hold in his laughter and everyone looks his way, wondering what the outburst is about. Hemming's dark scowl at being stared at overawes the younger men with Osgod, but Eadwin scowls back.

'I am sorry, my Lord', Hemming asks forgiveness for his rude stare, 'but this fool would try a saint'.

Eadwin lightens. He grins and answers, looking aslant at Saeward,

'Hemming, I would hardly see a saint in you. You are right, however. He *is* trying'.

Clicking my tongue I press Braenda forward to catch up with him again and rest a hand on his shoulder,

'There you are, Saeward. You have pulled off something others strive a lifetime toward - *renown at last!*'

'I have *you* to thank, for teaching me, Lord Ivar', he chortles, earning a dark look from Eadgar. The *aetheling* has warmed to me, although my kinsman was the first to rob him of his birthright.

Eadgar's scowl brings Saeward to his senses. The young fellow is usually the last to show anger, but he is the noblest here. He might one day be king, and Saeward *should* be worried about earning a scowl from him.

The rest of the ride goes on wordlessly, westward down the narrow track from the tall wayside cross, up over the next hill and into Kjell's hamlet, Kjelldale. A few souls watch us pass through along the broad track. To our right is a small church on a rise, raised likely by the man Kjell himself many years ago. Now all they have left of him is a hog-backed stone set amidst the grass and bushes that ring the small wooden church. One day someone will build something that will last, of stone, to think on him by.

By the time we reach Aigetun, a few miles on, we can see one another only by the light of a waxing moon. The dwellings on either side of the river, the same that runs through Harding's hamlet, are swathed in darkness. Only a few torches flicker in the light breeze to show there is life in this northern corner of the wapentake.

'Beorn-Ulf, where is this inn you spoke of?' Osgod stretches and rucks about on his saddle, trying to ease the soreness on his backside.

'Where the three torches burn, outside the long hall', Beorn-Ulf waggles a finger that can be barely made out.

Morkere brings himself to smile at last, sighing loudly,

'You know how glad that makes me feel?'

His brother glowers at Saeward, who now laughs loudly at something Hemming has told him, but Saeward cannot see him from where he has slid down onto the Cigesburh road.

Beorn-Ulf drops down from his saddle and vanishes through the hall's great door. When he comes back again he has a man and woman in tow. The man carries a paunch and he is balding, lightly bearded. The elderly woman, slight and bowed, tells us we are welcome and asks how many we are. When told of our number, the innkeeper scratches his head and, thinking hard, pats his belly. He squints at us and looks at the woman, who shrugs, and then up at Osgod,

'Is there anyone of noble birth?'

'Half our number', Osgod answers, staring levelly at him. 'Why?'

'The others will have to sleep above the stables. It is warm in there, from the horses –'

'Ah - that I can *well* believe', Osgod smirks. He turns to Eadgar, Morkere and Eadwin, to Osulf and then back to the innkeeper asking, 'I take it food is to be had, even this late in the evening?'

The innkeeper brims over, beaming broadly,

'My kitchen maids will cook you all a meal worth thinking back on, my Lord'.

Eadgar thanks him and slides down to the road, rubbing his thighs.

'However long I ride, I will never be used to these long days in the saddle!'

'We are all tired, my Lord', Eadwin speaks for the rest of us. He nods and sucks in the chill night air. Although summer is well upon us now, its warmth is lost on us up here after days of dampness.

The others eat with us before withdrawing to the stable, Saeward and Hemming grinning at me seated between Morkere and Eadgar, with Osulf glaring at me from across the spread. Osgod is on the other side of Eadgar and the two are well into their talking as they drink and eat. Morkere, on my left, sits sullen, huffy that he could not sit beside Eadgar. I am between him and the man who might bestow the earldom on him that he thinks should be his, once the outlanders have been thrown back into the sea.

Eadwin is less bothered with such lofty matters and has launched into the food set before us. Osulf, no longer staring at me, takes on the Miercan in talking about other lofty matters. But Eadwin cares as little about the land north of the Tese as he does about the land to the south of his erstwhile earldom.

Osulf gives up on him and starts on one of the thegns to his left, but he too is too taken by the food, worried he might not get his share. The Beornican ealdorman growls and yields to the needs of his stomach.

'We will soon be on my land', Harding tells me, seated beside Osulf. I have paid no heed to him, yet he seems to be in a forgiving mood. 'You are far away, I feel'.

'I am sorry. You are right', I fib. 'I am far, far away, thinking of days gone by'.

'And of your woman, I should not wonder', he beams, takes a draught of ale before breaking bread and dipping it into his broth. Whereas Eadgar does not seem bothered by Harding's lack of breeding, Morkere glares hotly at him

He thumps down his food and sits back, arms folded across his chest.

'The food is not to your liking?' asks the innkeeper. Morkere can only shake his head and begins to eat again, not wanting to draw scorn from his brother. Although having been an earl in his own right, albeit for only a year or so, he still stands in Eadwin's shadow. Aelfgar's sons are not happy with one another!

We are shown to where we are to rest for the night, most of us in rooms quartered by smaller booths. Eadgar, Eadwin and Morkere have rooms to themselves. I have brought a skin of apple ale with me and settle down with it for the long night. My thoughts wander again as I let the golden ale pass over my tongue, the nearest I shall get to tasting mead for now.

I must have fallen asleep with the skin undone. When I feel the ale's coolness over my side, there is nothing else to do but to take off my breeks until morning, when I ask someone to find me some more. As I climb back into the cot I feel a hand on my back. By the light of burning rushes in a stoneware flask beside the cot I see her behind me, naked above the cover, her full, round breasts welcoming.

'*Braenda*, I thought you had given up on me', I turn to her and let her arms snake around my bare midriff. When I am about to say more she puts a finger to my lips and kisses me over her finger. She next pulls my tunic over my head and presses her breasts to my chest, smothering my neck, jaw and cheeks with soft, warm kisses. As she wraps her thighs tightly around my back I enter her. We push hard, lustily against one another until we fall back, panting, with sweat beading our bodies in the fading light of the gutting rushes.

She is gone again by dawn, as always, sated by our coming together in the night. I reach for my breeks, struggle with pulling them on and go out into the chill yard to swill my arms and chest in the cold water of a horse trough. As there is no-one about, so I think, I pull my breeks down and swill my manhood.

A woman giggles and says out aloud,

'Now there is a man who could fulfil a woman's needs. Such a shame I have tasks to do in the kitchen!'

I pull up my breeks quickly and wheel around to see a young woman standing there, pail in one hand, besom in the other. She grins cheekily up at me, winks and then puts down both pail and brush,

'*Oh*, what am I saying', she breathes and leads me around the back of the hall to a short, low building that abuts onto the hall, into a store room. Shift pulled quickly over her head the maid heaves herself up onto the lid of an ale vat, clasps her full breasts and tells me, 'Fill me!'

How can I turn her away? Standing between her outstretched legs I pull my breeks down around my backside and pull her onto me. By God the woman is ready! When my thoughts stray back to Braenda and I know this must be forbidden fruit, but by now I can no longer hold back.

'What – is - your *name?*' she asks, her breaths rasping as I slip back and forth into her womanhood, warm juices overflowing around my crotch.

Without thinking I answer, pulling her to me, *harder*,

'I - *am* - *Ivar*'. My legs feel weak but I cannot stop now. I am in my stride and the woman is willing.

I do not see why I should know her name, but she kisses my neck, one hand around my shoulders the other holding her up against the board she is sat on, and hisses into my ear, her breath hot,

'I am – *Braendeswitha!*' Her head jerks back and she sighs throatily. By the time I have pulled back and opened my eyes she has pulled off her knotted headscarf and laughs, '*Got you!* Who did you think I was?'

'I knew *all along*', I lie, winking, pulling my breeks up again. 'I thought, this is Braenda trying to test me again so I shall have her again before she leaves'.

'*Liar*', she laughs, and plants a warm kiss on my mouth before turning to find her shift. 'You are a *good* liar, though, my love. Our paths will cross again before long. Believe me', she cups a hand around my jaw and presses her lips to mine. We part, looking back at one another once before she enters the hall with her pail and besom.

My way takes me back to my booth, to clothe myself and make ready for the first meal of the day. Hopefully it is not the only meal of the day, yet Harding has given forewarning of our being on his land soon. We may be given something to fortify us at Rudby before we go on to the crossing over the Tese.

'You look well', Osgod tells me between mouthfuls.

His booth was next to mine, and I think he may have heard something in the night. 'You seem happy with life this morning'.

'I feel well within myself', I smile as I take the pot from Harding.

'So you should, from what I heard', Harding chuckles. He stuffs porridge into his mouth and looks up at me as he chews. With a wink at me he looks across at the hall door at Morkere, and pulls a mock scowl.

Osgod turns on the bench to see his lord enter beside Eadwin, and goes back to eating. Morkere draws up behind him, seats himself across from Harding and glowers at him. The big man's eyes are on the woman who passes behind Morkere.

'Is that your woman, Ivar? What is *she* doing here with that pail and besom?'

'I might have asked her myself, but she had something else in store for me', I lick my lips and sit down to eat. When his guffaw thunders across the hall he sprays milky oats over Morkere.

A dark cloud brews over the young fellow. I feel the air thickening, and he brings tightly clenched fists down onto the table so hard everything jumps. His own full cup of ale leaps into the air and into his lap. He sits, staring with rounded eyes up into the darkness of the roof trusses.

Osgod does not know where to look for fear of laughing. He puts a hand over his mouth and bites on one finger to stop it. Eadgar shakes his head, but goes on eating and Eadwin overlooks his brother's foolishness. Harding arches his brows and goes back to his porridge, hoping nothing more comes from Morkere's side.

For myself, I have to look forward to the next time Braenda and I meet, and spoon what is left of my porridge into my mouth to keep from smirking.

17

'So far, in this corner of the earldom there are no Northmen. We are too far east here, away from the highway between Eoferwic and Dunelm, as far as Tese. Beyond the river is within reach of the Fleming Rodberht de Commines', Harding tells me as we ride. 'You would be too close to ride by without him hearing of your passing'.

'Why not ride along the coast road, to the east of Heorot?' I ask. 'There is a road that leads by Uiremutha and on north over the Tina near Nyburna'.

Harding sits astride his saddle looking at me, mouth open. At first raising his left hand as if to say something else, he lets it drop to his knee again and looks around. he sees Osgod and bids me ride on whilst he and Osgod talk with Eadgar.

'What was that about?' Saeward asks, having passed Harding on his way to me.

Glad to have him beside me, I answer,

'I have put forward that we ride along the coast to steer clear of being seen by the new Northman lord's scouts. They were going to ride for Scotland a lot closer under the outlanders' noses'.

'Sounds odd to me', he turns in his saddle as Harding pounds past on his horse and halts a little ahead before looking around.

'Were you looking for me?' I ask.

'*Ha!* I thought he was further back', Harding says, looking at Saeward. 'Eadgar thinks you are right. It was Eadwin who wanted to ride straight across between the Tese and the Tina by the shortest road. He is in too much of a hurry to flee this kingdom!'

'With that much haste, he would hinder the crossing over the Twida into Maelcolm's kingdom', I tell him.

'Are we going with them?' Saeward asks me.

I shake my head slowly and look at him before answering,

'You can, I am staying here in Deira'.

'Where will you hide out?' Harding stares, unable to believe what he has heard.

'I was hoping I could stay with you', I look ahead, over my mare's head as I answer. Will he grant me my wish?

'*I* am riding north with Osgod and the others. We will be stopping for a few nights at Baebbanburh before riding on to see King Maelcolm'.

'Would I be able to bide awhile at Rudby?' I ask.

Harding looks at me past Saeward, brow knit tightly. He is thinking, I can tell, and it seems hard for him to say 'no'. I should by rights stay at Aethel's steading, but there is no-one there to ask. Staying here within a long day's ride of Jorvik, Rudby would be easier overlooked by anyone seeking me. We ride on for a few more miles, not a word passing between us, until we see the first dwellings of Huttun against a darkening sky to the north.

'As long as you know you must help my men – chop wood for fires, hunt for the pot, mend roofs', he nods and squints against the sunlight behind me to the south-west and reins in his horse to let Saeward past, then guides his mare with a deft pull on the reins to ride beside me.

'That I can, and *will* do', I reach out my right hand.

He takes it glumly, and then tells me,

'I had thought of staying myself. Whether Osgod would want me with him, I cannot say. There is a woman back there in Aigetun I would like to wed'.

'Then we will be good friends for one another', I laugh and slap him on the back.

'I hope so', he purses his lips. 'I also hope there will be other friendship for me – a woman's'.

'We should only hope so', I wink. 'Braenda may even come, hopefully'.

On hearing my woman's name Harding shudders and crosses himself,

'With luck there will be no more trouble from spay-wives or whatever other evil beings that may choose to cross this land and elsewhere', he suddenly scowls. Is it the thought of having to spear his wife Aethelhun outside Theodolf's home?

'- Unless you do not wish it', I prod.

'No, Ivar, you are welcome. If your woman wants to, she can show at Rudby, even stay a while for as long as she wishes'.

Thus said, he grunts and rides forward to speak to someone else ahead. Hemming rides up from behind and asks,

'You are not going on with the *aetheling?*'

'No, Hemming. I shall stay behind, with Harding. We will ride with the rest of you as far as the bridge that spans the Tese, and then back. Are you riding on with the others?'

He nods, adding,

'I think Saeward and I will ride on with Eadgar, Osgod and the earls. We will see the lie of the land where King Maelcolm bides, and see what arises. We can lend our sword hands to the Scots' king, if he wishes to use them on any Northmen who dare set foot in his kingdom'.

'Then we shall see one another by and by, soon', I smile. He clicks his tongue and passes behind me to ride beside Saeward.

'You and I are to ride with the *aetheling*', I hear Hemming tell him. Saeward shows no feeling either way. He sniffs and draws a finger around his nose, wiping it, and shakes off the droplets into the wind. He looks back at me and nods, riding on side by side with Hemming.

We make a halt at Harding's steading by the Leofen, his men bringing out ale for us all. He leaves a couple of the skins of apple ale with one of the maids, which she takes to store in one of the outhouses. Whilst Osgod talks to Eadgar, Morkere and Eadwin, Osulf seeks me out. He raises a hand to show he means no harm,

'I understand you mean to stay with Harding. Is that so?'

'That is so', I answer, waiting for him to add more.

'You think we mean you harm in Baebbanburh?'

He raises his beaker, 'Your health, Ivar'.

'It is *not* out of fear you think I may have', I swear.

He chews over his words before letting me know his thoughts,

'You should know you will be welcomed if, or whenever, you think of riding north with the aetheling. We hold nothing against *you* as kinsman of Tostig. However, we are not answerable for the deeds of those who share our blood'.

This is new to me, as the first time I saw him, he and his kinsman Gospatric seemed only too willing to strike me as tackle Copsig. Even when we came to be in the same troop near Jorvik, he looked set to strike me from my horse. Now I learn they will welcome me in the north. What brought this on?

'Will you have more ale, Ivar?' Osgod has been watching me talk to Osulf, I think. He has a pitcher in one hand and is about to pour when he asks, 'Is it true you wish to stay here with Harding, sooner than ride on with us?'

When a maid passes with a platter of bread and cheese I help myself to a chunk of both and set my ale down on a tree stump. Whilst I chew I think of the way Osgod asked about my stopping here. As I turn the bread over in my mouth he waits for me to empty my mouth and begins to ask again. I stop him in mid flow with a raised hand,

'It is in the *way* you asked that made me think hard, Osgod. You know me well by now, I hope, and you should know that Harding and I have become firm friends since the days we rode to Baebbanburh. It is not that I do not *want* to ride with you, it is that I wish to be in Deira when Theodolf shows'.

Osgod breathes out and pours more ale into my beaker. He smiles and taps the side of his nose with one finger,

'It is Morkere and Eadwin who irk you?'

'Put that way, I have to say you could be right. You *are* right', I laugh, looking around, making sure neither of them has heard either of us.

'And your woman – is she about?' he asks, and   screws up his mouth when I shake my head.

'I saw her last night, but I do not know when I will see her next. She said it would be soon, but I have no way of knowing when'.

He thinks of something else to say, coming out only with something that sounds like ill feeling,

'What can be done by staying here?'

'When Theodolf comes north from Ceaster I can reach him quicker. He needs to be kept in check, not to overdo the fighting. I owe Hrothulf's son that much for past friendship'.

He nods, understanding maybe, and drains his own beaker.

I hold out my beaker and he fills it again, asking about Theodolf,

'Is it likely Theodolf will come back to his old haunts? He has a woman and child in the west, has he not, as well as a woman in East Seaxe? Surely he should seek out either of them, rather than ride all that way to Deira to live alone?'

'Firstly his woman at Wealtham is further away than Rhosgoch. He has fallen out her anyway. As for his other woman, I do not know whether she is still at Rhosgoch. I do not know if Theodolf knows. He is more likely to head this way', I add, 'to Aethel's steading'.

'I hope you are right, for your sake', Osgod finishes off his ale and puts down his beaker on the tree stump next to mine, then walks away to where Eadgar and Morkere talk together with Osulf listening.

'What did he want with you?' Harding asks. He has been wandering about aimlessly between the clusters of men, and has come over to me without my knowing. Saeward strides across the garth yard, hands full with ale and food. Harding half turns toward him and asks, 'What gives, Saeward?'

'You want to talk with Ivar?' Saeward asks and walks away again, heading for Hemming.

Harding chuckles,

'Sometimes I could cheerfully crack his skull'.

He rakes the soil with one boot and begins again.   'Would you grant me something?'

'For a friend, aye, I would'.

He sucks in air, and tells me what he wants,

'If the Northmen come this way, you should say you are one of my household. Give them an Aengla name like Wulf. I will give you clothing that you can wear around here, and when you leave again I can let you have your own back'.

'I thought you were going to ask me to do something that could cost me my life', I laugh and pat his back as we walk to his hall past Saeward and Hemming.

'You are done talking?' Saeward calls after me.

'Aye', I answer. 'Did you want something of me before we ride north to the Tese?'

'I only wanted to know if you will be on your way south to Tadceaster', he asks, looking wide-eyed at me. Hemming stares dully into the air, not knowing about Aethel's steading – nor caring, to look at him.

'I would have to know whether Theodolf was on his way before I left here. Otherwise it would be a waste of my time', I think back on whether Theodolf had said anything about going north. Surely he would not come all that way on his own from Ceaster?

'Give him my greetings if he does come', Saeward asks, offering a hand to take his farewell as Eadgar and the others mount.

'Harding and I are riding with you as far as the Tese', I tell him, looking up against the light at him with my right hand shielding my eyes. 'There will be time enough to take our farewells, you, me and Hemming. We will think on Eirik over the next few months, will we not?'

'Aye, we will', Saeward lowers his eyes. He seems downhearted at parting after these months of riding and fighting side by side with me.

'We will meet again soon', I use Braenda's words of farewell, and heave myself up onto my saddle telling him, 'believe me. Besides, we have miles to go yet before we reach the river, long enough to talk about the old days, eh? Look at it this way, when we meet again we will have more to talk about, and be happier to see one another for the time apart'.

'Come, *spur* your horse Saeward or you will not need to take your farewell of Ivar', Hemming chides, having reined in and turned his mare toward us.

'Well, what if I did *not* go with you?' Saeward tests our friend sorely at the best of times. Hemming purses his lips and turns his horse again. He raises one arm, and lets it drop heavily to his side in an unspoken 'farewell'.

'Leave me behind would you?' Saeward crows loudly after Hemming and laughs.

He grins at me and kicks his mare into a trot. I wait for Harding to catch up and we, all of us, ride for the Tese. We have at least an hour's ride before farewells are needed.

Eadgar rides at the head of our troop, Eadwin behind him to his right and Morkere on the left, both irked that Willelm has seen fit to overlook them in his handing out land and rights. Eadwin is still disgruntled that Willelm offered him his daughter Adela as a bride, and then withheld her hand in wedlock. A Bretlander was instead given the right to be the king's son-in-law and Eadwin was left to bemoan his *wyrd*. Morkere was by-passed as unfit for the earldom. This king would squeeze blood from a stone!

Would they get what they want from Maelcolm, either of them? He cannot offer them land without drawing the wrath of his own lords. What Willelm has done so far in this kingdom is little other than any lord would do elsewhere. Maelcolm can help, as Diarmuid did for Godwin Haroldson, in offering ships and men.

The fast-running waters of the Tese glint in the sunlight through the trees below Gearum. We see riders with long lances on the street ahead as we turn into the road down to the river.

'I thought you said the Northmen have not reached here yet', Eadwin snaps at Harding.

We pull back and gather, watching the foe from between bushes and trees. How many are there of us to them? We could overcome them, but we would lose too many to their lances before they yielded. Can we take them somehow without needless losses?   Eadgar draws us all together, whilst keeping lookouts near the roadside.

'Do we have bowmen?' he asks.

A few hold their bows over their heads, but in my eyes not enough. He thinks the same and looks let down,

'Osgod, what would you say?'

'We kept out of sight in the west until we were almost on them', Osgod offers. 'Ivar has fought them more often'.

'Ivar, have you any thoughts?' Eadgar tries not to look care-worn, but plainly wonders why he has Eadwin and Morkere with him if they have so little to offer.

'We can lure them into an ambush', I put to him. 'Send out two or three men on horseback to catch their eyes, and when they give chase our horsemen bring them through here. Bowmen could hide here and there, others with axe and dagger close behind them or drop onto them from the trees'.

'That worked in the Andredesleag when we rode to see which havens the Northmen's ships were docked in, to bring their men and weapons', Saeward cuts in when Morkere is about to say something.

'What were you about to say, Morkere?' Eadgar asks him before he bursts with anger.

292

When Saeward was sent away from Jorvik Morkere had threatened his life, should he ever be seen there again. Now Saeward is here and Morkere can say nothing against him, it is more than the fellow can bear. Eadwin puts an arm on his to steady him, pulling him back from doing something rash.

'I was about to say that, having seen the East Seaxan throw axes at Thorney, he might be the one who stops any of them fleeing', Morkere's eyes glint. It could be the sunlight breaking through the trees, or it could be hatred fuelling spite.

'Could you do that?' Eadgar asks Saeward and is rewarded by a nod.

'Aye my Lord, I could and *would*', Saeward answers, brightening at the thought of bringing more Northmen down. 'Could I have Hemming with me?'

'Which one –'Eadgar begins.

'I am Hemming', Saeward's fellow East Seaxan raises his arm to be seen.

'Will you see to it that none of the Northmen flees?' Eadgar looks from Hemming to me next, and asks me, 'You might wish to be with your friends, Ivar?'

'Gladly, my Lord', I answer. I am not as keen as I might seem, but I should stand by my friends before others.

Morkere smirks, making sure Eadgar has not seen, and offers more,

'Osgod might take Harding out to the right of us with a few others, and see to it that none of them leaves that way'. He looks at his thegn, asking, 'Would you *do* that?'

'I *would*, my Lord'. Osgod nods, and with a wink adds, 'I think your men would be grateful for your leadership if you were seen to be with us, to guide us'.

'There, Morkere. Your men look up to you!' Eadgar beams and turns to Eadwin. 'You shall be by my side'.

Eadwin grins smugly at his brother and shakes his head. He had warned Morkere about opening his mouth out of turn, and now he will either show himself to be as useless a leader as he was at Gata Fulford, or he will shine. I hope for his sake, and ours, that he shines.

We all ready ourselves for the Northmen. They would not lower their lances until they are close enough to smell the fear in their prey. There is little likelihood that Eadgar would be speared as long as he does not allow them enough room to show how good they are with their lances. If they are squeezed between us on each side, they will be harmless.

'Set back to allow our own men through, Northmen as well, before we press from behind', I tell Saeward and Hemming.

'I see them!' Hemming warns.

We pull our mounts around and wait behind an outhouse or barn at the top of the street. Osgod's men come hurtling past with all seven of the outlanders close behind them, lances still held upright. The first Northman passes close by, the leader, pennon fluttering wildly below the point of his lance. As the last one pounds past we close on them.

To our left Morkere, Osgod and a few others draw up, Morkere himself hanging back until his horse rears and dashes through the others. Another thegn and his men come in from the west and we have our foes trapped between us, unable to lower their lances and trying to keep us away with their swords, flailing like men drowning.

I briefly catch sight of Saeward crashing into the nearest, axe at the ready, bringing his arm back to sever the links around the Northman's midriff and bringing an ear-splitting scream from the fellow such as I have never heard before from a man. Hemming beside me on my right lays into the elderly noble.

This Northman gives as well as he gets but I have a young fellow ahead of me who wants to lay me out in the earth. He swings at me with his sword, almost catching his neighbour with the tip of his blade. In raising his sword arm he has laid himself bare and my axe catches him in his armpit. Hemming's noble and my youngster fall onto one another as they drop from their saddles.

The others are dealt with by Osgod's and Harding's men, until all seven lie, blood-drenched amid tangled tree roots. Hemming has been dealt a sharp blow on his shoulder by the nobleman's sword and bleeds steadily through his chain mail. One of Morkere's huscarls lies, almost beheaded, by his horse's front legs. His broken sword blade is lodged in the chest of one of the outlanders, the hilt still in the huscarl's hand.

'Ulfketil will have to be buried', Morkere stands over him, sheathing a sword as yet un-blooded.

'How do we bury a man when we have no shovels?' Osgod asks and shrugs. Morkere stares and Eadwin waves his brother away.

'Have they any between them?' Morkere points at the dead Northmen. '*Someone* must have a shovel, surely?'

Harding puts forward, looking along the street,

'We could ask someone who lives here'.

'There must be *some*one around'. Morkere sounds annoyed. They still have a few miles before they are safe across the river, and this is just holding them back.

Eadgar, astride his horse, does not seem worried. He watches everything happening around him as if it had nothing to do with him.

294

He does not see the horsemen coming from behind him, pennon fluttering from another nobleman's lance-head.

'There are more Northmen – *behind you*, Lord!' Harding's mare bucks as the newcomers close on us from the west, lances levelled.

Saeward is next to see the threat and turns to meet the foe. When one of them comes at Eadgar, the east Seaxan brings down his axe onto the lance, splitting it and sending wood shards into the air. Eadgar raises his shield against the flying shards of ash. One of the shards arcs back at the horseman, who has not seen it coming at him. Wood shears skin, an eye is lost, and next to be lost is the rider's life as Saeward's axe hurtles through the air and cuts deep through his helm into his skull.

As another comes at me I trick him with my shield into thinking I am about to strike him with my axe. Instead I punch him in the chest with the shield, knocking him across his high saddleback. It is as good as having another weapon. When his backbone cracks he wails and slides sideways off the saddle into the path of one of his comrades.

As a lance-head is pushed through the dying man's back and shows through his manhood, Harding uses the second man's bad luck to skewer him with a lance taken from one of the dead men.

The others take flight, straight into the path of unknown bowmen. Two drop like stones from their saddles, another is dragged along through thicket and thorn by his left stirrup. Only one is able to flee unharmed – eastward toward the bridge Eadgar needs to cross.

Eadgar watches as three men stride toward us,

'Who are these bowmen, who have come to help?'

'Who are you?' Morkere calls out to them as they come near enough to answer.

'I am Hringolf Brusason, and these are my brothers Arnkell and Hunding', the nearest answers.

'You missed one', Morkere mutters, a finger aimed at where the Northman had vanished through the woodland. One of Hringolf's brothers looks crestfallen up at the young earl, sucking in air, not knowing the outcome of his letting Morkere down.

Eadwin digs an elbow into his brother's shoulder and tells him what anyone should know about warfare,

'There is always *one* arrow drawn too quickly to catch its target. The riders might easily have run them through if they had waited too long!'

'That is true', Eadgar bears out Eadwin's words. 'Things happen quickly on the field of war'.

Morkere should know better than to cast doubt on other men's skills, having fled the fighting with his brother at Gata Fulford. Osgod and Harding are not the only ones here who know. Knowing better, Eadwin has no wish to air his brother's failings, having also run from Harald Sigurdsson as the Norsemen broke the Northanhymbran *fyrd*.

Eadgar brings down a veil over Morkere's lack of understanding for the bowman's failing,

'We are getting nowhere here. Your browbeating the fellow renders his brothers' feat meaningless and we should be away. The folk of Gearum will bury Ulfketil –'

'We will bury the fellow, Lord', Hringolf cuts in, bringing a scathing look from Morkere.

'Very well Hringolf, we will leave his burial in your hands. I have to thank you for your task in hand. Morkere, Eadwin, Osgod, we must ride! Farewell Hringolf and your brothers. Do not take the earl's manner to heart, these are trying times'.

'Farewell my Lord', Hringolf touches his forehead and watches as we ride past, his brothers with him.

'Do you know these men?' I ask Harding.

'I cannot say I do, no', he answers, baffled. 'I thought I knew everyone around here. I must ask about them when we get back to Rudby'.

Saeward leans in toward me and tells me,

'Hemming will not be able to make Scotland. I think with the cut on his shoulder he will lose the use of his arm'.

'What does Hemming say?' Harding asks across me.

'Hemming is a fool. He would ride on until he dies. Could I bring him back to Rudby with you and Ivar?'

'You are no fool yourself though, are you Saeward?' Harding acknowledges my friend's wish and tells him to bring Hemming to his garth when we have seen the *aetheling* over the bridge.

Saeward taps his forehead in thanks and takes Hemming's reins. I would say Hemming looks worse for wear already, in need of Saeward's healing skills, and I ask Harding to go back with them to Rudby whilst I ride on to the river. He thinks hard on this, but thankfully not for too long,

'Aye, Ivar. I see Hemming would need to rest before we were able to reach home from crossing the Tese'. On calling to Osgod that he must ride back with Saeward and Hemming, his fellow thegn nods and Harding turns his horse.

'Why is it that Hemming needs Saeward's care?' Osgod asks me, Eadwin and Morkere looking on.

Eadgar is some way down the track with a few of Osgod's men

around him and has not heard Harding ask to turn back. When we reach him he looks beyond us and asks,

'Who are the three riders going the other way?'

When Osgod lets him know Harding has taken the other two back to his garth, he looks nonplussed.

'Hemming is in needs of care?'

'He is, aye, Lord', Osgod answers, 'but Ivar will ride with us to the bridge in Harding's stead'.

'Does he *need* to come any further with us?' Eadgar presses, waving a hand at the men with him as well as the Miercan brothers. 'After all, we have you and these others to guide us'.

'You may as well ride back with them', Osgod reaches out a hand to take his farewell of me for now.

'Take care, Ivar', Eadgar waves, and beckons the others on. Eadwin nods to me but Morkere merely gives me a blank stare and turns his horse to follow the *aetheling* riding beside his brother. I watch them down the track, as far as the next bend where they are lost behind the trees, and turn Braenda. With a nudge from my knees she trots on and begins to canter when I give her free rein.

'Osgod sent me back with Eadgar's blessing', I tell Harding when he raises his brows at seeing me so soon.

'It may be they *can* do without you', Harding jokes. 'No, forget that. It was in bad taste, Ivar. A small band of men will not be as easily seen, and go on to Maelcolm's court without making the Northmen unduly aware of their passing. Come, we must press on before Hemming becomes feverish'.

The sun threatens to dip behind a bank of heavy cloud to the west when we come to the rise where a track drops down to the Leofen. Another leads on toward Huttun. Before we take the downward slope I see men around Harding's garth.

'Are they your men?' I ask him.

'Are *who* my men?' his head jerks around from taking in the landscape he has come to love. 'Good God, what are *they* doing here?'

'You know them?' Saeward asks, and props up Hemming.

'I do not know them but I *have* seen them before. I hope they have not come to rob me again'.

'Rob you? Are they thieves or outlaws?' I ask as we follow the track down to Rudby.

Harding tells me before I get much further along the track,

'They are Willelm Malet's tithe gatherers. I would not let them see any of you'.

'*What about Hemming?*' I ask, worried. What can we do with him before he passes away? I wonder. Saeward has the same worry etched on his brow. How do we get him to bed, to be cared for?

'One of my neighbours will take you in whilst I deal with the outlanders', Harding steers us in the half dark away from his garth to one of the smaller steadings that nestles beneath the brow of the hill.

When we come to the doorway of the first dwelling Harding calls, rather than thumps on the door,

'Styrbeorn, are you there?' He calls again and as we are about to leave the door creaks open and an elderly fellow stands there, rush light in hand. Styrbeorn calls after us,

'Who is that?' When Harding turns Styrbeorn's eyes open wide. He rasps, 'What is the matter?'

'Can I leave a couple of men in your barn?'

Styrbeorn looks toward Harding's home and asks,

'Are the outlanders at your garth again?'

'They are indeed. These fellows cannot be seen here. I think you should stay with them, Ivar', Harding counsels.

'I think so too', I am at one with him.

'Come', Styrbeorn raises his rush light and beckons me. 'Bring your friends. Stay with my ceorl whilst Harding deals with his guests. The other two can bed down in the hay loft. What is wrong with that one?'

'He is badly wounded. A Northman's sword cut into his shoulder', Saeward lets Styrbeorn know the worst. They could be here for weeks at least, until Hemming is healed.

'Help your friend bring him', Styrbeorn tells me. We will be faster, the pair of us, getting Hemming away from prying eyes. Harding's neighbour leads us to a low, narrow door, where we ease Hemming up a few creaking wooden steps to a small room. An opening in the wooden wall is covered by a miller's bag that has been opened down the seam to make it bigger and keep out the cold.

In the poor light we help Saeward pull off Hemming's mailcoat, taking care not to hurt him too much. He is a brave fellow, I have to allow, but the pain is too much for him and he cries out. It takes little more time to ease him onto a narrow straw bed and cover him with a spare horse blanket from Styrbeorn's store.

'You have tended to men's wounds before', Styrbeorn is in awe of Saeward's work, cleaning and dressing the wound.

Saeward asks me to bring some things from his saddle bags,

'I hope I have done enough. There is balm in my saddle pack to put on a dressing, you know Ivar?'

'I think I know', I pat him on the back in passing and almost fly headlong down the steps.

'Take care on the stair', Styrbeorn rhymes, stifling laughter.

'Now he tells me', I groan, trying to find my footing and catch my breath. The steps seem narrower going down than they did on our way up. Why is that? Saeward and Styrbeorn cackle in the loft as I make my way to where I saw the ceorl take our horses. I have the balm back in the hay loft before long and withdraw down the steps again, out of Saeward's way. Harding should be in his own garth by now, greeting the outlanders as if nothing untoward had happened.

He told us to wait until he sent one of his men, but I cannot wait. I have to see for myself. The way is dark out here, where cloud has drifted across the moon, and I stumble more than once on grassy tussocks. I curse myself for not waiting, yet must go on and see what is keeping them. Are these Northmen holding him, waiting for more armed men to come and take us?

One of them stands at the gateway, arms folded, waiting to be told to mount and ride away again. He looks bored when I near him, making myself out to be some fool from the hamlet, my mailcoat covered by a ceorl's cloak. The man yawns widely. Sleepy eyes are fixed on me until I stand, wobbling before him, as though almost overcome by drink. He tries to hold himself aloof.

'My Lord', I reach out a hand dirtied by my steadying myself against a tree the last time I stumbled.

He looks the other way, trying not to see me. Standing before him I cannot be missed, too tall for him to look over me. He reaches for his sword, but I have my dagger under his nose before he can lay his hands on the hilt. Slowly he reaches his hands into the air, but that is of no use to me. I want his hands together, to be bound. How do I tell him that? With my dagger tip still in his sight I hold my other hand up to it, to show him.

Fearfully looking down his long nose at my dagger, then up at me, he brings his hands together and I wrestle a length of binding I found in Styrbeorn's barn to twist tightly around his hands. He winces when I pull too tight for him to bear, and I pull again to see his mouth twist in pain. Having seen – or rather not *seen* but *known* of – Willelm fitzOsbern wriggling free of his bindings I do not want it happening again. I pull him by the loose end away from the gate, and bind him to a tall sapling, still keeping the dagger tip close enough to his nose that he will not be foolish enough to struggle.

When I am done I pull off his helm and he keeps his head bowed, knowing I do not mean to kill but stun him. There is a length of bough on the grass, short enough to use. The task is carried out without him

299

even flinching. He drops to his knees. My length of binding is not long enough for him to fall any further. Safe enough for me to see what keeps his fellows.

Someone plucks a lyre within the hall, but there is no merrymaking. The lyre player groans through a dreary lay as I steal in through the darkened door to the kitchen. Harding sits, half asleep on his high seat, listening to one of the tithe gatherers. The others watch, bored, as the lyre player bows and leaves.

The few Northmen clap and lift their cups in a toast to man of the household.

'Thegn Harding, we thank you for the food we have eaten, for the ale –'

The Northman is not allowed to finish. One of his men rushes back into the hall, shouting, prodding the hot, smoky air at Harding. His master stares at my friend and raps out an order to the two men at arms he still has. They thump across the floor toward Harding, one coming around his left past me. Not seeing me as a threat, he stands with his back to me, his fellows both looking across the hearth at Harding. One beckons him to step forward from his seat.

I bring my dagger smartly around the nearest one's throat. The other two still have not seen me as I pull their comrade into the dark, tear off the cloak and don the dead man's helm. Then I draw my sword. I hardly think, in this poor light, that even Harding would know I am here.

He rises and pulls back his cloak to show he is unarmed before walking forward past the hearth toward the cleric. The last Northman makes his way between the benches toward Harding, his sword still drawn.

The cleric says something to me, taking me for one of his men and I step forward. He turns to me when I come nearer and his eyes widen with fear. When I put a finger to my lips and go to stand behind him he says nothing. Afraid to warn his fellows, he shivers. I bring my sword up across the cleric's chest and tell him,

'Your man there, tell him to lay down his sword on the bench beside him. Do not try to say anything else, as this fine Aenglish blade will be christened in your blood!'

The cleric babbles and his man sets down the weapon, glaring at me.

'Now tell him to put down his dagger and take three steps back', I mutter into the cleric's ear. Shaking still, he passes on my order and the man's dagger glows beside the longer blade.

'*Tell him* to take three steps back!' I hiss into the cleric's ear. 'He will know what follows if he does not'.

The cleric whines and his bodyguard steps back, twice, to stand, feet apart, arms folded, daring me.

'Tell him again, *three steps!*' I draw my blade closer to the neck of the cleric's black robe.

Sobbing wretchedly, the cleric pleads for the man to step back once more, and hot tears fall when nothing happens. My blade rises to the cleric's collar bone before anything happens. The guard smirks and shakes his head at the cleric.

'Now tell him to come here, slowly', I order, and ask my friend, 'Harding, are you well?'

'Tired, Ivar, but I am well enough. I thought I told you to wait across the way with Styrbeorn'.

'I was tired too, Harding - tired of waiting. It seemed these good folk would stay all night', I break off and ask the cleric to tell this bodyguard to cross the floor to where his dead comrade lies.

The cleric begins to sob again when the Northman strides slowly by me and stops by the corpse. Looking down at his slumped fellow and back at me, he bends to pick up the sword lying there. He then slumps dead by his comrade, a long bladed scramaseaxe in his back.

Styrbeorn stands, smiling in the doorway through which I entered the hall. He peers through the smoke at Harding, sees he is well, and grins at me,

'I could not let you have them all to yourself, Ivar! Harding I am glad to see you are unharmed'.

'I may not be unharmed for long if these are missed in Jorvik', Harding lets his neighbour know his misgivings and sighs, winking at me. 'If I tell you to wait, Ivar, it is for the better. Now we will have to slay the priest'.

The cleric gives a start and dashes for the doorway, only to be stopped by one of Harding's ceorls coming in with a bushel of kindling for the hearthside.

'I thought we might need this', Toki grins toothily at the cleric as he speaks. Harding nods and chortles. How else would we have stopped our last guest from leaving early? Toki pushes the cleric backward with the kindling, and drops the bundle onto his feet by the fire when he can go no further back. The cleric groans with the pain, but holds an am up to ward off Toki.

'How do we speak to you?' Harding asks.

A look of bewilderment from the cleric angers Harding. Beetling his brow, he asks,

'What is your *name*, priest?'

'I am not a priest', the cleric maddeningly answers.

'Whatever you are, Northman, you have a name right?' Harding squints, trying not to show he is irked. In his shoes, I would counsel the cleric not to be so finicky about what he is and just answer.

'I am Canon Lodovic of Mesnon', he answers with a pout. 'And I am Frankish'.

'Well then, Lodovic, you know my name', Harding tries hard to be kind to the fellow, although he would just as soon bury him. This Lodovic of Mesnon, whatever he thinks he is, is under threat of his life – did he but know it. 'Tread warily, friend Lodovic. Frankishman, Northman or whatever you are, you could find yourself in the same ditch as these two if you choose to be awkward'.

'I will try', Lodovic answers wretchedly and swallows. Will he be helpful, or do we have to wring any other answers from him?

'You cannot but try', Harding smiles.

'As trying as you have been', I add, 'we might overlook your lack of manners if you do as you are bidden'.

Lodovic's brow furrows. Can he not understand the mess he is in, or does he think we owe him something, now seated on one of the bench ends awaiting his *wyrd,* or whatever these Franks believe?

'What Ivar means is that you have so far been less than helpful. What I need to know is, if you do not show back in Jorvik will they begin a search for you, raise the hue and cry? Your friends might not be missed, but *you* may well be'.

'The last man you killed', he looks at me in saying this. I shrug off the foolish claim, if anything to learn what he wishes to tell us about his friend. 'He was the nephew of the shire reeve, Willelm Malet. His Lordship *will* raise the hue and cry, as you say, fear not! You will be hunted down to the far corners of the kingdom –'

Saeward has entered the hall and crept quietly around behind Lodovic to cup one hand over his mouth. Styrbeorn now threatens Lodovic with his dagger blade and looks to Harding to know what to do with the outlander.

'We will have to do away with him', Harding mutters, rubbing his beard.

'The wolves are still out in the woods', Styrbeorn offers.

'We only have to bind him, hands and feet, and leave him amid the trees.

'That is a thought', Harding stares at the shivering Lodovic.

'*Threaten* us, would you?' I smile. A thought suddenly comes to me. 'We could empty his chest, stuff the silver into his purse and tie him to a tree – *gagged*. The Northmen would hardly believe whatever he told them then'.

Heads are nodded, and Lodovic looks fearful when I finish telling them,

'If not the wolves, then a passing bear might take a liking to him. He is well padded-out, would you say? Do you still have bears in these parts, Harding? With these tithe gatherers out everywhere, there will be little spare to leave out for our heavier furry friends', I watch Lodovic's eyes dart from one to another of us, fear building in them. 'There is another one of their number I left outside, bound to one of your saplings, Harding'.

'You could have told me', Harding scowls.

'Bring him', Styrbeorn tells me flatly.

'*I* will bring him', Saeward touches his forehead and vanishes through the hall door.

'How is the other one, your friend Hemming – he needs to rest awhile?' Harding asks.

'The East Seaxan is resting', Styrbeorn tells Harding, looking at me.

Saeward comes back pushing the Northman through the doorway ahead of him. Still groggy, the fellow looks at me first and then around the still smoky hall. Seeing Lodovic still alive he brightens.

'Tell your friend there', Styrbeorn growls at Lodovic, 'that he need not get his hopes up. You both live on borrowed time'.

Lodovic seems unable to understand Styrbeorn and I put the warning in other words he might know,

'Tell your friend you are both under threat'.

The warrior, such as he is, looks downcast on being told. His hands are still bound and he holds them up to me, hopeful of the bindings being cut. He looks even more downcast when he sees me shake my head.

'He should sit down', I say to Lodovic to tell his friend.

'Lest *I* see him as a threat', Saeward finishes for me, showing the shining blade of his dagger. Lodovic looks askance at him, but understands the meaning when Saeward runs his dagger blade along the Northman's hauberk sleeve to sharpen it.

My wish is passed on and the Northman thumps down on the bench beside Lodovic.

'His name is Thurbrand', Lodovic tells Saeward.

'A handsome name', Styrbeorn smiles, 'for such a fool. Shame these Northmen took on your grasping Frankish ways, eh, Lodovic?'

'Not that we need to know', Saeward sniffs, driving the tip of his dagger blade into the wooden bench beside the warrior Thurbrand, who sits there without showing fear. The cleric Lodovic closes his eyes as if in prayer.

18

A brisk wind from the south east cools an otherwise bright and cheerful summer morning. High, ribbon-like clouds seem drawn across the sky toward us, over blue-cast hills from the sea near Hviteby.

I have been standing by the doorway, asked to do so by Harding so that Lodovic and his friend do not try to flee. Saeward comes out with a cup of ale and on handing it to me yawns and stretches one arm, pulling his hand back, fist clenched. On raising my ale to him I take a draught and swill it around my mouth, swallow and take another mouthful before asking,

'What gives?'

'*What gives?*' he asks back, grinning. He yawns again and stretches both arms after putting down his ale by the threshold. 'You mean in there? Nothing has happened for some time. Harding is asleep still, as is Styrbeorn'.

'Arnbern guards our guests, fear not', he reads my thoughts again. What was once uncanny, I now think as being everyday. I drain the cup and turn for the door. Again he reads me, 'I shall watch out for you. Get some sleep, however little'.

Tired, I nod and enter the hall, resting my right hand flat on his shoulder as I pass him. He pushes me in, laughing,

'Friendship waits, Ivar, however *sleep* does not'.

I awake when someone thumps the bench at my head.

'Ivar, we will leave soon', Harding stands over me, food in hand. I suddenly know I am hungry, sit up, feel for my sword on the floor beneath me and stand.

'Food', I say, 'I need to eat'.

'Porridge is in the pot over the fire. Take care you do not burn yourself. Bowls are at the end of the table near the hearth', Harding finishes what he has in his hand, belches and rubs his belly. 'I needed that. Styrbeorn has gone back to his dwelling to see to Hemming. We, you, Saeward and I, will take our guests a little way south from here, beyond Aigetun. We can bind them to any thick-trunked, straight-grown tree - leave them for the bears and wolves'.

'That sounds fair to me', I answer, and nod, laughing.

'Or *outlaws* may take their lives after emptying Lodovic's purse', Harding smoothes his beard, mouth twisting upward in a wry grin.

'*Or worse*', Styrbeorn, back with us again booms loudly, 'they could loosen their bindings and make off back to Jorvik'.

'What a doom-merchant you are, Styrbeorn! It would be a long walk for them, and that silver will weigh heavy on the Frankishman. Besides, I hardly think they could get out of Ivar's knots. You know he has been a seaman? I daresay he could tie them strongly enough to keep them there for a lifetime'.

Styrbeorn wakes Lodovic with his deep laughter. The cleric rubs his eyes and sits, pulling his friend upright with him. The pair of them look up at us, bleary-eyed.

After leaving Rudby well behind, Aigetun in the mid-morning sunlight is alive with folk. Children run after us, slapping the tightly bound Lodovic and his Northman friend. Not that Thurbrand would understand the words used, but he must understand their meaning.

When earth is lobbed at them both some catches Harding. He turns and yells at those who follow us too closely,

'*Hey*, if you must lob earth at these two, wait for your thegn to get out of the way!'

Cowed, they fall back and blow duck noises at Harding. Even our hostages laugh. Saeward snarls at Lodovic, stilling his laughter and the other one ducks his head in time before Saeward catches him with a wooden club he has taken to carrying.

With Aigetun left behind, all the shouting and yelling fades and our track leads us on to Eseby and Kjelldale. Harding reins in and tells us,

'We can halt here. I think here would be as good as anywhere else to tie these two to a tree'.

Lodovic looks around, at us and at Harding. His jaw drops, knowing what is about to happen. He has not forgotten what we talked about doing with him and his last bodyguard.

'Are you leaving us here?' he wails.

'We are going to tie you both to a tree', Harding answers, tongue-in-cheek. 'Fear not, we will tie you so that you can talk together, eye to eye if you can stretch your bindings with the tree trunk between you!'

Saeward guffaws and slides down from his saddle.

'*You*, come here', he beckons to Lodovic. The cleric looks at me, although I cannot think why. Does he think I would stop this? I would sooner leave him somewhere wilder. After all, I think we are still too close to Aigetun.

When Lodovic stumbles timidly, Saeward reaches out, grabs his hands and pulls him to the tree,

'Why so fearful, Frankishman, when we have so many good things in store for you?

Lodovic struggles, flailing with maiden-like thumps on Saeward's mailed chest. He is easily finally bound with his rounded stomach onto the tree, the rope pulled tight around his shoulders, back and legs.

When Harding and I help Thurbrand down from his horse he does not struggle, nor does he hold back. Taller and better built than Lodovic, he would be more of a threat. This Northman behaves oddly for someone who can only guess at what could happen out here. Do they have bears and wolves in Northmandige? Foxes even, might take a liking to their flesh. I know they have *them*.

With the pair of them bound, Harding stands with us to take in our handiwork,

'Handsome pair, are they not?' he chuckles, playing with his beard, once fiery and now flecked with iron grey. He still has the fire within him, however, as witnessed by his yells when I showed unasked last evening.

'Am I forgiven?' I ask, thinking back to when his eyes nearly popped at the sight of me, and holding in my glee at taking the Northmen unaware. He reddens suddenly, and Saeward warily reaches for his dagger hilt.

'What is that for?' Harding glowers at Saeward.

'I thought something was going to happen', Saeward calmly takes his hand away from the dagger hilt and smiles at Harding.

'Where did you find this bloodthirsty lout, Ivar?' Harding asks, looking at me and winking. 'No, Saeward, I was about to cough. The need has passed, thankfully. I think our task is done here. What to do with their dead, though?'

'We should have left them out on the moor for the beasts', I put forward.

Harding shakes his head thoughtfully, looking down at his boots. He scratches at his upper lip and turns to look at Lodovic against the tree and throws his hands wide, asking,

'When would we have the time to *do* that? We would have to keep them bound at Rudby and there could be more on the way'.

'It is not the time of the year for digging up roots for the pot', Saeward begins, 'but we could plant some'.

Harding pops at me, jerking a thumb at Saeward,

'What can he *mean?!*'

I cannot think what has entered my friend's head and stare heavenward, as if in prayer. What can he mean?

'What are you babbling about, Saeward? What is this about roots and planting?'

'We could dig them in with whatever grows in the fields around them. That way any more guests you have would never know they have ever been here', Saeward answers blandly. I might add the look he wears is of annoying smugness, having thought up something like this

306

so easily.

Harding seems taken aback at first, but laughs like a child when it sinks in. He thumps Saeward on his back and almost chokes as he gets out the words he is looking for, just what I thought,

'Such a blindingly straightforward way of looking at things, your friend has!'

'*I* thought so myself', I nod, climbing back into my saddle.

'It comes from toiling in the fields', Saeward tells us, as if it was something we did not know.

'You might yet toil in the fields again, Saeward, if you keep that smug look', I warn him.

'No, leave him. He is right, Ivar. *We* did not think of it, and he did. Give him *some* thanks for thinking of it', Harding almost pleads.

Saeward seems to have found another friend.

We turn our horses back for Rudby, clattering through Aigetun once again. It is late afternoon when we reach Harding's hall and Toki stands outside, waiting in a state of upset.

'What now, Toki, why the sweat and fear?' Harding looks past his ceorl at a young Northman lord.

'Are you Thegn Harding?'

'I am, aye. Who might you be?' Harding flushes, wondering what his new guest wishes.

'My name, friend, is Geoffroi de Mesnil', the outlander tells him. 'My men are nearby, awaiting me. I was told a Lodovic of Mesnon might be in these parts with bodyguards. You know what some are like, I daresay?'

'Oh indeed? I could not have said better!' Harding brushes past this new nobleman to reach his high seat. No ill is thought of Harding's manner, plainly, when this Geoffroi de Mesnil enters the hall ahead of me. Toki comes in behind Saeward and stands ready for Harding to ask for ale to be given the new guest.

There is nothing to be seen of last evening's blood-letting. The dead are nowhere to be seen, benches as they should be. What does the fellow *really* want? He may say something about looking for Lodovic and his men, but I think there is an underlying threat here. Could he have been sent by their king to spy out the land for those who had attacked his stronghold in Jorvik?

'Bring ale for our guest Toki', Harding takes off his sword belt and hangs it over the back of his high seat. 'My Lord, what can I do for you?'

'As I say, I am looking for this man Lodovic. He had a small chest for the tithes he sought from the thegns in these parts. Are you sure you have seen nothing of him? It is odd, as he told the shire reeve, Willelm Malet that he was coming only as far as the river Tese. He has been seen in Treske and Allertun –'

'Have you been to Gearum?' Harding offers helpfully.

'You think he might have gone that way first?' asks de Mesnil, sipping at the ale, sticking out his tongue and putting it down on the bench beside him. I would say he will not finish that drink.

'Is the ale not to your liking?' Harding asks cheekily, trying to take de Mesnil's thoughts away from Lodovic. 'Would you like a wine?'

'You have *wine?*' The Northman brightens, forgetting his errand with this talk of drink.

Harding nods and turns to Toki standing behind him,

'We *did* have some. Toki, ask Arnbern if we have any of that wine left that we bought in Jorvik before the Yuletide?'

Toki leaves, glad to be out of the way, and Harding turns my way,

'Ivar, you have never tried the red wine I had?'

I catch the Northman looking sidelong at me, as if he knew my name but he looks away again, taking in the setting. I had best be on my guard if his men come.

'Wine is not to my taste, Harding', I answer.   'Your ale tastes good, I will give you that. Does Tofig's woman still brew your ale?'

'She does, aye', Harding nods briskly. He cranes his neck around to see his ceorl and laughs as he asks, 'Tofig, does she still put in more barley than the brewers say is enough? I believe she said it keeps us sweet'.

Tofig has come into the hall behind Arnbern and nods jerkily, saying nothing as he makes his way out of the main hall toward the kitchen. He is not easy around those he calls '*offcomers*'.

Arnbern is not long in coming with a thick glass flask of deep, rich red wine. Where it came from I do not know, and there is every likelihood Harding knows little about it either.

'I have the wine'. The irked look Arnbern wears is something to behold, I must say. He sets down the wine with a thud on the table beside the Northman, stepping back before leaving again.

'Are you sure you would not like to try this wine, Ivar?' Harding waves toward the flask. When I shake my head he sniffs and waits for Arnbern to show again with cups before offering it to de Mesnil. 'My Lord, I believe this wine will be to your taste'.

Looking down into his cup for some time, shaking it and sipping, Geoffroi de Mesnil makes out he is a man of taste. The show might be believable if he could see the wine from the side of the cup, but Harding's cups are of horn.

Saeward looks bemused. He has seen men with wine. Usually Wulfwin had the wine brought and poured into what he called Roman glasses, in a way he said they did at the court of the Holy Father. He itches to say something to belittle the Northman, but on seeing my frown thinks better of it and slurps his ale instead. De Mesnil, still up to his foolishness takes some of the wine and swills it around in his mouth. He looks around, and then spits it onto the wood floor, wetting the straw.

Harding sits back in his seat, eyes popping at the sight of this outlander spitting on his floor in front of him. He stands and blurts out,

'My Lord, is it so bad that you must be rid of it in that fashion?'

Before de Mesnil can answer, Saeward says for him,

'They do that, Thegn Harding. That is something my Lord Wulfwin did before offering wine to his Frankish guests at Wealtham – although not in front of anyone but his discthegn'.

'I must beg your forgiveness, Thegn Harding', the Northman adds. 'We do that at tastings, amongst fellow wine drinkers'.

'I understand', Harding sits again. He *says* he understands, but I somehow doubt it. If he lives long enough in this kingdom, the likes of de Mesnil may learn that it is not done with your host seated close by. You drink your ale or mead, or whatever, and it drops down inside your throat to ease your thirst or to make you feel better.

De Mesnil looks at Saeward and me in turn and offers the flask,

'It is a *good* wine!' He frowns at us shaking our heads, then looks up to Harding on his seat, 'Will you drink with me? It is a shame to drink this good Apulian wine alone'.

'Very well, my friend', Harding answers, putting down his ale. He asks Arnbern to bring him another horn cup and lets the Northman fill it for him. They touch cups and share the wine, then raise their cups to us.

'To you', says de Mesnil, downs the cupful and pours himself more, finishing that in the twinkling of an eye. He is soon full of himself, laughing at his own wit and seems to forget Harding or us after another cup or two.

'At this rate he will no longer know who or where he is', I tell Saeward in a hoarse whisper.

'What then?' Saeward asks, laughing with de Mesnil. 'Why whisper? He is well gone!'

Looking at and listening to the Northman would tell anyone he *is* past caring now, so I unburden myself openly to Saeward,

'I should say he has already forgotten about his men out there, wherever they might be. They could be here soon, wondering what has happened to him. Things will not be so boring then, when they come banging on Harding's door, calling for their lord to be freed'.

Toki hastens in through the door to Harding and stands close to him, telling him something.

I lean toward Saeward and tell him, as if he needs to hear from me, 'What did I say?'

'Ivar I think you are just as drunk as he is', Saeward answers.

'Am I...? What makes you say that?'

'You are swaying, your speech is a mite slurred. Hold off drinking and let *him* drink himself under the bench!' Saeward stretches out a hand, finger around his ale cup aimed at de Mesnil.

'Were you going to do something about him if his men had not come?'

'I had thoughts of planting him out there with the other roots', I grin, and when Saeward breaks into laughter I laugh with him.

The Northmen have still not come for their lord, as I thought. Instead three fellows are shown to where Harding sits, watching his guest leaning against the nearest table, helping himself to yet another cupful of wine.

'Thegn Harding', the first man greets him. All three are dressed in dark green, breeks and short-coats, and carry bows. Are they the men who attacked the Northmen with us at Gearum, stopping them fleeing across the river?

Watching de Mesnil from the corner of one eye, Harding beckons to me across the hall, asking when I am close enough for him not to wake de Mesnil from his daze,

'You know Hringolf and his brothers, Ivar, *from Gearum?*'

I think back to their bowmanship and grin welcomingly.

'Who have we here?' one of the brothers asks, Arnkell or Hunding, meaning the Northman.

'This fellow is Geoffroi de Mesnil', Harding smirks.

He steps down from his seat and shakes the bottle that de Mesnil thumped down onto the board. 'He has finished off my last flask of red wine on his own'.

'You are not going to ask him for the silver to pay for it?' Hringolf asks, grinning lopsidedly.

'Is that what you would do? He is a guest in my hall. I offered him it and had some myself. The others', he points to Saeward and me', wanted none of it. So we let him get drunk on it'.

'Is it that good?' Hringolf asks, and strides across the floor to lift the Northman's head from the table. He lets it go again, to thump down onto the oak planks. De Mesnil is still fast asleep and Hringolf raises his left brow. 'Would you like to try some, Arnkell?'

One of his brothers ambles across from the doorway and looks down at the outlander. He bends and sniffs at de Mesnil's cup, and stands again. Looking around, he sees the flask and smoothes his beard, telling Hringolf,

'Must be good - if he is still under after that handling I think I would like some!' Arnkell looks hopefully at Harding.

'*You* want some of it?' Harding laughs from his high seat. He shakes his head, laughing quietly, 'Too bad, friend, *he* finished off the last flask. Arnbern will take it out again. *Someone* might use the glass for something'.

Grinning foolishly, Arnkell asks,

'Do you think if we stood him on his head he might let us have some?'

'There would be a lot else that came out!' Hringolf bellows with laughter at his brother.

'You can smell it on his breath', I offer. 'Get drunk on that alone!'

'Aye, you might finish up under the table!' Saeward slaps the bench beside him and sits down, across from the still-sleeping de Mesnil.

'Where are his men?' I suddenly ask, coming back down to earth with a jarring thump.

'They are around *somewhere*', the third brother tells me from the shadows beside the door.

'Are they not likely to come looking for him?' I ask, cuffing de Mesnil across his head as I pass the end of the table to speak to Harding.

'*Hardly* – last I saw of them they were tucked up under mother earth's blanket, amid the roots in Harding's field beyond the Leofen', Arnkell smiles at me.

'They are dead?' Harding is wide-eyed.

'Burying men alive is not my calling', Arnkell sucks in air and whistles through his teeth.

'I had to ask', Harding growls, 'you know that!'

'Pay no heed to my little brother, Thegn Harding. He has a turn like that every now and then. He can be just as prickly with those he knows. We are left with knowing what to do with this one?'

'Kill him?' Hunding is ready with his dagger under the Northman's throat.

'Steady with that blade!' Harding snaps. 'I do not give my maids needless work! We dealt with a couple of his fellows earlier'.

'How *did* you deal with them?'

'I took the silver from the tithe box they had with them and filled the pockets and purse of one of them, a Frankish cleric by the name of

Lodovic', Harding tells them gleefully. 'We tied him and another outlander, a man-at-arms, to a tree not far from Kjelldale. Hopefully the bears or wolves will soon take a liking to them. We could tie this one to the same tree. If the Northmen find them they might take it that Lodovic had filled his purse with their king's silver, and when they smell the wine on de Mesnil's breath he will suffer the anger of his masters!'

'Good thinking, if it works!' Hringolf thumps down onto the bench beside our guest and ruffles his short hair. 'Odd, the way they cut their hair'.

'High at the back and over the ears, like a thrall you mean?' Arnkell looks closely at the sleeping man.

'King Harold's men wore their hair short, but not as short as this!' Saeward aims a thumb at me, 'You should have seen *him* when he was a huscarl of Harold's'.

'You were a king's huscarl?' Hunding peers at me, having neared us, mid-floor of the hall.

'I was', I answer, biting my lip to hold back that I was one of Tostig's first. These days, I know better than to give away that sort of knowledge. Few around here are as understanding about that sort of knowledge as Harding. Saeward was not so keen to learn about my past in the north, either. He does not raise it, and nor does Harding.

Hunding folds his arms across his chest, spreads his feet and makes known his own knowledge about me,

'As I think back on it, you were a huscarl at the Earlsburh as well'.

The hush that follows is deafening. The elder brother stares at me, as does Arnkell. I feel awkward in my skin, as I am sure does Saeward. Harding's mouth clamps shut and he stands, ready with his right hand on the pommel of his sword.

'You need not fear us doing anything, Harding', Hringolf tells him, still looking me up and down.

'You were his kinsman', Hunding goes on.

'As was I also kinsman to King Harold', I tell him.

'That goes without saying, being brothers', Hringolf buries his head in his hands, thinking. He pulls his hands down and asks me, 'You know Copsig was made earl north of the Tese?'

'Aye, we came to warn Earl Gospatric about that'.

I go on,

'Earl Osulf was ready to slit *my* throat for being one of Tostig's kin'.

'I would not go as far as that', Hringolf smiles and slaps Harding on the back as our host comes between him and Arnkell.

'A man must stand by his kin, no matter what', Arnkell tells me. He flashes a smile and pushes the Northman back over the bench, to fall onto the floor and into wakefulness. He looks up and stares sleepily at each of us in turn.

Hunding stands over de Mesnil, dagger at the ready, but Hringolf pulls him away and asks me,

'You know Hrothulf?'

'I *knew* him and know his son, aye', I wait for him to say something else. He seems puzzled, so I add, 'Hrothulf died fighting the Northmen in the south. His son Theodolf lives still, but I know nothing of his whereabouts'.

'I do', Arnkell grins, and puts a foot on de Mesnil's chest to stop him getting to his feet.

'Last I saw him he was in Ceaster, suffering from a lance wound', I look at Arnkell, hoping to learn of Theodolf's whereabouts.

'He is back at the woman Aethel's steading near the Hvarfe, trying to muster the strength to draw a bow'.

Arnkell grins broadly at me. I stand, slack-jawed at hearing news of my friend.

'You know him?' I ask.

'It was Hrothulf who showed me how to be a bowman. Neither of us knew then that Theodolf would ever be a bowman himself. It was only when he told me that I learned he had been with you in the south, fighting the Northmen. Was he good?'

I draw myself to my full height, nodding slowly,

'Fighting the Northmen again, at Lunden Brycg he saved the stallari Ansgar's life. He has saved mine more than once before and after the great fight on Caldbec Beorg'.

He scratches his gristly chin, straightens his jaw and raises his brow to ask,

'*That* good, eh – the *aetheling* has seen his skill?'

'He has also seen my friend Saeward's skill with the axe', I add, 'As has King Diarmuid in Leinster'.

'Who is that – *which one?*'

Hringolf looks around. The only man he sees is Saeward and, jabbing back over one shoulder with a bent thumb he raises his brow again, 'That one?'

My wink tells him what he needs to know.

'You have skill with the axe', Hringolf elbows Saeward. 'Can you show me?'

Saeward scowls, screwing up his mouth, and almost spits his answer,

'I can try out my skill on *you,* or would you like me to bury the blade in the skull of one of your brothers - ?'

'*Saeward*', I hiss, 'there is no call for that! Show him on a tree!'

'I thought he *was* a tree', Saeward smirks.

'Droll, are you not, fellow?' Hringolf grins and winks at his brothers. 'We shall have some fine sport with *you*, Saeward'.

'What, at this time of day?' I look across the hall at the still open door, at the greying dawn light.

'What better?' Arnkell asks. 'It is now light enough to see where to aim our arrows, or for Saeward to aim his axe'.

'As I thought', Hringolf draws thumb and fingers down a matted beard. He laughs, pointing down at de Mesnil, Arnkell's boot still pinning him down on the floor, 'We can use this wretch to aim at, as a target'.

'Suits me', Harding sniffs. 'If we kill him here, he can be buried along with the others amid the turnips. Who knows, their bones might prove useful'.

'You would have to grind their bones down for that, Harding', Hunding offers his own wisdom in land husbandry.

'Otherwise your crops might be spoilt', Arnkell adds.

Did these three hold their own land before the Northmen came and turned them out?

'I shall have the roots pulled up for the pot', Harding vows, looking at Saeward as if he means to ask the East Seaxan to do it for him. 'My three ceorls should be able to do that whilst the daylight lasts'.

'What else did you think of doing with him?' Hringolf asks, breaking bread that has been left out all night, not yet gathered in by Harding's ceorls. He tosses it to the floor for the hounds that lie still at the back of the hall, but they only raise their heads and stare at it before setting their jaws back down across stretched out forepaws. Hringolf shrugs and looks at me.

'You wish for some food?' Harding asks.

'It would be a start', Hringolf yawns.

He thoughtfully holds his hands across his mouth to hide the gaps in his teeth.

'No, I was wondering which tree we should tie *him* to before we see Saeward's skill'.

'I have a stout silver birch at the back of the hall – why?' Harding's eyes open wide at the thought of his tree being cut to ribbons by Saeward, Hringolf and his brothers. 'No, use one of the trees beyond my garth instead! There is a tall beech a little way up the hill, tie him to that!'

'We have a walk ahead of us', Hringolf tells his brothers. 'We shall sate our hunger after dealing with the Northman. Are you ready, Saeward, Ivar -?'

'Pick him up, Arnkell', Hunding waves.

'What did your last thrall die of?' Arnkell chortles. 'Come, Hunding, lift him by his shoulders!'

Hunding groans and shuffles across the straw-bedecked floor to heave de Mesnil up onto his left shoulder. The pair of them struggle out through the door, the chill morning air meeting us as we leave the hall to climb the hill toward Huttun. We reach the tree and lean the outlander against it whilst Harding follows us with a length of binding.

Geoffroi de Mesnil is bound to the south side of the tree, his long shadow being added to the even longer one of the tree.

He eyes us boldly, not caring for his own life.   If he ever held any hopes of coming away alive, he has another think coming. Saeward will not miss, nor will any of the brothers. What I can foretell is that he will meet a grisly end at the hands of these three.

Someone slithers, cursing downhill in open-toed sandals. When he comes closer, beneath the boughs of neighbouring trees, we see he is a priest. He slips and falls on one knee and flaps his arms about like a fledgling testing its wings. He shouts loudly at us,

'What are you doing, you heathens? You call yourselves Aenglishmen and you would do this? Have you no *souls*?'

Harding strides forward to meet the young priest, who sweats from running all the way from the higher hamlet in his heavy robe,

'Father Aelfberht, what ails?'

'*You* ail, Harding!' Flustered, Father Aelfberht struggles to his feet and rails at Harding. 'Will you go against your Christian teaching and slay this poor outlander like the heathen that you really are?'

Arnkell turns and smirks, walks along the hillside and pushes Aelfberht to the ground. He pins the priest down with one hand asking,

'What is it to *you*, priest? You church men would as soon have the outlander for king as the rightful *aetheling*!'

'Aye, go back and tend to your two-legged flock before we tie you to the tree with him!' Hunding turns on the priest, hitting him over the head with his bow and drawing blood.

'Brothers, brothers', Saeward comes between them and the priest. 'What is it with you, that you would harm an unarmed man? Leave him be, send him back uphill. He can watch from nearby what we do to those who attack our kingdom, thinking they can do what they will. Be off with you, Father Aelfberht. Get fat off your flock and leave the likes of us to do God's work!'

'*God's work*, is it, to kill the unarmed? You forget *so soon* what you just said?'

'He would just as soon do the same to us, Father Aelfberht! Now *fly*, whilst I still think of you as a priest and not an annoying little fly that I would swat with the flat of my axe blade. You can watch from here, or further away, but you will watch or *leave!'*

'Best leave whilst you still can, priest', Hringolf tells him, testing the blade of his dagger with his thumb, drawing blood to underscore his meaning.

Would he let his brothers kill a priest, or do it himself?

'Heathen war-makers, what do you hope to gain?'

The priest stares balefully at him, pulling back all the same, up the grassy slope to where he thinks it is safe for him. What *he* hopes to gain is beyond me, but he is still under threat. Hringolf is not one for playing with words.

Arnkell looks up and laughs. There is no warmth in it and the threat is clear as he jerks his head sideways up at Father Aelfberht amid saplings planted by Harding's ceorls,

'The fool thinks he is safe up there, does he?'

Hunding cackles as he sharpens arrow tips on a whetstone taken from his belt pouch, and aims the arrow at the priest with his hand to bring home to him how close he really is to ending his days there and then. Saeward might have a fight on his hands if he tries to stand up to Hringolf and his brothers on behalf of Aelfberht.

'Are we ready?' Hringolf asks loudly of Arnkell and Hunding. This is more for the priest's sake than anyone else's. I can see him peer around the side of one of the bushes, the branches shaking in his hands.

De Mesnil growls from where he stands, bound hand and foot to the beech tree, blindfolded and angry enough to curse us,

'I hope you rot in hell, Aenglishmen!'

'You might be so good as to keep our seats warm by the hearth whilst you await us there, eh?' Hringolf thunders back, smirking.

He passes behind Hunding and rasps,

'They make me sick, these outlanders. He will sing another song when the arrows bite!'

Hunding crooks at finger at Harding, who walks toward him and blenches when the young giant tells him,

'Bring the priest down here, to see better what we are at! He might want to be closer'.

'Aye, so he can feel the strength of your arrows when they hit the tree trunk beside his right ear', Arnkell smiles coldly, 'or give the Northman a blessing before he leaves us for the netherworld'.

'Come, priest, be part of this show? If you like, we can let you feel some of our iron so that you know what to fear if you again come between us and one of theirs!'

I stride uphill with Saeward to my right, Arnkell and Hunding beyond him. Aelfberht sees us from his 'hideaway' and sets off stumbling uphill again, with Hunding chasing after him. Arnkell goes wide away from his brother and cuts off Aelfberht from the upper track. He has to climb the hillside again, through thorn bush and gorse with Hunding now in full cry, baying as if on the hunt. Saeward stays to my right as we scale the hillside.

Aelfberht is now caught by long thorn stems, unable to flee, his robe slowly being ripped to shreds as he tries to pull away. Saeward chops at the thorns to get to the priest and Aelfberht eases, thinking he will be freed. I come from the other side, pushing away the gorse as I close on the priest.

Behind him Hunding nears, mouth twisted hound-like, snarling, and Arnkell laughs loudly as we push ever nearer.   Saeward is the first to get to him, hacking at the thorns that have seized on Aelfberht's robe. He holds a hand out that is gladly taken, and drags the priest to him,

'Do as I say and no harm will come to you!' Saeward snaps at Aelfberht. Hunding closes on him and strikes out with his dagger, but Saeward ducks and scythes with his long-handled Dane axe at Hunding's waist.

'*Hey*, what do you think you are at?' Hunding leaps back, narrowly missing being shorn in half.

Arnkell comes up behind the now freed but ragged Father Aelfberht and catches one arm, wrenching it back so that the priest falls back painfully into the thorns. He raises a fist to pummel the bleeding priest but I pull his arm back.

'*Fool*, what is it that has got into your head?' I shake Arnkell and push him back, away from Aelfberht. 'We do not kill priests in this kingdom!'

'Dim-wit, no-one was going to *kill* anyone!' Arnkell, having steadied himself comes at me, hoping to pummel *me*. Saeward has his hands full with Hunding.

Neither of us sees Aelfberht creep away uphill until he is some way off. Arnkell pushes past, no longer set on fighting me,

'*Now look what you have done!*' He yells at me, then at his brother to leave Saeward and hunt the priest. We follow them to make sure Aelfberht comes to no harm. These two have lost their wits, it seems, the thrill of the chase gone to their heads. They are not the men I took them for when I first set eyes on them.

317

Hunding's blood is up, his older brother no better.

Aelfberht is now nowhere to be seen, hiding, no doubt from the men-beasts who would tear him apart before getting him back down the hill. The four of us stand, searching the hillside for the tell-tale torn black priest's robe. The day is older now, the sun having come out from behind the clouds, casting shadows down the hill. He is nowhere to be seen.

'*Now* what do we tell him?'

'Tell him what you were going to tell him', I sneer. 'Tell him you were going to kill a harmless priest!'

'I might tell him we had to kill *you*', Hunding snarls at me, brandishing his dagger in a threatening manner.

'Or we might have to tell him we had to fall back after the Northmen had killed you', I hint at the likelihood. 'After all, he would not know otherwise'.

'*What* Northmen -?'

'Any Northmen we can think of who might have strayed into this wapentake', I look levelly into his eyes. It would take more than the likes of him to frighten me. He slides his dagger back into its hilt glares. His brother struggles through the gorse ahead of Saeward and pushes Hunding ahead of him, back downhill.

'Say nothing about the tussle', Arnkell warns Hunding.

The younger man tries to hide his anger at losing the priest and thrashes through the gorse and thorns downhill ahead of us. He makes it plain by not looking back who he thinks is to blame when we come back to Hringolf.

'Well, *where* is the priest?' Hringolf looks at Hunding who sneers at me before letting his brother know the worst.

'Ask them', Hunding jerks his head toward Saeward and me, and strides to his elder brother's side to look us both over with him.

Arnkell walks over to Harding, still watching over de Mesnil. He murmurs something like, 'Look at these two fools, letting the priest free', to which Harding hisses an answer that I would be hard put to forget,

'I would say you two are the greater fools!'

'Why so?' Arnkell is put out by Harding's sharp answer.

Nonplussed, he raises his hands and thumps his forehead with clenched fists.

'How is it you cannot see, that when you talk of throwing axes and loosing off arrows at someone, they will be frightened?' Harding thumps Arnkell's skull with a bent forefinger and draws his sword when Arnkell reaches for his dagger.

'Hey, little brother, are you such a dolt that you draw your dagger on a *friend?*' Hringolf bellows. 'From what Hunding says, you threatened Father Aelfberht with his life! Did our father raise fools, or were you not listening when he told you never to bare blades at a man of the cloth?'

Both Arnkell and Hunding seem to feel let down by their elder brother. Down in the mouth, Hunding sulks. He grips his bow hard enough for his knuckles to whiten and scowls when Hringolf asks for an answer,

'What do you say, both of you – *either* of you? It is no use telling *me* you are sorry, though. Harding lives here, and he must bear up to his neighbours. I would have thought that when you went after the priest, you should have *told* him we were not going to harm him!'

'He must have thought you *meant* to harm him whilst drawing blood from your hand with your shining blade', I tell Hringolf.

He looks up into the air behind my head and mumbles,

'You may be right, Ivar. For now we have to deal with the Northman', he turns and thumps Hunding on one shoulder. 'Get ready with your arrows'.

Hunding, scowling, rubs his shoulder, pain showing as he swings his arm back and forth to ease it.

'Ready?' Hringolf asks, watching as Arnkell ambles up to stand to Hunding's right, draws an arrow from his bag on the ground. He stands, an arrow over the bow, waiting. To the right of Arnkell Saeward weighs his axe in both hands.

'Are we to take this way out, by binding a Northman to a tree and killing him that way, or do we give him a man's death in which he might wield his sword?'

'What do you mean, Dane?' Hringolf asks and raises an arm for his brothers to hold back.

'One of us could take him in a fight, one on one', I answer, going on, 'such as I'.

'You want to *fight* him?' Hringolf seems happy, eyes twinkling, looking at his brothers.

'As in a *holmgang*', I answer, nodding.

Hringolf stares hard at me, hardly believing his ears,

'You mean we have to mark out the ground?'

'Aye, to look like an eyot in a wide river', I nod.

'As there are no eyots nearby, we peg out the ground as it would be'.

'There is an eyot on the Tese', Harding offers. Hringolf shakes his head and Harding holds up his hands, giving in, 'Too far away?'

Hringolf's answer is in the way he looks upward.

'Here is good enough', I put in.

'We have to whittle pegs from branches and then push them into the soil', Hringolf groans. 'Where have you some softer soil around your garth, Harding?'

Harding tells him,

'Behind the hall, where the old midden was, would be the best'.

'Fight amid your old shit? That should be a good laugh!' Hringolf cackles, 'Smelly too, is there nowhere else?'

'It hardly smells any more', Harding offers, tongue-in-cheek. I would not be keen to fall onto it.

'The outlander might not have the strength to put up a worthwhile fight', I tell Hringolf. 'It may not prove worthwhile watching if he yields too soon'.

'You do not mind feeding this Northman, to build his strength for a fight?' Arnkell asks Harding.

'Whyever should I not?'

Harding tells Arnkell and Hunding to unbind de Mesnil, and calls for Toki to bring food and drink for him. When Toki shows with a platter of food he gives his master an odd look before slapping down the platter and cup on a dry tree stump. He leaves again to bring ale to wash down the food.

'You understand you will fight Ivar to the death – *your* death?' Hringolf asks de Mesnil.

The Northman eyes me steadily, and nods before setting about the food. Bread, cheese and meat are speedily and eagerly wolfed down, followed quickly by ale. His mouth turns up at the taste of the ale, and is told that is all there is to drink since he downed all the wine Harding had in store. He nods glumly and sets about the food again, drinking more ale and so on.

When he has finished eating he belches, finishes off the ale and stands.

'You are ready now?' I ask and he nods again in answer. 'Your sword belt awaits you outside. Are the pegs out?'

'We have four pegs in the earth, with twine between them', Toki lets me know, touching his forelock.

'And that is as much as we need', I wink at Toki and he leads the way out into the sunlit garth.

'Are you not going to fight with a sword?' De Mesnil has seen me take my axe from Braenda's saddle. He looks worried, and well might he be, but I did let him pick his weapon. His sword looks well-made and could do me some harm if I let it come too close to!

'You have a fine sword, if I may say. There is no way I would let you shave my beard with it in anger. Come, my good man. Let us have this over and done with. May the best man win, eh?' I let him go first, with Arnkell and Hunding on either side close behind him. Saeward comes with me and Harding follows us all out.

Before we reach the pitch he looks once over one shoulder at me, coughs and walks the last few strides with his sword drawn. He shoves it into the earth and rubs his hands to rid himself of sweat.

Harding passes him and asks,

'Would you like to dip your hands into flour, to keep your hands from sweating and keep a good grip on your weapons?'

De Mesnil clenches his fists, looks closely at them and nods. Tofig brings a flour bag and the Northman follows my lead. He pushes his hands quickly through the white powder and pulls them out again, blowing off much of it.

I take my share and rub my hands well, keeping most of the flour on them. I have no way of knowing how long the fight will go on. I mean to be the one standing when it is over. My axe hefted over my shoulder, I stride to the far side of the pegged-out square.

'Who will keep tally?' Hringolf asks.

'I would have thought you were the fittest of us for that task', Harding answers, cosying up to the fellow. Hringolf first scowls, and then grins at Harding to show his thanks for the flattery.

'Are you buttering me up, Harding?'

Harding reddens,

'You are the best able to watch over this fight, no more. Would you sooner I did it?'

'No, friend – I *can* do it', Hringolf says sheepishly as the outlander glowers across the pitch at them both.

'I think he wants to get this over with', I tell Hringolf when he at last puts his feet to the twine. 'He is in a hurry to die!'

De Mesnil growls angrily,

'*Whatever you say –*'

When laughter breaks out around him the Northman reddens. He snatches his sword from the earth and shakes it, sweeps the blade across the scant grass and bellows,

'*Can we begin at long last?!*'

'Have you got somewhere to go?' Hunding cackles.

'I think he has a freewheeling nun somewhere that he wants to take care of', Arnkell laughs wildly at his own wit.

'Very well then', Hringolf catches my eye and nods. De Mesnil takes his sword in both hands and spreads his feet. He seems to be ready. 'The first man to step outside the twine loses'.

De Mesnil smiles sourly and sidles around me.

When I turn to watch him he has the sun behind him. This is Brand all over again! I turn away from him, watching him from my left side, and he comes out of the sun with his sword high. Keeping out of the way of the slashing blade, I bring my axe around as he passes and catch his midriff. Links fly everywhere, and the gash I have made in his hauberk has gone through to graze his skin.

Nevertheless it is only a flesh wound. He turns and, in doing so brings the sword around level with my shoulder, threatening to slice me across the top of my chest. I arch my back as the blade hisses through the air past me, and follow him around with my axe blade, catching flesh again. He yells loudly but stays on his feet. Where have I caught him this time?

No-one shouts, there are no cat-calls to put him off his stride. Everyone here watches, rapt. The air is still before he takes his sword hilt in both hands and brings the weapon down at me. I feel the twine against the back of my boot and sidestep, then forward around his left and, one-handed, swipe at the small of his back with my axe butt. He falls forward, toward the twine, but braces himself against going over and turns smartly, if woodenly, to draw his blade against my right side.

Out of the corner of one eye I catch sight of the blade coming out of the sun at me and swerve out of reach. In swerving, however, I catch my right boot on a hole in the earth and go down onto my left knee.

De Mesnil seizes his opening and swipes my axe out of my hand with the flat of his sword, then stands over me. Hands on the hilt, blade down at me, he snarls and brings down the tip of the sword onto my chest. Digging my elbows into the soil beneath my back I bring my left boot around to hook behind his and topple him. When he goes down onto his knees I stand sharply and kick him over onto his right side to hamper his sword arm. His right arm is over the twine but no-one sees, and I bring my axe blade down onto his left side.

Blood sprays across the pitch as the cold steel of my axe bites through chain mail, into his waist. He tries to raise his sword arm, but with my right boot on it he is pinned to the grass.

'Try to cut me with a soiled sword, would you?' I roar, axe raised, ready to cut into his chest. 'This is to show you what happens when you fight a kinsman of Harold Godwinson!'

He glares back at me, angry to the end, and spits as he curses,

'I hope you die a *lingering* death, Ivar Ulfsson!'

His end is quick, not that he earned it!

Harding has Tofig and Arnbern take the corpse somewhere to bury it. Geoffroi de Mesnil will lie in an unmarked grave, far from his homeland. Had he cut into me with that sword, I would be laid into the earth, the soil from his blade having worked into my blood.

Luckily I have lost only a few links from my mailcoat and suffered only grazes without drawing blood. The lingering death will have to wait another day.

'*You* were lucky after taking a tumble like that,' Saeward tells me, peering closely at where the missing links came from, 'not even a flesh wound!'

'Aye, you *were* lucky', Hringolf adds as he pokes a bony finger through the gap in the links.

'Even I thought that would be the end of you', Harding pats me on my back.

'That is a task for someone better skilled in fighting than he was', I answer. 'God knows, there are men enough who have tried!'

19

From the doorway of Harding's hall I watch the sun sink to the west below the steep bank of the dale. Night will be a while longer coming, as the trees near the bank top still catch the light. Shadows lengthen and leaves shimmer in the breeze like bright stones in a king's crown.

I am here, still in the land of the living as they say, still breathing the air all men share. Geoffroi de Mesnil has been laid to rest amid Harding's cooking roots. Tofig and Arnbern have worked hard to bury him and make the rake marks look as if they had been made all at the same time.

'His fellows are unlikely to find him, short of digging the whole field to the north of the river', Harding tells me, handing me a cup of ale. He laughs uneasily, asking, 'Do you see that happening?'

'I thank you, friend. No I do not see it happening, unless...' I have had a thought.

'Unless *what* – out with it, Ivar! Unless what –'

'...Unless Father Aelfberht had been watching everything. He may have watched your ceorls burying the Northman as well'.

'*God* –', Harding looks down at his boots, and into the darkening sky. 'He is likely to stop the first Northmen he sees to send them down here! You, Ivar, with Saeward, the brothers and me will have to leave.'

'We can rest the night here, even until midday. Where would they come from?' I look around, along the hilltop, to see whether we would know they are here before we wake with our hands bound. They would have to ride down one of the two tracks, from east or west, whichever way they came overland. That would let us know which way to leave. There is no way they could take us unaware, as we have eyes everywhere. The Aengle in Huttun above us, are no fonder of these outlanders than we are, surely - would it come to taking sides?

'My household ceorls will watch the roads like hawks. If they come through Huttun they have to pass Styrbeorn's holding before they come to mine, and he will have *his* eyes on the road', Harding tells me, draining his cup. 'More ale, Ivar -'

'I shall come in with you to drink. My bones need resting, old man that I am', I chuckle.

Harding stares hard at me, and begins to laugh hoarsely. He cackles,

'Aye, *old man* - God rest your weary bones!' He stifles his laughter when we enter his hall, and goes up to his high seat. 'Ivar come sit by me, on my right, where Aethelhun once sat! Hringolf, come sit on my left'.

'What was the laughter about as you came to the door?' Hringolf asks, fingering the cup before him, toying with it.

'Oh dear, friend, has no-one seen your empty cup? Where is Arnbern?' Harding makes out as if he had not heard Hringolf ask about what his laughter was about.

'The laughter', Hringolf growls, 'what was it about, why did you suddenly stop?'

'It was not about *you*, friend. Ivar here said he needed to rest his *old* bones!' Harding's grin freezes when he sees Hringolf draw his dagger from its sheath. 'Did you think it was about you?'

Hringolf looks up at our host, his blade on the bench,

'Harding, friend, why would I *of all men*, think that?'

Arnbern shows and shuffles to the ale vat, to bring a pitcher full for our cups.

'A man could die of thirst here!' Hunding grumbles.

Arnkell cuffs him across the back of his head. When he stands, fist ready to take his brother to task, Hringolf roars loudly Hunding hurriedly takes his seat. As it is, Hringolf was only sneezing and – looking the other way - cannot have known about his 'little' brother's spat. Saeward holds back from laughing out aloud at Hunding's antic and slurps ale from his cup before holding it up for Arnbern to fill on his way past.

'Food is on its way!' Arnbern calls out on his way back to the kitchen, vanishing through a door at the other end of Harding's hall. Almost as soon, another door opens and a pair of maids enters the hall with bowls of hot broth to set before us. They in turn vanish again and Arnbern shows this time with more steaming bowls. A platter of bread follows, borne by another hall maid ahead of a lad struggling with a deer carcass.

Arnbern helps the lad take it to the hearth where, between them they spear it onto the spit.

'Turn that now, Sighvat', Arnbern tells him and looks around to see if our cups need filling again. He shuffles across the hall floor to the vat and brings the pitcher back with him.

'Leave the pitcher with us, Arnbern', Harding tells him. 'We can help ourselves when we have need'.

Arnbern nods wordlessly and leaves again. The maids enter again with more platters, small, cold roots and dried, salted meats to sharpen our taste buds until the meat is ready on the spit.

Saeward licks his lips and raises his cup to Harding,

'We should drink to Harding, open-handed thegn and cherished friend that he is!'

'*Aye*', Hringolf agrees, 'all hail to Harding, long may he live!'

325

'And long may he be our host!' Arnkell raises his cup. He drains it and looks around for the pitcher.

'*Here*, glutton', Hringolf laughs, lifts the pitcher for his brother to see and thumps it down again. 'Use your own damned legs!'

Hringolf does his best to finish the task, I can see, but his brothers are rough and ready. Their father must have had a hard time bringing them up on his own. Handled well, they might be good men, but they could just as easily turn bad as we saw when trying to bring the priest back to the garth. He might not have thought so badly about them had they behaved, but that was down to a misunderstanding, a wrongly read signal from Hringolf.

Still, I cannot fault their bowmanship, and the eldest keeps them in line insofar as they know who they are fighting *against*. They must also wander far and wide, having known Theodolf is back at Aethel's steading.

All thoughts of fighting are forgotten when Arnbern comes back to the spit to see how Sighvat fares. He claps his hands and lets us know the meat is ready. I can see Hunding dribbling in the hope of being given a good share. When Arnbern hands him a dish of meat he almost whines like a hound,

'Is this *all* I get for bringing the hart down?!' He has angered Hringolf, I can sense, but the threat comes only in the words,

'For *now*, Hunding, eat what you are *given*. There is more to go around. Nor is there any need to eat like a hog, or I shall put you with the hall hounds! See how much you get *then!*'

'*I* brought the damned hart down, Hringolf. Never forget that!'

'And *I* shall bring *you* down, little brother!' Hringolf fumes. 'Soon enough, some poor, forlorn woman will take you for her husband, but for now *we* are your close kin, Arnkell and I. See this as your way of thanking me for teaching you. Now be a good lad and get on with your share'.

Hunding sniffs and snatches up the meat that sits before him on his platter in both hands. I try not to look, but what enters my thoughts now is that I fell sorry for the woman who weds him.

In an odd way it brings me to thinking of my uncle, another Hunding. A fairer fellow I have hardly seen. He let me find my own way in the world, often asking after me from where he lived near the river in Jorvik. My half-brother Osbeorn and I once sailed across the eastern sea with him in his ship, '*Braendings Slange*', to where he said he once hid from the Jomsvikings near the mouth of the Dvina. This was some time before I went with Tostig to Jorvik. Uncle Hunding spent much of that time in the east, but I did see him now and then at his staith on the Ose before he died – some say drowned at sea on his way between Faeroe and Iceland.

This Hunding licks his fingers before grabbing at his ale cup and pulling one of Harding's maids back onto his lap. Before Harding can say anything Hringolf has his *'little brother'*, as he calls him, nose down on the floor with both hands up behind his back.

Hunding snorts like a bull but can only whine,

'You said one day I would have a woman!'

'Not *this* way, and not one of Harding's *maids!*' Hringolf seethes with pent-up fury. I have the feeling he would do more in the way of scolding in his own home, but here he stops short of beating Hunding.

'He *only* pulled my skirts!' The maid begins to weep at the sight of Hunding on the ground, his nose pressed against the hot hearth stones and Harding asks Hringolf to let the young fellow up. When Hringolf lets go of Hunding the maid brings a dampened cloth to clean his dirtied cheek and jaw, fussing over him as she dabs every last little smudge.

'*Well I never* – the young hog has found himself a friendly sow!' Arnkell laughs, slapping his things and leaning back.

Hringolf thumps his younger brother off the bench, to lie on his back in the grubby straw beside the hearth. Hunding shoves him away and gets to his feet.

'That is no way to speak of your little brother!' Hringolf towers over Arnkell, the *runt* of the clan. Arnkell is a hand's width taller than I am, if that gives you an inkling of Hunding's height. Hunding looks much like Theorvard did when I first came across him near Akeham, but does not have Theorvard's breeding.

Saeward, who has been keeping his own counsel all this time, now speaks up,

'Hringolf, you do the work of both mother and father with these two. How do you put up with them?'

'*Not easily!*' Hringolf laughs and picks up more meat. He slaps it down on Hunding's platter, telling him, '*There*, little brother, you will need to keep your strength if you are to become a breadwinner! What is your name, sweet thing?'

The maid reddens, finishes dabbing Hunding's jaw free of the dirt and straw that has stuck to him, and rises.

'I am Earngerd', she answers before throwing Hunding a look of understanding and leaves us for the kitchen.

Arnkell, having taken his seat again, slaps the table and whistles after her, shouting out aloud,

'Well, well – it looks as though he will be the first of us to feather his nest, brother! I had better look out, or I shall be the last one to have to look for a bride'. He lifts his cup, holds it up to Hunding and slurps the rest of his ale.

'As I said, it is not easy'. Hringolf shakes his head at Arnkell's lack of manners and adds, 'Still, it seems at least one cloud has a silver lining'.

Someone outside bangs hard on the door and Tofig shuffles across to let in whoever is there. Styrbeorn puffs and pants, and yells out loudly enough to be heard up in Huttun,

'There are riders coming, with long spears. They are as yet only on their way east from the old Eoferwic road, but there are a score of them!'

'*God rot* these outlanders! Why do they have to come *now?*' Harding thumps both fists down onto the table before me, rattling cups, platters and eating knives. The meat smells too good to leave, but we must ready ourselves to leave again. This will be a night out on the land again, waking in a dew-soaked bed roll!

Harding snaps at his ceorls and maids,

'Douse the fires, pack away the meat!'

'I could wrap some for you, my Lord', Tofig offers. 'A few skins of ale can be put over the back of a pack horse'.

'*Good man*, Tofig. Put cheese and bread with it. Get Toki and Arnbern together, with the women, and go to your kindred. This hall will stand empty for a while until we are able to come back – *as long as the Northmen do not burn it down!*'

The garth suddenly comes to life, with men and women rushing about seeing to this and that. Horses are saddled, and weapons looked at, sharpened and sheathed. Saddle bags are filled, bed rolls stowed away. Harding barks out his wants and needs, and everything is in uproar. I look forward to the day when this Northman king and his underlings are back where they belong!

'What can you do?' Saeward sighs aloud.

'What I would like to do –'

I do not finish. Earngerd passes Hunding, shoving something into his hands as she vanishes into the hall again.

He opens his palm and looks at a small ring, a keepsake – to make him think of her, and looks at me. I can only smile and wink before Hringolf shoves him toward the gate with Arnkell, the three of them melting into the darkness. Styrbeorn hastens back to his own dwelling, to gather things together for the ride – to where?

'Where would we ride for?' I ask Harding.

'East, and then south to the moors I think, Ivar', he mutters, then tells Tofig to share whatever food and ale there is amongst the others. He turns to me and begins to speak, but is sidetracked when Toki enters. 'What is it?'

His ceorl, out of breath from running tells his master,

'Outlanders are closing on Huttun, this side of Leofetun'.

'We have a little time then, before they show here', Harding tells me, asking next, 'Are the horses ready?'

'Aye, Harding, ready and awaiting you', I answer. Suddenly I think back. Where is Hemming? 'What about Hemming? Saeward, ask Styrbeorn if he is –'

'Hemming died of his wounds. I told you, Ivar', he peers at me from under bushy eyebrows. Weeks – no, *months* of riding here and there, being chased through Mierca to Ceaster, fighting in Jorvik and at Gearum, has all played havoc with us both. Not thinking straight, even forgetting Hemming's death, I need to pull   myself together or I will be a threat to others as well.

'These last weeks have stampeded past us, Ivar. You are not the only one to feel it. Until we were told the Northmen were heading this way I had almost forgotten where we were'.

Harding seems to be losing himself, too, would he but own up to it. We are each of us under strain –

'You are right, Saeward. I see no way out of this hectic life either for a long time. The weeks have passed like grain past the quern stone – I am sure you know my meaning', I tap my sword hand on his shoulder briefly before turning to mount Braenda. My thoughts then turn to my woman, whom I have not seen since leaving – where, Ceaster? Have I not seen her since that long ago? I must be losing my wits, not being able to think back on sowing my seed!

Hemming now, who next - Theodolf? If he is back at Aethel's steading, who is looking after him? Now seated in my saddle, I think hard before telling the others,

'I think we should ride for Tadceaster', I tell Harding.

'Will it be any safer there, so close to Jorvik?' he asks by turn, looking sideways at our East Seaxan friend.

Saeward either has not heard Harding, or he is so used to us all talking about 'Jorvik' instead of 'Eoferwic' he no longer cares. This is not the Saeward I know of old. He has come a long way since those days on the road north with Harold's huscarls, yelling at them for calling the *burh* Jorvik?

Harding swings himself up into his saddle and taps Saeward on one shoulder,

'Ivar thinks we should ride south again'.

'Aye, I heard', Saeward answers, watching something above and behind us. He points up behind us and calmly heralds, 'Right now, though, I think we ought to be a long way from *here*'.

Harding looks up at where Saeward points and yelps like a scalded pup,

'Whoever saw them at Leofetun did not know there were others closer! Come, quick *this way*, east through the trees to the ford'.

Our flight to the Leofen ford stirs a flock of wild geese at their grazing. As they rise, honking from the field side we press our mounts to a headlong gallop through the ford, spraying water everywhere, the track we follow taking us out of the deep dale toward Stochesleag. We shall not make a halt there, lest the Northmen have been told we fled that way. They are likely to have been given new mounts at Leofetun. Stopping anywhere so soon will render us into their hands.

'*Hold*', Harding calls out, 'I think my horse is lame!'

'Where do we get another horse here?' Saeward asks. With thick, high bushes and tall trees on either side of the track, neither of us can see a steading nearby for Harding to buy another mount.

'I have to stop and look first!' Harding tells him. 'Give me a little time'.

On lifting one of the mare's back legs, Harding groans loudly,

'It *would* have to be a stone in her hoof! I can walk her into the next field to the right down here –'

Saeward cocks an ear and calls back to Harding,

'I hear the rumble of hooves!'

'Aye, *I* can feel it too, but needs must!' Harding answers.

He looks about and points to our left,

'Through there – *be quick about it!*' He drags his limping mare along the wide, tree-lined track and leads us into a thicket. When his mare grumbles, threatening to whinny, he puts a soothing hand over her muzzle and strokes her neck slowly.

Seven riders pass closely, their mounts sweating after galloping from beyond Rudby. Soon they can only be heard, not felt any more, still pounding the packed earth eastward. If they are going that way, then we must find another way around Stochesleag. I think there is a road south, before we enter the small *burh* that should lead us to the foothills before climbing up to the high moor.

'There is a smith across the field here, who will sell me a new horse if the stone in my mare's hoof is not all that is wrong with her', Harding tells me as he leads the way to a narrow boundary track. On looking around, neither I nor Saeward can see anything that looks like a smithy. There is not even smoke from a hearth. All there is to see is a clump of low trees and tall bushes.

Harding looks both ways along the broad track we are to leave. He asks Saeward if he can hear anything, and on seeing him shake his head beckons us onward.

'Your friend hears thing I cannot', Harding tells me, behind his hand.

'Aye, and I also heard *you* mumbling to him', Saeward chortles, gazing around, not looking at either of us.

'How is it you have such good hearing, friend?' Harding asks him.

'It takes years of pilfering the lord's game, believe me', Saeward grins and puts a finger to his lips.

'Is there someone coming?' I ask him.

'No, I do not want to talk about my past, lest I give myself away'.

Harding laughs out aloud, a belly laugh that seems to rumble like an empty keg being rolled on hard earth.

Saeward touches his nose with one finger,

'I will only say it was before you came across me, Ivar. The thegn on whose land it was is long since dead, but his son is still about and may have given his oath to the Northman king. My life could be forfeit if he knew'.

'He will hear nothing from either of us', Harding swears, his right hand across his great chest, 'will he, Ivar?'

'By no means', I nod with Harding.

He stops, holds up a hand to quieten us, and calls out,

'Grimolf, are you there?'

'Who is it?' I hear someone call back, gruff, deep, threatening.

Harding chides in a friendly manner,

'Have you forgotten me *already*, Grimolf?'

'*Ah*, Harding I might have known it was you! Wake the whole neighbourhood, go on!'

'*Wake* the neighbourhood – what neighbourhood? Grimolf, were you *asleep?*' Harding laughs, unable to believe his ears. 'You were asleep at *this* time of day – what about your *work?*'

'*What* work? No-one brings me any work now the outlander has his shop in Stochesleag!' Grimolf punches the doorpost of his workshop, cracking the wattle. 'Damned old fool is too old to do the work himself anyway and has to hire younger men. Yet *still* they flock to him. Charms and witchcraft he uses. A man for whom he made a war axe is said to be the bane of this king's nobles!'

'What is the man's name?' I ask.

'What does it matter –'Grimolf begins before looking at Harding and thinks better of it. 'Men call him the Wend, whatever that means. It might mean the iron he makes the weapons from turns into something else, other than what we think it to be'.

Grimolf spits into the fire, raising a small cloud.

I ask more from Grimolf,

'You know where he comes from?'

His eyes narrow almost to slits, but he tells me,

'They say he is a *freed* man, from the Danelaw shires somewhere. You know him?'

'From what you tell me, I could well know him – dark skinned and with a topknot?'

'Aye, whatever hair he still has on his head is tied on top of his skull. A *real* heathen, he looks. Like something that crawled out from the netherworld, one of the dark elves!' Grimolf laughs at the thought.

'You are not thinking of going there, with the Northmen scouting around in Stochesleag?' Harding pulls back his long, matted wavy hair back with his gloved hands. He shakes his head at me, eyes popping. 'First you asked me to take you to Baebbanburh, where the Beornican lords were as likely to skin you alive as listen to you – they knew Copsig was on his way anyway – and *now* you want me to come with you into that hornet's nest down the road? Have you lived too long, or something, that you want to risk *our* lives as well as your own?'

'I can go on my own if you are worried about being taken by the Northmen. It is a long time since I last saw old Volund', I tell him.

'You say his name is what, *Volund?* Who gave him that name?' Grimolf comes up to me and stares up into my eyes. 'Are you the Dane they say goes by the name of Ivar Ulfsson, the one the Northmen turn hamlets upside down to find?'

'Is that what they say?' I cannot help grinning. Am I so sought after in my late years?

'Are you *still* thinking of going into Stochesleag to find this Volund?' Harding asks, still worried – perhaps even more so after Grimolf saying about me being prey for every Northman in the kingdom. Saeward shows nothing, whether worried or happy at the opportunity to free more of the outlanders from their earthly fetters. We shall see.

'I see a shadow across my threshold', someone says in the darkness beyond the door. 'Someone I have not seen since leaving the Eastern Sea who comes to look for me'.

'Are you the man they call the Wend?' I ask, and shudder at the thought of seeing my old friend after all this time. After all these years can it really be him, or will I be taken to task for my foolishness?

'And you might be the man they know in this land as Ivar Ulfsson?

332

You once knew me by another name'.

Laughter fills the small workshop, echoing around the walls, and the old man steps into the cold light of an Aenglish summer dusk,

'*Ivar*, I thought I would *never* see you again after the Svear thrallmaster took me!' He hugs me, bear-like strength gripping my upper body, plants wet old man's kisses on my cheeks and forehead. He looks around at Harding, Saeward... aye, and Grimolf.

'You are old friends, then?' Harding does not seem shocked at the sight of this old man being so moved at meeting me so far from home.

Now that I see him again after all these years, Volund hardly looks older than when I last saw him. Grimolf sees him as an old man, past his best, but there is still the darkness in him that I felt when being around him all those years ago.

It may well be true he has dealings with otherworldly beings, as Grimolf says he has, to bring about un-godly weapons. Yet he has helpers, *men*, not dark elves or trolls, to make these tools of death that he might utter dark words over when they are still being wrought. Men once told tales of the small, dark folk in their howes, hammering and beating through the dark hours to bind themselves to their master. Thus also came about the ring that skalds spoke of loudly in their lords' halls on dark winter feasting nights, the ring sought by the hero Sigurd, fought over by Fafnir and cursed by mankind in their Midgard hovels. The ring that brought the never-ending darkness, the Fimbulvetr or long winter, was wrought by *Andvari* – the name we gave this Wendish weaponsmith!

'*Andvari* – that was the name we gave you!'

He beams broadly at me, and then reaches out for something on the wall. Grimolf gives a start, seeing Andvari bring down a shining blade from its cradling behind the fire.

'*Watch out!*' Grimolf yelps, ducking out of the way as the blade falls from the old man's hands onto the floor, ringing on the stone setts around firebed and anvil as it settles, still, shining in the red-gold of the dancing flames.

'I am old and weakening, Grimolf. *Forgive me*. Can you pick up the blade for me? It awaits only a hilt and sheath, and they should be ready by tomorrow when Earnwulf and Ingi come to help me'. Andvari smiles at me, 'It will be yours, Ivar, something to help you when threatened by your foes, to think on me by'.

Looking longingly at the blade I ask him,

'What do I owe you for this, Andvari? What would you ask of me?'

Grimolf hands me the blade,

'As it is meant for you –'

I take it as if it were a babe-in-arms, and hold it up to one of the rush lights. The flickering flame glows eerily back at me, you might be forgiven in thinking from within the hard steel. A wolf's eye stares back at me, shaped on the blade by Andvari's craft.

The old man rests a long, bony yet strong hand on my arm and takes the blade gently from me,

'Be back by dusk, as you came this evening Ivar'.

'I shall be back, and tell me what I can do for you', I rest my shield arm on his back and take my leave.

Saeward asks, whispering hoarsely into one ear,

'Can we afford to stay around for that long?'

'You will be safe if you stay out of sight, with Grimolf at his workshop', Andvari tells Saeward.

'Well I hope *I* will be as safe with this one in my home!'Grimolf grumbles, looking sideward at me.

Andvari smiles all-knowingly,

'There is nothing to worry about, take my word'.

How did he know I would *be* here? Without Grimolf telling us I would never have known of *his* whereabouts and would have cheerfully ridden on south to Tadceaster. I have to ask one last thing before I go,

'Do you ever think of Ubbi?'

'You knew him well?' Andvari seems to light up afresh. 'His father freed me from the Svear some years ago. I learned much anew about the craft of weapon-making from their smith, and he in turn from me. You know Aenglish swords are sought after as far away as Holmgard and Miklagard? Some that were bought from our workshop have been used to part the Turk from his earthly *wyrd*'.

Harding's brow rises, his eyes opening wide at talk of Aenglish sword-making being so well known, so far away.

'It is true', Saeward nods. 'Lord Harold told me he had seen weaponry in Frankia that he could say was crafted by a Northanhymbran'.

'By the way you talk, Saeward, you come from far off in the south. Am I right? You, too are one of Ivar's ilk?'

'I am a lowly land worker, or *was*, until Ivar and I crossed paths on the way north to Eoferwic for only the second time. Life has been anything *but* boring since then. Now that I know he is much sought-after by our new masters, it will be still *less* boring!'

'Well spoken, Saeward', Andvari slaps his back and leads us out into the open, where our horses crop the lush grass around his workshop a short way east of Stochesleag. He bids us a fond farewell when we are mounted, 'We will meet again next evening, Ivar'.

I wave cheerily as we head west again. There is little enough sleep, small as his dwelling is.

Sleep comes to me only after a long time of lying on my back, looking up at Grimolf's patched roof. My dreams are of the fine sword made for me by my old friend.

The night has not passed quickly enough for my liking. We whiled away the day searching through nearby woodland for something to eat. Now, with the light fading we are ready to ride back to Stochesleag. In the west the sun has dipped below the tops of the trees and only the sky that way is still blue. To the east clouds are closing from the south-east. The sea will be anvil black this evening! If the weather closes on this corner of the shire, then any Northmen around would stay put where they have put in.

Andvari, otherwise known as Volund – after the god-like smith – stands at his doorway to greet us just as the rain begins to slant against the wall of his workshop,

'Come in, *come in,* Ivar. Ingi and Earnwulf are finishing your sword. They do well together, do you not my lads?'

One of them has a hand spare and waves it in answer. Both men sweat like hogs in the heat, but the hard work is over. The other smith looks up and winks at us, stares at Grimolf and goes back to what he was doing before he looked up.

'I was talking about sending some work your way, Grimolf', Andvari tells him. 'We have way too much for this workshop, and as the outlanders leave again in the morning we shall have little sleep'.

'When they are gone you will have *less* work, surely?' Grimolf asks, but I could see his eyes open wide with talk of work being turned his way.

Andvari looks Grimolf steadily in the eye and sighs deeply, almost as if he lamented it,

'When they have left we shall still have much to keep us busy until well after the Yulefeast! No, Grimolf, I would say some of it could be passed to you. Furthermore I would tell the good folk here that your skills are as good as those of these fellows'.

'If that is how you see it', Grimolf shrugs. He will not turn away this work out of false pride, I know, but he dare not show it too much lest Andvari sees him as being needy for work.

Andvari takes Grimolf's hand in friendship, to tell him not to see him as a taskmaster but as a fellow craftsman,

'Bring your tools into Stochesleag. I will get my men to help if you wish. I know of a workshop that would suit your needs'.

'I like my own workshop, friend. Thanks all the same'. Grimolf keeps hold of Andvari's hand and puts his own on top.

'Your meaning is well taken, Andvari. Any work you can put my way will be welcome'.

Andvari's eyes light on me again. He smiles broadly to show his liking for me as a trusted friend from the old days,

'Meanwhile, Ivar, come - watch Ingi's deft hands working on your blade. He has learned well, I think. My hands are no longer as clever. Some of these fingers will not always do as I wish, more is the pity. When we are young we think we can go on forever, and it is old age that teaches us how things really are'.

'*Surely* – 'I begin to tell him that he cannot have lost so much of his skill that he cannot pass it on, but he waves away my avowal.

'It is how it is, and none of us can alter the way things go over the years. One day you will proudly pass on this sword to your son, whom I believe you will name after the man you know as your father'.

How can he know I have a son, or is there something Braenda has not told me, and how can he know what name I will give any son I have? There have been times when my thoughts have strayed to Jarl Ulf Thorgilsson, my father. What does he mean by saying 'the man I know as my father'?

For now I watch Ingi's craft, his finishing skills put to the test on a gift from his master to me. Ingi is tall, as is Earnwulf, his copper-hued hair tied back and beard of a ruddy hue as anyone would see the god Thor. Yet he is of Aengle stock, a southern neighbour of the Jutes who came before any other folk from the northlands.

Ingi, on the other hand, is swarthy and shaggy-maned like a hill pony. There are many here of Danish blood, whose mothers are of Aengle or Celt stock. Their given names are from the Danelaw, but that is as much as they owe their fathers.

Their arms ripple with the strength of weaponsmiths, yet what they are doing now is fine work on hilt and matching sheath. The backing for the sheath is fine woodwork overlaid with leather. Loops have been added for me to thread my sword belt through. This sword will be masterful in its finishing, fit to make any man jealous!

These two are almost done when I hear footfalls behind me. I do not look up, however, rapt as I am with the skills of Ingi and Earnwulf. Someone's hands fasten on my arms and as I turn Ingi looks up and tells the armed men who have come to seize me,

'He is Ivar Ulfsson'.

Andvari has not foreseen this and is as taken aback as I am by Ingi's treachery,

'*Ingi*, why did you do this?'

'When our new masters have taken over the land they will be in need of weaponsmiths they can trust', Ingi's lip curls downward as he answers.

Earnwulf adds, smirking,

'Your day is done, Wend. This is *our* workshop now! The Northmen will leave you alone if you let them take away the outlaws'.

Andvari scowls, his whole being darkens. Eyes light like hot coals and Ingi steps back, afraid, to fall into the white hot coals of the hearth. Earnwulf cannot believe his eyes as dark shadows cloud the workshop. The young Northmen who have hold of me fall back, scared out of their wits by something they do not understand. Andvari is nowhere to be seen, but from the darkness hands take shape that tighten around Earnwulf's neck. This is the work of a dark master – is my friend Andvari one of them?

Outside I hear our horses snorting, whinnying in fear. Grimolf dashes into the workshop and stares, wide-eyed at the sight of Earnwulf turning blue, eyes popping, mouth wide open. His feet are no longer on the stone floor and his arms flail. He tries to scream but nothing comes of it, his life deemed forfeit for betraying his master and us. His spent, lifeless shell falls limply onto the workshop floor.

Harding rushes in after Grimolf and gapes at the sight of Earnwulf's limp corpse and Ingi's charred carcass by the hearth. Behind me the two young Northmen have been overcome, unable to flee even through an open doorway. He grins lopsidedly, not knowing what to say, but there is enough wit there to ask me,

'It was too much for these two?'

'You might say that', I grin back, and hear myself ask, 'Where has Saeward got to?'

'He has told of the horses' reins – *just*', Harding tells me and looks around for Andvari.

'*Where is the old man?*' Grimolf asks for them both.

I look around and see a shadow behind the hearth wall,

'Down there, I think'. I tell him, and see my sword lying beside the anvil where it fell. The sheath has fallen into the hearth and burns brightly still. All that good work has gone to waste, even if it was the treacherous pair that made it.

Harding and I walk around the hearth wall and spy Andvari sitting, back to the stone wall, knees drawn up and arms resting limply on bony knees.

He squints up at us and nods, holding his arms out to be lifted to his feet,

'Aye, it *is* me. Set me on my feet, will you – both?' He is ashen, hollow-eyed, as if he had run many miles without rest. We put him on his feet and stand him against the wall.

'What happened?' I ask, unable to believe my eyes.

'You do not trust the proof of what your eyes tell you?' Andvari asks, tongue-in-cheek. He seems to be his old self again, and laughs at us, 'You look as if you had seen a ghost?'

'Not so much a ghost perhaps', I begin to think again, yet still unsure of what I did see.

'As what – you said not so much a ghost?' Andvari pushes his body away from the wall and comes to stand before me,

'Not so much a ghost as a dark master', I answer, thinking to see the same dark master rise in a cloud above me.

'*No* Ivar, the dark master is gone', Andvari walks away to look at what is left of Ingi. He kicks the legs out of his way and peers down at Earnwulf. '*What a* waste! They were such good workers, too. Now I will have to find someone else I think will rise to the test – what about Grimolf here?'

'I think Grimolf is scared of you', Harding tells our host.

'You are not afraid of me, are you Grimolf?' Andvari asks, beckoning him to his side. 'You would have to work hard to keep your fears at bay. What do you say, are you up for the trial?'

'If you think I will come up to scratch', Grimolf spreads his arms and shrugs.

'You are willing to learn?' Andvari rests a hand on Grimolf's shoulder.

'There may not be as much for me to learn as you believe, but I am willing to throw my lot in with you', Grimolf takes Andvari's hand. 'If it is a partnership you wish, I can bring my tools and anvil. My waggon has stood idle for some time and I have no horse to draw it. The old mare was a bit tough, too!'

'You ate your *horse?*' Harding looks deeply shocked at Grimolf.

'I ate the old mare, aye. I still have the young one, or else what did I ride here? That waggon needs *two* horses to pull it, with all my things. That anvil is no feather, as you will understand when we lift it!'

'Who said anything about staying that long?' I chortle. 'The Northmen will soon be back, I would warrant'.

20

Saeward's mare is harnessed alongside Grimolf's on a waggon that I would say had seen better days. He tells us it was used to haul war gear for the Stochesleag wapentake two years since, when Morkere called on the *select fyrd* to fight Harald Sigurdsson and Tostig at Gata Fulford.

'But then I had both horses and this waggon was a lot newer', Grimolf tells us, as if he needs to. He is full of himself, at one with a world that has suddenly shown to be friendlier, 'With Andvari I can show these folk around here the mettle of my skills!'

'Aye, Grimolf, you shall have a new start in life', Harding nods wisely as Saeward cracks the whip in the air to set the horses on their way. The rumble of heavy iron-rimmed wheels on a narrow, broken stone track is deafening.

We turn left at the main track into Stochesleag, until-

'*Back*, Grimolf! Get this waggon back!'

Harding has seen something that worries him. Saeward jerks hard on the leather reins that pull on his and Grimolf's horses. Harding on the far side grasps his side of the waggon, I on mine. Grimolf leaps down to bodily push the horses back until the waggon rumbles unbearably slowly backward into the undergrowth. Once back far enough Grimolf hastily seizes branches from either side to cover the front of his waggon.

Rasping, short of breath, he climbs back onto the waggon, to be pulled under the branches by Harding. Saeward has already leapt down to hide beside the great iron-banded hulk and I wheel Braenda around to hide behind tall bushes.

It is not long before the steady clop of hooves on the hard earth nearby tells me there must be at least a half-score of the outlanders, twelve or more, who pass beneath the high canopy of trees to Stochesleag. I soon see them through the tall bushes. They talk loudly, their banter cocky as if they had nothing to fear. Laughter rings out in the cooling evening air.

Then they are gone, unaware they were being watched. We wait a while longer, making sure they do not come back on hearing the creak of Grimolf's waggon.

Looking around I nudge Braenda out onto the broad track again and beckon Harding. He waves Saeward and Grimolf forward. The horses strain to haul the waggon backed onto Grimolf's overgrown track and Saeward drops down to heave,

When he yells, '*Hey, you two, give us a hand!*' Harding waves him down and covers his mouth with the other hand.

Grimolf growls at Saeward beside him,

'I think he means they might still be within hearing'.

'They cannot be that close, if he thinks they will not hear the creaking of your waggon', Saeward laughs.

'They might have heard you booming in the stillness, Saeward!' Harding hisses when they close on him. 'I shall stay here and watch out until you are around this bend in the track'.

'What, over the noise of their hooves and all that shouting?' Saeward shakes his head and taps it with a forefinger to mean he thinks Harding's fears are unwarranted, far-fetched, not worth worrying over.

We are some way along the track before the drumming hooves of Harding's mare can be heard behind us – at least I hope it *is* Harding's mare! When he shows around the trees I breathe out again.

'What is it, Ivar? You look as if you had seen a ghost!' Harding laughs hollowly as he pulls up alongside me. 'Come, Ivar, stir yourself! Andvari will wonder where we are'.

I nudge Braenda into a trot after the others and we reach Andvari's workshop soon after. He awaits us outside, arms folded,

'What kept you?'

He seems to be smirking, but I put it down to a trick of the light. Would he have known of the outlanders riding this way along the track?

Saeward tests out his wit on the old man,

'We thought perhaps you had sent along some of the outlanders to welcome us'. I do not know whether my East Seaxan friend wholly trusts the Wend. It might be something to do with his heathen skills...

'Your wit belies your good name', Andvari cracks and turns to Grimolf, looking over his few tools and things in the back of the waggon. 'You have *everything?*'

'I would have brought more', Grimolf cracks, 'thinking you might not have room. No, Andvari, this is *all* I own. At one time I had more, but I have had to trim down my belongings over the years'.

'Take what you need of mine, Grimolf', Andvari holds out a hand, which is taken and shaken in friendship. Once Andvari was not as open to outsiders, but that was before he became a freed man. Now he seeks friends, although he had made one or two mistakes of late. Grimolf will be both friend and helper to the ageing Wend.

We lend our weight to Grimolf, helping unload his tools and other belongings. Last off the waggon is the anvil.   He clambers up onto the back and heaves it single-handedly toward the tailgate before standing to take breath.

'You need help unloading that, I think', Andvari tells him with a twinkle in his eye.

'Take your ease, sit astride the anvil and I shall see what I can do for you'.

We stand around, awaiting some sort of trickery whilst Andvari closes his eyes. A black fog enfolds us, and Saeward clutches at me, afraid. Harding comes closer to me, too, and looks about. Unable to see anything beyond the sudden darkness, he thumbs his beard and looks up into the air. The stars are still clear, high in the heavens, and when I look down again the anvil is close to the hearth, where it should be with Grimolf still astride.

Andvari opens his eyes again, smiles, claps his hands and hails Grimolf,

'You look *truly* at home there, friend!'

'I *feel* at home!' Grimolf laughs uneasily, 'Where is the ale, master?'

'Now friend – *that* is something you will have to find at the inn! My skills do not reach to brewing'.

Grimolf, now at the door waves us to follow him.

'*For shame* – Let me reach into my purse to pay for it!'

Saeward is unsure,

'Will the outlanders not be there?'

'What if they are?' Grimolf pats Andvari's back. 'My new partner will make sure we are unseen - *can* you do that?'

'Something like that', Andvari sniffs, and looks up at Harding, Saeward and me. 'In asking the three of you to take off your mailcoats will warrant that you stay unseen!'

'I would never have thought of that!' Harding chortles and we pull off one another's mailcoats.

'Nevertheless I would say we should keep our daggers at hand', Grimolf offers. We put on our belts after sliding the sheaths onto them.

Andvari has thought of something else,

'Leave your sheathes and daggers here, and I will give you something more in keeping, to make you look like field ceorls'. He walks to the back of his workshop and brings out three rough leather belts and sheathes. Sliding in roughly-made knives, he hands them to us. 'Those fine heirlooms you have would mark you out here! Thinking on it, I would say you wear these smocks over your fine tunics'.

'I understand', I nod. Harding and Saeward pull on the smocks and belts with me and stand, ready to go drinking.

'This is new to me', Andvari beams, 'walking with four fine fellows for a drink. If anyone asks, you are here for ploughshares I made for you. I have some in the workshop'.

'That sounds right', Harding sighs, his brow creased.

'It would suit you, Harding, albeit lowering your standing from thegn to free man', I tell him as I push him forward, out of the workshop and onto the road.

'Where is the inn?' Saeward stands in the middle of the road, turning on his toes.

'Follow me', Grimolf beckons. 'I would have thought you could *smell* it from here!'

After only a few more yards I believe him. Whoever does the brewing must throw in more barley than anyone else, it smells oddly sweet. Do we have to go in there?

'*God* what does that smell of?' Saeward has taken in a noseful of it. He stops in his tracks and looks to me. When I shake my head we all come to a halt. Grimolf cannot understand why we do not wish to go further and stands in front of me with arms folded.

'It is miles to the next inn!' he snaps and glowers at Saeward.

Andvari is no happier than we are,

'If they do not want to go in there, there is no way you should try to make them. Harding, have you lost your sense of smell?'

'I need a drink', Harding groans.

'So do I', I tell him, 'but I have my pride'.

Grimolf has thought of something, a sort of bargain,

'We could go in and see what it is like. We can always come out again with a couple of skins of ale', Grimolf tells us. 'What do you say to that?'

'Very well', I answer, nodding slowly.

'Aye, we will wait here for you', Andvari adds.

Grimolf and Harding leave us and enter the inn, only to burst out through the doorway again.

'There are a score or more of the Northmen in there, all *dead!*' Harding tells me.

'What of the innkeeper or his kin?' I ask.

'No-one stirred when we entered. That may be what you could smell, the *dead* men', Grimolf is wide-eyed.

'*Who* could have slain them?' Andvari asks.

I stride to the door, only to be overcome by the stench.

'They had to have been taken unaware, all at the same time'. Back outside again I feel sick from the smell.

'What were you looking for, Ivar?' Saeward asks, wondering what could make me want to go in after saying I would not. He looks me up and down in the pale moonlight and offers, 'Did you want to know what they died of?'

I answer, still reeling from the stifling stench of death,

'I think I know now. The ale had been meddled with'.

Walking the field after men have fought and died out in the open is one thing. Here the inn doors had been pulled shut, the fire in the hearth left burning. Men lay on the benches and on the earth floor, stomachs blown out with maggots crawling all over them. It is no wonder the smell turned my stomach!

'The barley may have been worm-ridden', Saeward says, playing with the small hairs of his beard as he mulls over what might have brought on the deaths. 'Aye, Ivar, the barley must have been worm-ridden!' he says again.

'Surely they must have known that *before* drinking?' Harding scratches his head.

Andvari thinks out aloud,

'The Northmen would not think twice before drinking if they did not know the smell'.

Harding's brow furrows deeply at that, but Andvari goes on to ask me,

'Hunding, before you tasted their apple ale, did you think anything of the way it smelled?'

I wonder how he knew I had tasted it.

'You have tasted it', Andvari presses, nodding.

'I have indeed tasted it, and it did not smell 'off', however. I think I would have known if it were, having been in Northmandige with Harold and Thorfinn'.

He peers at me in the darkness, reading my thoughts.

'What do we do?' Harding wants to know.

'What do you want to do?' I ask. '*I* think we should leave here now, all of us, before any of their fellows come and call on the *burh* to stump up the Murdrum fine for killing their kind. These here all seem to have been young men. Some of the riders we had to hide from may have been nobles, and left their young men behind to their own ends. There may have been the odd one or two who could give orders, but if they could not tell their drinks did not taste right before the worm struck...'

'What is the *Murdrum* fine?' Harding asks, slack-jawed, waiting for an answer.

I cast my thoughts back, to what I heard once,

'When a Northman is slain or whatever, the folk around must prove know nothing of it. If they have no way of proving their lack of knowledge of the killing, they must pay the fine between them. If the *burh* or hamlet cannot raise the fine, their homes are burnt to the ground and they are driven off to fend for themselves in the wild'.

Harding scowls darkly and swears under his breath,

'Dirty outland scum that they are, we should kick their arses black and blue until they have to sit in the sea to cool off!' He swears loudly, and thumps one fist into the other, ready for a fight.

'They are thoughts we all cherish, but we must make those thoughts live, Harding!' I tell him.

'We must make them suffer!' Saeward adds and Grimolf laughs out aloud.

'So say all of us!'

There is no-one about anywhere, and no-one has been out since we came with Andvari and Grimolf. Where *is* everyone? Are they in hiding, awaiting the worst? It dawns on me then, that the folk of Stochesleag must have known about it, fled before others came and the reckoning would begin.

I tell Andvari and Grimolf,

'You had best come with us. Life will not be worth living here when their fellows show up again'.

'I can always go back to my workshop – what am I talking about?' Grimolf curses.

'If you like, we can help you take your things back', I offer, hoping he turns me down.

Grimolf laughs, and sucks in air through his teeth,

'By all means, if that slaving was not too much for you'.

He turns and sets off back to Andvari's workshop, trudging slowly at first and then picking up his feet. 'We should stir ourselves, and quickly!'

'He is right', Harding turns after Grimolf and the rest of us, Andvari, Saeward and I, follow closely behind.

Working like madmen, we stow all the tools and heave Grimolf's anvil back onto the waggon. Some of Andvari's things go with Grimolf's, the rest having to be left behind. Andvari's skills may not be enough if he is on his own, wrong-sided by the Northmen when they turn up – and they will be angry at *any* men they can find.

We are mounted, Saeward and Grimolf back on the waggon and Andvari resting on the anvil. As we are about to leave, the sound of many horses comes from the road outside, more than passed earlier when we hid behind the bushes.

'What do we do now?' Harding hisses.

'We leave – as quietly as we can with four horses and a creaky waggon-full of blacksmithing tools', I answer. 'But we will have to wait for them to pass'.

The creak from the waggon when it starts sounds as loud as a church bell and we stop again. Nothing stirs – the Northmen's leaders will be tearing their hair out in the inn! Still, we must be gone from here, come what may. The waggon creaks off to a slow, noisy start again. We all cross our fingers and hope the outlanders make so much noise between them in the inn that they cannot hear us here, loud though the groans and creaks from Grimolf's waggon are!

After what seems an age we are out of Stochesleag, heading west again. The dwelling houses, barns and outhouses are well behind us and the outlanders still have not begun to follow us. Then again, why would they follow us? Which way would they go, and how long ago would they think the good folk of the *burh* had fled? They might not think it worthwhile searching and see to burying their own – or set fire to the inn with them inside. I think they might be overcome with the smell of their dead if they tried to do the Christian thing!

'I see fire back there', Andvari says out aloud to anyone who can hear him over the creaking of the waggon and clopping of hooves.

On turning to look over my left shoulder I see flames shoot high into the sky. As I thought, they have taken the easy way out and put a torch to the inn. When I catch Harding's eye I nod back at the flames for him to look.

'*God*, they have set fire to the inn!' Harding rides alongside the waggon and slaps Grimolf's right arm to show him.

As Grimolf looks back, Saeward cracks the whip over the horses' heads to stir them. The horses pull harder and the waggon rumbles louder, Harding and I press our mounts to trot after them.

I hope we do not see them before dawn, but the night is well lit by the moon. Anything is likely and we have almost reached the end of Grimolf's track when I hear the pounding of hooves some way off behind us.

'Can we get this thing going any faster?' I shout at Saeward. He cracks the whip again and the waggon lurches on. Will we be there before the riders overtake?

'Nearly there', Grimolf calls out, pointing. I do not know the last time I looked forward to hiding behind bushes, but I feel fear gnawing at me. The pounding of hooves sounds closer and the waggon hardly seems to roll any faster!

Harding and I grasp either corner at the back of the waggon and press our mounts harder. The waggon lurches again and Andvari almost falls off the back over me. Grimolf laughs and Saeward curses as we launch into the greenery at the head of his track. The tail of the waggon is hardly through the bushes, come to a halt, before the riders pass on their way westward.

Harding watches them round a bend in the track before asking something that had not entered my head,

'Were they after *us*, or were they on their way to the Dunelm road, to ride north? I am not sure they even knew we were here.'

'I was not going to ask them why they came this way',

I answer and tell Saeward to crack his whip again. We will have to get used to Grimolf's small home for a day or two before we head south again.

Saeward flicks the whip and we lurch along our way again, along the narrow, overgrown track. I would say it is a wonder the waggon does not come off the track, Saeward not knowing how wide it is in the dark.

'The bushes and weeds have overgrown everything along the trackside', Grimolf shouts over the groaning of the wagon as it lumbers in the darkness. 'Still, it is wise to head on watchfully, as it bends sharply one way or the other. You will see'.

Morning dawns dully after overnight rain kept me awake, drumming on the thick thatch. Some has seeped through and stands in a puddle around my sword and axe by the door.

'Your roof needs looking at', Harding seethes. 'I could hardly sleep in the night for rain dripping onto my shoulder'.

He stretches before turning to look at Grimolf.

'You could have turned over', Grimolf chuckles wickedly. 'I hoped I could forget about this hovel when I was told I would share Andvari's workshop. Now I shall have to see to it'.

'There are worse things that could beset you, Harding', Saeward grins and shows the marks on his back where he was birched in Jorvik after killing Garwulf. Grimolf turns away, sickened. 'This was done by Aenglishmen in the name of the law in Eoferwic. I have yet to be caught by the outlanders, so I do not know yet what they might have in store for me'.

'No doubt they will think of something fittingly grisly', I tell him, grinning. For Harding's sake I add, 'One young outlander noble caught us *thrice* but lost his hold on us again – *careless, eh?*'

'He really thought he had you this time, as I see it', Saeward laughs out aloud.

'So he *did.* Near Oxnaford the third time he was almost overcome with glee at catching me again'.

'If Theodolf and I had not followed you, what would have become of the three of you, I wonder?'

Saeward folds his arms, as if asking for thanks.

'Very well, Saeward. I thank you – again. How many more times should I thank you? We both have Theodolf to thank for being freed the first time we were caught together', I turn the talk to our young friend. 'It is a shame Oslac is no longer with us to thank you'.

'And Thor –'

Grimolf is open-mouthed. Harding looks put out.

'*Thor?* Are you talking about a Norse god saving you from the Northmen?' Grimolf is aghast.

Harding still looks puzzled but says nothing hoping, by the look of him, to be enlightened.

'Thor was, *is* a weaponsmith who has a workshop in the *burh* of Lunden', I tell them. Andvari eyes me, unbelieving when I go on. 'He is also a Christian priest, no less'.

'A Christian priest who goes by the name of Thor? What would you have me believe?' Andvari shakes his head and smiles sidelong at Grimolf. They both begin to laugh, even after Saeward tells them it is true.

'I knew a Christian priest called Hrafn', Harding puts in. 'He dwelt in the church near the south-western wall of Jorvik where they say Tostig was buried – I forget the name'.

'One day you may meet this weaponsmithing priest', I tell Harding.

Soon we will have to head south, Harding, Saeward and I, in the afternoon or evening.

'Harding, where is this kinsman of yours, whose home lies on the moors?' I ask, having said nothing about our way for days. Asking again may show I have not forgotten.

'He lives not far from where we rode north with the *aetheling* Eadgar, Morkere and Eadwin – a little west from that on the side of the moors at Havneby, in Bilsdale'.

'That is how far from Jorvik?' I ask, looking at Saeward as I do so. He does not even flinch, but smiles wearily to show he no longer cares what name we give the *burh*. I feel in my bones we shall be back there again before long. For now we will be on our way to find Theodolf.

'Havneby is near the rim of the moorlands, uphill east of Treske. We could ride for Tadceaster by way of Treske, and cross the great dale to the North Road', Harding tells me all this with his eyes closed, drawing with a finger in the air. Grimolf smirks, but stops when Harding opens his eyes and stares at him.

'That sounds like a long way around', I do not like the sound of it, but what else can we do with all these Northmen everywhere. Jorvik must be swamped by them!

Harding asks me testily,

'Is there another way, Ivar?'

I would have to think – hard. For now I close my eyes and nod. When I look again, Harding stares at me, and then looks sidelong at Saeward.

'Have *you* thought of anything better?' Harding is prickly and Saeward shrugs, jaw set, eyes lowered.

'In this weather you could ride late in the afternoon. You would not have to wait until dark', Grimolf tells Harding.

'I need to eat', Harding switches.

'You can have oatmeal', Grimolf stands and begins looking into bags. 'There is meat, too'.

'What about bread?' Saeward asks.

'What *about* bread?' Grimolf mumbles, still looking through his bags. 'It would be stale by now, anyway'.

'I have bread', Andvari opens one of his bags.

'It must be stale, *surely?*' Harding looks idly over at the old man, then looks back to Grimolf who still searches for something only he knows of.

'Push a finger onto it, if you will not believe me', Andvari does not like Harding's manner but says nothing.

He holds out the bread, but Harding keeps his hands to himself, by the look of him thinking this to be more witchcraft. Andvari sniffs and offers me some, which I gladly take from him. Saeward is also offered some, and takes a wedge with meat offered by Grimolf. The meat is salted boar, and tasty!

'You can live well in these woods', Grimolf chats and pulls open a bag of oats, takes a bowl and dips it into the bag, handing the full bowl to Harding, telling him, 'Ewe's milk is in there'.

A stone vat stands in one corner, away from the light. Harding lifts the lid and looks in,

'Is this fresh?'

'I hardly think so. If you want fresh there is a miller who lives a short way off, south of here in the woods'.

'How far is that?' Harding puts down his bowl.

'Not far, that way', Grimolf shows Harding, but the thegn gives up. He scoops some of the milk from the vat and pours it onto the oats. He has no inkling of how to make oatmeal ready to eat.

Grimolf fusses with his bags, lights a fire in the hearth and swings a small pot over the crackling flames,

'Put the oats and milk in there, add salt and some more oats and milk for me'.

Andvari holds up a hand to ask,

'I should be happy for some oatmeal. I should be glad for anything'.

'We will all have oatmeal then', Grimolf tells Harding, staring hard at Andvari, 'so put another few handfuls of oats into the pot and add more ewes' milk'.

Harding ought to learn something about cooking before the day is out! Yet he seems unwilling to learn. Whilst Andvari busies himself with making porridge, Grimolf lays out meat and cheese.

The morning meal goes quietly, and all anyone can hear for a while is the chomping of jaws as first porridge, and then boar meat, cheese and ale are downed. It is no feast, but it will keep the wolves at bay for now. Fruit, kept in a barrel beside the milk vat, is apples. No plums or damsons, berries or pears, only apples kept in cold water. Anything else needs to be eaten quickly, I would say. As they say, beggars cannot be choosers.

'We ought to look at our blades – axes, knives and swords', I tell Harding and Saeward after we have eaten, 'oil them and run the whetstones over them'.

Harding eyes me before answering,

'I am glad you thought about that. There is something else'.

'What?' I await the worst. Is his horse lame, or is it that he wants to go home now?

He strokes his beard thoughtfully before letting me know what it is that suddenly come into his head?

'I think I should see to the priest Aelfberht'.

'*See to him?* Do you mean to kill him?' I ask.

'If it comes to that, aye', Harding sniffs and runs a finger under his nose. 'What would Saeward say?'

'He may fight you over it'.

Harding stares at me in the gathering gloom and I go on,

'You know, the priest is only doing what his master, Archbishop Eadred tells him. The Church thinks Willelm is king by right and only a few of them are ready to take him to task. Some have already left these shores, I think you know', I pick at an apple seed caught between my front teeth

Harding thinks long and hard before asking next,

'Of the ones who have stayed and do not feel they owe Eadred any loyalty, what would they say if I slew a priest for betraying us to the Northmen?'

'If Saeward is against it, do you not think they will not be? You are asking much from me, too, you know, if you think I would be happy at the slaying of an unarmed man of the cloth', I have to tell him.

'What, even for betraying us to the outlanders?' Harding reddens.

'For whatever he has, or may yet do', I answer.

Saeward, having entered the hovel again after going out to ease himself, fixes him with a cold stare. Harding shifts awkwardly on the chair, trying not to look back at the East Seaxan. The thought of killing a priest does not warm Saeward to Harding.

'Can you stop staring at me like that?' Harding snaps.

Saeward looks away, at me, at Grimolf, and cuts into an apple with his dagger.

'I would say think again about 'seeing to' Father Aelfberht', I tell Harding in the early afternoon.

He scowls and looks at Saeward, who seems to have dozed off, elbows on the table in front of him, hands holding his head. Grimolf is in his workshop, talking over the anvil with Andvari. They will be out there for some time, I should guess. It is time for me to test out a few home truths on Harding,

'You know a thegn must uphold the law of the Church as well as that of the king. The king you swore your oath to is dead now, so that leaves the Church. Killing a priest would put you beyond the fold, never mind the Northmen's laws. *No* man would shelter you, think on that'.

'Not even you?'

'Not even me', I nod.

'Would you *betray* me to the Northmen?' Harding hisses. He glares at me and sits back, arms folded across his chest.

'I would not betray you, but you would have to seek out others to be your friends. I cannot bide the thought of killing a man who will not wield a weapon, or who has never learned the skills even a fyrdman would need to know'.

Harding stays seated, looking up into the rafters of Grimolf's hovel. He shifts once or twice, but does not rise. Then, looking at me he asks,

'Will you ride with me to Huttun, to make sure I do *not* kill him?'

'What could you want from him?' It makes no sense to me, why Harding should want to see Father Aelfberht. He was against Arnkell and Hunding harming the priest, so what has come over him? He is not the same man we rode with from Jorvik. Has killing his wife turned him after all this time?

'I need to know why he would turn against his own kind', Harding tells me.

It does not ring true, and he might be lying. Out on the track he might even try to get away from us and reach Father Aelfberht another way. We would then have to find the priest and, if the worst comes to the worst, kill Harding to save the priest.   It does not bear thinking of!

'When did you see yourself riding to Huttun?' I ask. We are some way into early evening now, and Grimolf said he thought we should ride south before nightfall. Whether he was thinking of his own welfare or ours is of no matter to bother us.

We would need longer to ride west to Huttun, wait for Harding, if he did catch us out on the way, and quieten him before riding south with him. We might even have to bind him to his horse to keep him from himself.

'I want to ride as soon as we can be ready', Harding nods sideways at Saeward as he looks at me. 'Wake him up'.

'Saeward we are to ride now', I wake my friend, rocking him by his shoulders.

'God, what is it now with Harding - has he something aforethought?' Saeward shakes himself fully awake and stretches, arms straight out from the shoulders.

'We are to ride with him to Huttun to keep him from striking down the priest', I yawn as we gather our belongings, stride through the yard door and stand around Grimolf.

'You are ready to go?' Grimolf only asks out of habit. It is the way of folk around here. He knows the answer. Andvari smiles at me in a way of blessing our undertaking. We shake hands, Grimolf, Andvari and us, before leading our horses out from the small stable – luckily there *were* four stalls – and mounting together.

Saeward has long since mastered the noble art of mounting, and makes a show of raising one leg over his saddle back. Harding, meanwhile, takes it slowly in the way of a man burdened with cares. Is he thinking of losing us out there, once we are underway? I swing myself onto Braenda and wait for Harding.

Grimolf bids us a loud farewell, Andvari nods at me when I turn in the saddle to look back at them both. Will I see him again?

The track is soft, the rain-laden undergrowth on either side almost hiding it from sight in the poor light. Above, leaden clouds pass eastward, pushed by a fresh westerly wind toward the coast around ten miles away. The sea-swell will have been hard for seafarers through the day.

When we reach the greater track it is heavier going than when we came last with the waggon, just as well for us with the weight it had to bear – even better for the horses, and harder for us to hear the Northmen's mounts coming.

Pulling up the collar of my cloak when the rain slants down again, I see Saeward and Harding doing likewise ahead of me. We are unlikely to meet any of our masters, I hope. In the downpour I wonder why we need to be out in it. There has to be a better way of seeking out Father Aelfberht than being soaked to the skin – and then we have to make our way back again, to follow the track for the moors. It will be even worse up there!

Father Aelfberht answers his door to us, startled at the sight of Saeward and me. He wrings his hands as if in prayer until he sees Harding and wails to him for help,

'Thegn Harding, help me. They want to *kill* me!'

'Fool, they are here to stop *me* killing you!'

The priest does not know where to put himself and makes a start at fleeing, only to be cornered by Saeward against a writing slope and the door beside it.

'*Behave* yourself, father!' Saeward chides. 'Be a *man*, for God's sake!'

'He has never *been* a man, as such', Harding mocks.

'I must say I have seen more manly women!' I tell him, holding my nose. The priest smells as if he had filled his breeks!

'You hear that, Father Aelfberht? Shame on you! I will have to ask for the archbishop to send a better shepherd!' Harding laughs as Saeward mocks,

'I heard once that the king of East Aengla, Eadmund, fled the fight to hide in the church at Byrig. The Danes made him look like a hedgehog with arrows but the Church made a hero of him!'

'That fits'. Harding chortles, 'What do you say to that, Ivar?'

'I believe Haesten Ragnarsson asked him if he thought he would fly like an angel if they slew him, but he merely sagged limply in his bindings with arrow flights sticking out of him like a hedgehog.. There were nobler *Church*men with him!'

Harding turns to Saeward,

'And you say he ran from the fight, Saeward?'

'It is what I heard, aye'. Saeward looks from Harding to me, 'At least that is what Ivar told me once'.

Harding, annoyed with the priest turns on him, grabs Aelfberht's collar and snarls, his mouth close to the cleric's ear.   Not so long ago Harding saw me as an outsider, almost akin to the Norsemen who attacked Jorvik. Now I can do no wrong by him. .

'I will have no Danes in God's home!' Aelfberht's upper lip twists upward in a show of dislike.

'*My* forebears were Danes, priest. What do you say to that?' Harding lets go of Aelfberht and wipes his hands on his cloak. 'You smell, priest! Do you ever wash your clothes?'

'I do the Lord's bidding!' Aelfberht wipes his mouth with the back of his sleeve.

'No-one said a priest should wear filthy clothes', Harding growls.

'A priest should be a shining beacon to us all', Saeward adds. He glares back at Aelfberht when the priest stares balefully at him.

'This is getting us nowhere', Harding throws up his hands and Aelfberht backs away, fearful of being struck.

'What did you *think* you would achieve in coming here?' I ask him, as angry with him as with Aelfberht, for wasting our time.

'To be honest, Ivar, I no longer know'.

Saeward gives a half-smile and offers,

'I thought we came here to teach the priest a lesson about trustworthiness'.

'I keep faith with the Lord, *and our anointed king!*' Aelfberht snaps and backs away again. When we merely look at him he seems to rally.

'That is all very worthy of you, Father Aelfberht, but it is Eadgar you should hold with, not Willelm', Harding tells him, walking toward him.

He cowers again, unsure still of what is in store for him. I daresay he sees himself as a likely martyr, but he does not have the nerve for that sort of thing. He would hide behind his mother's skirts if she were here! Who thought him fit for the priesthood? However, we are not here to pander to his hopes. A ticking-off is as much as he can look forward to, as long as he does not rile Harding too much.

'Cowardly scum, *stand up like a man!*' Saeward thumps Aelfberht in the stomach, 'You are not *fit* to wear a priest's robes!'

Harding stares, eyes wide open, at Saeward.

He looks down at Aelfberht, on his knees, holding his stomach. Does he think he has been stabbed? Saeward has a hard fist. Being hit by him might make anyone think he had used a weapon.

Aelfberht looks put out that he will not meet his maker this evening, but it does not stop him from being sick over Saeward's boots.

'Leave the wretch be', I tell Saeward. 'He is not likely to fulfil his duties otherwise. We ought to set out for the south now, Harding. There is no telling when we will next see the outlanders. Come, Saeward, let him alone and we can get to our horses'.

Saeward nods gloomily and slaps Harding on his back,

'Aye, come Harding, we have wasted enough time on this dross'.

'We can better deal with him when we have thrown the Northmen back into the sea', Harding follows us out into the moonless night. The small church looms eerily against the night sky, lighter now only because the clouds have broken up, still shifting busily eastward.

As we mount Harding asks why I spoke about riding south.

'There are many ways that lead southward', I answer. 'You know that. His Northman friends are hardly likely to send men scurrying over the moors when we could as easily be on the Jorvik road'.

Harding grunts as he clambers into his saddle,

'I only hope you are right'.

'I would never have held you for the worrying kind', Saeward chuckles as he presses his mare into a canter. 'Where do we go from here?'

21

'They would never have thought of us following this road', I wonder aloud.

'What was that?' Harding wheezes, looking back at me, but my answer is blown away in a sudden gust of wind. He shrugs, turns to look ahead again and rides on.

We have bypassed Stochesleag, not that we thought there would be anyone there. Even the Northmen would have left once they learned that no one was about any more, to answer for the deaths of their men in the inn. Here and there we have had to walk our horses, so our climb is slow through the dale above Brogtun. To our left, through the trees the tiny hamlet of Urra slumbers beneath a newly overcast sky, only one or two hounds barking to mark our passing. Rain threatens again and we have a long, hard climb ahead.

'The Northmen would never have thought of us following this road, surely?' I say out aloud what I had muttered to myself.

'Hopefully the outlanders have seen no use in following the Helmsleag road', Harding answers, looking up into the air.

Rain begins to drum on our helms, spatters on our shoulders and runs off our cloaks. I can barely see shapes in this darkness further than the trees on either side of the road. Only fools would stray out of doors in this miserable weather. We are the fools who have strayed!

'How far is it from here to Havneby?' I ask. Talking lets each of us know he is not alone, we are sharing the gloom. It is with hardship that we learn one another's strengths. With luck the weaknesses will not be tested too hard.

'We should be there before dawn', Harding peers through the darkness at me.

'How do you stand for this poor summer weather in these parts?' Saeward asks.

Is it aimed at Harding, or at me? As it is, Harding answers for us both, cackling at Saeward's look of sheer wretchedness,

'Ivar would know from being in Northanhymbra, that sometimes it is hard to tell whether it is summer or winter, and often the fore year, summer, afteryear and winter can be seen in one day!'

A sudden squall from the west drenches us, driven through a gap in the trees. When it passes Saeward swears,

'Damned heathen weather that you get here, how is it you stay cheerful?'

'I have known it this bad in East Seaxe, Saeward', I take him to task. 'Often when the wind comes off the sea the land around

Wealtham floods, *you* know that!'

He says nothing. There is nothing he *can* say. Wulfwin would pour scorn on him for such an outburst. We mount when the road levels off a little, the stillness around us broken only by hoofbeats on the packed earth and stones.

We pass a few dwellings around a bend in the road. A hound barks loudly out of sight in a yard. No one stirs, at least not that we would know out here on the track. The way is ours and ours alone. None would envy us this night's ride.

At last Harding tells us to turn right, downhill off the Helmsleag track, and uphill again for much of the way on a narrow, winding packhorse track. Wet through, we and our horses plod doggedly on, side by side. The few level stretches along the track are hardly worth mounting our horses for before the track climbs sharply again, only to dip around a sharp bend and uphill, *steeply* uphill.

Soon Harding lets us know,

'We are almost there'.

'God has saved us!' Saeward raises his chin skyward, claps his hands together, his mare's reins between them.

Harding chuckles and tells us over one shoulder as he pushes open a wooden gate,

'We stay a night or two at Wulfheard's home', Harding tells us over one shoulder as he pushes open a side gate. A long-legged, golden-haired hound bounds up to him and wags its tail, thumping Saeward's legs. His eyes drooping with tiredness from the hard climb out of Stochesleag, Saeward is much too weary to be annoyed. 'Do not mind Gold-hair. He has not seen me for a year or more – now where is Wulfheard?'

'Who is that?' A woman shows in the doorway, wrapped in a cloak. Bare legs and feet tell us she has been awakened from her slumbers.

'It is Harding, Thorgrima', he hands me his mare's reins and strides forward to greet her. 'Where is Wulfheard?'

'He is in Jorvik, Harding. He rode there last week with Thegn Wulfric. Did you not see him?'

'*Last* week, you say?' Harding is nonplussed. '*When* last week did they ride there?'

'At the end of the week', Thorgrima knows from the way Harding looks at her, that something is amiss. She sobs, and would drop to her knees but for Harding holding her up.

He holds her to him whilst she sobs bitterly on his chest. When Thorgrima's sobs quieten Harding asks,

'Where is Thegn Wulfric now, do you know?'

'He is not back yet, either. His wife asked after Wulfheard yesterday. None of us has seen either of them since they left. We thought they had gone to meet you and Thegn Osgod', Thorgrima wails into her hands.

'We shall be riding that way', Harding tells her. When Saeward is about to say something about steering clear of Jorvik Harding puts a finger to his lips and goes on, 'I shall look out for them, fear not Thorgrima. Go back to bed, try and rest. You do yourself no good worrying. We will rest here awhile and ride on when we have rested. Golden-hair will guard you'.

Frail Thorgrima is helped back to her bed by a maid and we follow into Wulfheard's hall, leaving a wet trail on the wooden board floor.

Carrying a torch, a man comes forward from the shadows to meet us. He is known to Harding and they greet one another.

'Hallfred is Wulfheard's discthegn, Ivar. He will show us to where we can rest. After we have eaten we will ride on. We cannot stay here for as long as I thought we might, not with Wulfheard under threat in Jorvik'.

All I can do for now is nod, words being useless anyway.

We follow Hallfred through the hall, through a side door into a darkened room. With a torch he lights rushes in an iron basket and leaves us, bidding us rest well. Saeward sinks onto a cot and drifts into deep sleep before either Harding or I can tell him to undress, at least take off his cloak and helm.

I shuffle across the small room to him and pull off his cloak, hanging it over the cot-end. Before I fall asleep myself I take off his helm and set it down on the floor. Sleep takes me after I take off my own cloak and helm, almost when I lie down on a second cot.

Dreaming of my woman Braenda, of Aelfberht and of Andvari and whatever else comes to me in my sleep. Only when someone knocks my boots after what seems like no time at all do I sit up and look around. The fight to open my eyes is as hard as I can ever think. When I make out who it is standing over me, I sit up with a start.

'I wondered how much longer you were likely to sleep', Harding grins. 'Watching Saeward awaken not long ago was the nearest I have come to seeing a dead man rise!'

I sit on the side of the cot and shake my head to stay awake. It would be too easy to fall asleep again and I hear myself ask,

'For how long have I been asleep?'

Harding sniffs and tells me of having to cheer Wulfheard's wife, swearing we would soon be on our way,

'...I was hoping to have eaten and been on our way by now. You

357

have put paid to that, you *and* Saeward'.

'Harding, if I had known –'

'You were dead to the world, Ivar. Fear not. Eat, you and Saeward, and we can ride on'. Harding pats my back and leaves to see to something.

'Feeding time, I think', Saeward yawns, pulls on his boots – Harding must have pulled them off – and strides to the door with me close behind. We follow the smell of oatmeal cooking, and find Harding seated on one of the benches halfway down along one wall, an empty bowl resting in his lap.

'Help yourselves to porridge. Bread is freshly baked, by the hearth. There is ale is in the vat, but not freshly brewed. It tastes a little stale but will wet your throat'.

We eat, drink, talk a little and thank Hallfred for the food and ale. Harding walks with him to the door, bids him farewell and beckons us to follow him to the stable. Braenda is still munching on hay when I lead her out, pull her blanket over her back and tighten the straps under her belly after heaving up the saddle. When at last we are ready we file out of the garth to follow another narrow road to Helmsleag across a lightly wooded moortop.

Yesterday's heavy, iron grey clouds have gone and bright sunlight floods the uplands. Everywhere I look it is more like summer again. Before we get too hot we furl our cloaks, stuff them into our saddle packs and make for the south.

Birds sing around us, a kestrel hovers over moorland rocks and deer crop the grass close to the trees before vanishing between them on seeing us. All is well with the world – *for now*. There will come a time, soon, when we will have to count our scanty blessings again.

Harding leads us to a road that will take us to the north of Jorvik, to skirt around to the east of the burh where we left a week or so ago.

'We need to be careful', he tells us when we catch sight of the Foss again.

'I still have the monk's robe', Saeward tells him, winking at me. 'There might be some use for it. These Northmen never take on men of the cloth for fear of being scolded by their betters'.

'You might be safe, but what about us?' Harding chafes.

'There must be a church nearby', I put in. 'There might be spare robes. Priests are safe, too'.

'You have some grounding now, in how a priest should bless anyone who asks', Saeward tells me.

'*How is that so?*' Harding's head jerks my way.   Saeward chuckles as I tell of our narrow escape,

'At Exanceaster Saeward and I went over the wall with a priest who spoke the Northman tongue. He was to learn of anything the Northman king meant to do, and that was where we met Hemming'. I say nothing about Saeward killing Hemming's friend Guthfrith. That might test Harding's friendship toward Saeward, even though it was a blunder.

There is a small church not far from our ride, seen from the road, its side door a little way open.

'Wait', Harding reins in.

'An open church door - what can be wrong with that?' I ask, and then see his meaning. 'Someone may be watching the church, you think?'

'What would you say? Saeward, can you put on your habit and walk?'

'I also need to take off my boots and put on sandals', Saeward answers, dropping down onto the stony road from the saddle. He pulls out the habit and the sandals and sets about turning himself into a man of the cloth.

'Take your time', Harding tells Saeward when he at last looks right. He has even taken off his woollen boot liners and pulled up the hood. 'If you think anything is wrong, do not go in'.

Saeward touches his forehead to Harding and sets off to the church whilst we hide amongst the trees to watch him.   The field beside the road runs almost to the nearest church wall, which makes watching him easy. We can see the heavy studded creak shut with a dull thud before Saeward reaches the church. He turns and looks back at us before turning back to the church. When Harding groans beside me I feel foreboding and wish for Saeward to turn and walk back.

He pushes the door open and looks inside, then vanishes from sight.

'God, what kind of fool is he?' Harding grinds his teeth and I find myself groaning inwardly. Has Saeward lost his wits?

'*Now* what do we do?' My mouth feels dry and, just as I begin to fear the worst the door creaks open again. Saeward shows in the doorway to wave us in. Why am I suddenly so fearful about the unknown?

'What can this mean?' Harding thinks we are being lured into a trap. My own thoughts are that Saeward has been threatened with his life and that our going to help him will ease his lot.

I share my thoughts, adding,

'We should take our time going there, keep his horse ready and make good our flight before anyone can catch up with us'.

Harding raises his own misgivings,

'What if they have hold of him?'

'Then we have a fight on our hands', I answer, reaching for my axe, as suddenly brave as I was fearful.

Saeward is still at the door when we reach him. He beckons Harding to enter and I take both horses in hand, watching the road as I do so lest the Northmen have set a trap.

Harding shows at the door again and calls me in,

'Ivar, you would never guess who I have found here. I shall hold the horses whilst you come in'.

The door creaks again as I push it back with my left hand, my right gripping my sword hilt. My eyes see nothing at first in the damp, chill blackness. When I get used to the dark I see someone, a woman, seated by the wall closest to the altar.

'It is good to see you again, Ivar'.

My heart leaps into my mouth at the sound of her words and I ram the hilt down again.

'Braenda, I wondered whether...*when* I might see you next!' As I say the words I stride toward her. Then I see the bundle in her arms, a small child swathed in a blanket. Yet the next words I utter are, 'What is it that brings you to this church?'

'It is the only safe haven, Ivar, when the Northmen are out looking for you'.

She holds up the bundle for me to see the child, and asks under her breath,

'Do you want to see little Ulf?'

'He is - *my* son?' I must seem wooden to her. I can only stand there, staring at the tightly closed eyes, the upturned nose, and the open, bud-like mouth. My eyes feel damp suddenly. This is *my* son? 'Has his big sister seen him yet?'

Braenda flinches, then a smile comes to her mouth. Yet it is not a warm smile – it is the smile of someone who has bad tidings to tell. Nevertheless the bad tidings stay unspoken, so I do not press for an answer. One day I will learn the truth behind the sadness – or have I been told and forgotten?

'The Northmen are looking for me, you say?' I bring the talk back to what she first told me. 'Is that why I have not seen you?'

'You have not seen me because I was carrying your son', is all she tells me.

'Where did you learn that I am being sought?'

'I hear things. Word has it you were here with the thegns and fyrd, and sent away the shire reeve. The king chided him before his men. Now you are sought to right a wrong in his eyes. He will make you swallow your pride the hard way if you are caught, and the king will have your skin to cover his shield when the shire reeve is done with you'.

'You have heeded their words well, Braenda', I tell her. 'Is that what they told you to tell me?'

'Ivar, who is this 'they' you speak of?'

I begin to tell her who I mean,

'Willelm Malet or Rodberht fitzRicard might have told you –'

'I was not told by anyone, Ivar. They are *my* words. If you will not heed them I can do nothing for you. Hold your son in your arms, my love. Feel him breathe and then go on to risk *ever* seeing either of us again', she pleads. At all other times we have met, she has been on top of things - *and* on me – but now she seems to have lost her iron grip over me. Or am I reading this wrongly?

When little Ulf wakes and smiles up at me I feel weak within - I would sail away with them both to a safe haven, to my half-brother Svein's kingdom. If I do that, do I leave my friends here to the mercy of their foes? Would Saeward, Theodolf and Harding ache for their homeland? Would it pain them if others lay blame on them – me, even - for running from the struggle?

'We will go somewhere safe', I tell her, handing back my son. I would see them both again, soon I hope.

'You say that', Braenda's eyes narrow, but she keeps a smile for sake of the babe in her arms. 'Do you mean what you say, or are you giving me false hope?'

'I mean that', I tell her. 'For now I have to help Harding find his friend Wulfheard'.

'In Jorvik – you are on your way there, are you not?'

I shrug and hope it does not come to that. If we could, let it be that we find him and his thegn before entering the jaws of hell. Why do I think like this now? I should not be fearful for the sake of my woman and son – would he look up to me if I were to tell him one day that I gave up my sword and axe to keep him safe?

'Believe me, Braenda. If it could be otherwise, would I risk your love?' This sounds like madness, and I think I have said these self-same words to her before.

'You would risk your neck, Ivar. Would you know where to find us?' She frowns and little Ulf smiles up at her, yawns and goes back to sleep. Braenda stretches to kiss me on the mouth, and calls to Saeward, 'Can you open the door for me, Saeward?'

Then she is gone. It is almost as if she had not been here, as if I had dreamt her being here. As if reading my thoughts again, Saeward asks,

'You think you dreamed of her being here?'

'I was beginning to think so, aye. *Was* it a dream?'

'She was here. It was no dream'.

I thank him and tell them both,

'*We* should be on our way, too'.

They nod and follow out of the darkness, into the daylight and we mount again to search for Wulfheard and the thegn.

I cannot help thinking, about what Braenda told me about not seeing her and the child again. That sounded like a threat, like an 'or else'. Surely she did not want me to turn and run from my *wyrd*?

Everything that happened in the church seems to fade into nothing when we near the Foss. At the sight of horsemen with lances we take cover amongst the bushes and wait for them to pass. But they do not pass, they mill around, waiting for something – or some*one*. Have we been seen? Harding's mare snorts and he looks around, first at us and then through the undergrowth. He shakes his head. With the stamping and grinding of stones on the road under their horses' hooves they could not have heard Harding's mare.

More horsemen come, greetings are traded and laughter fills the air as the two young nobles jostle playfully before riding on northward, side-by-side.

Harding and I wait until all the horsemen are beyond the nearest trees before taking the road again, on foot. Saeward stays with the horses, amongst the trees and bushes well out of hearing from the road. Monk Bar looms against the sunlight. Men on foot guard the way in, looking everyone up and down.

With our cloaks over our chain mail, packs slung over our shoulders we enter the burh past the guards. Eyeing us closely, the outlanders say nothing. Another of their kind strides outward to the gateway, and stops before us.

'Where are *you* going?' he barks throatily at us.

'My Lord', Harding almost bows, and points to the left, 'we are here to see our brother Wulfheard in his new workshop. It is near the Ose Gata Brycg, down that way'.

The Northman glowers at Harding and nods us on, other matters weighing heavier on him by the way he strides back and forth to stop others at the gates.

'That was good thinking', I tell Harding.

'We must keep our mouths shut from here, Ivar', he answers, 'I am sorry, but I feel there will be eyes on us. Clothed the way we are, we look like craftsmen – even with these boots. We only have to hope we are not searched'.

I nod to show I have heard him. We pass onward through the heart of Jorvik, mingling with others going the same way, past a market. Everyone here seems cowed. He elbows me a little further and jerks his chin upward to the left. My eyes follow his, to the left at a new wooden stronghold that overshadows the Foss. As my eyes wander, I see another where I know the eastern end of Skelder Gata to be. Harding has seen it as well, and elbows me.

Onward, we walk downhill to the bridge and cross.

There are Northmen everywhere we look, watching idly over passers-by from their mounts. I feel someone's eyes on me, although not for long. Everyone who goes by is stared at, or past. There are also armed men on foot, clustered for their own safety. They fear any attack from downriver, and they fear attacks from those thronging by. Some young nobles stand, swords drawn, by the bridge whilst their fellows struggle with something – or someone.

We are halted by outlanders who stand shoulder-to-shoulder across the width of the bridge as someone is brought from the eastern side. Two men, chained, ragged, bruised and bloodied, are being pushed – almost thrown - and pulled toward the bridge.

Harding groans under his breath and watches as the pair are jostled across the bridge and up the slope toward Mickel Gata Bar. When they are out of sight Harding tugs at my cloak and leaves Ose Gata eastward, to where the two men were driven from. When he thinks no-one is watching, or listening, he tells me why he has brought me here,

'That was them', he sucks in air through clenched teeth. 'Nothing can save them now!'

'That was Wulfheard and –'

'*Hush!* Aye Ivar, that *was* Wulfheard and Thegn Wulfric being driven along - from the Earlsburh I should think. Like as not, that shire reeve must have taken the Earlsburh for himself'.

'*That* would make Morkere happy!' I chortle.

'Morkere be blowed! He did not fit here in Northanhymbra, Ivar. *Mark my words*, many of us would have kept Tostig as earl, but there were those who saw him as too able for their good. It was Copsig who lost Tostig his earldom, filling his own coffers. We have to be careful here, though, Ivar. Copsig's kin are still about, biding their time I should not wonder'.

'Well Copsig is now no more', I begin, but Harding puts a hand over my mouth.

'*Be still!* No more about *him* either, Ivar. His brothers would as soon dish *us* up to the Northman shire reeve as anyone else. They may have been told who it was slew Copsig. No more, now'.

Understanding that we may be under threat I nod in answer. I was never told Copsig had brothers here, so the less said the better. We make our way back to Monk Gata by way of Stan Gata, past the burnt-out shell of the great church of Saint Peter, and turn right. A few unlucky souls dig amongst the charred timbers for anything they might sell to buy food, and scatter as we stride past.

The guard at the gate has too much on his hands this time as we leave the *burh*, searching a two-wheeled waggon for weapons. He must have been set the task of stopping anyone or anything he did not trust. Harding grins when one of the men with the waggon argues with him over what he thinks is a weapon.

The Northman waves a trimming knife in the air and almost catches one of his mounted fellows with it. Howls of laughter meet his efforts to stow the knife away again and we hasten away, out of sight of him before he turns our way again.

Saeward is sat on the grass when we part the bushes again. Around him are bowmen, five in all, who aim their bows at us as soon as we step into the open.

'Who are you?' one of them asks.

'I might ask the same', I answer, drawing my sword. 'Firstly, why is our friend seated on the grass, and where are our horses? We are on our way west to a friend near Tadceaster, and we do not aim to walk there!'

One of the bowmen winks at his friends and grins broadly at me,

'You might have to, if they have been bought'.

'And *where* have they been taken for sale?' Harding growls loudly at him, pushing my hand down on the hilt.

Another of the bowmen laughs hoarsely and points the way to where our horses have been taken,

'Treske – if you run hard you might save your horses from their new owners!'

Saeward stands and brushes straw from his cloak,

'So what do we do now?'

'If you run fast enough, you might make Tadceaster by morning', the first one tells us.

'Harding, we have to teach these fools a lesson', I murmur, grinning back at the spokesman.

Harding nods. He elbows Saeward, showing him his own sword hilt and draws the weapon, scything at the nearest man. Saeward shoves another of them in the way of an arrow that has been let loose at him, and cuts down a third. My blade slices across the chest of the fourth and the last man takes flight.

'Do we give chase?' Saeward asks, to Harding shaking his head.

If we are quick enough we might find new mounts nearer Jorvik.

Their owners might be put out at losing them to us, but our need is greater. Although saddened at the loss of Braenda, I understand I would not have owned her forever and put all thoughts of finding her out of my head.

By evening we are worn out, resting in a field beside the road some miles to the west of Jorvik and not far off the eastern bank of the Hvarfe. We have had to give the *burh* a wide berth and are still looking for mounts.

We are stirred by the clop of hooves on the packed earth road nearby and Saeward stands to look.

I snap at him,

'*Get down!*'

Someone calls out from the road.

'Saeward, why hide in that field amid the barley stalks?'

It is my turn to stand.

'I know who that is!' I yell, thrashing through waist-high undergrowth at the side of the road. 'And he has our horses!'

'When I saw Braenda being led along with Saeward's old mare on the road north of Jorvik, I began to think. I knew, Ivar, you would never · sell your horse, and my gut feeling was that you lived yet, both of you', Theodolf still has hold of Braenda's reins when I clamber into the saddle. He goes on, 'The fellow who led your horses was a dolt who could not ride – did his friends really send him *on foot* to sell your horses? I thought Harding had gone home – how come you are still together?'

'There were a few Northman slain on my land, and the priest led others to my garth', Harding takes the reins of his mare from Theodolf's hands, and I am given mine. Saeward limps up to his mare and heaves himself into the saddle.

'I hope you taught the weasel a lesson!' Theodolf chortles and grins impishly at Harding.

Harding's mouth curls back, showing yellow teeth,

'I should have, and believe me I felt like it. But Saeward does not hold with attacking clerics'.

'*What*, even turncoats?' Theodolf stares at Saeward.

'Aye, *even* turncoats', Saeward snaps back.

'They carry no weapons, and cannot stand up to armed men'.

'You forgot Thor!'

'I did *not* forget Thor - nor even did I forget some of our abbots or bishops who know how to wield a sword in anger!'

'Then what kept *this* one from being flayed alive?' Theodolf laughs.

'He was a *toady*. Killing him would have solved nothing, or given me fulfilment, as the Northmen already overran my land', Harding answers for Saeward.

'The Viking days are well and truly over', Theodolf smiles coldly and presses his horse into a trot. We follow him, down to the Hvarfe and through the swirling waters of the ford. 'Every time I come here I think of that time when the pair of you outwitted my father's henchmen. Hrothulf learned a lesson from that, I think!'

'He did indeed, Theodolf', I agree, laughing inwardly. I can see everything so plainly, the fat priest with Hrothulf's arrow in him, his small horse - and Hrothulf's men falling either side of us.

'You made off with our silver', Saeward tells Theodolf. Loud, rasping laughter from Harding draws scolding from the East Seaxan, 'You would not have laughed like that, had it been *your* silver!'

'I think you misread me, Saeward. It is the thought of Theodolf sneaking off with a bag –'

Harding is not allowed to finish and scowls at Saeward when he is told,

'It was two purses of silver!'

'*Whatever*. You got them back, did you?' Harding will not be browbeaten by a ceorl, such as is Saeward.

Saeward falls silent, sulking. I slap him across the back and chide him for being so churlish. Is it the loss of his horse – however short the time was he had to do without - that has upset him like this?

'Thinking back on what happened afterward gives me nightmares', Saeward tells me. 'Being flogged before all these folk in Eoferwic was *shameful!*'

'You did kill the fellow, Garwulf', Theodolf tells him.

'With *my* axe', I add, 'that I no longer have'.

'Aye, Theodolf, for killing my brother Beorhtwulf in a drunken brawl!'

'Well, Theodolf', I break in, 'I saw the fool hit his brother with his fist. Neither Earl Morkere nor his brother Eadwin would do anything about the killing, yet they were ready to haul me over the coals for the killing of the other old fool Sigurd!'

'No-one would miss either of *them*', Saeward puts in.

'You killed Garwulf – how?' Harding leans forward in his saddle to hear Saeward's answer.

'I threw Ivar's axe at him, felling him in the woods close to Aethel's steading', Saeward says proudly.

'How far was he from you when you threw the axe?' Harding asks further, taken by Saeward's feat.

'About from here to that tall oak tree there', Saeward shows him.

'*God*, I wish you had been with me at Gata Fulford! Think, if we had felled Harald Sigurdsson -'

'Just think of it', I nod, grinning. 'He did it again in the south, bringing down a young Northman from his horse when it was turning away from him'.

'*God*', Harding says again.

'Good thing he is with *us*, eh?' Theodolf winks at Saeward. He gives a start, his mouth twists, and then he grins at me, making out all is well.

'Has your wound healed well?' I ask my young friend, but I am not happy with his answer. He would need to stay away from the fighting for a long time yet, or his will be a short life. I would not want him dying on me, and having to tell Aethel he died needlessly.

He would only try to lie about it, I tell myself, and listen as he tells me how he has made a home for himself at Aethel's steading. He has done a lot, as I see when we ride into Aethel's thwait. It is no wonder Theodolf has pains in his side, but he has to rest. We will have to make him rest, for *our* sake if nothing else.

'Feel free', he tells us, his open-handedness taken up gladly. Harding lies down on one of the benches and is asleep before Theodolf can ask if he will have ale from the vat.

'You have brewed ale?' Saeward stops in his tracks as he walks back to the door for something.

'The barley and everything was freed from the clutches of the Northmen, on the road to Tadceaster. They were being attacked by outlaws and I thought I might help myself whilst their backs were turned'.

This is the Theodolf we all know. Aside from a few aches and pains – and who does not have them – he is at one with the world again. He looks fleetingly look down at Harding, grins and goes to the corner to scoop some of his ale into an earthenware ewer.

Meanwhile I look around Aethel's home.

Little is new in there that I can see, and then I look into the room I was given before Hrothulf, Aethel, Theodolf and I rode south. The door brushes against a wider bed that takes up most of the floor. A child's cot stands at the far side of the bed, and a broad bag lies in one corner, a woman's things spilling out onto the floor. I would say from this that he and Gerda were together again with a young one on the way.

'You have seen have you?' Theodolf asks. When I turn he is there, behind me, eyeing the room.

'I have', I turn back to look at the room and ask,. 'Is Gerda here with you?'

'Gerda –', he shakes his head. 'No, the last I saw of her was when she stood in the road watching after me as I rode after you with Saeward. This is *your* woman Braenda's doing, although I have not seen her for a week or so'.

'You have no thoughts about seeing Gerda again?' I ask. The scowl he gives me is by way of a warning not to say her name again. He had almost brushed her from his thoughts, I can see now. He may be looking for another woman here, near Tadceaster, or he may just be resting.

He smiles, and by way of making amends offers a drink, leading the way back to the main room,

'Come, friend, have some ale'.

As Theodolf pours for me he looks across the room to where Saeward sits astride a bench by the hearth,

'Would you like more ale, Saeward?'

'Aye, I would like *some* ale', Saeward rumbles.

'You could have helped yourself. You know you are welcome', Theodolf hovers, ewer still in one hand, cup in the other, to make yourselves at home here.

'I keep seeing Garwulf in the ingle', Saeward says, staring as if it were yesterday that we pulled him out, cowering from Aethel's attack. He needs cheering up,

'We should catch and roast a hart, have some ale. Who knows, Braenda may be here by the time the meat is done'.

Saeward blinks and asks who will bring down the hart, to which Theodolf answers that he will. He leaves the dwelling and comes back with his hunting bow, brandishing it in the manner of a prize. He grins broadly and calls out,

'Help yourselves to more ale. I shall be back soon'.

'What was that?' Harding sits up on the bench, blinking and rubbing his eyes, staring up at Theodolf. 'Where are *you* going?'

'I am going hunting, Harding, for your supper', Theodolf laughs and leaves.

'He has been gone a fair while', Harding looks out at the gathering gloom. I see storm clouds nearing when I look out from the doorway.

Walking back to the bench, I answer,

'He may not yet have a hart'.

'These woods abound with deer', Harding answers. 'It should not have taken this long to find one old enough for the kill. Where is he?'

'He might have found drawing the bow harder than he thought he should, and his pride will not let him come back without the hart he said he would bring', Saeward takes another draught of ale.

'We should look for him, surely?' Harding goes to the door again.

'*What is it?*' Saeward gives a start, looking at me.

'I thought I heard something', Harding opens the door and looks out. He shrugs, closing the door behind him, and walks back to where his cup stands by the bench legs. He raises the cup to his lips but does not drink, staring instead at the door, where our young hunter leans against a doorpost. He looks drained.

'*Theodolf*, what ails?' I ask, striding across the room to help. His shoulder has slid down the post and he drops to his knees, knuckles resting on the floor. There is a pool of blood that spreads across the floor by his right side.

Saeward comes to help me lift him to his feet.　　It is only when we have his arms over our shoulders that Harding points. I raise his left arm from my shoulder and look down to where Harding was looking. The short flights of a crossbow bolt stand away from his chest, blood staining his tunic. How far he has struggled like this I cannot think. All thoughts of a late summer feast are gone as we help him to his bed.

Does this mean the Northmen are close by here, and do they know about Aethel's safe haven? It may no longer be as safe, plainly, as we thought.

'We have to leave', I say to nods from Harding and Saeward.

'There is nothing I can do for him this time', Saeward tells us, 'save to say a prayer for him and ease his passing'.

'We will stay with him until he dies, and bury him close by', I tell them, looking down on him on his bed. His eyes are lightly closed as if he were dozing.

Hopefully Saeward can help him through his pain.

'Who could have known he would come to this?' Saeward asks, holding a palm over Theodolf's brow.

'When we first saw him, he seemed oddly free of the world around him', I add, cradling Theodolf's head.

Harding coughs and smiles,

'You mean, like Hrothulf you thought him backward?' He looks down at our young friend, the first to see him come in through the door.

'I would not say backward, more otherworldly', I have to say. 'We soon learned otherwise. He has saved the lives of many men with his bow, and it seems odd now that he died by the bow'.

Theodolf's eyes open and he smiles, but I do not think it is at us he smiles. There is something else here beside us that may be a spirit. Whatever it is, he seems to welcome it. Tears well in Saeward's eyes as he stands back to let the spirit take Theodolf, and I stroke his cheek with my thumb before I stand back.

Then he is gone. Another friend has passed on.

Come morning we are riding through the woods again. Theodolf has been buried with his war bow, and we must be careful not to be taken unaware by the crossbowman who parted him from his young life.

Bewildered as he was once by life's trials, Theodolf's heart was set right. He understood his part in trying to free the kingdom from the outlanders, to even the score for the death of his father – or to be rid of any blame he felt for bringing it about, as he thought. Was Hrothulf the welcome spirit that took him?

'Where are we going now?' Saeward asks. He sounds tired. Overnight we keep watch, each of us taking a turn by the door for the time it takes a short candle to burn out.

We finish the food we found, put some way for later and drink to Theodolf. With our stomachs full we can ride most of the day before we need to eat and rest again.

'I know an inn on the other side of Tadceaster, near the river', Harding tells us. 'We will be safe there, away from the road and prying outlanders'.

'You know the innkeeper?' I ask, to keep the talk going. Riding silently along after losing a good friend we will sink into our own thoughts. We need to stay sharp until we are safe out of sight for a while at least.

'I know his *wife*', Harding grins.

'*Oh* – like that, is it?' Saeward laughs.

We laugh, Harding loudest before letting us know,

'She is my daughter, not my *lover!*'

'Well – daughter, lover, *whatever* – do you think we will be safe from prying eyes at this inn?' I ask.

'I *know* we will be safe', Harding grunts.

'We thought we would be safe with Theodolf at Aethel's home', Saeward sniffs.

'We will be *safe* – there is an end to it!'

HERE BEGINS A NEW TELLING

I hope you enjoyed reading 'BETRAYED', the fourth book in the saga of Ivar Ulfsson's part in the struggle against the rule of King William and his allies. If you have not yet read the previous three books in the series, book one 'RAVENFEAST', two 'OVERTHROWN' and three 'OUTCAST' will give you the perspective to understand the timeline for this part of the saga.

Additionally you might like to follow progress on the series on the following:

alancaster149.hubpages.com/hub/RAVENFEAST.

See also www.northworldsagasite.webeden.co.uk and turn to the Books/Contact page (2) where you will find updates on future titles in the series as well as a historical synopses of eras in pre-and post-Conquest eras of British history from Hengist and Horsa to Henry 'Beauclerc', third son of William 'the Conqueror' (also known as Henry I).

Lightning Source UK Ltd.
Milton Keynes UK
UKOW03f1924071014

239772UK00001B/3/P